THE BURGLAR
ON THE PROWL

THE BURGLAR ON THE PROWL

LAWRENCE BLOCK

HarperLargePrint

An Imprint of HarperCollins*Publishers*

LARGE TYPE
M
BLOCK, L

This is a work of fiction. The characters, incidents, and dialogues are products of the author's imagination and are not to be construed as real. Any resemblance to actual persons, living or dead, is entirely coincidental.

FIRST HARPER LARGE PRINT EDITION

Printed on acid-free paper

Library of Congress Cataloging-in-Publication Data

Block, Lawrence.
    The burglar on the prowl / Lawrence Block. — 1st ed.
        p. cm.
    ISBN 0-06-019830-3 (Hardcover)
    1. Rhodenbarr, Bernie (Fictitious character)—Fiction. 2. New York (N.Y.)—Fiction. 3. Thieves—Fiction. I. Title.

PS3552.L63B856 2004
813'.54—dc22
                                                            2003055848

ISBN 0-06-058979-5 (Large Print)

04 05 06 07 08   WBC/RRD   10 9 8 7 6 5 4 3 2 1

**This Large Print Book carries the
Seal of Approval of N.A.V.H.**

Here's a book for

MAGGIE GRIFFIN—

great reader,

great friend,

webmaven,

consigliere,

and

good right hand

AUTHOR'S NOTE

Once again, it's my great pleasure to thank Writers Room, of Greenwich Village, where some preliminary work on this book was done, and Ragdale, of Lake Forest, Illinois, where it was written.

A good thing about writing, so they tell me, is that you can do it anywhere. Well, the hell you can. But I can, in these two blessed places, and I am forever grateful to them.

 **ONE**

"The man," said my friend Marty Gilmartin, "is an absolute . . . a complete . . . an utter and total . . ." He held out his hands, shook his head, and sighed. "Words fail me."

"Apparently," I agreed. "Nouns, anyway. Adjectives seem to be supporting you well enough, but nouns—"

"Help me out, Bernard," he said. "Who is more qualified to supply **le mot juste**? Words, after all, are your métier."

"They are?"

"Books are your stock-in-trade," he said, "and what is a book? Paper and ink and cloth and glue, to be sure, but if a book were nothing more than those mundane components, no one would want to own more than one of them. No, it's the words that constitute a book, sixty or eighty or a hundred thousand of them."

"Or two hundred thousand, or even three." I'd read **Grub Street** recently, and was thinking about the less-than-eminent Victorians George Gissing wrote about, forced by their publishers to grind out interminable three-volume novels for a body of readers who clearly had far too much time on their hands.

"That's more words than I require," Marty said. "Just one, Bernie, to sum up"—he glanced around the room, lowered his voice—"no, to **impale** Crandall Rountree Mapes like an insect upon a pin."

"An insect," I suggested.

"Far too mild."

"A worm, a rat." He was shaking his head, so I shifted gears and exited the animal kingdom. "A bounder?"

"That's closer, Bernie. By God, he **is** a bounder, but he's much worse than that."

"A cad."

"Better, but—"

I frowned, trying to conjure up a thesaurus spread open before me. A bounder, a cad . . .

"A rotter?"

"Oh, that comes close," he said. "We'll settle for that if we can't do any better. It's just archaic enough, isn't it? And it's better than **bounder** or **cad** because it's clearly not a temporary condition. The corruption is permanent, the man is putrid to the core." He picked up his glass, breathed in the bouquet of aged cognac. "**Rotter** comes very close indeed to conveying just what a thoroughgoing shitheel goes by the name of Crandall Rountree Mapes."

I started to say something, but he held up a hand to stop me. "Bernie," he said, wide-eyed with wonder, "did you hear what I just said?"

"Shitheel."

"Precisely. That's perfect, the quintessential summation of the man. And where do you suppose the word came from? Not its derivation, that would seem clear enough, but how did it get into our conversation? No one says **shitheel** anymore."

"You just did."

"I did, and I couldn't guess the last time I uttered it." He beamed. "I must have been inspired," he said, and rewarded himself with a small sip of the venerable brandy. I couldn't think of anything I'd done to merit a reward, but I had a sip from my own glass just the same. It filled the mouth like liquid gold, slid down the gullet like honey, and warmed every cell of the body even as it exalted the spirit.

I wasn't going to drive or operate machinery, so what the hell. I had another sip.

We were in the dining room of The Pretenders, a private club on Gramercy Park every bit as venerable as the cognac. The membership ran to actors and writers, men in or on the fringes of the arts, but there was a membership category called Patron of the Theater, and it was through that door that Martin Gilmartin had entered.

"We need members," he'd told me once, "and the main criterion for membership at this point is the possession of a pulse and a checkbook, though to look around you, you might suspect that some of our members have neither. Would you like to become a member, Bernie? Did you ever see **Cats**? If you loved it, you can join as a Patron of the Theater. If you hated it, you can come in as a Critic."

I'd passed up the chance to join, figuring they might draw the line at prospective members with criminal records. But I rarely turned down an invitation to join Marty there for lunch. The food was passable, the drink first-rate, and the service impeccable, but the half-mile walk from Barnegat Books led me past eight or ten restaurants that could say the same. What they couldn't provide was the rich atmosphere of the nineteenth-century mansion that housed The Pretenders, and the aura of history and tradition that permeated the place. And then there was Marty's good company, which I'd be glad of in any surroundings.

He's an older gentleman, and he's what fellows who read **Esquire** want to be when they grow up— tall and slender, with a year-round tan and a full head of hair the color of old silver. He's always well groomed and freshly barbered, his mustache trimmed, his attire quietly elegant but never foppish. While enjoying a comfortable retirement, he keeps busy managing his investments and dipping a toe in the water when an attractive business venture comes his way.

And, of course, he's a patron of the theater. As

such he goes to quite a few shows, both on and off Broadway, and occasionally invests a few dollars in a production that strikes his fancy. More to the point, his theatrical patronage has consisted in large part of underwriting the careers of a succession of theatrical ingénues, some of whom have actually demonstrated a certain modicum of talent.

Dramatic talent, that is to say. Their talent in another more private realm is something upon which only Marty could comment, and he wouldn't. The man is discretion personified.

We met, I would have to say, in highly unlikely circumstances. Marty had assembled a substantial collection of baseball cards, and I stole them.

Except, of course, it was more complicated than that. I hadn't even known about his card collection, but I did know that he and his wife were going to the theater on a particular evening, so I planned to drop in. I got drunk instead, and Marty (who had cash flow problems) reported his collection as stolen, so that he could collect the insurance. I wound up with the cards—I told you it was complicated—and cleared enough selling them to buy the building that houses my bookstore. That's remarkable enough, but no more so than the fact that Marty and I wound up friends, and occasional co-conspirators in the commission of a felony.*

And felony, it turned out, was very much what Marty had in mind this afternoon. The putative vic-

*The Burglar Who Traded Ted Williams

tim, you won't be surprised to learn, was one Crandall Rountree Mapes, aka **That Shitheel**.

"That shitheel," Marty said with feeling. "It's abundantly clear that he doesn't give a damn about the girl. He doesn't care about nurturing her talent or fostering her career. His interest is exclusively carnal. He seduced her, he led her astray, the cad, the bounder, the rotter, the . . ."

"Shitheel?"

"Precisely. My God, Bernie, he's old enough to be her father."

"Is he your age, Marty?"

"Oh, I suppose he's a few years younger than I."

"The bastard," I said.

"And did I mention that he's married?"

"The swine." Marty himself is married, and living with his wife. I saw no need to point this out.

By now I had a good idea where the story was going, but I let Marty tell it at his own pace. In the course of it our cognac vanished, and our waiter, an aging cherub with glossy black curls and a bulging waistcoat, took away our empty glasses and brought them back replenished. The minutes ticked away, the lunch crowd thinned out, and Marty went on telling me how Marisol ("A lovely name, don't you think, Bernie? It's Spanish, of course, and comes from **mar y sol,** meaning sea and sun. Her mother's Puerto Rican, her father from one of those charming little countries on the Baltic. Sea and sun indeed!") was indeed abundantly talented, and quite beautiful, with an aura of genuine innocence about her that could break one's heart. He'd seen her in a showcase presentation of Chekhov's **The Three Sisters,** of which the less said the better, but her performance and her incandescent stage presence drew him as he had not been drawn in years.

And so he'd gone backstage, and took her to lunch the next day to discuss her career, and squired her to a play he felt she simply must see, and, well, you can imagine the rest. A small monthly check, barely a blip on his own financial radar, meant she could quit waitressing and have more time for auditions and classes and, not incidentally, Marty, who took to visiting her Hell's Kitchen apartment at the day's end, for what the French call a **cinq à sept,** or a little earlier, for what New Yorkers call a nooner.

"She was living in South Brooklyn," he said, "which meant a long subway ride. Now she's a five-minute walk from a few dozen theaters." Her new digs were also a short cab ride from Marty's apartment and an even shorter one from his office, which made the arrangement convenient all around.

He was besotted with her, and she seemed equally impassioned. With the shades drawn in the West 46th Street walk-up, he'd shown her a few refinements her younger lovers had never introduced, and he was pleased to report that the vigor and energy of youth was no match for the art and sophistication of experience.

It was a veritable Eden, that apartment he'd found for her, and all it lacked was a serpent, which soon appeared in the person of that acknowledged shitheel, Crandall Mapes. I'll spare you the details, which is more than Marty did for me; suffice it to say that a sobbing Marisol had told a heartbroken Martin Gilmartin that she couldn't see him anymore, that she would always be grateful to him for his generosity, and not least of all for the gift of himself, but that she had lost her heart to the man with whom she knew she was destined to spend the rest of her life, and possibly all eternity as well.

And that man, Marty was shattered to learn, was the shitheel himself. "She thinks he's going to leave his wife for her," he said. "He has a new girl every six months, Bernie. Once in a while one of them lasts a full year. They all think he's going to leave his wife, and one of these days he will actually leave her, but not the way they think. He'll leave her a rich widow, when a heart attack does what I'd like to do and takes him out of the game for good."

If Marty was unusually bitter, it was explained in part by the fact that Mapes was not an entirely faceless rival. Marty knew the man, and had more than a nodding acquaintance with him. He'd run into him at shows and backers' auditions, and he and Edna had actually been to the Mapes home, a fieldstone mansion in Riverdale. The occasion was a benefit for Everett Quinton's Ridiculous Theater Company, which was looking for a new home after having lost its longtime house on Sheridan Square. "You paid a couple of hundred dollars for dinner and an intimate performance," he recalled, "and then they did what they could to persuade you to write out a check for another thousand or two. Dinner was all right, though the wines were no more than passable, but Quinton's a genius and I'd have made a contribution in any case. And Edna was glad for a look at their house. We all got the grand tour. They didn't show us the basement or the attic, but they did drag us through all the bedrooms, and there was a painting in the master bedroom, a seascape."

"I don't suppose it was a Turner."

He shook his head. "It was just passable," he said, "like the wine. Your basic generic sailing ship. The only thing significant about the painting is that it was tilted."

"That shitheel!"

He raised an eyebrow. "I'm not compulsive about it," he said, "but it bothers me to see a picture hung at an angle. It goes against the order of things. Even so, I'm not ordinarily the type to go around straightening the paintings in other people's houses."

"But this time you did."

"I was the last one to leave the room, Bernie, and something made me stop and return to the painting. You know that line of Coleridge? 'As idle as a painted ship / Upon a painted ocean.'"

I recognized the line—two lines, actually—as from "The Rime of the Ancient Mariner," a poem which, unlike most of the other imperishable works we'd had to read in high school English, I'd actually liked. " 'Water, water, everywhere,' " I quoted back, " 'And all the boards did shrink; Water, water, everywhere, / Nor any drop to drink.' "

He nodded approvingly. "Most people think the last line is 'And not a drop to drink.' "

"Most people are wrong," I said, "most of the time, about most things. Was the painted ship silent, upon its painted ocean?"

"It was," said Martin Gilmartin. "But what was behind it spoke volumes."

 **TWO**

A wall safe," Carolyn Kaiser said. "He was straightening the picture and he felt something behind it, and it was a wall safe."

"Right."

"And Marty's idea," she said, "and the whole point of inviting you to lunch, was that you could run up to Riverdale, let yourself into Mapes's house, and open the safe."

"I'd like to think it wasn't the **whole** point of lunch. After all, we're friends. Don't you suppose he figured he'd enjoy my company?"

"Goes without saying, Bern. If I ever join a fancy club I'll invite you for lunch all the time. Right now I'm afraid this is as fancy as it gets."

We were at the Poodle Factory, Carolyn's place of business, just two doors down from my bookstore on East 11th Street between University Place and Broadway. This was a Wednesday, and ordinarily we'd be eating our sandwiches at Barnegat Books, having lunched at her dog grooming salon the day before. But instead I'd joined Marty on Tuesday,

and we'd been at the bookstore Monday, so it was
her turn to play host and mine to show up with the
food. Accordingly I'd picked up a couple of stuffed
pitas and two portions of an indeterminate side dish
at Two Guys from Kandahar, the latest incarnation
of the hole-in-the-wall around the corner on
Broadway. The only soft drink they carried was a
hideous blue-green thing flavored with pistachio
nuts, so I'd stopped next door for a couple of Cokes.

"These are good," she said, "but how authentic
do you figure they are? I mean, do they even have
pita bread in Afghanistan?"

"Does it matter? I mean, do they have tacos in
Beijing? Or calzone in Tirana?"

She saw my point. We were, after all, in New
York, where half the taco stands are run by Chinese,
and most of the pizzerias by Albanians. "You're
right," she said. "But getting back to Marty. This is
something different for him, isn't it? The jobs he
steers you to are usually friends of his who want to
be burgled so they can collect the insurance. This
Mapes doesn't sound like a friend—"

"Not unless you consider **shitheel** a term of
endearment."

"—and I don't suppose he's going to be in on the
burglary. What's in the safe?"

"Cash."

"How does Marty know that? Don't tell me it
was open."

"If it had been open," I said, "he could have
taken the money himself. Not that he would have,

because at the time he didn't have anything against Mapes. He didn't much care for him, he'd always thought of him as a weasel and a fourflusher, but this was long before Marty had met Marisol."

"Who was probably still in high school in San Juan."

"Oakmont, actually."

"Wherever. Oakmont? Where's that, Bern?"

"Pennsylvania. It's outside of Pittsburgh."

"So's Philadelphia," she said. "Outside of Pittsburgh, that is. How does he know about the cash?"

"Things Mapes let drop. I don't know what he said exactly, but the implication was that he got paid now and then in cash, and that it stayed out of the bank, and off the books."

"I hardly ever get cash anymore," she said. "It's almost all credit cards nowadays. Which is fine, because they don't bounce the way checks used to. Do you get much cash?"

"When it's less than ten dollars, almost everybody pays cash. And just the other day I had a sale that came to forty-eight dollars and change, and the guy handed me a fifty-dollar bill. But that's a rarity."

"The forty-eight-dollar sale? Or getting paid in cash."

"Both. When it's a two-dollar sale from the bargain table, sometimes I just put it in my pocket. But most of the time I ring the sale. I mean, I'm not looking to skim cash from the business. I'd rather show as much store income as possible, and declare it and pay taxes on it."

"Because your other job's tax-free."

"That's the thing about burglary," I said. "There's no tax bite, and very little paperwork."

"I'm not gonna ask about the pension plan, Bern. Anyway, what does Mapes do?"

"He's a doctor."

"And he gets paid in cash?"

"Not entirely, but there's a fair amount of cash involved."

"But everybody has medical insurance," she said. "Who pays cash?"

"I don't have medical insurance."

"Well, no. Neither do I, Bern. We run our own businesses, and the cost of medical coverage would bankrupt us. Fortunately my health is good, so it doesn't come up very often, but when I have to go to the doctor I wind up writing a check. That way at least it's tax deductible."

"Right."

"Of course maybe Mapes is an old-fashioned doctor," she said, "like the one I go to over in Stuyvesant Town. You don't need an appointment, you just walk in and take a number like you were at Zabar's. And it's fifteen or twenty dollars for your basic office visit. But the guy's a saint, Bern, and Mapes doesn't sound much like a candidate for canonization."

"He doesn't, does he?"

"So what kind of a doctor is he?"

"A plastic surgeon."

"You're kidding, right? A guy does nose jobs and gets paid in cash?"

"According to Marty," I said, "most plastic surgery is elective. The insurance companies won't reimburse you for it. If you want breast enhancement or liposuction or rhinoplasty, it's going to come out of your own pocket."

"Or out of my checking account, because if I shell out that kind of money I'd at least like to get the tax deduction. It's still deductible, isn't it? Even if it is elective?"

"I think so."

"So?"

"People who wind up with a lot of cash of their own," I said, "are always looking for ways to pay cash that won't show up. Say you're skimming a hundred thousand dollars a year off the top of your business."

"Which would be a neat trick, in my business. I mean, skimming the surface wouldn't do it, Bern. I'd be going through bedrock and halfway to China."

"It's a hypothetical example."

"Not a dog grooming facility at all. Got it."

"You've got all that cash," I said, "and what are you going to do with it? You can buy your wife a diamond necklace, that'll work, but then you may not be able to insure it, or somewhere down the line someone might ask you where it came from. If you're a collector, of course, you're in the clear. You can buy stamps and coins and rare books until the cows come home, paying cash for everything, and your hobby'll soak up every spare dollar you've got. But another thing you can do—"

"Is pay the plastic surgeon?"

"You'd have to write a check to the hospital," I said, "and you could deduct that, but maybe the surgeon lets you know that he wouldn't mind getting his fee in cash, and that he might even shave it a little in return for cash payment. That way everybody comes out ahead."

"Neat."

"Very neat," I agreed. "Also, I gather that Mapes has some acquaintances on what I'd call the wrong side of the law, if it weren't that I spent so much time on that side myself."

"Criminals."

"Of one sort or another, yes. The scuttlebutt, according to Marty, is that he's the go-to guy when somebody like Tony Soprano needs an illegal operation."

She looked puzzled. "An illegal operation? You mean an abortion, Bern? Last I heard, they were still legal."

"I mean if you want a gunshot wound stitched up," I said, "by someone who won't report it. Or if you walk in with a poster off a post office wall and ask him to make you look different from the picture, and incidentally how about removing some of the tattoos and distinguishing marks they mentioned? I don't suppose Mapes gets a lot of those, but I bet they pay top dollar and they don't try to put it on their MasterCard."

She thought it over, nodded. "Bottom line," she said, "he takes in a fair amount of cash. And keeps it in a wall safe."

"That's how Marty figures it."

"And how do you figure it, Bern?"

"I figure he takes in a lot of cash," I said, "and he keeps **something** in the safe. If it's not cash, it's still going to be something worth taking. The thing is, I know he's got a safe, and I know where it is. I even know what picture's in front of it."

"A painted ship on a painted ocean."

"A poorly painted ship on a poorly painted ocean."

"You figure the safe'll be easy to open?"

"A wall safe? I never yet found a really difficult one. And if he's got the mother of all wall safes, well, all that means is I'll have to pull it out of the wall and take it home and work on it at leisure. That's another thing about wall safes, they're portable. They have to be or you couldn't stick them in the wall."

"Are you gonna do it, Bern?"

"I told Marty I'd have to think about it. He really wants me to do it. He offered to come along on the job, and even said he'd be willing to waive his end."

"What was he gonna wave his end at?"

"**Waive** with an **i**. He'd get a finder's fee, and if he came along, too, he'd get a share. But he said he'd be willing to go the whole route and not get a nickel for his troubles. Of course he probably knows I wouldn't take him up on the offer, but the fact that he made it in the first place shows how strongly he feels. He doesn't care about the money. He just wants to see Crandall Mapes get one in the eye. Whatever he's got in the safe, it's either cash or something he bought for cash. So it's not insured, which makes it a dead loss to the good doctor."

"You figure Mapes is really that big a shitheel, Bern?"

"Well, I don't suppose he's one of nature's noblemen. At the very least he's a bounder, and probably a cad in the bargain. Marty's got a particular reason to hate him, because he took Marty's girl away from him before he was done with her. Personally, I've got nothing against Dr. Mapes. He hasn't done anything bad to me, and he's not likely to, since I haven't got a girlfriend for him to steal."

"Neither have I."

"But I don't have to hate a man in order to steal from him. I've never bothered to justify what I do, because I recognize it's not justifiable."

"You've said it's a character defect."

"It is, and I probably ought to do something about it. And maybe I will, someday."

"But not today, huh, Bern?"

"Not today," I said, "and not tomorrow, and not the day after tomorrow."

"What's the day after tomorrow?"

"Friday."

"Thanks, Bern. If I didn't have you for a friend

I'd have to go out and buy a calendar. What happens on Friday?" I just looked at her, and she put her hand on her forehead. "Duh," she said. "That's when you're gonna do it. Friday night? I guess that means you'll be ordering Perrier at the Bum Rap."

We meet every day after work at a gin mill around the corner for a ritual Thank-God-It's-Finished drink, to unwind after a high-pressure day of washing dogs and peddling books. On those occasional evenings when the work has just begun for me, my standard tipple is Perrier water. Scotch, my usual drug of choice, mixes well with any number of things, but burglary, alas, is not among them.

"But that's okay," she said, "because I won't be there myself." She cocked her head, winked. "I've got a date."

"Anybody I know?"

"Nope. Well, I shouldn't be so quick to say that. You might know her. But I don't."

"You met her online."

"Uh-huh."

"Which service? Date-a-Dyke?"

"They're the best, Bern. They're much better than Lesbe Friends at screening out the teenage boys. What's the deal with adolescent males and gay women, do you have a clue? Why are they so fascinated with us? Because I can assure you it's not reciprocal."

"You mean to say you don't have fantasies of being a fifteen-year-old boy, or fooling around with one?"

"Oddly enough," she said, "I don't. Bern, you were a fifteen-year-old boy once."

"That was before computer dating and online chat rooms."

"Yeah, but it wasn't before Sappho. Did you have a thing about lesbians?"

"I did have a thing," I said, "though I couldn't figure out what to do with it. As far as lesbians were concerned, I barely knew they existed. I had a pretty elaborate fantasy life, but as far as I can remember it was pretty much dyke-free."

"I just have this image of a hot chat room conversation, with two gay women pulling out all the stops and telling each other just what they want to do and how they'll do it, and each one of them is actually a boy. I just thought of something."

"What?"

"Well, the boys who do this. I mean, they may be crazy but they're not stupid, right?"

"So?"

"So don't you figure they know their online buddy is about as much of a lesbian as they are? And if they know, and get off on it anyway, what does that make them?"

"Happy," I suggested.

"I guess. Anyway, you get a lot less of that crap with Date-a-Dyke. There's no chatting, you just post messages back and forth. And if you click you make a date to meet."

"And this'll be what, your fourth date?"

"Only the third, Bern. I had one all set a week ago, and she canceled."

"Cold feet?"

She shook her head. "Warm memories. She and her ex were going to try to make it work after all. So it was just as well she canceled, because earlier she'd said she was footloose and fancy-free, that her last relationship was a horror and she never wanted to see the bitch again. If she was going to be carrying all that baggage, well, I'm glad I didn't waste an evening on her."

"Figures."

"The one I'm seeing Friday," she said, "is a paralegal at a law firm that represents lenders in commercial real estate transactions."

"She probably tweaked it a little to make it sound exciting."

"So it's not glamorous. It's not as though washing dogs day in and day out is gonna get you on the cover of **Vanity Fair**. Anyway, she sounds interesting. Of course, without a photograph it's hard to know if you're going to be attracted to one another."

"No photos on Date-a-Dyke?"

"That's one way to keep the boys away. You'd think it'd be the other way around, that they'd have trouble finding photos to post, but they just download them from somewhere else." She rolled her eyes. "Teenage boys sending each other naked pictures of the women they're pretending to be. Some world we live in, huh, Bern?"

"What's her name, the woman you're meeting?"

"If we hit it off, she'll probably tell me sooner or later. Right now we're on a screen name basis. She's GurlyGurl."

"She probably won't show up dressed to go duck hunting."

"I think the screen name's partly ironic, actually. She's not ultrafemme, but she doesn't drive a Peterbilt semi, either."

"Somewhere in the middle."

"Uh-huh."

" 'I'm not a lipstick lesbian, but I play one at the office.' "

"Something like that, Bern. She sounds pretty interesting. Even if it's not a romance, it should make for a fun evening. So I'd have to say I'm looking forward to Friday."

"Me too," I said.

 **THREE**

I went back to the bookstore and opened up, and I can't say my afternoon would have been any less exciting if I'd been, say, a paralegal at a law firm representing lenders in commercial real estate transactions. GurlyGurl must have earned more than I did that day, and I'll bet she's got medical coverage, too.

I closed up around six, brought in my bargain table from its place on the sidewalk, made sure Raffles had dried food in his food dish and fresh water in his water bowl, and that the bathroom door was ajar so he could use the toilet. I met Carolyn at the Bum Rap, and we ordered our usual scotches, hers on the rocks, mine with a splash of soda. Maxine brought them and we drank to something—crime, most likely—and worked on our drinks. Somewhere in the middle of our second round, Carolyn asked if I wanted to come over to her place for an evening in front of the television set. It was Wednesday, she pointed out, and that meant **The West Wing** and **Law & Order,** both of which would go perfectly with some take-out Chinese from Hunan Pan.

"Can't," I said.

"You've got a date?"

"The last date I can remember," I said, "is 1066."

"The Battle of Hastings?"

"If I'd been there," I said, "I'd have been on Harold's side. That's how well dating works for me."

"You could try the computer, you know."

"Yeah, right."

"And even if you don't, Bern, you'll meet someone. It's just a question of time."

"By the time I meet someone," I said, "I'll have forgotten what it is you're supposed to do with them. No, I haven't got a date tonight. I've got to go to work."

"Tonight? I thought that was Friday."

"Tonight too."

"But you're drinking, Bern."

"I'm not drinking alone, though, am I?"

She frowned. "Bern, you never have a drop of alcohol before you go out burgling. It's a firm rule of yours, and just about the only one."

"I don't play cards with men named Doc," I said, "or eat at places called Mom's."

"Or drink before you burgle."

"Or drink before I burgle," I agreed. "Three sound rules, I'd have to say."

She thought it over. "You're working tonight, but it's not going to involve breaking and entering."

"I shall not break," I said. "Neither shall I enter."

"Are you doing an appraisal?"

My antiquarian book business sometimes has me working evenings, appraising a client's library for insurance purposes or making an offer to a potential seller. But that wasn't what I had on tonight's agenda.

"It's burglary-related," I said, "and it demands a reasonably cool head, but not necessarily a sober one. I'm taking the subway up to Riverdale for a look at the Mapes estate."

"A reconnaissance mission. Do you want company?" She frowned. "But I'd have to be back by nine o'clock. This is gonna sound silly, but I really don't want to miss **The West Wing**."

"It doesn't sound silly. Tonight'll be boring, anyway. All I'm going to do is look at the house and walk around the neighborhood." I picked up my drink, observing its pleasing color. "Friday's when I could use company, but you're tied up with GurlyGurl."

"Wait a minute. I thought Marty was going with you."

I shook my head. "He'd be willing, but there's no way I'd want to take him along. Remember, he knows Mapes. If he's spotted in the area, if there's anything at all to connect him to the burglary—"

"And you were going to ask me to come with you? Why didn't you say something?"

"Well, as soon as I found out you had a date . . ."

"I'd have broken it. I can still break it, I'll just e-mail GurlyGurl and tell her something came up."

"No, don't do that. This'll be your third connection through Date-a-Dyke, and everybody knows the third time is the charm. Besides, I always feel a little guilty involving you in my crimes."

"As long as we don't get caught," she said, "you've got nothing to feel guilty about."

"That's not the way they teach it in Sunday school."

"Too bad." She frowned. "What time?"

"I really don't want you breaking your date."

"I got that part. What time are you gonna be doing it?"

"I don't know. I haven't worked that out yet. The Mapeses have tickets for the Met. There's an eight o'clock curtain, so they'll most likely leave the house around seven."

"And that's when you'll go?"

"No, that's a little early for me. I figure I'll set out around nine. They're seeing **Don Giovanni,** and that lasts close to four hours, and by the time they get home—"

"I can come," she said.

"But your date with GurlyGurl—"

"Didn't I tell you I'd be skipping the Bum Rap Friday? I'm meeting her in the lobby of the Algonquin at 6:15. That gives me plenty of time to run home and put on jeans and sneakers and meet you wherever you say."

"Suppose the two of you hit it off?"

"Then I'll probably be a lot better company on the way to Riverdale than if we hate each other. So?"

"I mean really hit it off," I said, "and decide to have dinner together, and then decide to, uh—"

"To do all the things the fifteen-year-olds dream up in the chat rooms. Relax, Bern. It's not gonna happen."

"But if you both really like each other—"

"If that happens," she said, "and I really hope it does, although God knows the odds are against it. But if it does, we'll have a second round of drinks, and then we'll tell each other how much we enjoyed the meeting, and we'll shake hands, with maybe a significant little squeeze at the end of the handshake. And then we'll meet again online and arrange a dinner date."

"That sounds complicated."

"It's a lot simpler to go over to the Cubby Hole and drag some drunk home with you," she allowed, "but most of the time it doesn't work and you wind up going home alone, and when you do get lucky, who do you wind up with? The kind of woman who lets herself get picked up in dyke bars, that's who."

"Oh."

"What I figured I would do, Bern, is have my drinks with GurlyGurl, and then pick up a barbecued chicken on the way home, and after I shared that with the cats I'd go over to the Cubby Hole and make a night of it. But I'd a whole lot rather go with you to Riverdale. Can you really use the company?"

"Well, I'll want to drive. The subway's fine for

tonight, but when you're carrying things that don't belong to you, public transportation's not the safest way to go."

"You need me," she said firmly. "Suppose you can't find a parking place?"

"That's what I was thinking."

"We're in business," she said. "I'm your hench-person, just like old times. And of course I won't breathe a word of it, Bern, but GurlyGurl's going to notice that I have an air of mystery about me." She grinned. "So? What could it hurt?"

 **FOUR**

I didn't really have to go home first. I was dressed all right in what I'd worn to work that morning. They haven't got a dress code in the subway, and I don't suppose they've got one on the streets of Riverdale, but one wants to avoid calling attention to oneself, and the only thing my khakis and polo shirt might call to anyone's attention was the relative poverty of my sartorial imagination.

It was spring—I may not have mentioned that—and, if the thermometer dropped a few degrees with nightfall, I might feel the chill in a short-sleeved shirt. Even if it didn't, I'd had a pair of stiff scotches at the Bum Rap, and it wouldn't hurt me to give them a little extra time to wear off. There was nothing on the agenda that required a sober head or quick reflexes, but my mission, while lawful enough all by itself, was part of a larger campaign that was as felonious as a monk. I'd had a slice of pizza on my way from the Bum Rap to the subway, and I suppose that had a sobering effect, but why not make assurance doubly sure? Why not stop home, and even make myself a cup of coffee while I was at it?

As it turned out, it didn't cool off that much, but I couldn't know that ahead of time, when I stopped at my apartment for my windbreaker. It was tan, a shade or two deeper than my slacks, and completed the costume of an ordinary guy, Mr. Middle of the Road, leading a blameless and certainly law-abiding existence.

My apartment's in a prewar building on West End and 70th. Much of my life centers in the Village—the bookstore's there, of course, on East 11th, and Carolyn's apartment on Arbor Court is less than a mile south and west of our two stores, in the West Village. She walks to work every day, and it's often occurred to me that it would be nice to be able to do the same. I suppose I could as things stand, but I'd have to allocate two hours to the process, and so far it's never seemed like a good idea.

Moving to the Village hasn't seemed like a good idea, either, because it's just not feasible. My apartment's rent-stabilized, which means that it costs me around a third of what it would otherwise. If I gave it up I'd have to pay at least three or four times as much for an equivalent apartment downtown. Or, if my nighttime activities brought me a really big score, I could buy a co-op or condo downtown—and then shell out in monthly maintenance about as much as I pay now for rent.

Besides, I'm used to the place. It's not much, a skimpy one-bedroom with a view of another apartment on the other side of the airshaft, and I've never taken the trouble to improve its furnishings or décor.

Well, wait a minute. That's not entirely true. First thing I did when I moved in was build in book-shelves on either side of the fireplace. (On the rare occasions when I actually have someone over, she invariably asks if the fireplace works. No, I explain, it's retired.) And the second change I made, a few years later, was to construct a hidden compartment at the rear of the bedroom closet. That's where stolen goods go, until I manage to figure out how to unload them. It's also where I keep my Get Out of Dodge kit, which consists of five to ten thousand dollars in cash and a pair of passports, one of them genuine, the other a very decent facsimile.

Plus, of course, the little collection of picks and probes and thingamajigs and whatchamacallits that come under the general heading of burglar's tools. Unless you're a licensed locksmith, the mere pos-session of such implements is enough to earn you a stretch upstate as the guest of the governor. It's occasionally occurred to me to pick up a locksmith's license, just to keep from getting nailed for posses-sion of burglar's tools, but they'd laugh themselves silly if they saw my name on an application. Or at least I think they would; maybe the people who give out the licenses don't check the names against a master list of convicted burglars. If not then I'd have to say the system's flawed, and wouldn't that be a shock?

I made a cup of coffee and drank it, and I went to the closet for my windbreaker, and somewhere around eight o'clock I went downstairs and walked over to 72nd and Broadway to catch the West Side IRT. I had my hands in the pockets of my windbreaker, and in a trouser pocket I had my burglar's tools.

And for the life of me I couldn't tell you why.

I suppose it must have been automatic. I was going to work, even though I knew my work would be strictly limited to reconnaissance. But a man on his way to work takes the tools of his trade along with him, and that was precisely what I did.

Halfway to the subway station, I realized what I'd done. I thought about going home and putting the tools back where they belonged, and I decided it was a fool's errand. No one was going to put his hand in my pocket, with the possible exception of myself. I wouldn't be doing anything illegal, so no cop would have a reason to frisk me. And it wasn't as if I were walking along with a loaded gun on my hip. They were burglar's tools, that's all. They weren't apt to go off on their own.

Riverdale's a part of the Bronx, but don't be ashamed of yourself if you hadn't known that. They're doing everything they can to keep it a secret. In the classified ads, under **Houses for Sale,** there's a special section of listings for Riverdale after the Manhattan listings. Then come the Bronx listings, following along after them.

The subway's elevated by the time it gets to the northern reaches of Manhattan, so you can watch through the window as the train crosses the Harlem River and presses on through Kingsbridge and into Riverdale. If you do, you won't spot a billboard that proclaims "RIVERDALE—PART OF THE BRONX AND DAMN PROUD OF IT!" It'd make a nice billboard, but so far no one's been prompted to put one up.

And, when you get off at the last stop at 242nd Street and make your circuitous way south and west on Manhattan College Parkway, so named because it winds its way around the ivied campus of Manhattan College, you might be excused if you leapt to the conclusion that you were in, uh, Manhattan. Manhattan Community College is in Tribeca, and Marymount Manhattan College is on East 71st Street, and you'll find the Manhattan School of Music on Broadway and 122nd. They've got Manhattan in their names, and they're in Manhattan, but Manhattan College, curiously enough, is in Riverdale, and Riverdale is in the Bronx.

Ah, well. **The Bronx?/No, thonx!** wrote Ogden Nash, some seventy or eighty years ago. Even then the borough got no respect, and time has not been kind to its image. Riverdale, with its fine old field-stone houses and its very preppy Riverdale Country

Day School, understandably blanches at being mentioned in the same breath as, say, Fort Apache.

I mused on all of this as I tried to find the Mapes house and found myself wishing I'd brought a map along. I have a Hagstrom atlas of the five boroughs at home, and I'd studied the map of Riverdale and plotted my route, but it would have been handy to have the map in front of me now. The atlas says it's pocket-size, but only if you're a kangaroo. I'd thought of tearing out the relevant page, but I'm too much of a bookman to mutilate a useful book on a whim. I have a folding map of Manhattan that I could have taken along, but what good would that do me? Riverdale, despite the likely wishes of its inhabitants, is not to be found thereon. The mapmakers know damn well it's in the Bronx.

There were a couple of convenience stores on Broadway at the foot of the subway terminal, and one of them would probably have been happy to sell me a map of the Bronx, if I promised not to say where I got it. But I didn't even think of that until I'd walked far enough on the winding stretch of Manhattan College Parkway to scramble my mental compass. I was damned if I was going to go back and buy a map and start over, so I kept on going, and took a right on Delafield Avenue and a left on 246th Street, which got me under the Henry Hudson Parkway and within shouting distance of the Hudson River. I kept myself pointed toward the river and hit streets I remembered from the map, and I took a wrong turn here and there but figured it was just part of getting to know the neighborhood, and wasn't that part of my assignment?

And then I was on Devonshire Close, a dead-end street that ran north a single block from another street with the irresistible name of Ploughman's Bush. Riverdale is hilly, and Devonshire Close perched on the slope of a rise, with the houses on the east side of the street—Mapes's was among them—situated at the top of the slope. They were large houses and they stood on good-sized lots, with their lawns angling down to the sidewalk. The lawns looked too steep for easy mowing, and about a third of the homeowners had finessed the problem by substituting a ground cover, ivy or pachysandra, for the usual grass. Mapes had grass, though, and his lawn looked well tended, his shrubbery neatly trimmed. Well, he was a plastic surgeon, wasn't he, given to reshaping things to their aesthetic betterment? He might not be out there with hedge clippers himself, but he'd damn well make sure the job got done.

You couldn't see the Hudson from where I was standing, but when I walked up the driveway to where the house began, there was just a sliver of river visible. You'd see more from the first-floor windows, and you'd have a good view from either of the two higher floors. There's something in the human spirit that longs to look at water, and I think that may explain why so many people have fish tanks in their houses and apartments. It's not the fish, it's the water, and I knew that the folks on Devonshire Close didn't need to stare at tanks full of guppies. They'd be able to see the Hudson.

I returned to the front walk, where all I could see was the baronial manse of Crandall Rountree Mapes, and for the time being that was plenty. It was quite a house, but then so were all the others on the block. A few were of red brick, and two were of Tudor-style half-timbered stucco, but the rest were made of stone, which you'll recall is the very same material they build castles out of. The houses on Devonshire Close weren't castles—I didn't spot a single moat or drawbridge, and not even a portcullis—but there was nevertheless something distinctly castleish—castlesque? castleine? Castilian?—about them. They felt substantial, which was ideal from my point of view, but they also felt impregnable, which was not. **No one's getting in here,** roared the lion's-head brass knocker in the center of the massive oak door. **Go home and start over,** murmured the thick stone walls. **Don't even think about it,** growled the windows, all so neatly outlined at their borders with metallic tape.

The tape indicated the presence of a burglar alarm system, and an extra escutcheon plate just below the Rabson lock on the front door told me the system was a Kilgore. I'm familiar with the Kilgore, and even bought one to increase my familiarity, and for a change familiarity bred not contempt but grudging respect. I couldn't bypass it, not without running an electric drill that would draw more attention than the alarm itself. I could turn it off once I was inside the house, I knew how to do that, but first I had to get in, and the Kilgore system was sitting there smugly and telling me I'd have an easier time getting into Fort Knox.

The thing is, you can get in anywhere. I've never had a look at Fort Knox, and can't see why I would want to—I'm not even certain there's any gold there, are you?—but I'm sure it would be possible to get in. It wouldn't be easy, but you can sail a long ways from Easy before you reach the shores of Impossible.

And the Mapes house wasn't Fort Knox. It might be tricky, but there would be a way in. There always was, and the idea was to spot it now so I'd know just what to do come Friday.

First, though, I walked back to Ploughman's Bush and circled the block. I'd been standing in front of the Mapes house for several minutes, and I didn't want to attract any attention. If anyone had spotted me, I'd give them a chance to watch me walk away, and while I was at it I could get a fuller picture of the overall neighborhood.

I took five or ten minutes, and when I came back the big stone house with the manicured lawn and shrubbery looked just as I had left it, with the same lights glowing in the same windows. I couldn't tell if anyone was home or not, because just about everybody with a house leaves lights on routinely, figuring that a darkened house is an invitation to burglars. (To this burglar, a completely unlighted house suggests that the occupants are at home and asleep, though admittedly that doesn't hold until the late hours.)

Apartment dwellers are more apt to darken the place when they go out, figuring reasonably enough that anyone wishing to kick the door in would do so without being able to tell whether the lights were on or off on the other side of it. The occasional break-in was just a chance you had to take, whereas a high Con Ed bill was a certainty, month in and month out.

But people in houses feel more vulnerable, and also feel they ought to be able to do something about it. For a while you could spot the empty houses by the lights that stayed on all night, blazing away at four in the morning to announce their owners' absence, but nowadays everybody has lights on timers, winking on and off in realistic fashion.

It's all part of the eternal game, a domestic version of the arms race. They keep coming up with better locks and more sophisticated alarm systems, and reprobates like me keep finding ways to get past the locks and around the alarm systems. The same technology that reinforces a door provides me with a new way to get through it.

Were the Mapeses home? There were ways to find out no matter how clever they were with their lights. I could call them on the phone and see if they answered. Voice mail and answering machines muddy the waters some, and when a machine picks up there's no guarantee there's nobody home. The next step is to ring the doorbell. Even if they don't come to the door—and why should they, if it's the middle of the night?—you almost always get some indication of occupancy. They switch on a light, they walk around, they make noise, and the painstaking burglar slinks away, and lives to steal another day.

And, finally, there's something else, an instinct you tend to develop, a sense you get just standing outside of a door as to whether or not there's someone with a pulse on the other side of it. It's not infallible, that instinct, and it's subject to influence by such forces as impatience and wishful thinking, but it's there, and you get to a point where you learn to rely on it.

And what did it tell me?

It told me I was standing in front of an empty house. There was no evidence pointing me toward this conclusion, no logical argument against their presence. It was just a feeling I had.

But what difference could it possibly make? I wasn't here to break and enter. There would be plenty of time for that on Friday, when I wouldn't need my intuition to let me know the place was empty because **Don Giovanni** would guarantee it. And I'd have a helper along, and a car to carry me and my helper and our well-gotten gains quickly and safely away. All I had to do now was figure out how, come Friday, I was going to get inside of the goddam place.

The first thing I did was check the windows. I'd already spotted the metallic tape on the first-floor windows (which a burglar from Britain or the Continent would call the ground-floor windows, due to a cultural predisposition to begin counting at the top of a flight of stairs rather than at the bottom). Sometimes, though, a homeowner will save time and money by wiring the more accessible windows into the alarm system but leaving out those he figures are too remote for a burglar to get to. After all, does he really want to have to close every window in the house before he sets the alarm? He might want to leave the odd upstairs window open for ventilation. Simpler, isn't it, to leave the upper windows untaped? And just as safe, too, right?

Simpler, perhaps; safe, perhaps not. If a window a flight up would provide Kilgore-free access, how hard would it be to bring along a telescoping aluminum ladder long enough to get me up and in? And, if that turned out to be the sesame that would open the Mapes house, I could pop into the garage tonight and see if they might not have a ladder I could borrow. I'd put it back when I was finished, and in the same condition I found it.

I took a good look, and knew I didn't have to break into the garage because a ladder wouldn't do me any good. The windows on the second floor had metallic tape on them. (There was a chance, slim but real, that the tape on the upstairs windows was just for show, just as there's a chance that a 100-to-1 shot will sweep the Triple Crown. It's possible, sure, but you wouldn't want to bet the rent money on it.)

How about the basement windows? They're small, and their panes get broken and aren't always replaced right away, and basements are dirty and cluttered and yucky, home to spiders and centipedes and things that go slither in the night, and you don't go there unless you have to, so who would even think that a basement window might be a burglar's way in? Could he even fit through a basement window if he wanted to? And why would he want to?

The basement windows were all rimmed with the same metallic tape. That was disappointing but not surprising, and at least I hadn't had to crane my neck to find out I wasn't going to get in that way.

And the third-floor windows? I couldn't tell from where I stood, and I couldn't see what difference it made. I'm all right with heights, but I'm not crazy enough to climb two stories on a housebreaking expedition. Even if I could find a ladder that would reach that far, and even if I could brace it so that it wouldn't slip out from under me, I wasn't willing to spend that much time that exposed to the gaze of anyone who happened to glance my way. There are any number of illegal things you can do that can appear innocent to a casual glance, but climbing into a third-story window is not one of them.

Okay, forget the windows. Forget the doors, too. What did that leave?

The house, like all the others on the block, had been built at least three-quarters of a century ago. It was obviously prewar (which will always mean World War II when you're talking about New York real estate, no matter how many wars have been fought since then, just as antebellum will always refer to the War Between the States, and antediluvian will always indicate Noah's flood, unless you happen to live in Johnstown) and my guess was that it had been built in the 1920s. I could find out for certain, but it didn't matter. What was significant was that it had almost certainly been equipped originally with a coal furnace, and that meant a coal cellar, and that meant a chute down which the delivery vehicle could pour the stuff.

That in turn meant a wooden cellar door, probably built to lean against the rear of the house at an angle of somewhere between forty-five and sixty degrees. Remember the song "Playmate"? Oh, sure you do, and it's got nothing to do with magazine centerfolds. **Playmate, come out and play with me/And with my dollies three/Climb up my apple tree/Shout down my rain barrel/Slide down my cellar door/And we'll be jolly friends/ Forevermore.**

They don't write 'em like that anymore, but then neither do they make cellar doors you can slide down. They did when they built the Mapes house, however. People kept them locked, generally securing them with a padlock, but how the hell did you tie a padlocked wooden cellar door into a burglar alarm system?

There may be a way, but the whole thing became academic when I went around to the back of the house and tried to find the entrance to the coal cellar. They'd had one, sure enough, but somewhere along the way it had been removed, with brickwork and concrete filling in where the opening had been. I could get in, all right, but not without a jackhammer, and they tend to draw attention.

Rats.

There's always a way in, I told myself. It makes a nice mantra, but even as I ran it through my mind I found myself beginning to doubt the universal verity of it. What if there wasn't always a way in?

But there had to be. It was a big old house, sure to be chock full of crannies and nooks (or, if you insist, nooks and crannies) and window seats and stair cupboards and rooms no one ever went into. That was fine, but they were all on the inside, and on the outside there was nothing but stone, along with two doors and more windows than I troubled to count, all of them wired into an alarm system that I couldn't knock out unless I found a way to create a power failure for the whole neighborhood.

I was trying to figure out just how I might manage that, which comes more under the heading of idle speculation than the exploration of a real possibility, when I opened my eyes and saw something that had been in front of them all along. How had I missed seeing it? The answer, of course, was that I had indeed seen it, but that it had somehow failed to register. I'd seen it and known what it was, but what I hadn't recognized was what it **meant**.

It meant I was in like Errol, that's what it meant.

 **FIVE**

Turning around and walking down the driveway and away from the Mapes house was one of the most difficult things I'd ever done.

Here was the house, an unassailable fortress, and here I was with a perfect way to assail the daylights out of it. And I'd come prepared, my picks and probes at hand, and my hands easily enough encased in the pair of Pliofilm gloves I'd tucked into a pocket. And who was to say I hadn't been the beneficiary of unwitting wisdom when I brought along the gloves and the tools? Maybe I'd somehow been given to know that an opportunity would knock. Now that it had done so, how could I fail to answer?

I hadn't phoned, hadn't established that they were out for the evening, but the house felt empty to me. I read somewhere that a house can actually sound empty, that occupied premises hum inaudibly with the energy of the people within. I don't know about that, but I know I can sometimes sense a human presence. I didn't sense it here, and I had some corroborating evidence from the garage; a peek had shown a fat and happy Lexus SUV parked to one side, with plenty of empty space for a second vehicle alongside it.

God, I was itching to do it, chomping at the bit, salivating like all of Pavlov's dogs rolled into one. My fingertips tingled, and the blood surged in my veins, and it took a measure of self-discipline I hadn't known I possessed to get me out of there.

Not that getting away from the Mapes house cut off the siren's song. There were other houses just like Mapes's, an inner voice reminded me, and every single one of them was sure to have the same happy flaw that would lay it wide open to an enterprising burglar. Why not knock off one of them now? Or even two of them, if time permitted. Why the hell not?

Because a burglary in the neighborhood would put everybody on edge, I told myself, and increase the risk on Friday night. To that the inner voice, resourceful devil that he was, had a persuasive counterargument: a burglary a few doors away, two days before I hit Mapes, would make Friday's burglary look like part of a string, and Mapes an incidental victim rather than a designated burglaree. Thus nobody would think to look for someone with a grudge against the man, turn up Marty, and work backwards from there.

Knock off that house on the corner, the voice murmured, and they won't look twice at Mapes. They'll see a pattern, and they'll stake out the neighborhood, waiting patiently for the burglar to strike a third time. And he won't, and nobody will ever figure it out.

You can't argue with a voice like that. What you can do is keep walking, and that's what I did—head lowered, hands in pockets, shoulders drawn protectively inward. The voice babbled on. Thanks for sharing, I told it, and walked all the way to the subway, and climbed the platform and caught a train home.

The first thing I did was return my windbreaker to the closet. While I was there, I opened up my hidden compartment—easy enough, if you know how—and stowed my burglar's tools and the gloves. I made myself a cup of tea and sat in front of the television set. **The West Wing** was history, and **Law & Order** was already in its second half, with prosecutor Jack McCoy pulling a dirty trick in an overzealous try for a conviction. Once upon a time TV cops and DAs were all good guys, and then there was a stretch where some of them were bad guys, and now the medium and the viewers have matured to the point where a character can be both at once.

Something unrelated to the story kept me watching even as it made me lose track of the storyline. There was an extra, one of the dozen folks in the jury box, who looked like a woman I'd had a very brief fling with a couple of years ago. I hadn't laid eyes on her since, and had in fact lost track of her entirely.

And I couldn't tell if it was her or not. She'd done a little acting, although she hadn't gotten very far with it. She'd also done a little writing and a little singing, but what she'd done the most of, and what had kept her in panty hose and eyeliner, was waitressing. **Law & Order** is filmed in New York, not California, which is one reason the supporting actors and bit players on the show look like actual human beings, so it was by no means unlikely for a New York–based singer/writer/actor/waitress to turn up in the show's jury box.

If the camera had stayed on her for any length of time I probably could have said one way or another if it was Francine. But it didn't, and consequently I couldn't. They just gave you a glimpse of the jurors every now and then, and it was enough to assure me each time that yes, there was a definite resemblance, but not enough to let me know for sure. And, because I figured maybe the next view would be conclusive, I kept waiting for a shot of the jury and paying next to no attention to the rest of the story.

And it ended with the jury reaching a decision (they acquitted the bastard, so McCoy's ethical lapse was for naught) while I remained not a whit closer to one of my own. I was hoping someone would demand that the jury be polled, but no, instead they cut to a shot of Sam Waterston and Fred Thompson in their office, with Waterston embittered and Thompson philosophical. Then they rolled the credits at the speed of light, but it didn't matter, because she wouldn't be listed there anyway. Bit players with non-speaking parts don't generally make the crawl.

So I sat around thinking about Francine, not that there was much to think, since we'd only been seeing each other for a couple of weeks, say a month at the outside. If I remembered correctly, the night we finally went to bed together was the last night of the relationship, not because it was a disaster but because we really weren't destined for each other, and we'd both kept it going just long enough to get through the bedchamber door, just to make sure we weren't missing anything. Once our mutual sexual curiosity was quenched, there was really no reason for either of us to hang around.

I tried to figure out just how many years had passed since Francine and I had our moment together, and I decided it was more than three and less than six, and that was the best I could do to narrow it down. And then I found myself working out just how many women had passed in and out of my life since then. I don't remember what number I came up with, but it really didn't matter, because any number, high or low, was going to be depressing. I mean, suppose I'd had thirty girlfriends since Francine. Suppose I'd had two. See what I mean?

What made it even more depressing was that lately I didn't even seem to be playing the game. I wasn't even coming up to bat anymore, let alone taking a good healthy cut at the ball. I hadn't been out on a date since sometime the previous fall, when I chatted up a woman who'd dropped into my bookstore late one afternoon, closed up a few minutes early, took her for a drink and to a movie at the multiplex over on Third Avenue, and then put her in a cab and never saw her again. I had her phone number, and of course she knew how to reach me, but neither of us said "I'll call you" and neither of us did. She'd never walked into my store before, and she never did afterward, either.

And the last time I'd actually been to bed with a woman . . . well, I don't know when that was. I'd had a genuine girlfriend for several months, and that had come to a bitter end sometime during the winter, not this past winter but the winter before. Then sometime the next spring (which is to say last spring, which would make it approximately a year ago) I'd acted out.

Acting out. I'm not sure when we first started calling it that, or what we used to call it before that convenient term came into widespread use. Misbehaving, maybe. Whatever you want to call it, I reacted to having my heart broken by doing three things in dogged succession. First I stayed more or less drunk for the better part of a week, but all that did was give me head-banger hangovers and a perfectly suitable case of postalcoholic remorse. Then I started chasing women in a rather frantic fashion, and even managed to catch some, though the ones I landed were the sort any self-respecting sportsman would have thrown back. Finally, I went on a burglary spree, in the course of which I must have averaged a break-in a night for close to two weeks. I was a one-man crime wave, and the risks I took don't bear thinking about, but at least I wasn't suicidal about it. I didn't have a deep unconscious desire to get caught, and nobody caught me, and when I finally came to my senses and settled down again, at least I had a tidy sum tucked away in my rainy day account. I came out of it ahead, which is more than I could say for the drinking and the woman-chasing.

And since then . . . well, since then I'd been as sexually active as a priest who took his vows seriously. I'd helped Carolyn compose her listing for Date-a-Dyke ("LOOKING FOR A SPRING FLING? Five-foot-two, eyes for you. Bright and cute and funny, you can think of me as the long-lost bastard daughter of L. L. Bean and Laura Ashley. Love scotch, love New York, hate softball, and limit myself to two cats. My meaningful relationships always lead to heartbreak or LBD, so how about a meaningless relationship?") but wouldn't hear of cobbling up an equivalent listing for myself. It was, I told myself, a phase I was going through. I was evidently not yet ready to have a woman in my life, and when I was I would automatically change the vibe I put out, and women who now had the good sense to steer clear of me would suddenly think I was catnip. Just a question of time, I told myself. Time. That's all.

So when **Law & Order** packed it in I watched the first five minutes of the local news, then surfed my way around the channels, watching thirty seconds here and two minutes there, not getting caught up in any of it, perhaps because I didn't stay with any-thing long enough to give it a chance to catch me. I thought about calling Francine ("Hi, I saw you on **Law & Order** tonight, and I swear I couldn't take my eyes off the jury box. You absolutely lit up the screen!") and looked for her number, but I'd recopied my address book since we stopped seeing each other, and she hadn't made the cut. I reached for the phone book and put it back when I realized I couldn't remember her last name. Then I channel-surfed some more, and then I turned off the TV and stood up.

All of the foregoing is by way of explanation for what I did next, and maybe it explains it, but it doesn't justify it. The whole thing's embarrassing, so I won't dwell on it. I'll just report it in plain English.

I went to my closet, opened up the hidden com-partment, gathered up my tools and gloves, put on my windbreaker, changed my mind and swapped it for a blue blazer, and went down the stairs and out of the building.

And on the prowl.

 **SIX**

On the prowl.

The phrase has a wonderful ring to it, doesn't it? It sounds at once menacing and exciting, deliciously attractive in an unwholesome way. Byron, someone observed, was "mad, bad, and dangerous to know"—which evidently made the son of a bitch irresistible. Can't you picture him going on the prowl?

When a burglar goes on the prowl, he's improvising. Now improvisation is vastly useful in the arts, and in jazz it's fundamental; when a jazz musician gives himself free rein to improvise, he finds himself playing notes and creating phrases he hadn't thought of, unearthing the music from some inner chamber of his private self. When I play a record and listen to some solo piano by, say, Lennie Tristano or Randy Weston or Billy Taylor, I can get lost in the intricacies and subtleties the pianist is working out on the spot, creating this beauty as he threads his way through the notes.

That's great if you're a musician, and what I

really should have done was stay home and play some of my old LPs, admiring the way those fellows could prowl the keyboard. Because improvisation in burglary is different. It's a foolproof method for minimizing rewards while maximizing risk, and what kind of a way is that to run a business?

It is, I should point out, not a career I would recommend for anyone. It's morally reprehensible, for starters, and the fact that I evidently can't give it up doesn't mean I'm not well aware of the disagreeably sordid nature of what I do. Such considerations aside, it's still a poor vocational choice.

Oh, there are attractive elements, and let's acknowledge them right in front. You're your own boss, and you never have to sit through a job interview, never have to convince anyone that you have the requisite experience for the task at hand, or, conversely, that you're not overqualified. No one has to hire you and no one can fire you.

Nor, like the ordinary tradesman, are you dependent upon the good will of your customers. That's just as well, as ill will is what they'd bear you, and it's all to the good if they never know more about you than that you've paid them a visit. But you don't have to drum up business, and you don't have to deal with suppliers, and no avaricious landlord can raise the rent on your business premises, because you don't have any.

Your business is essentially unaffected by booms and busts in the national or world economy. There's a built-in hedge against inflation—the value of

what you steal keeps pace with your higher costs—
and depression won't throw you out of work. (The
competition's a little keener in bad times, as otherwise solid citizens decide to find out what's behind
Door Number Three, but that's all right. There's
always enough to go around.)

You don't need a license from the city or state,
either, and there's no union to join, no dues to pay,
and no paperwork to fill out. On the other hand,
there's no pension plan, and since you don't pay
taxes neither do you qualify for Social Security and
Medicare and all the other benefits that sparkle
like diamonds in the setting of the golden years.
No sick days, either, and no paid vacation. No
health care. Bottom line, you're pretty much on
your own.

You set your own hours, of course, and you'll
never find yourself putting in a forty-hour week.
Even allowing for study and research, you're not
likely to work forty hours in the course of an entire
month. Once you get down to cases, time is of the
essence, and burglary, unlike some other pursuits,
does not reward the chap who makes the whole
thing last as long as possible. The idea is to get in
and get out as quickly as possible.

All of this sounds pretty good, doesn't it? Even
the drawbacks—no pension, no security, no guar-
anteed annual wage—are part of the image of the
romantic self-sufficient loner, making his rugged-
individualist way in the world. You can almost hear
country music playing in the background, and

Merle Haggard urging you to chuck the effete urban rat race and move to Montana like a man.

Well, there's a downside. For one thing, you never get to feel like a useful and productive member of society, because you're not. Even if you can shrug off the natural guilt that comes from taking things that don't belong to you, even if you rationalize it by arguing with Proudhon that all property is theft, there's nothing to give you a sense of accomplishment.

A construction worker, walking past a skyscraper, can say to himself, "Hey, I built that." An obstetrician, lamenting the endless escalation of his malpractice insurance premiums, can console himself with the thought of all the children he brought into the world. A chef, a hooker, a bartender, even a drug dealer, can rejoice at the day's end with the thought that any number of people feel better for having been his or her customers that day.

And what can a burglar tell himself? "Hey, see that house? I broke into that house, robbed 'em blind. Stole everything but the paint off the walls. Made out like a bandit. And that's just one of my houses . . ."

Great. And that's not the worst of it, either.

Because here's the thing: you can get caught. And, if they catch you, they'll throw you in prison.

For all I know, you may have romantic ideas about prison. Maybe you figure you'll finally get to read Proust. Maybe you watched **Oz**, overlooked the less savory aspects, and decided it would be neat

to be a part of all that high drama and snappy dialogue. Well, put those notions right out of your
head. I've been there—just once, and just briefly,
thank God and St. Dismas—and I have to say I
learned my lesson.

Because it's really horrible inside. All the freedom that makes burglary attractive is taken away
from you, and people are forever telling you what to
do. The guards are unpleasant, and your fellow
prisoners are no bargain, either. I mean, consider
what they did to get locked up there. All in all, I
have to say you meet a better class of people on the
D train.

And you won't read Proust, either, or **War and
Peace,** or any of the worthy works you've promised
yourself you'd get around to if you only had the
time. You'll have plenty of time, but it's noisy
inside, noisy all the time, with people yelling and
banging things and doors slamming. If **Oz** had
shown that aspect of prison life realistically, nobody
could have heard the snappy dialogue. The background roar would have drowned it out.

The right or wrong of it aside, burglary just doesn't
make sense. I know I should give it up, and believe
me, I've tried. I couldn't tell you how many times
I've sworn off. Once I actually managed to stay away
from it for a couple of years, and then I knocked
off an apartment, and I was hooked again. It's an
addiction, a compulsion, and so far I haven't found

a 12-Step program that addresses it. I suppose I could start up a chapter of Burglars Anonymous, and we wouldn't even have to find a church willing to rent us a meeting place. We could just break into a loft somewhere.

Until then, the best I can do is remember the lesson I learned in prison. It wasn't the one they hoped to teach me—**Thou Shalt Not Steal**—but a pragmatic variation thereof—**Don't Get Caught.**

The way to avoid getting caught is to keep risk to a minimum, and the way to manage that is to size up each potential job in advance and do as much planning and preparation as possible. Consider the Mapes house, if you will. I'd been provided in advance with some useful information about Mapes—the location of his safe, the likelihood that it would contain cash, and the happy knowledge that it was cash he hadn't reported to the government, which meant he might very well choose not to report the burglary to the authorities. I'd established who lived in the house—just Mapes and his wife, his kids were grown and had long since moved away—and learned that Mr. and Mrs. Mapes had season tickets to the Met, and that's where they'd be come Friday night. I'd dropped by Lincoln Center—it's just five minutes from my apartment—and determined that the opera they were seeing would keep them in their seats until close to midnight.

And then, two nights before the event, I'd gone up for a look-see. I'd assessed the locks and the alarm system, probed the defenses, and kept at it until I saw a way through them. Then I'd gone home, prepared to devote another two days to refining my plan and working out the details.

That didn't mean nothing could go wrong. Here's another maxim: **Something can always go wrong**. Either of the Mapeses could come down with a migraine and decide that it was no night for Mozart. Mapes's daughter-in-law could have kicked her spouse out of the house—if he was a shitheel like his father, God knows she'd have ample cause—prompting the junior Mapes to come home with his tail, among other things, between his legs, ready to hole up in his old room until his wife came to her senses. I could let myself in and find him there, a former college athlete who still worked out regularly at the gym, and who'd lately added a course in martial arts, all the better to defend the family home against a hapless burglar.

I could go on, but you get the point. Something can always go wrong, but that doesn't mean you just plunge blindly ahead, kicking in the first door you come to.

And here I was, on the prowl. Walking the darkened streets, gloves in one pocket, tools in another, risking life and liberty for no good reason. I knew what I was doing, and I damn well should have known better.

I was acting out, that's what I was doing. I felt crummy because I didn't have a girlfriend and I was leading a purposeless existence, and I wanted to do something to change my mood, and I didn't have the urge to get drunk or chase women, somehow knowing that neither would do me any good.

I caught a cab, had the driver drop me at the corner of Park Avenue and 38th Street. I walked the streets of Murray Hill, knowing I was making a big mistake, knowing nothing good could come of this, knowing I was courting disaster.

And here's the worst part of all: It felt wonderful.

 **SEVEN**

The first place that looked good to me was a house on the south side of 39th Street a little ways east of Park. I studied it from across the street and decided nobody who lived there had to worry where his next meal was coming from. I crossed the street for a closer look and spotted a plaque that identified the place as the Williams Club. (That meant that the members had all attended Williams College, not that they were all guys named Bill.)

For a moment or two I found myself thinking it over. On the plus side, I could pretty much take it for granted that the place would be empty. They'd shut down for the night, and there was no nonsense about leaving a light on to ward off intruders. The windows on all four floors were dark as a burglar's conscience. Some clubs, I knew, had sleeping rooms they kept available for out-of-town members, or local members with marital problems, but any such residents would be lodged on the top floor, and they'd never hear me moving around below, or do anything about it if they did.

Nor did I expect to encounter a state-of-the-art security system. As far as I knew, there had never been a break-in at a private club in New York, so why spend a few thousand dollars of membership funds to prevent something that wasn't going to happen? There'd be a lock on the door, and I was sure it would be a good one, but so what? The better the lock, the greater the satisfaction when the tumblers tumble. Where's the fun if they leave the door wide open for you? Where's the sense of accomplishment?

But it's not enough to get in. You have to get out, too, and with something to show for your efforts. I was fairly sure they had a decent wine cellar, and a cozy billiard room, and a welcoming bar, but I couldn't see myself waltzing out of there with a couple of bottles in hand, however splendid the vintage.

There wouldn't be any cash. You don't part with cash at a private club. You don't even need plastic, you just sign for everything, and write a check once a month. There'd be paintings on the walls, no doubt in elaborately carved and gilded frames, but they'd likely be portraits of whatever Williams had founded the school, along with various college presidents, distinguished alumni, and star athletes. If you wanted to turn them into cash, you'd have to cut them out of their frames—and then sell the frames, because no one would give you anything for the portraits.

I walked on. Not without some reluctance, I

have to say, because I'd already imagined the plea-sure I'd take walking silently through the darkened rooms of the club, a fine if somewhat worn carpet underfoot, the heavy drapery redolent with the aroma of expensive cigars. Maybe there'd be a humidor of cigars behind the bar, and I could take one to the reading room, along with a glass of tawny port or a small snifter of brandy. I could sit in an overstuffed leather club chair with my feet on a matching ottoman and a lamp lit at my shoulder, and I could dip into one of the books from the club library, and—

Go home, an inner voice suggested, but I barely heard it.

I wanted a brownstone.

In the loosest sense of the word, that is. Strictly speaking, a New York brownstone is a structure three or four or five stories tall, with a façade made of—surprise!—brown stone. The term, however, has stretched to cover similar structures fronted in other materials, including limestone and even brick.

If brownstones can vary some on their outsides, it is within their exterior walls that they approach infinite variety. Many were built originally as single-family homes; typically there's a parlor floor, usu-ally a half flight up from street level, with a higher ceiling than the two floors above (where the bed-rooms are) or the semi-basement below. Others started out as three- or four-family residences, with one apartment per floor. (Tenements, with four apartments to a floor, sometimes sport façades of brown stone, which does tend to confuse things.)

Over the years, a vast number of one-family brownstones have been chopped up for multiple occupancy, some of them converted into rooming houses, with a couple dozen individual tenants. These conversions have themselves occasionally been reconverted in the process of neighborhood gentrification, turned into three-family dwellings or even all the way back into single-family houses.

Murray Hill was a neighborhood that had never declined significantly, and as far as I knew none of its brownstones had ever had more than one apartment to a floor. Many were still one-family dwellings. A few had commercial tenants on the lower floors, with residential apartments above. Some were private clubs—I'd already stumbled on one of those—and a few were entirely commercial, but the greater portion had people living in them, and looked to be better targets of opportunity than the apartment buildings, which almost all had doormen or security cameras or both.

Although the uniform might lead you to think otherwise, the average New York doorman is a less formidable bulwark of security than the Beefeaters posted at the Tower of London. Under the right circumstances, I'm more than willing to try to flimflam a doorman. But these were by no means the right circumstances. I didn't know the names of any of the tenants, didn't have a particular apartment targeted, and knew I'd be a lot better off with a brownstone.

So I walked around trying to decide which one to hit.

I must have wandered around for a good half hour, and it may have been closer to forty-five minutes. That's a lot of time to devote to an essentially random choice, almost on a par with feeling every last ticket stub before drawing one out of a hat. There's a limited amount you can learn about a house by strolling past it, and all I can think is that I may have been trying to outlast the impulse, to walk and walk and walk until the compulsion to burgle left me and I could go home and get some sleep.

No such luck. I stopped abruptly in front of a brownstone (with a façade of actual brown stone, as it happens) on East 36th between Lexington and Third. There was a travel agent on the ground floor, while the parlor floor was occupied by a gallery dealing in tribal art; the window was lit, and most of what I saw was Oceanic, along with a handful of African pieces, including a Benin bronze leopard and a mask that looked Dogon to my admittedly untrained eye.

The gallery figured to have some sort of security system, but I'd have passed it up even if the door had been wide open. You couldn't walk down the street with your arms full of primitive tribal artifacts. That'll draw attention, even in New York.

And, even if you got away with it, where would you sell the stuff?

I mounted the steps, checked out the nameplates next to the three doorbells. (The basement travel agency had its own entrance a half-flight down from street level.) **Ladislas Szabo Gallery,** read the bottommost nameplate. The one above it said **J. Feldmaus,** while the top one said simply **Creeley.**

Creeley or Feldmaus, Feldmaus or Creeley. I'd have to decide, but I didn't have to decide yet. First I had to get into the building.

There was a double set of doors, one leading into the vestibule, the other leading from that little antechamber into the building's interior. Both sported locks, but neither put one in mind of the Gordian knot. I studied the first one, stroked the cylinder with the tip of my forefinger, and wouldn't have been overly surprised if that had been enough to make it pop open. But it wasn't, so I took out my ring of tools and glanced over my shoulder before I got down to business.

And saw a police cruiser from the local precinct, just moseying along, keeping an unblinking eye on things.

And, if they were looking my way, what could they see? Just a harmless-looking fellow, respectably turned out in khakis and a blazer, fitting his key in the lock with no more difficulty than you'd expect after a round or two (or three or four) at the gin joint around the corner. The lock was a sweetie, I could have opened it with a toothpick, and it surrendered in no time at all, and only when I was within the vestibule did I take another look at the street. The police car was nowhere to be seen.

Comforting, though, to know they're on the job.

I took a moment to put on my Pliofilm gloves— now that would have caught a cop's eye, a man putting on clear plastic gloves before unlocking his own front door—and then I opened the inner door with not much more difficulty than I'd had with its outer cousin. I closed it quietly and stood there with no more light than filtered in from the street, stood there listening to the house.

It was, as far as I could tell, as still as a tomb.

I climbed a flight of stairs and stopped in front of the door of the Feldmaus apartment. The name, a new one on me, was German, and I knew just about enough of that language to translate it as **field mouse**. Creeley is Irish, I think, or possibly Scots-Irish, and I've no idea what it means. A creel is the woven basket a fisherman keeps his catch in, but I can't see how that could enter into the equation.

Creeley or Feldmaus? Feldmaus or Creeley?

All things being equal, one's best advised to take the apartment on the lower floor. One less floor to climb up, and, more to the point, one less floor to descend from on the way out. No light showed beneath the Feldmaus door. I listened for a long moment at that door, heard nothing whatsoever, took a breath, and rang the Feldmaus bell.

And once again heard nothing, nothing but the bell itself, but waited, waited patiently, and was just about to ring again when, yes, I heard footsteps, and then the sort of grunt you utter when you bump into something, probably because you're stumbling around in the dark. The footsteps stopped, then resumed.

Was the top-floor tenant male or female? I didn't know, and slurred my way accordingly. "Mis' Creeley?" I called through the door.

The footsteps stopped again, and the silence was eloquent. Then a male voice, thickened with sleep and irritation, said, "Up a flight."

"I say, terribly sorry." For some reason I was affecting an English accent.

"Fucking idiot," Feldmaus said, but the words didn't have much force to them. I headed for the stairs, and heard his footsteps heading back to bed.

A flight up, I went through the same routine at Creeley's door. I determined that no light showed below it or through the keyhole, then put my finger on the buzzer and buzzed away. When I heard Creeley's approaching footsteps, I knew just what I would do. I'd say "Mister Feldmaus?" and I wouldn't have to fudge the first word, because I'd established that Feldmaus was a man. (There might be a Mrs. Feldmaus as well, for all I knew, but that was neither here nor there.)

Then Creeley, Ms. or Mr., would tell me Feldmaus was a flight below, and I'd excuse myself, using the same English accent that had served me so well thus far. And then I'd go downstairs, not one flight but two, and then I'd go out of the building and, please God, catch the first cab I saw and go home.

But I didn't hear any footsteps.

I rang again, and got the same non-response. I put my ear to the door and listened to the silence.

There were three locks on the door. I unlocked all three of them, or at least I thought I did, but the one in the middle was unlocked to begin with, so picking it only served to lock it, as I found out when I went to open the door. I picked it again, retracting the bolt I'd unwittingly extended, and now the door opened.

And in I went.

 **EIGHT**

What a feeling!

I don't know that I can possibly convey what it felt like. I can tell you that my senses were keener than normal, that the blood sang in my veins, that there was a tingling in the tips of my fingers, but the more precisely I record such phenomena the more pathological the whole thing sounds. What I'm hard put to get across is the sheer exhilaration that possessed me, combined with an all-encompassing sense of well-being, and even of appropriateness. I was, it seemed to me, precisely where I ought to be, doing precisely what I was supposed to do.

Which, when you stop and think about it, is palpable nonsense. I was in point of fact where I was manifestly **not** supposed to be, where the law of the land told me in no uncertain terms I was not allowed to be. And I was doing what I was unquestionably not supposed to do.

But I can only tell you how it felt.

And it felt terrific.

• • •

For a few minutes I just stood there, monitoring my own response, enjoying every particle of it. The apartment was dark, and I let my eyes grow accustomed to the dimness. When they were equal to the task, I took a moment to lock all three locks. Then I had a look around.

The room the door opened on was the middle room of the apartment, and it was a combination kitchen and dining room. To the left, fronting on 36th Street, was a very large living room; in back, with windows looking across a courtyard at the buildings on 35th Street, was a bedroom almost as large as the living room. Any one of the three rooms would have served as a perfectly decent studio apartment, so Creeley, whoever he or she was, had an abundance of living space by New York standards. (To keep things in proportion, it's worth noting that a welfare mother holed up in a broken-down trailer on the outskirts of Moline, Illinois, would have at least as much square footage, and a front lawn and back yard in the bargain.)

There were blackout shades on the bedroom windows, which I lowered, and curtains as well, which I drew. I wondered if perhaps Creeley worked nights and slept days, which would account both for the blackout shades and the tenant's absence. It would also give me all the time in the world to finish my work.

I turned on a bedside lamp and had a look

around. The bed—queen size, of Danish teak—
was made, the pillows plumped. That alone suggested Creeley was a woman or lived with one,
because what man living alone bothers to make the
bed? Oh, I suppose military service gets some men
in the habit, but my immediate thought was that
Creeley was of the female persuasion, and a glance
at the mahogany dresser, topped with little jars and
bottles of makeup and scent and such, cinched it.
Creeley was a lady, and a reasonably girly girl at
that, with dresses sharing her closet with the suits
she wore to work, and the jeans she wore for play.

I left the bedroom, closing the door far enough to
block most but not all of the light, and with what
leaked out I made my way through the kitchen to
the living room, where some light came through the
front windows from the street. The living room
windows had floor-to-ceiling drapes, heavy velvet
things that must have been hanging there since the
Korean War. I drew them shut and turned on a lamp
or two and made myself at home.

Sometimes I think that's the best part, when you
can just take a few moments to slip into another
person's life as effortlessly as you've slipped into
their abode. I stretched out on the sofa, sat in the
matching armchair, browsed the small bookcase
(mostly trade paperbacks, proclaiming their owner
as hip and sophisticated but cost-conscious, pre-
tentiously lacking in pretension). I ambled into the
kitchen and opened the refrigerator. Eggs, bacon, a
few kinds of sausage, and an array of cheeses from

Murray's on Bleecker Street. No milk, but a half-pint of heavy cream. No beer, no bread, no bagels. No carbs, I noted, and recalled that one of the books in the bookcase was the latest work of the late Dr. Atkins. Ms. Creeley's refrigerator suggested that she practiced what he preached.

And to good effect, judging from the sizes of the clothes in her closet. If she'd ever been a chubbette, she'd long since banished her fat clothes to the Salvation Army.

Her first name, I learned from the Con Ed bill in her desk, was Barbara, and other bills and payment stubs confirmed this. I didn't find a checkbook, and assumed she kept it in her purse. Barbara Creeley lived alone, I knew, and generally slept alone, I could tell, though she evidently had High Hopes.

And how did I know all this? Well, the wardrobe told me she lived alone. If she had a boyfriend who stayed over with any degree of regularity, there'd be a few garments of his left at her place for convenience, and there weren't. The queen-size bed had surely been purchased with the intention of sharing it at least occasionally, and the mattress, with its shallow depression on one side and no evidence of wear whatsoever on the other, told me that she slept alone, and always on the right-hand side of the bed.

Yes, I checked. Yes, I pulled back the covers and felt each side of the mattress for firmness. Not out of prurient interest, I assure you, but out of a fierce curiosity that may well be every bit as shameful. I disturbed her bedclothing, I thrust my gloved hands into her linen. Of course I made the bed again afterward, but that didn't erase the psychic stain, did it?

Some years ago a friend of Carolyn's was burglarized. Whoever it was who did it didn't take much—he couldn't, she didn't have much—but she told us that what she'd lost was the least of it. "He was in my **place**," she said, shuddering. "He was touching my **things**. I feel like burning all my clothes and having the place tented and fumigated. I feel like moving out, I feel like going back to Nebraska, and you know how I feel about Nebraska. God, I feel so utterly **violated**."

I understood completely. I'd had the same feeling myself, when my own apartment had been inexpertly tossed. Tossed, I might say, was the operative word; the swine had taken all the books off my shelves and scattered them in a heap on the floor. I'd realized in a rush just what I inflicted upon the people I visited. I told myself it wasn't the same, that I never made a mess or damaged anything I left behind, but so what? The violation was the same.

Ah, well. Someday I'll reform. In the meantime, I might as well enjoy it.

I got to work.

There's a line that originated in the Army Corps of Engineers and has since had widespread circulation on T-shirts and bumper stickers and such. The wording varies, but the gist of it is that, when you're up to your ass in alligators, it's hard to remember that your original purpose was to drain the swamp.

Similarly, when I'm immersed in another person's life, or at least the glimpse of it I get by rummaging through their furnishings and worldly goods, I'm in danger of forgetting what brought me there in the first place. Which, pure and simple, is greed.

Crooks are greedy. It's not nice to admit it, but there's no way around it. Otherwise we'd be content to live on what came to us honestly, but we're not. We want more, and what I wanted—what had brought me here—was whatever Barbara Creeley had that was worth taking.

She made a decent living, that was clear from her address and from the clothes in her drawers and closet, but that didn't necessarily tell me she had anything I wanted. Maybe she saved her money, or spent it on travel and high living. Maybe she kept all her money in the bank and anything valuable in a safe-deposit box.

I gave her three rooms a systematic search. By the time I was ready to call it a night, I had turned up the following: a pair of earrings, with what looked to be rubies and diamonds, set in what was definitely gold; a watch for evening wear, a Graubunden, with a platinum case and band; a gold charm bracelet with eight or ten charms in the shape of different animals, along with fifteen gold coins attached as charms, none of them of any particular numismatic value but all of them, like the bracelet itself, worth their weight in gold; and, in the freezer compartment of her refrigerator, in among enough steaks and chops and roasts to comfort Dr. Atkins in the hereafter, a brown manila bank envelope containing $1240 in twenties, fifties, and hundreds.

That wasn't the only jewelry she had, of course. There was a high school class ring, gold and onyx, that was not without value, and a whole array of earrings and bracelets. There was a gold locket on a gold chain, and in it were pictures of a man and woman whom I took to be Barbara Creeley's parents.

All of these things were worth taking from a pure dollars-and-cents standpoint, but I've found that I tend to balance the cash value of an artifact against its likely sentimental value to its owner. Why deprive this woman of her class ring and her locket for the few dollars they would bring me? I'd be hurting her far more than I'd be helping myself, and it didn't seem right.

Now if my unwitting hostess had been not Barbara Creeley but Elizabeth Taylor, say, and the object in question had been not a high school ring but a diamond necklace, I wouldn't care if Richard Burton gave it to her and she couldn't look at it without getting tears in her violet eyes. Sentimental value only goes so far. But I didn't notice a pearl richer than all my tribe in the Creeley jewel box, so I took what I've told you about and left the rest. It's not conscience, not inherent decency, just a sense of proportion.

I tidied up as I went along, and when I was finished I went through the whole apartment, making sure I left everything as I'd found it, except of course for having removed the few items I've mentioned. I took a last look around, turned off the lights in the living room, opened the velvet drapes, and had just turned from that task when I heard footsteps on the stairs.

Hell.

I moved quickly through the apartment, killed a light in the kitchen, switched off the bedside lamp. The footsteps paused at the second-floor landing, and I had a moment where I hoped, all logic notwithstanding, that this was not Barbara Creeley on the stairs but someone planning a late visit to J. Feldmaus.

No such luck. The footsteps resumed, and I heard human speech (What other kind is there? Parrot?) but could not make out what was being said. Either Barbara had company or she was talking to herself. Well, the locks would delay her, and by the time she got past them I'd be down the fire escape.

I opened the curtains, raised one of the blackout shades, and took hold of the window.

And the damned thing wouldn't budge.

I checked to see if it was locked, and learned it was worse than that. The damned thing was nailed shut. Evidently Barbara (or some previous tenant) had been paranoid about an intruder coming in off the fire escape, and had taken up hammer and nails to safeguard herself. Cross-ventilation wasn't a problem, you could still open the window from the top, but you couldn't get out that way. What was she going to do if she had a fire?

More to the point, what was **I** going to do?

They'd reached the top of the stairs now, and it was clear there were two of them, because I could hear two voices, one basso and one soprano, or perhaps mezzo. So Barbara, who typically slept alone on the right side of the bed, had found someone to bring home with her. That made it her lucky night, but it certainly wasn't mine.

She had trouble with the locks, and I gave thanks for that. It sounded as though she and her companion had had a few drinks, not infrequently the case before two people decide to go home together, and her dexterity had gone the way of her inhibitions. Sooner or later she'd get it right, however, and then where would I be?

I raised the shades, opened the curtains. And now what? The closet? Twice in my career I've hidden in closets, and both times I went undetected, but somehow I knew the third time would be the charm. I couldn't hope to get away with it again.

"Jesus, gimme the fucking keys," said young Lochinvar, and I knew my time was running out.

I hit the floor and dove under the bed.

 **NINE**

I tried not to listen.

I'd been willing enough to snoop around in Barbara Creeley's private life earlier, but that was different. She wasn't around at the time, and all I was doing was going through her things and getting what sense I could of the person who owned them. Now, though, she was in the apartment with me, and so was he. It wasn't hard to guess what they were going to do now that they'd managed to get through the door, and unless an excess of passion made them rip off their clothes and do it in the kitchen, they were going to do it right on top of me.

I'd been home, for God's sake. I'd put away my burglar's tools, I'd stowed them in my hidden compartment. I was all settled in for the night. Why couldn't I have gone to bed?

But no, that would have been too easy. So instead of lying comfortably in my own bed I was wedged underneath Barbara Creeley's. There was no room to spare, and there'd be even less when a pair of bodies piled on top of the mattress.

And if anybody looked under the bed, well, then I was sunk. It was not a refuge I could leave in a hurry. All I could do was stay there and wait for the cops to drag me out.

"Kinda sleepy," the woman said.

"Yeah, well, you're gonna get the best night's sleep you ever had," the man said.

"Ca' keep m'eyes open . . ."

"Roofies'll do that."

"How'd I get here?"

"You live here, you dizzy bitch. Jesus, you're built nice, aren't you? Hang on now, just let me get your clothes off."

"Sleeeeepy . . ."

In spite of myself I listened, and somewhere along the way it dawned on me what I was listening to. One thing he'd said—"Roofies'll do that"—was enough to clue me in, once I'd allowed it to register. Roofies is one of the names for Rohypnol, that miracle of modern medical science known as the date-rape drug. Barbara Creeley, who'd already been burglarized (even though she didn't know it yet), was about to get raped (even though she didn't know that, either).

It struck me that I ought to do something, but what? If I tried to squirm out from under the bed, I'd alert him long before I was in a position to do anything. I'd gone in headfirst, more or less, so I'd be coming out feet first, and by the time my head cleared the bedframe he'd be in a position to break something over it. And even if I somehow got out before he reacted, well, then what? I never studied martial arts, never put on a pair of boxing gloves, and the last time I was in a fight was when I was eleven years old. My opponent was Kevin Vogelsang, and he gave me a bloody nose, which I probably deserved for chirping "Tweet, tweet, tweet" at him. (His last name means Birdsong. If it had been Feldmaus I'd very likely have gone "Squeak, squeak, squeak" at him, and gotten the same bloody nose. I was a real pain in the ass when I was eleven.)

The point is I've never been much at physical combat, nor am I the hulking sort who can intimidate an opponent by his mere physical presence. In fact I had a feeling it might be the other way around. I hadn't had a look at the Roofies guy, but he had heavy footsteps and a deep and resonant voice, and I'd formed the image of a large fellow who spent a lot of time at the gym lifting heavy metal objects. There was always the chance that my strength would be as the strength of ten because my heart was pure, but what good would that do me? His strength was very likely the strength of eleven, even if his heart was darker than the inside of a cow.

My impulse was chivalrous, but you couldn't have told as much from what I did, which was stay right where I was, as idle as a painted ship upon a painted ocean, while the scoundrel had his way with her.

• • •

I'll draw a veil over the next ten or fifteen minutes, if it's all the same to you. I couldn't shut out the sounds, nor could I stop my mind from inventing pictures to go with them, but I'm going to keep all that to myself. Barbara Creeley had to endure it, but at least she didn't have to know about it, and neither should you.

I said she didn't know about it, but that's not to say she was unconscious throughout. At one point her voice rang out clear as a bell: "Who are you? What are you doing?"

"Shut up," he explained.

"What's going on?"

"You're getting laid," he said, "but you won't remember a thing in the morning. You'll just wonder why you're sore down there, and where the wet spot in the bed came from."

And he laughed savagely, but she didn't say anything, and I guess she must have slipped back under the fuzzy blanket of Rohypnol. According to what I'd heard and read about the drug, he was right that she wouldn't remember much, if anything. A couple of Roofies, ground up and stirred into a drink, made the drinker essentially comatose, albeit with occasional interludes of apparent lucidity. Sometimes the victim even participated in the lovemaking (if you want to call it that), making the usual moves and uttering the usual grunts and sighs, but not from a truly conscious plane, and without anything much imprinting itself on her memory.

There you have it—Rohypnol, clearly a drug for our times. What beats me is why anyone would want to use it. Where's the pleasure in having sex with someone who's not even capable of knowing what's going on, let alone matching your moves with moves of her own? Isn't it a little like romancing an inflatable doll?

Then again, they evidently sell quite a few of those dolls, enough to warrant mass-producing them. There would seem to be a substantial number of men who don't care if their partner's having a good time, or if she's even there at all. And I can see where a woman all goofy on Roofies might have it all over a plastic lady. You wouldn't get winded blowing her up, and you wouldn't have the worry that she might suddenly deflate at **le moment critique**.

I guess Barbara Creeley functioned satisfactorily in her role as a flesh-and-blood inflatable doll, because her partner seemed to be having a good time. He moaned and grunted a lot, and said "Baby, baby" and that sort of thing, and made a lot of noise as he reached the finish line. Then the bed stopped creaking and rocking above me, and all was mercifully silent for a moment, and then his weight shifted and he got up from the bed.

"Not bad," he said. "You're a pretty good piece of ass for a dead girl." And he laughed that deep-throated laugh I'd heard earlier, and said, his tone mock-earnest, "Well, darling? Was it good for you?" and started in laughing all over again.

I stayed where I was. **Not bad for a dead girl.** But it was just a drug, wasn't it? Just a couple of Roofies, enough to sedate her but not enough to kill her. He couldn't really mean it literally, could he?

While I lay there and wondered about it, he clomped around the apartment, making more noise than a man generally makes getting dressed. I heard him yanking drawers out, spilling things, and I had a pretty good idea what was going on. But I couldn't do anything about it. I kept knowing what the son of a bitch was doing, and I kept being unable to do anything about it.

Eventually he walked off, and I didn't hear him for a while and wondered if he might have left. Then his footsteps returned, and I heard a buzzing sound. I couldn't place it, until he spoke and cleared things up for me.

"Your name's Barbara," he said, with the air of having just discovered this fact. "Hey, Barbie Doll, how about if I give you a shave? Be a nice surprise for you when you wake up. Make things a little smoother and sweeter for the next man in your life, too."

The shaver went on buzzing.

"Nah, the hell with it," he said, and there was a noise which it didn't take too much imagination to identify as the sound of the electric shaver hitting the floor. "So long," he said. "Sleep tight, you stupid cow."

He slammed the door on his way out, and he didn't stop to lock the locks. I heard his heavy foot-steps on the stairs, and I heard the door slam down on the first floor. And then, when I didn't hear any-thing more, I set about wriggling and squirming, and the heroic devil-may-care burglar got out from under the bed.

He'd left a godawful mess behind. I'd figured out the noise he was making was a by-product of a search for something to steal; having taken what he could sexually, he was looking to turn a cash profit on the night as well.

Her black leather handbag was on the floor where he'd flung it, its contents strewed all over the place. I scooped up a lipstick and a comb and her checkbook and a set of keys and returned them to her purse. Her wallet, a little French purse of green leather with gold tooling, lay in a corner where he'd flung it; I picked it up and saw that her driver's license was halfway out of its frame, and figured that's how he'd learned her name. The license iden-tified her as Barbara Anne Creeley, gave a date of birth that made her thirty-two years old, and showed a picture of a pretty woman with dark hair and about as winning a smile as anyone can manage while being photographed by some **schmendrick** from the Department of Motor Vehicles.

I carried the wallet over to the bedside, past the heap of clothing she'd been wearing. She was sprawled on her back, her head angled to one side, and her mouth was open, which never helps one to look one's best, but it was the same woman, no question about it, and she'd have struck me as prettier if she'd been less pitiable. She was naked, and that bothered me enough so that I covered her with a sheet, even at the risk of waking her. But of course it didn't wake her. She was alive, her breathing was deep and even, and she was in no danger of waking up, not for hours.

I went through her wallet and saw that he'd left her credit cards. Her bank card was there, too. He couldn't use it at an ATM unless he knew her PIN number, but he might have taken it anyway, and I was glad to see he hadn't. He was an amateur, it was clear to me, and not a real thief at all. There are some burglars who will rape a woman if they encounter her in the course of a burglary, not because they're rapists by inclination but because she's there and they like her looks so what the hell. Similarly, there are some rapists who, having enjoyed a woman's favors, feel they might as well put a few dollars in their pocket. He was in the latter category, and that's why she still had her credit cards, but that's also why the place was such a mess; it was all part of the rape.

And of course there was no money in her wallet.

I put her purse in order, with the wallet in it. I found the various drawers he'd upended, restored their contents, and put them back where they'd come from. It seemed to me that he'd taken some of the jewelry I'd passed up, but I was glad to see he'd missed the locket with her parents' pictures, although he'd managed to take her class ring, the son of a bitch.

In her bathroom, he'd hurled a couple of bottles against the wall, but all but one were plastic and didn't break. I cleaned up the one broken bottle, and got rid of the shards of glass so she wouldn't cut herself. I found her Lady Remington that he'd switched on and then hurled to the floor, and wasn't surprised to discover that it no longer worked. The pink plastic case was cracked, and when I moved the switch nothing happened. I laid it in the wastebasket, then changed my mind, wrapped it in a paper towel, and tucked it away in a jacket pocket.

I got the place as neat as I could, short of scrubbing the floors on my hands and knees, and then I went in for a last look at her. It was the closest I'd been to a naked woman in longer than I cared to remember, and all I felt was sad.

I went to the door, opened it. Then I sighed heavily and returned to the bedroom for one final stab at chivalry. It didn't take long, maybe five minutes, after which I let myself out of Barbara Creeley's apartment, picked her locks shut, and went home.

 **TEN**

If Crandall Oaktree Mapes is a shitheel—"

"Crandall Rountree Mapes."

"Whatever. If he's a shitheel just for taking Marty's girlfriend away from him, Bern, what does that make this guy?"

"There must be a word," I said, "but I can't think of it."

"Well, for openers," Carolyn said, "I'd have to say he's a prick. You never got a look at him?"

"For all the time he was there, I was under the bed. All I got a look at were the dust bunnies."

"It's good you didn't sneeze."

"It is," I agreed. "It's good I didn't even think about sneezing, because it was unpleasant enough without having that to worry about. But no, I never got a look at him. I decided he was six-four with a washboard stomach and shoulders out to here, but that was my imagination. All I really know is he had a deep voice."

"I know women with deep voices, Bern. You can't tell too much from a deep voice."

It was Thursday, a few minutes after noon, and we were having lunch at my bookstore. Carolyn had gone clear over to the Second Avenue Deli for sandwiches piled high with the best corned beef and pastrami and tongue in town. What, I'd asked her, was the occasion, and she'd replied that there was no occasion beyond the fact that she'd spent much of the previous night dreaming about delicatessen.

"I missed dinner," she said. "I was on the computer for hours, browsing the listings on Date-a-Dyke, and I figured instead of wasting time eating I'd go over to the Cubby Hole and snack on the bar food. So I went to bed with nothing in my stomach but a couple handfuls of Beer Nuts, and I had this endless dream where they kept making my sandwich but never got around to bringing it to the table. And by the time I woke up I knew just what we were gonna have for lunch today. It's good, isn't it?"

We were working on the sandwiches and sipping our Cel-Ray tonic, and it turned out to be just what I wanted, even if I hadn't had a dream to tell me so. Corned beef is Raffles's favorite thing in all the world, and Carolyn had brought a little extra and slipped it into his food dish, where he was at once eating it and talking to it, a ritual he goes through with kosher corned beef and nothing else. Siamese talk to their food occasionally, or so Carolyn tells me, but Raffles is a tailless tabby, allegedly a Manx but lacking the characteristic body shape and rabbity gait of the typical Manx. His only Manx trait, really, is the tail he doesn't have, and I've often suspected that he's a Manx manqué, but I could be wrong about that. He's certainly not Siamese, but he sounded like one when he had corned beef in his dish, so that's how you might have pictured him if you'd been hiding under the bed, with nothing to go by but his voice.

Carolyn said, "How do you figure a guy like that, anyway? I mean, it goes without saying that he hates women, but why would he want her unconscious?"

"I don't know. Maybe conscious partners tend to give him bad reviews."

"I guess Barbara Creeley couldn't tell him he was a lousy lover, since she didn't have a clue what was going on. Still, you'd think he'd want someone capable of responding. Maybe his first girlfriend was English."

"I suppose it's possible."

She put down her sandwich. "That was a joke, Bern. You know the old one about the Frenchman who finds a girl on the beach and starts making love to her?"

"I know the joke."

"Someone comes along and tells him she's dead and he's horrified. 'Soccer blew,' he said. 'I thought she was English!' "

"I know the joke. Soccer blew, huh?"

"That's what they say. Frenchmen, they say it all the time. Soccer blew. Don't ask me what it means."

"I wouldn't dream of it."

"Bern? That was pretty decent of you, straightening up before you left. You must have been anxious to get out of there."

"Well, I felt sorry for her. I wanted to do something."

"It sounds as though you did everything but wash the windows."

I shook my head. "All I did was straighten up a few things. I was going to put her clothes away, but I figured I'd just put them in the wrong place. Besides, there was no way to keep her from knowing she'd been out of it when she got home, or that she'd had sex. But I couldn't leave her stuff in a heap on the floor, so I folded her things and put them on a chair."

"And put the stuff in her purse, and so on. Bern, do you suppose he left her any souvenirs?"

"Souvenirs?"

"Like a pregnancy she wasn't counting on, or an STD."

"Oh," I said. "I'd say probably not. He used a condom."

"Really? You wouldn't figure him to be that considerate, would you?"

"I think he was considering himself," I said, "and practicing safe sex more for his own benefit than for hers."

"And maybe to keep from leaving evidence."

"Evidence?"

"You know, DNA. She could go to the police and they'd take a swab and be able to identify him if they ever caught him. From his DNA."

"If he was concerned about that," I said, "he'd probably have taken the condom away with him."

"He left it there?"

"On the floor."

"Yuck. What did you do?"

"I got rid of it."

"How?"

"I picked it up and flushed it down the toilet."

"You touched it? Double yuck. How could you even do that, Bern?"

"I was wearing gloves."

"Oh, right."

"And I couldn't just leave it where I found it."

"No, of course not. You know something, Bern? Barbara Creeley was lucky you were there."

"Oh, absolutely," I said. "It was her lucky night all around."

"I mean it, Bern. If you hadn't been there, that prick would have taken her watch and her charm bracelet and her diamond earrings."

"Instead, I took them."

"But you put them back, Bern."

"Well, I felt sorry for her. An unprincipled son of a bitch slipped a drug into her drink and brought her home and raped her, and now I was adding insult to injury by stealing her stuff."

"Except you got there first."

"Even so. I'd already picked up the jewelry he left behind and put it away, and I figured if I put the good stuff back, she might not even know she'd been robbed. There were a few things missing, but what kind of moron would snatch a class ring and pass up a bracelet dripping with gold coins?"

"She'll just think she must have misplaced the ring."

"If I could manage to find out who he was," I said, "I'd pay him a visit one of these nights and get her ring back for her."

"Unless he's sold it by then."

"Oh, he won't sell it. He won't know where to go with it, and anyway he'll want to keep it for a souvenir. Something to remember her by, the son of a bitch."

"That'd be neat, if you could steal it back. How would you get it to her? Just drop it in the mail?"

"Or let myself into her apartment and put it in the drawer it came from."

"Perfect. She'd just think she missed it the last time she looked for it, that it was hiding under a piece of costume jewelry." She frowned. "Or else she'd worry that she was losing her mind. But at least she'd have her ring back."

"I always leave a place as neat as I found it," I said, "though in his case I might make an exception. But it's academic, because I don't have any idea who he is or where he lives."

"And you got rid of the only thing that would identify him." When I looked blank, she said, "You flushed it down the toilet, remember?"

"Oh, right."

"Not that you could run around giving DNA tests to every guy with a deep voice. Bern, I know you didn't break into her apartment out of an urge to do her a good deed. But that's what you wound up doing, and she was lucky you were there. Didn't you tell me you even put money in her wallet?"

"A few dollars."

"How much?"

"Well, there was no way to know how much she started with. I didn't think she'd carry too much cash. I wound up tucking a hundred and twenty dollars into the bills compartment."

"A burglar who gives you money. That's gotta be a first, Bern."

"You think?"

"And that's in addition to putting back everything you took—the bracelet and the earrings and the watch."

"Right."

"And the envelope full of money you found in the fridge. Bern? You put that back, didn't you?"

"Well, no," I said. "I didn't."

"Oh."

"I took a hundred and twenty bucks out of it," I said, "and that's what I put in her wallet. But I kept the rest."

"Oh."

"Chivalry only goes so far."

"I guess."

"You're surprised," I said.

"Yeah, kind of. I guess I was starting to see you as a knight in shining armor."

"I'm afraid the armor's a little tarnished. I went

there to steal, Carolyn. I put back most of what I took, but I wanted to come out a few dollars ahead on the deal."

"So you made a profit of . . ."

"Eleven hundred and twenty dollars," I said. "Minus cab fare."

"Well, that's a better hourly rate than you make selling books."

"No kidding."

"But considering the risk . . ."

I shook my head. "I don't even want to go there. It was crazy, going on the prowl like that, and I just hope I got it out of my system, at least for a little while. The thing is, I knew how irrational it was, and how dangerous."

"But you did it anyway."

"I did it anyway. It's not much of an exaggeration to say I couldn't help myself, and I really couldn't keep from hanging on to the money in the brown envelope, either. I can tell myself that I'm a pretty literate guy and a decent fellow. I don't go out of my way to offend people, and I certainly wouldn't slip Rohypnol into a lady's drink. But there's no getting around it. When all is said and done, I'm a burglar through and through."

There's a bell hanging from the door of the bookstore, so arranged that it makes a not-unpleasant jingling sound when the door opens. I was already into my last sentence when I heard the bell, and I suppose I could have chopped the words off instantly, but I didn't.

"Now ain't that the truth," my visitor said. "Truer words were never spoken, not by Mrs. Rhodenbarr's son Bernard, at any rate. A burglar through an' through, that's what you are, all right, an' all you'll ever be if you live to be older'n Methuselah."

I felt, if not as old as Methuselah, as though I could easily pass for his younger brother. "Hello, Ray," I said. "How's crime?"

He sighed and shook his head, and when he spoke the jaunty banter was gone. "As if you didn't know," he said. "You really put your foot in it this time, Bernie. You screwed up big time. I don't know how the hell you're gonna get yourself out of this one."

 **ELEVEN**

"T hat's a nice suit," I said. "Armani?"

"Close," he said, and held back the lapel to show me the label. "Canaletto. Another of your Eyetalians, an' you can't beat 'em for suits."

Whichever fine Italian hand had crafted his suit, the price tag would have been too high for a policeman's income, but then Ray Kirschmann had never attempted to live on what the city paid him. Fortunately no one would look at him and guess that his suit cost a bundle, because it had stopped looking expensive the minute he put it on. It was, as I'd said, a perfectly nice suit, but whatever suit he wore wound up looking as though it had been carefully tailored for another man, and a differently shaped one at that. The suit of the moment, navy with a subtle gray stripe, was too roomy in the shoulders and too tight at the waist, and the stain on the sleeve didn't help, either. It looked like spaghetti sauce, which was another thing the Italians were acknowledged to be good at.

"As for you," he said, "I have to say you look

good in stripes." I was wearing a striped polo shirt, a red and blue number Lands' End had introduced a year ago with an excess of optimism; I'd picked it up last month from their catalog of overstocks. "It's a damn shame," he went on, "that the prisons quit issuing striped uniforms, because they'd look great on you."

"They still wear them in cartoons," I pointed out. "When a cartoonist wants you to know that somebody's a convict, he always puts him in stripes."

"Is that a fact? Well, I guess you'll be stayin' out of the funny papers, because what they're gonna put you in is one of them orange jumpsuits. I'm glad you think that's funny, Carolyn. Maybe you'd like to explain the joke to me."

"I was just trying to picture you in an orange jumpsuit," she told him. "I figure you'd look like the Great Pumpkin."

"You'd look like a beach ball," Ray told her, "but then you always do."

"Always a pleasure, Ray."

"Pleasure's mine," he said. "An' for a change you'll come in handy. You can lock up after I take your pal here downtown."

"Wait a minute," I said. "It's beginning to dawn on me. Ray, you're serious."

"Serious as a positive biopsy. You been gettin' away with it long enough, Bernie, but I don't see how you're gonna get out from under this one."

"Well, maybe you can help me," I said. "For

starters, why don't you tell me what I'm supposed to have done?"

"I got a better idea. Why don't I ask the questions an' you tell me a few things?"

"Well, I suppose we could try it that way."

"For starters, where were you last night?"

"Home. I was watching **Law & Order**."

"I didn't watch it myself, but I can tell you what happened. The cops put a great case together and the rest of 'em screwed it up. That's what makes it a good show. It's always true to life. You were home, huh?"

"All night long." I decided to hedge a little. "Of course **Law & Order** doesn't come on until ten, and it had already started by the time I got home."

"Whatever you did before ten o'clock is your business, Bernie."

"Actually," I said, "you could say the same for whatever I did **after** ten o'clock, but it happens I was home, and I made it an early night. I must have been asleep well before midnight."

"And slept right through?"

"Except for getting up to pee, and I couldn't tell you when that was because I didn't look at the clock. I suppose I ought to keep track of that sort of thing, in case a minion of the law comes around asking questions, but—"

"The question's not when did you pee," he said. "It's where did you pee."

Carolyn said, "What, did you miss the toilet, Bern? That's disgusting, but I understand a lot of guys do it. It's a natural consequence of the biological flaw that makes you pee standing up. But I didn't know it was considered a police matter."

He was looking at me, waiting for my answer. "I went to the bathroom," I told him.

"The one in your apartment."

"Oddly enough," I said, "that's the very one I used."

"In that case," he said, "do you suppose maybe you can tell me what the hell you were doin' in the East Thirties?"

I'll admit it, the question shook me. Here's what I'd figured—someone had pulled some kind of break-in somewhere in Riverdale, and some eyewitness, presented with a book of mugshots of known offenders, had picked me out as someone who'd been seen lurking in the neighborhood. But any lurking I'd done had been in the early evening, and Ray said he was only interested in where I'd been after **Law & Order.**

It didn't seem like anything to worry about. One witness who thought he might have seen me in Riverdale a few hours before a break-in—well, I hadn't done anything, and wouldn't have left prints or trace evidence, so I couldn't believe Ray expected to get anywhere with this. Most likely he was just going through the motions.

And then he mentioned the East Thirties.

Where the hell did that come from? The only

person who could have reported the break-in at the Creeley apartment was Barbara Creeley herself, and there was no way she'd think she was the victim of a burglar. The odds were she was still deep in the throes of a booze-and-Roofies hangover and hadn't yet discovered that her class ring was missing, not to mention the very cold cash from her refrigerator. When she did, she could only assume it had been taken by the miserable son of a bitch who'd brought her home. If she reported it—and I could see why she might not want to—and if she had any memory at all of the pickup, it would be Lover Boy's description she'd give the police. It certainly wouldn't be mine, as the woman had never laid eyes on me.

I didn't know what to say, but I had to say something. "The East Thirties," I said. "In Manhattan, you mean."

"No, in East Jesus, Kansas."

"The East Thirties. You mean Kips Bay, over by the East River?"

"Try a little north and west of there," he said. "Try Murray Hill."

"Murray Hill," I said. "Murray Hill. I went to school with a fellow named Murray Hillman, but—"

"We know you were there, Bernie."

"I suppose you've got a witness."

He shook his head. "Better. What we got is photographic evidence. Ever hear of security cameras?"

Of course I'd heard of them, and they were one

of the reasons I'd stayed away from apartment buildings. But there hadn't been a security camera in the Feldmaus-Creeley house. I'd looked, I always look, and I'd have spotted it before it could have spotted me.

"You're bluffing," I said, "and I don't know why, because I don't even know what I'm supposed to have done. Which I think you really ought to tell me before we go any further."

"You think so, do you?"

"I really do, Ray."

"Whatever you say, Bernie. Sometime a little after midnight a couple of mopes walked into the lobby of one of them white brick apartment buildings on the corner of Third Avenue an' 37th Street. They overpowered the doorman, duct-taped his feet and ankles, slapped another piece of tape over his mouth, an' locked him in the parcel room. Then they went around to all the security cameras an' opened 'em up an' took out the tape."

"It seems like a lot to go through," I said, "to steal some videotapes."

"Go ahead an' be a wiseass, see what it gets you. Next thing they did was go upstairs to the penthouse apartment, which was on the top floor."

"Good place for it."

"They forced the door, and overpowered the man and woman inside the apartment, who'd sublet the place as Mr. and Mrs. Lyle Rogovin, which may or may not have been their real names. They trussed them up with duct tape, same as the doorman, an' went to work. There was a safe in the Rogovin apartment, big heavy monster, not what you'd expect to find in a residence. They got it open and cleaned it out and left."

"And you think I had something to do with it."

"I know damn well you did, Bernie."

"Because you know me, and you know how I operate, and I have a long history of overpowering doormen and binding them with duct tape and forcing my way into apartments when the owners are home."

"No, you've never done anythin' like that in your life."

"Of course not," I said, "so why are you wasting my time and yours with this nonsense?"

"And mine," Carolyn said.

"You want to go back where you belong so you can hose down a Rottweiler," he told her, "feel free. No, it's not your style, Bernie. An' I don't think for a minute that you roughed up the doorman or held a gun on the Rogovins."

"Then why on earth—"

"What I figure you did," he said, "what I flat out **know** you did, is open the safe. That box was a Mosler, an' it took real talent to get into it, an' if there's one thing you've got a shitload of it's talent. In one area, anyway. I don't know if you can carry a tune or draw a straight line, but you can open any lock ever made without breakin' a sweat. That's what they wanted you for, an' that's why you were all over the neighborhood, walkin' around as nervous as a long-tailed cat in a room full of rockin' chairs." He glanced over at Raffles, who was once again sunning himself in the window. "No offense," he said. "You figure that's how he lost his tail, Bernie? Got hisself run over by a rockin' chair?"

"He's a Manx," I said. "He was born that way."

"An' I guess you were born that way yourself. With a talent for locks, I mean, not that you were born without a tail, although that's probably true too, now that I come to think of it."

"Ray," I said, "am I missing something? Besides a tail, I mean. What I don't get is where I come into all this. I know, you just told me, I'm the guy they brought in to open the safe. But why me?"

"They heard you were good."

"No, what makes **you** think it was me?"

"I told you, Bernie. We got your pitcher."

"My pitcher? Oh, my picture."

"That's what I just said."

"Right. But you said they took the tape. The security cameras were out of commission."

"In that buildin', yeah. But not in the rest of the neighborhood. Jesus, Bernie, you walked past an ATM machine at the Chase bank at the corner of Third and 34th. An' you walked past a whole lot of buildin's. You must have been walkin' around for an hour or so, waitin' to get the call to go over to the penthouse an' crack the safe. What you got to remember, Bernie, is that they got these cameras all over the place. They're not just in lobbies an' elevators. You walk down a street, any street, you might as well go ahead an' smile, 'cause it's a good bet you're on **Candid Camera.**"

"You say you've got all these pictures of me. You know, security camera pictures always tend to be blurry and out of focus. How do you even know it's me?"

"You want me to tell you what you were wearin'? Khakis an' a blue blazer. An' a polo shirt, but not striped like the one you got on today. It was a solid color shirt, but don't ask me the color, 'cause that I couldn't tell you."

"You've got pictures of me," I said, "but all I'm doing is walking around, and the last I heard that was still legal. The pictures don't establish that I was doing anything wrong."

"They didn't," he said. "Not until you opened your mouth and lies started pourin' out of it."

"Huh?"

"I asked you where you were last night," he said, "an' you said you were home, watchin' TV an' goin' to bed early an' never stirrin' except to pee. Right in your own bathroom, you said. You recall sayin' somethin' along those lines?"

"I wasn't under oath," I said, "so it's not per-jury, but you're right. I lied."

"Now tell me somethin' I don't know."

"The reason I lied," I lied, "is I was ashamed to admit where I was." I turned to Carolyn. "Because you're here," I said.

"What's Shorty here got to do with it?"

Carolyn gave him a look. I said, "Oh, hell. There's a woman I've been seeing, and it's a sick, hopeless relationship, and I swore to Carolyn that I wasn't going to see her anymore. And I went out last night looking for her."

"I bet you went lookin' in Murray Hill."

"As a matter of fact I did. That's where she lives, but she wasn't home, so I went around looking in some of the bars and coffee shops she's apt to frequent."

"And did you find her?"

"Finally, but it took forever."

"Bernie, I can't believe what I'm hearing," Carolyn chimed in helpfully. "You actually started up with that neurotic bitch after you swore up and down you were through with her."

"I know, I know. It was a mistake."

"The two of you are somethin'," Ray said. "One lies an' the other swears to it. This femme fatality, has she got a name?"

"Of course she's got a name."

"Yeah, well, don't tell me, not just yet. First we'll try a little experiment." He took out his notebook, tore out a sheet of paper, ripped it in half, and gave half to me and half to Carolyn. "Since you both know this woman," he said, "whyntcha both write down her name?"

We did, and he collected the slips. " 'Barbara,' " he read. "An' Barbara. I don't know how the two of you pulled that one off, but it don't really matter. I don't buy the whole story for a second."

"Fine," I said. "It happens to be the truth, but you don't have to believe it. Take my picture and show it to those people."

"What people?"

"The Rogins, or whatever their name is."

"Rogovin."

"Fine. Show my picture to the Rogovins and ask them if they can identify me. When they can't, maybe you'll go bother somebody else."

"Can't do it, Bernie."

"Why not?"

"They took two bullets apiece in the side of the head, an' they're never gonna be able to identify anybody."

"Ohmigod."

"You didn't know, did you? I had a hunch you didn't. Your partners must have sent you home before they capped 'em." He frowned. "Bernie, you don't look so good. You're not gonna puke, are you?"

I shook my head.

"I know it's not your style," he said. "Not the rough stuff, and not the triple homicide."

"Triple? I thought you said there were just two of them."

"Yeah, well, the doorman was taped a little too well. He died of suffocation by the time somebody found him."

"God, that's awful."

"It's about as bad as it gets. I don't understand you, Bernie. Why would you want to work with people who would do something like that?"

"I didn't work with anybody."

"You usually don't," he allowed. "An' that's wise, because the worst thing about partners is they'll always rat you out to save their own asses. An' that's exactly what you're about to do, my friend."

"What?"

"Give up the murderin' bastards you worked with last night. We'll pick 'em up and you'll turn state's evidence an' testify against 'em, an' you'll get off with a slap on the wrist an' a stern talkin'-to from the judge. That doesn't sound so bad, does it?"

"No, but—"

"Matter of fact," he said, leaning on the counter and lowering his voice, "there's no reason you got to walk away from the whole deal empty-handed. I figure you an' me, we worked a lot of angles in the past, we can probably work somethin' out here. Share an' share alike, if you get my drift."

It wasn't that elusive a drift. "While we're on the subject," I said, "what exactly did they get from the safe?"

"I should be asking you that, Bernie. You're the one who was there."

"Except I wasn't."

"Aw, Bernie," he said, shaking his head. "You're disappointin' me, you really are."

"Well, I don't mean to, Ray, but—"

"Let's go."

"Huh?"

"What, you want to hear the whole spiel? 'You

have the right to remain silent, di dah di dah di dah.'
Do I have to give it to you word for word?"

"No, that's good enough. You're serious? You're taking me in?"

"You're damn right I am. Three people are dead an' you're mixed up in it up to your eyeteeth. You bet your ass I'm takin' you in. Now have you got somethin' you want to tell me?"

"I think I'd better exercise my right to remain silent." I turned to Carolyn. "Call Wally Hemphill," I said, "and tell him to do something. And would you do me one more favor? Wrap up the rest of my sandwich and put it where Raffles can't get it. I don't know how long it'll take Wally to spring me, but I'm sure to be hungry by the time I get out."

 **TWELVE**

The first time I met Wally Hemphill, I'd just been arrested, which is when I have the most urgent need for an attorney. I'd called Klein, who'd served me in that capacity for many years, only to learn that, in the time since I'd last had the need for him, the man had died. You don't figure your lawyer's going to do that, and it threw me, but I wound up with Wally, who was training for the New York marathon. And I have to say I was glad of that, because I figured it would keep the weight off and the cardiovascular system in tiptop shape. It takes a while for an habitual felon to bond with his lawyer, so you want to pick a guy who's going to be around for the long haul.

Wally went on training for marathons, and running them, until he blew out a knee. Then he met a nice girl and got married, and they had a kid, and then either he found out she wasn't so nice after all, or she found out he wasn't, or the discovery was mutual. They got a divorce and she packed up the kid and moved to Arizona, where she'd apprenticed herself to a potter. "She's throwing clay pots," Wally said, "and as long as she's not throwing them at me, I say the best of luck to her."

After the divorce he'd taken up martial arts, and you can make of that what you will. It didn't stress his bum knee, and the skills he developed gave him increased self-confidence when dealing with some of his less savory clients, but the chief benefit, he assured me, was spiritual. "You've got to try it," he told me. "It'll change your life."

I'd tried running, though I never got to the marathon level, and I have to say it had changed my life. It made me feel better, and I stuck with it for a few years, and then I stopped, and that made me feel better all over again. When I've got more time, I told Wally, and he gave me the knowing smile of the spiritually advanced human being. "When you're ready, Bernie," he said gently. "You just let me know."

He showed up downtown at One Police Plaza, which is where Ray had taken me, and by late afternoon he had me out of there, and took me around the corner to a teahouse one flight up from a store that sold lacquered Chinese furniture. We sat at one of those low tables with a recess in the floor for your feet, and a little slip of a girl came over and taught us how to make tea. I'd never needed instructions in the past, I just dropped the tea bag in the cup and poured hot water on top of it, but this was a more elaborate procedure involving a pot full of water with a can of Sterno under it to keep it at the boiling point, and a whole system for making the tea in small batches which we were supposed to drink from these tiny china eyecups.

"This is the real stuff," Wally said, knocking back a quarter of an ounce of liquid the approximate color of tears. "Drink up, Bernie."

I did, and noted the extreme subtlety of the flavor. It tasted, I have to say, an awful lot like water.

"Amazing, right? And there's no place like it this side of Hong Kong."

"Really? You'd think there'd be a line halfway around the block."

"That's the thing," he said. "Nobody knows about it. Bernie, they've got nothing. That's why they cut you loose without putting up much of a fight. I mean, what have they got? They can prove you were within a few blocks of the place around the time those people were being robbed and murdered. Well, so were several thousand other people. They can't establish that you were in the building, let alone the penthouse apartment where the crime took place. I've got to wonder what Kirschmann was thinking of, hauling you in when he knew they couldn't hold you. Unless . . ."

"Unless what?"

"Well, unless they turn something up searching your apartment."

"They're searching my apartment?"

" 'Fraid so, Bernie. The fact that they had you in custody persuaded some tame judge they had grounds for a warrant, and they're over there right now. You don't look happy. Want to tell me what they're likely to find?"

"Nothing illegal," I said. There's a Mondrian on the wall, and it happens to be an original, but everyone assumes it's a copy, and it's been hanging there for years.* My burglar tools were back in my hiding place, along with both passports, and they could make a little trouble for me if they found them, but I didn't think they would. They never have in the past.

"Nothing from the break-in last night," Wally said.

"I wasn't there, Wally."

"Just making sure. Nothing from, uh, any other place you might have been?"

He hadn't asked what I'd been doing in Murray Hill, but that didn't mean he didn't have a good idea. Not a thing, I told him, and he seemed satisfied.

"More tea, Bernie?"

"Uh, sure."

"When I think of all the coffee I used to drink," he said, "it's enough to give me the jitters. Tea's better for you, you know."

"It must be."

"It's got these compounds in it, I forget what they're called, but every day it seems they're finding something new that they do, and that's good for you. All I know is I find it invigorating. How about you, Bernie?"

*The Burglar Who Painted Like Mondrian

"I'm invigorated," I said.

"Me too. You been seeing anybody new, Bernie? Getting anywhere in the love life department?"

I shook my head. "How about you?"

"Zilch. Between my practice and my workouts in the dojo, I don't have a hell of a lot of time on my hands. Still, the old urge is always there, you know what I mean?"

"I know what you mean."

"What I'd really like to do," he said, "is get something going with our waitress. You happen to notice her?"

"I wasn't paying too much attention."

"I think she's beautiful. The Mysterious East and all that, and those silk robes she wears drive me nuts. I think they call them cheongsams."

"Is that a fact."

"All I know for sure is I'd like to get into hers. I'd ask her out to dinner, but I can't."

"Why not?"

"She doesn't speak any English. I mean, even if I managed to make myself understood, and even if she was willing to sit across a table from a round-eyed foreign devil, what would dinner be like?"

"I don't know. How are you with chopsticks?"

"I mean the conversation, Bernie. We couldn't even make small talk. I've been thinking of learning Mandarin."

"You're kidding."

"Well, it could come in handy. The Chinese population keeps growing, and some of them need lawyers. Don't you think they'd be more comfortable with an attorney who understood their language?"

"They'd probably be more comfortable with one who was Chinese to begin with."

"You're right, dammit. The only reason to learn the language is so I could talk to the waitress. The thing is, I think she likes me."

"Oh?"

"Every time I come here," he said, "she goes through the whole rigmarole, teaching me to make the tea. And I'm here three or four times a week, so it's obvious I know the drill by now. So why go through it each time? I figure she likes spending time with me."

"That's possible."

"Well, what other explanation could there be?"

"Maybe she doesn't remember you from one day to the next, because all Caucasian guys look alike to her."

"You think?"

"Or," I said, "maybe she figures you're not bright enough to retain the information from one tea-brewing session to the next."

"You really know how to make a guy feel good," he said. "I can't tell you how glad I am I brought up the subject in the first place. Bernie, I've got to ask you a question. I know you weren't on the scene last night, you're about the least likely person I can think of to be involved in something like that, but do you know anything about it?"

"Only what I heard from Ray."

"You were never approached? Like somebody invited you in on the job, and you said you'd pass, but you'd keep mum about it?"

"What makes you think that, Wally?"

"Well, it might explain what you were doing in the neighborhood, and why you couldn't tell Kirschmann. Maybe you hung around to see how the whole deal went down."

I shook my head. "Nothing like that. I'll tell you this much, I had a reason to be in Murray Hill, although I have to admit it wasn't a very good reason. And it was something I wasn't willing to share with Ray Kirschmann, and it's not something you need to know about."

"Got it."

"And it had no connection whatsoever with the Rogovin burglary, which incidentally I wish people would stop calling a burglary, because that's not what it was. It was a home invasion, and that's something I've never been involved in."

"First thing I told them. 'If you know anything about the man, you know it's not his style.' "

"And nobody tried to recruit me for it. The first I heard about it was when I got arrested for it. And if anybody **had** tried to enlist me, I'd have turned them down—"

"Just what I said a minute ago."

"—and the last place I'd have gone was Murray Hill, because I'd have wanted to be a long ways away when they pulled the job, preferably in the company of two judges and a cardinal."

"So you'd have a solid alibi. I get the point, Bernie, but let me put it this way. You know people. You hear things."

"I try not to associate with criminals, Wally."

"So do I," he said. "Present company excepted, of course. But much as I try, my line of work makes it difficult. And so does yours, so there's a chance you'll talk to someone who knows something, and if you do—"

"I could do myself some good by passing the word."

"A whole lot of good. Of course I realize that might go against your code of honor. Nobody wants to be a rat."

I shook my head. "Not where these clowns are concerned," I said. "I'd love to see the cops pick them up, and not just because they'd stop bothering me. They killed three people, for God's sake. It's jerks like that who give burglary a bad name."

⊙ THIRTEEN

They came to the Poodle Factory," Carolyn said, "sometime around two. Ray and two uniformed cops. They had a warrant to search Barnegat Books, and they wanted me to open up for them. On account of I'd locked up after Ray took you downtown. I said just because they had the right to search your place didn't mean I was under any obligation to shut down my own place of business and open up for them, and Ray said I was absolutely right, but if I didn't open up they'd have to force their way in, and that would mean using a bolt cutter on the padlocks and window guards. So I figured you wouldn't want that, and I did what they wanted me to. I hope that was right."

"Absolutely."

"When the place was open Ray told me I could go back to work, and I told him I wasn't budging until they were gone and the store was locked up again. See, I wanted to be there while they searched the place. I didn't want them making a mess, or upsetting Raffles."

"How did he take it?"

"I think he just assumed they were customers. But then he's just a cat, or he'd have spotted them as a bunch of illiterate lip-movers. At any rate, they didn't knock themselves out searching. It'd take hours to search a bookstore thoroughly, and they didn't even try. They rummaged around your back office and looked behind the counter, but they didn't take books off the shelves or anything."

"The place looked fine to me," I said. "I didn't even know anybody had been in it."

"You went there?"

"On my way here," I said. We were at Carolyn's apartment on Arbor Court, a West Village cul-de-sac that's so quaint and charming hardly anybody knows how to get there. When Carolyn first moved in, she'd had to start from the right place every night or she couldn't find her way home. Her apartment's as quaint and charming as the street it's on, with the tub in the kitchen and a sheet of plywood on top of it to transform it into a table, at which we were currently seated, tucking into some Bangladeshi takeout from No-Worry Curry. I'd spent too much time in the teahouse to agree to Chinese.

"I figured you'd lock up," I said, "but I wanted to make sure. And I had the rest of that sandwich waiting for me."

"It almost wasn't, Bern. One of the boys in blue had his eye on it. I told him if he laid a finger on it I'd have him up on charges. Scared the crap out of him."

"It wouldn't have worked with Ray."

"If I thought Ray was gonna eat it," she said, "I'd have poisoned it. He had his nerve, running you in."

"It's a pretty horrible crime. He's going to do whatever it takes to solve it."

"But he couldn't have thought you had anything to do with it."

"He probably didn't, but it was a case of leaving no stone unturned."

"If he was without sin," she said, "then he'd have the right to turn the first stone." She frowned. "I think I know what I meant, but I'm not sure it's what I said."

She asked about Wally, and I recounted our conversation at the teahouse, and she said that was the whole thing about tea—the higher the quality, the subtler the taste, until eventually you were drinking the very best stuff and it had no taste whatsoever. "With No-Worry Curry," she said, "you can damn well taste it."

"Of course, we may not be able to taste anything again for the next few days."

"It's worth it," she said. "Believe me." She mopped her forehead with her napkin and sighed with satisfaction. "So after you finished drinking tap water in the guise of tea, you went straight to the bookstore?"

"I went home first."

"To see how they left your apartment. And?"

"You could tell they'd been there," I said, "but I have to admit they didn't make that much of a mess. Maybe the new commissioner's sending them to charm school. What's the matter?"

"I was trying to picture Ray in charm school. He'd sit in the front row, and when the teacher walked in and introduced herself, he'd fart."

"Funny, he always speaks highly of you."

"The hell he does. He can't stand me, and thank God for that, because this way I can hate him without feeling guilty. I gather they didn't find your hiding place."

"No, I was pretty sure they wouldn't."

"So everything's okay, right? And you're off the hook for the Rogovin murders. Not that you were ever on it, but now you're off."

"I wouldn't be surprised if Ray dropped in to yank my chain from time to time," I said, "but he's apt to do that anyway. I hope they wrap up the case in a hurry, though. If only to get those creeps out of circulation."

"That poor doorman," she said.

"What about the Rogovins?"

"Well, them too, of course, but didn't Ray say those might not be their real names?"

"Just because a person's name isn't Rogovin, that doesn't mean it's okay to kill them."

She rolled her eyes. "If they were using false names," she said, "maybe they were crooks. And no, that doesn't make it all right to kill them either, but it might mean they were involved with the guys who broke into their apartment, co-conspirators in a dope deal or something, and they betrayed their partners and that's what got them killed. Hey, you read the papers, Bern. That kind of thing happens all the time."

"I guess."

"But the doorman was just minding his business," she said, "which consisted of minding the door, and he wound up dead. So I feel sorry for him. I feel sorry for the Rogovins, too, but not as intensely."

"I guess I follow you."

"Not that it matters who I feel sorry for or how sorry I feel, because it doesn't do any of them a bit of good. Right?"

"Don't ask me," I said. "Ask Wally Hemphill. He's studying martial arts, and it's making him spiritual, so a question like that should be right up his alley."

I hung around and we watched some TV, and then I picked up a book and read for half an hour while she booted up the computer and dealt with her e-mail and worked her way through the message boards and newsgroups she subscribed to. Then I guess she found her way over to Google, the search engine, because she was able to report that one Saul Rogovin had pitched for several minor-league baseball teams in the 1950s, while a woman with the memorable name of Syrell Rogovin Leahy had published a couple of novels, before turning to mystery fiction and adopting a pen name.

I said, "A pen name? She was born with a pen name."

"Anyway," she said, "I can't find any Lyle Rogovin, and I don't know what his wife's name was so I can't look for her. You want to hear the good news?"

"Sure."

She grinned. "My date's on for tomorrow night with GurlyGurl. She says she's really looking forward to it."

"I'd call that good news."

"Me too. Bern? What about after?"

"After?"

"In Riverdale. Are we still on?"

I took a moment to think about it, because, curiously enough, I hadn't thought about it at all. Tomorrow was Friday, and Carolyn had an early date with GurlyGurl, and Crandall Mapes and his wife had a date with Wolfgang Amadeus, and then Carolyn and I had a late date with the wall safe in their bedroom.

Since we'd set the date, I'd committed one burglary and been arrested for another, but that was all water over the dam or under the bridge, as you prefer. The Mapeses were still opera-bound, and I was still a burglar, and Mapes was still a shitheel, and I could only assume the money was still in the safe, so why change a good plan at this late date?

"Sure," I said. "We're on. Why not?"

It must have been around ten when I left Carolyn's apartment. I caught the subway at Sheridan Square. That's a local stop, and I could have changed to the express at 14th Street, but I was comfortable and stayed put. I got off at 72nd Street and walked home, trying to remember if I needed anything from the deli. It seemed to me that I did, but I couldn't think what it was.

I turned at West End, and when I got to my building I found that the doorman had deserted his post. Some of the building staff still smoke, and they can't do that indoors, so they generally step outside for a cigarette. But we've got a couple of antitobacco activists in the building, and they'd complained about having to run a gauntlet of cigarette smoke on their way in or out, and some of the guys had taken to slipping around the corner when they felt themselves going postal with nicotine withdrawal. I figured it would all sort itself out, as soon as the mayor quit pussyfooting around and made smoking illegal anywhere in the five boroughs.

Meanwhile, though, the lobby was wide open. If it was someone else's building, I'd have sailed in and set about looking for someone to burgle. But I lived here, so all I did was get on the elevator and go up to my apartment.

I had the key out, and I don't know what made me try the knob first, but I did, and it turned and the door opened. Stupid cops, I thought. The least the inconsiderate bastards could have done was lock up, but no, that was too much for them.

And I pushed the door open and followed it into my apartment.

I hadn't taken two steps before the penny dropped. The cops hadn't left the door unlocked. I'd already been home, for God's sake, and determined that they'd locked up after themselves, and then I'd gone out, heading first to the bookstore and then to Carolyn's place, and I'd damn well locked up after myself, because I always do. And even if I didn't, the snap lock would have engaged automatically and kept the door from opening.

Which meant someone else had come here after I left, and if I'd had any sense at all I'd have realized as much the minute I tried the knob and found the door unlocked. And, armed with that realization (and nothing else) I could have spun on my heel and gotten the hell out of there.

But it was too late for that now.

 **FOURTEEN**

If anybody had been waiting to ambush me, there wouldn't have been much I could do about it, short of hopping into a time machine and taking a cram course in the martial arts. But there was no one looming behind my door, no one pressed up against my wall. Whoever had broken in had left, and that was all to the good, although it would have been worlds better if they hadn't come around in the first place.

Unlike the cops who'd dropped in earlier, these sons of bitches (or this son of a bitch, though I tended to think in the plural) had not been to charm school. They'd been through my apartment as if they were a tornado and it was a trailer park. They'd stopped short of outright vandalism, and thus hadn't smashed or slashed anything, which is to say they'd done their dirty work without malice—but you could say the same thing for the tornado, couldn't you?

They'd taken my Mondrian off the wall and set it

on the floor, but they hadn't damaged it, nor had they thought to take it away with them. Either they hadn't recognized it or they'd assumed, as everyone does, that it was a worthless copy.

I didn't know what they'd come looking for, but I'd bet it was worth a good deal less than the Mondrian, which would probably bring a couple million dollars at auction, assuming the seller had clear title and a provenance for it. On the underground market, well, who knows what it might bring? I've never been tempted to find out, because what could I buy with the money that I'd enjoy as much as the painting?

And I really enjoyed looking at the painting right now, because it was a lot more pleasant to look at than the rest of the apartment.

They'd done quite a job on it. The books were off the shelves, though they'd at least piled them more or less neatly on the floor. The drawers, dresser and desk, had all been pulled out and upended. The clothes were shoved over to one side of the closet, and, at the rear of the closet, damn it to hell, my custom-designed hiding place, impervious to police searches, had been opened and ransacked.

And ruined in the process. I'd had it constructed like one of those cunning wooden boxes they sell at places like the American Craftsmen's Guild, where you have to push this piece of wood to the left in order to snick this other piece back which enables you to nudge this third piece to the right, at which point the lid pops open. It takes no time at all when you know how it works, but no one's born with that knowledge, and it's not that easy to dope it out, especially if, like all my previous visitors, you don't realize there's a secret cupboard in front of you.

They'd known what they were looking at, though, and hadn't wasted time trying to crack the code. Instead they'd applied brute force, and that was the end of my hidey-hole.

They'd left the passports. I guess they weren't worried that I might skip the country. And they'd left my burglar tools, which, judging from the way they'd forced the door, they wouldn't have known what to do with. They'd also left the electric shaver with the cracked plastic case, the one I'd picked up in Barbara Creeley's apartment.

But they took my money. Last night, when I put my tools away for the second and final time, I'd added the $1120 from Barbara Creeley's icebox to my Get Out of Dodge fund. While I was at it, I counted the stack of bills, so I'm able to tell you just how much the bastards got from me. The grand total, including the night's proceeds, had come to precisely $8357. (And yes, that's an odd sum, because I always make sure I have some small bills in my emergency stash. If you're running for your life, you don't want to have to break a hundred-dollar bill at a toll booth.)

Eight thousand bucks and change. They hadn't come for the money, that was clear, but they found it, and it was money, so they took it. And the hell of it was that I couldn't really blame them.

After all, I'd have done the same thing myself.

The first thing I did was pick up an armload of books and start reshelving them.

That, granted, was pretty stupid. Anyone drawing up a list of priorities for someone in my particular situation would be apt to put the orderly reshelving of my personal library down toward the bottom of the list, somewhere between making a laundry list and flossing. The books were in short stacks on the floor, where I could walk around without tripping over them. They were in a sense safer there than back on their shelves, in that they were in no danger of falling anywhere.

But I'm a bookseller, spending the greater portion of each workday in a used bookstore, buying books every day from people who would rather have money, and selling them in turn to people who'd rather have books. The books usually go out one or two or three at a time, but they come to me in larger quantities; while occasionally a book scout like Mowgli brings in one or two choice items he's turned up, I'm more apt to acquire books by the shopping bag or wheelbarrow or truckload. When I buy a whole library, the books go to my back room, where they repose in cartons until I get around to dealing with them, which I generally do a carton at a time, lugging the box out front and putting the individual volumes in their proper places on my shelves.

That's a task I fit in when I can—and, since an antiquarian bookseller's workday is rarely conducted at a breakneck pace, there's generally plenty of time for it. When things are slow, when there's nothing else to do, I find some books and set about shelving them.

So that's what I was doing, and while I did it I tried to figure out what to do next.

First of all, damage control. The feeling of violation aside, what had I lost?

Well, money. Over eight thousand dollars, which is still a tidy sum, even if it's not what it used to be. (My grandfather Grimes paid eight thousand dollars for the house my mother was born in, while nowadays there are people in Manhattan—rich ones, admittedly—who pay that much every month in rent.) It hurt to lose the money, but that's the thing about money: it's always painful to lose it, but it's never more pain than you can stand.

Because all it takes to replace it is other money. Barbara Anne Creeley couldn't replace her class ring, but I could replace the eight grand, and when I did the pain I now felt would go away. So I hated to see my Get Out of Dodge fund depleted all the way to zero, but I knew I'd build it up again, one way or another.

Besides the money, all I could see that I'd lost was time, the time it would take me to make my apartment look as it had before my visitors had come. A certain number of hours, plus a certain number of dollars to replace the lock they'd broken and, now that the horse was stolen, add a more serviceable lock that would lessen the likelihood of the same thing happening again. And some more dollars for a cleaning woman, to whisk away the traces of an alien presence. My neighbor Mrs. Hesch had a woman who cleaned for her once a week, and I'd recruited her occasionally in the past, and could do so again. That would have to wait until the books were on the shelves and the drawers back where they belonged, so general tidying came first, but—

Oh, hell. I was forgetting the damage they'd done to my formerly secret compartment. The fellow who built it for me had moved to the West Coast—Washington State, if I remembered correctly—and I had no idea who I could find to do work like that. If I could reach him I could ask him to recommend someone, but I didn't know what town he'd gone to or if he was still there, and his name was David Miller, so I could forget about trying a computer search. The thing about computer searches is that they make finding a needle in a haystack as easy as falling off a bicycle. Nothing to it. But finding the right David Miller would be more like trying to find a particular needle in a needle stack. I knew better than to try.

Well, I'd find somebody. There was no rush, because for the time being I didn't have anything to hide.

I picked up another stack of books, and resumed the task of stowing them on the shelves. As important as putting my place in order, I thought, was dealing with the people who'd done this. Because it was pretty clear that they'd come looking for something, and my eight thousand dollars wasn't it. It had been worth taking, but it wasn't worth breaking in for, not to those bastards.

Because they had to be the same gang that broke into the Rogovins the night before.

I mean, who else could it be? No professional burglar for profit would single me out, and no snatch-and-grab junkie opportunist, looking to grab something he could turn into smack or crack, would wend his wobbly way into a doorman building, and—

Ohmigod.

I rushed out into the hall, rang for the elevator, then turned around and darted back into my apartment. My tools were in the ruins of my hidey-hole, where my visitors had left them, and I snatched them up and hurried back to the elevator, which had come and gone while I was getting my tools. Rather than wait for it I took the stairs, hurtling down them, terrified of what I was going to find.

The doorman at 34th and Park had suffocated. It was presumably an accident, tape meant for his mouth covering his nose as well, but maybe someone had decided that an extra piece of tape on the nose would avoid leaving a witness as a loose end.

And even if it had been an accident, who was to say they wouldn't make the same mistake again?

I went to the parcel room, tried the door. It was locked. I put an ear to it and listened, and couldn't hear a thing but my own heartbeat.

I got out my tools and went to work.

 **FIFTEEN**

Whoever they were, I guess they must have stocked up on duct tape when some genius in Washington suggested you could seal your windows with it in the event of a terrorist attack. They'd evidently got to Kmart before the supply ran out, so they had plenty, and they weren't stingy with it when it came time to immobilize Edgardo, who was unfortunate enough to be on duty when they came calling.

They'd taped his wrists behind his back, and then they'd sat him down in a straight-backed wooden chair and taped each of his ankles to the chair's front legs. Then they'd wound tape around his middle, fastening him to the back of the chair, and somewhere along the way they'd slapped a piece of tape over his mouth. But they'd left his nose uncovered, thank heavens, and he was still alive.

But that was about as much as you could say for him. He'd made a valiant effort to free himself, rocking to and fro on the chair until he managed to tip it over, but all that did was make his position that much more uncomfortable. He'd wound up more or less on his side, with his feet in the air and his head tilted downward. That way the blood could rush to his head, but it didn't have to rush, it could take its time, because Edgardo wasn't going anywhere.

He was so positioned that he could see a patch of floor and not much else, and when I opened the door he had no way of knowing who it was—someone come to rescue him, or the same guys coming back to finish the job. But it was somebody, so he made as much noise as he could, issuing a string of nasal grunts that were eloquent enough in their own way. If nothing else they let me know he was alive, and I matched his eloquence with a sigh of relief and rolled him over so we could get a look at each other, and so that I could set about getting him loose.

I picked at a corner of the tape covering his mouth, got enough of it free to get a grip on it, and told him to brace himself. "This is going to hurt," I said, and I was right about that. I gave a yank and got the tape off, and I swear the poor bastard's eyes popped halfway out of his head, but he didn't make a sound.

I don't know how he held it in. He's short and slim, with a boyish face, and I suppose he grew the mustache to make himself look older. It was a sparse and tentative mustache, and thus had the opposite effect, making him look like somebody who was trying to look older. And now it was all at once considerably sparser and more tentative, because a substantial percentage of it had come off along with the duct tape, and how he kept from screaming in agony is beyond me.

What he did do, when he had the chance, was rattle off a long frenzied speech as fast as he could talk. It was in Spanish, so I didn't understand a word of it, but I could tell it was heartfelt.

"Easy," I said. "You're okay. They're not coming back. You'll be all right now, Edgardo."

"Edgar."

"I thought your name was Edgardo."

He shook his head. "No more. Now is Edgar. Is more American."

"Fair enough. Hold still and I'll cut you loose."

There was far too much tape to try ripping it off, and I'd thought I would have to run upstairs for my Swiss Army knife, but I remembered that we were in the parcel room, and of course there was a box-cutter on the desk. It gave me a turn to see it there, as box-cutters don't seem nearly as innocent as they did a few years ago, but it was just what the job demanded, and I managed to cut the tape without cutting Edgardo—I'm sorry, make that Edgar—and before too long I had the chair standing up and him sitting in it.

"Now," I said, "just sit tight, okay?"

"Tight? How I sit tight?"

"It's an expression," I said. "**Un idioma**. Never

mind. Just stay here, and I'll get you a glass of water. You want a glass of water?"

"Hokay."

"I'll be right back with it. I'll get the water and I'll call the cops, and—"

"**No!**"

"No? Look, Edgar, you could have been killed, and the guys who did this to you already killed three other people, and one of them was a doorman just like you. Of course I'm going to call the police."

He looked on the point of tears.

"Why not?"

"INS."

"You want me to call the INS?"

"Ay, **Cristo**! No!"

"Oh," I said. "You don't want me to call the INS. And you don't want me to call the police because you're afraid they'll call the INS." He was nodding enthusiastically, clearly pleased that he'd finally made himself understood by this gringo idiot. "But you're not illegal, are you? How could you get hired here without a Green Card?"

It took a few minutes, but he got the point across. There were, it turned out, Green Cards and Green Cards. Some of them were issued by the Immigration and Naturalization Service, while others were the product of private enterprise. The latter would serve to placate a prospective employer, but someone from the INS would be able to tell the difference, and one more hardworking and productive New Yorker would be out on his **culo**.

I started to tell him the police had better things to do than run interference for the INS, and that all they'd want from him was whatever he could tell them about the men who'd wrapped him up like a Christmas present. But halfway through I changed direction, because I wasn't convinced of the truth of what I was saying.

To paraphrase the song from **My Fair Lady**, when a cop's not near the suspect he suspects, he suspects the suspect he's near. A lyric like that's not ever going to make the charts, but it's sadly true all the same. Edgar was clearly the victim in this case, but when they couldn't get anywhere else with what they had, some bright-eyed cop would decide they ought to take a harder look at the doorman, on the chance that he might have been in on it all the time.

And, when his Green Card turned out to be a little gray around the edges, making them even more suspicious of its holder, they'd have no choice but to inform the Immigration and Naturalization bozos, who'd pick up Edgar the minute the cops came to their senses and cleared him. And away he'd go, back to Nicaragua or Colombia or the Dominican Republic, wherever he'd lived back in the good old days when his name was still Edgardo and he earned three dollars a month cutting sugarcane.

"No cops," I agreed, a little belatedly. "And no INS. Come on upstairs and we'll get you cleaned up and get a couple of glasses of water into you. And maybe some coffee. **Una copa de café,** eh?"

"A cup of coffee," he said, helpfully. "**Sí, como no?**"

There were two of them, although he only got a look at one, and not a very good look at that. The way they worked it was simple enough. He'd come on duty at ten, and maybe twenty minutes later the first man, taller and heavier than Edgar—a description that fit the greater portion of the adult male population—came up to him, asking for me. He was wearing dark trousers and a zip-front jacket in tan suede, and he had a blue Mets cap pulled down over his forehead. And a shirt, but Edgar didn't get enough of a look at the shirt to remember it.

He rang my apartment, and when I didn't answer he reported the fact to my caller, who hefted the briefcase he'd been carrying. He wanted to leave this for Mr. Rhodenbarr, he told Edgar, but it was important, and he wanted to make sure it was safe. Was there a room for parcels? Something with a lock on the door?

There was, Edgar assured him, and he'd put it there. The man said he wanted him to put it there now, just to be on the safe side, and that he'd make it worth Edgar's while. He'd accompanied this last phrase by rubbing his thumb across the tips of his index and middle fingers, a gesture that, north or south of the border, meant some money would sweeten the deal.

It struck Edgar as an unusual way to earn a tip, but then America was an unusual country, with ways he hadn't entirely figured out yet. So he got the parcel room key from the drawer of the lobby desk, and led the man into the corridor beyond the bank of elevators and unlocked the parcel room door.

He'd no sooner accomplished this task than the man reached around and slapped him across the face, which seemed wholly gratuitous but turned out to have a purpose behind it, as he learned when he tried to cry out and discovered that his mouth was taped shut. The man gave him a shove, and he stumbled into the parcel room, and moments later another man came in, and the next thing he knew he was as I'd found him, secured to the chair with his hands taped behind his back. Well, not quite as I'd found him, because the chair was still upright at that point, and remained so until his efforts to escape sent it crashing to the floor a while later.

And that was that.

A team of cops might have found more questions to ask him. At the very least, they'd have asked him the same questions over and over. But they'd have wanted to make sure he wasn't hiding anything, and I was willing to give him the benefit of the doubt. I was also willing to give him coffee, of which he drank three cups in less time than it took me to drink one, and the use of my bathroom, which seemed only fair after I'd loaded him up with all that coffee.

After a few minutes I heard a little cry of shock and dismay, and a moment later he came out of the bathroom looking absolutely horrorstruck. I wondered if there was another of those damned waterbugs in the bathtub. They come up through the pipes, and they're huge and disgusting, but he'd grown up in a tropical country, for God's sake. He must have seen worse.

Then, shaking, he touched his finger to his upper lip.

"Oh, right," I said. "I didn't realize you hadn't seen it yet. I can't see any way to save it, Edgar. Let me lend you a razor and you can shave it off."

He looked questioningly at me, and I mimed the act, scraping away the mustache I didn't have with the razor I wasn't holding. He looked crestfallen, and rattled off a burst of rapid-fire Spanish. I don't know what it meant, but if I had to guess it would have been something along the lines of **But then I will resemble an idiot child and no one will ever take me seriously.**

I shook my head firmly. "You're better off without it," I insisted. "You can always grow it back, but the first step is to shave it."

I gave him a fresh disposable razor and a can of shaving cream, and he closed the door, and when he opened it again he looked about seventeen years old, which was only about six months younger than he'd looked before any of this happened.

I told him he looked fine and asked him if there was anything else he could use—an aspirin, a bite to eat, maybe a quick shower—but all he wanted was to get back downstairs and resume his post. He'd been away from it for far too long, he said, and it would be bad if he got reported to the super, who, while married to Edgar's sister's husband's cousin, could only cut him so much slack.

Besides, he said, the lobby was unattended, and that wasn't safe. Anyone could walk right in. The tenants paid a lot of rent, and they had a right to have him on duty, watching out for their interests.

And off he went, grateful for the coffee, grateful I hadn't insisted on calling the cops, and eager in spite of all he'd been through to get back to work. You can see why the INS would want to send a guy like that back where he came from.

 **SIXTEEN**

Since my clean-shaven doorman had put himself
back to work, I felt I could do no less myself, and
resumed work on my apartment. While I was at it I
called a twenty-four-hour locksmith and told him
what replacement parts he'd need to make my lock
sound again. While he was at it, I said, he could
bring an extra Rabson cylinder and a Fox police
lock. It took him fifteen minutes to get there and
the better part of two hours to install everything,
and the price he charged me added a little more
injury to the insult and injury I'd already sustained.
I wrote him a check and went to bed, fully expecting to sleep until noon, but at eight o'clock my eyes
popped open of their own accord and I started a
day I didn't have a great deal of hope for.

But a shower and a shave helped, and breakfast
didn't hurt, either, and by the time I opened up the
bookstore I felt almost human. I fed Raffles and
flushed the toilet for him—he uses it, but not even
Carolyn can figure out how to teach him to flush
it—and dragged my bargain table outside, and sat

behind the counter waiting for the world to beat a path to my door. When it failed to do so, I looked around for something to do, and remembered I had a box of books in the back room that needed to be shelved.

I walked halfway there, then spun around and returned to my stool behind the counter. I'd done enough shelving lately, I decided, and I picked up a book that had come in with the others, but that I'd set aside to read first before I gave my customers a crack at it. It was the new John Sandford novel, and I was about fifty pages into it, and with minimal interruptions I figured I could manage another fifty pages by lunchtime.

The cops in Sandford's books are apt to tell each other jokes, and one of them was funny enough so that I was chuckling over it when the phone rang. I picked it up and said, "Barnegat Books," and a voice that I recognized but couldn't place wished me a good morning, and asked if I happened to have a copy of **The Secret Agent,** by Joseph Conrad.

"Hold on," I said. "I think so, but let me check."

I went to the fiction section, and there was the book, right where the miracle of alphabetical order had led me to place it. I carried it to the counter and told my caller I did indeed have a copy.

"It's not a first," I said, "but it's a nice clean reading copy. Twelve dollars takes it home."

"Put it aside," he said. "I'll pick it up sometime today."

I could have asked his name, but that might have

been awkward, since there was something in his manner that led me to believe he thought I already knew who he was. Besides, what difference did it make? If he didn't show up, I'd put the book back on the shelf in a day or two. I had a lot more to worry about than a twelve-dollar sale.

"I've got a lot more to worry about," I told Carolyn, "than a twelve-dollar sale."

"I'll say."

"I wonder what they were looking for. They took my money, but that's not what brought them there in the first place. What do you suppose they wanted?"

"I don't know, Bern. What have you got?"

"Eight thousand dollars less than I used to have. Closer to nine thousand, if you count what I had to pay the locksmith. Aside from that, nothing. If these are the same jokers who robbed the Rogovins, and they'd pretty much have to be, then I don't get it at all. There's nothing on earth that connects me to the Rogovins. I never even heard of the Rogovins until . . ."

"Until Ray walked in and arrested you."

I nodded slowly. "That's got to be the connection," I said. "They committed a crime, and I was arrested for it. The cops made a mistake when they arrested me, but the newspaper story didn't mention that part, so the guys who committed the crime don't know that."

"They don't know they committed the crime? What do you figure their problem is, Bern? Short-term memory loss?"

"They know what they did," I said. "What they don't know is that I didn't do anything, that I was picked up because I happened to be lurking in the neighborhood for another purpose altogether. All they know is I got picked up, and that means there may be a connection between me and the Rogovins."

"Like what?"

"Like somehow I got to the Rogovins' safe before they did, and whatever they were looking for and didn't find, well, maybe I've got it."

"What do you figure it was?"

I shook my head. "Haven't got a clue," I said.

It was lunchtime, and I'd actually done a little business during the morning. I'd sold eight or ten books, including a gorgeous coffee table volume of photos of the Bronx in its heyday, which, alas, has long since come and gone. And Mickey Tolleris, my magazine guy, had come in empty-handed and staggered out with a carton full of back copies of **National Geographic** and **Playboy**. I don't put magazines on the shelves, you never sell them unless you're a specialist with a deep stock of back issues, but there are certain magazines I hang on to when they come into the store. Collectible pulps, of course, and all the genre magazines, mystery and science fiction and westerns, but also **Playboy** (if the centerfold's intact) and **National Geographic,** which enough people collect so that a fellow like Mickey can maintain a market in them. He gave me cash, and so did the folks who bought books, but I was still a long way from recouping the previous night's losses.

I'd picked up our lunch—hamburgers and fries, I wasn't feeling very imaginative—and we were at the Poodle Factory, and I'd brought Carolyn up to speed. If you wanted to call it that; it felt more to me as though I was spinning my wheels.

"What I think," I said, "is that it may not matter what they were looking for."

"How can that be?"

"Well, it matters to them," I said, "and it probably matters to the police, who'd like to find someone to hang the case on, since they're not going to be able to hang it on me. But the important thing is that those guys—I wish I knew what to call them, incidentally."

"The perps," she suggested.

"The perps," I agreed. "The important thing is the perps came looking for the—shit, I don't know what to call **that,** either."

"The McGuffin."

"Thank you. The perps came looking for the McGuffin, just on the off chance that I had it, since my name had been dragged into the affair. And they looked, and they didn't find it, and—you know what? It's a good thing they found my hidey-hole.

Because they saw right away that that's where I keep stuff, and the McGuffin—the McGuffin?"

"That's the word for it, Bern."

"They saw that the McGuffin **wasn't** there, and that's where I would have stashed it if I had it, so obviously I don't have it. Which means that they can leave me the hell alone."

"And you think they will?"

"I don't see why not."

"And you don't think you ought to go to the cops?"

"What for? Look, I promised Edgar I'd keep the INS away from him, and all I know that they don't is that one of the perps—the perps?"

"Bern . . ."

"That one of the perps is taller and heavier than Edgar, which doesn't narrow things down much. Oh, and either he likes the Mets or he beat up some Mets fan and took his cap. If I don't share that with them, do you figure I'm withholding valuable information?"

"I guess not. Bern, you know what's a good thing? That you weren't home when they showed."

I thought of the Rogovins, and gave a nod and a shudder.

"If you had been—"

"But I wasn't," I said, and figured it was a good time to change the subject. "No drinks at the Bum Rap tonight, right? Because you've got a first date with GurlyGurl, and after that you've got a date with me."

"It's still on?"

"Now more than ever," I said. "After last night, I've got the best possible reason to run up to Riverdale. I need the money."

 **SEVENTEEN**

I took less than an hour for lunch, and was behind the counter and ready for business a few minutes before one. When I thought about it later, I decided that the fat man must have been perched in a doorway down the block or across the street, waiting for me to come back and open up, because I'd no sooner reached for the John Sandford novel and found my place in it than the bell tinkled to proclaim his arrival.

That didn't mean I had to stop reading. I gave him a welcoming smile and a little nod and left him to browse my shelves, which is what just about everybody does upon arrival, unless they've got books to sell me, or they want directions to Grace Church. His hands were empty, so any books he wanted to sell were still on his shelves, and I didn't get the feeling he had the urge to seek out a moment of peace and quiet among the Episcopalians around the corner, so I closed my book and waited to find out what he wanted.

I'm sure it's politically incorrect to call him a fat

man, on the general PC principle that the last thing you should do is call a spade a spade. There's probably an acceptable euphemism for it, but I've thus far been spared knowing what it is, so I'll go on calling him fat in the hope that you won't object, and the certain knowledge that he won't.

And he was fat, all right. You see people who are uncomfortable in their fatness, as though all this extra weight just happened to them while they were thinking of something else, and now that they've got it they don't know what to do with it. Well, he wasn't like that. One look at him, the way he held himself, the way he moved, and you somehow knew he'd been fat all his life, a fat baby who'd blossomed into a fat little boy, gone through the awkward years as a fat teenager, and emerged at last as a fat grownup. He didn't have one of those pot bellies that look as though you're trying to smuggle a beach ball through Customs, didn't have skinny arms and legs sticking out of a fat torso like a potato imbedded with toothpicks. No, he was fat all over, and I got the feeling it was fine with him.

He was wearing a blue suit, and if it hadn't been made to measure then it had at the very least been tailored to fit him, and by a tailor who knew what he was doing. It didn't make him look thin, nothing could have, but it did make him look fit and natty and prosperous, and what more can you ask of a few yards of wool?

His shirt was white, with a spread collar, and his tie was this year's width, with regimental stripes of navy and scarlet. I can't tell you about his shoes because I didn't notice them when he walked in, and by the time I looked him over he was standing too close to the counter for his feet to show. But I'll bet they were good shoes. I've never yet known a fat man who didn't spend good money on shoes, and put a lot of care into their selection.

"Mr. Rhodenbarr," he said, making it not a statement but not quite a question, either. When I nodded, confirming his identification, he gave me a smile that showed a lot of teeth. They were perfectly white and perfectly even, so much so that one could hardly avoid the suspicion that they were not perfectly real. But then you could have said much the same thing about the smile.

"A pleasure," he said firmly, and stuck out his hand, which, it will not surprise you to learn, was fleshy. I shook his hand. If there's a way to avoid shaking a hand that's thrust at me, I've yet to figure it out, and I always wind up taking the proffered hand before I have time to wonder whether or not it's something I really want to do. In this case, though, I was perfectly willing to shake hands with the man. He was probably a customer, and even if he wasn't he was cheerful and pleased to see me, so why would I want to leave him standing there with his arm hanging out?

While we were shaking hands, Raffles seized the moment to leap down from his spot in my sunny window and come over to the counter, where he began circling the fat man's feet, rubbing against his ankles in the process. He goes through this routine with me when I open up in the morning, it's his way of letting me know he wants to be fed, as though it would never occur to me without this daily reminder. But he'd been fed already today, and couldn't logically expect a stranger, however well-fed himself, to do the honors.

This would have been a good time for me to check out his shoes, while I was looking down to watch Raffles polish them, but I was too busy noting the cat's uncharacteristic behavior to notice what he was rubbing up against. Anyway, I'll bet they were expensive shoes, and that he had a dozen pairs every bit as good in his closet.

He released my hand and looked down at Raffles. "A pussy cat!" he cried, with evident delight. "I love pussy cats. But what happened to his tail?"

"He was born without it," I said, wondering if I was telling the truth. "He's a Manx."

"Ah, of course. From the Isle of Man."

"Well, not personally—or do I mean cattily? His forebears were from Man, but Raffles was born right here in New York."

"I love pussy cats," he said once more, and demonstrated his affection by reaching down to give Raffles a little scratch behind the ear. The little devil purred, and the fat man scratched him some more, and Raffles purred some more, and then trotted off and leapt onto an open spot in the cookbooks section, on the fourth shelf from the bottom. From there he gazed at us, and if he'd had a grandparent from Cheshire instead of the Isle of Man, I do believe he'd have been smiling.

"It would be nice to be able to have a cat," the fat man reflected. "If I ever had a bookstore, I would definitely keep a cat in it. I think it was a very wise choice you made."

"Thank you."

"And now," he said, "I believe you have something for me, Mr. Rhodenbarr."

"I do?"

"I believe so."

He smiled again, same as before, and I decided that maybe those were his teeth after all. I was sure he would choose his dentist with as much care as his tailor, and dentistry has come a long ways in recent years. With regular visits to a first-rate dentist, you can have a mouthful of teeth so perfect that anyone would guess they were false.

But what could I have for him?

Oh.

"The Secret Agent," I said, and he beamed. I reached behind me, picked Conrad's novel off the shelf. I started to hand it to him, and he started to reach for it, and I drew it back a few inches. "But that wasn't you on the phone before, was it?" He hesitated, and I answered my own question. "He sent you to pick up the book for him."

That got me the smile again, and a nod to go with it. I handed it to him and he looked it over, but in a curious fashion; he didn't page through it, didn't even glance at the title or copyright pages, but instead turned it over and over in his hands, as if to absorb the essence of it through his palms. I've seen collectors do something similar with first editions or fine bindings, but this was just a reading copy.

But he was picking it up for the man who'd called, and might not know much about books beyond the fact that a cat fit nicely into a bookstore. Maybe he thought this was what you did when somebody handed you a book.

"Yes," he said with satisfaction. "How much do you want for it?"

"Same as I said on the phone. It's marked twelve. With tax it comes to a little over thirteen, but we can round it off. Thirteen'll be fine."

"Thirteen," he said. Something rather like amusement showed in his blue eyes. He turned to his left—toward Raffles, actually—and took a dark brown leather notecase from his breast pocket, standing so that his body screened its contents from my view. He counted out thirteen bills, or what he said was that number, pronouncing "Thirteen" with the same curious inflection as he returned the notecase to his pocket. He turned to face me again, folded the sheaf of bills in half, and palmed them discreetly to me.

Something made me want to count them, but I told myself not to be silly. The likelihood of his shorting me seemed remote, and did I really care if I got eleven or twelve dollars instead of thirteen? I matched his discretion pound for pound, taking the bills in hand and conveying them smoothly to a pocket. I wrote out a receipt, tucked it into the book and the book into a book-sized brown paper bag, and handed it to him.

"A great pleasure," he said, smiling the broad smile again, and spun neatly around, walking right over to Raffles and scratching him one more time behind the ear. "A truly delightful pussy cat," he said, while Raffles put everything he had into a full-throated purr.

Then the fat man spun once more on his heel and headed for the door.

Even as the bell was tinkling to announce his departure, I drew my hand out of my pocket. I looked down at what I was holding and saw he'd made a mistake, because the top bill was a hundred. Then I fanned the bills, and they were all hundreds.

I may be a thief, but my thieving pulls up short at the bookshop door. I don't rob my customers, or permit them to rob themselves. He'd just forked over $1300 for a twelve-dollar book, and that's more sales tax than anybody should have to pay, fiscal crisis or no fiscal crisis.

I hurried out from behind the counter, yanked the door open and stood on the sidewalk, looking around for him. He was two doors along toward University, standing at the curb and waiting to cross the street. "Hey!" I called, and got no response. If I'd known his name I'd have tried that, but I didn't, so what I called out was, "Hey! **Secret Agent!**" and started jogging down the sidewalk toward him.

He turned at my voice, but maybe he'd have been

better off if he hadn't. He might have seen the car coming, whatever good that would have done him.

I don't know what kind of car it was. I should have, because I saw it coming. I watched it pick up speed, then saw it stop abruptly with a great squeal of brakes. Then I saw the window open on the passenger's side, and saw a gun muzzle protrude from it.

Then I didn't see anything, because my instincts somehow guided me to the appropriate response, which was to throw myself down on the pavement so that a parked car screened me from the guy with the gun. He wasn't pointing it at me, but that could change.

And did, I learned later, because the muzzle turned out to be that of an automatic weapon, and the shooter swept it to and fro, spraying bullets left and right. And straight ahead, of course, which was where the fat man was standing. Several slugs found the car I was hiding behind, and one made a neat hole in the window of an importer of European antiques and went on to lodge in a Country French breakfront of no particular distinction. Others went other places, but a great many went where they were supposed to go, and they didn't do the fat man any good at all.

I didn't know all this just yet, because I hadn't moved. I did turn my head so that I could see what little was visible beneath the car that had just taken a bullet for me, and what I saw was this: the door of the shooter's car opened and somebody, presumably the shooter, hopped out, scurried over to where the fat man lay, reached down, picked up something that could well have been a book-sized brown paper bag, and got back into the car and closed the door. Whereupon the car burned rubber getting out of there, took a right at University without slowing down, and inspired a good many other drivers to honk their horns in righteous indignation.

I don't remember walking over to where the fat man lay, but I must have, because the next thing I knew I was standing there looking down at him. He must have been hit a dozen times, and the blood had poured out of him. He wasn't smiling, and who could blame him?

"Bern?" It was Carolyn. "I came out when I heard shooting. What happened? Who's he? And where'd all the money come from?"

I looked down and saw I was holding the $1300 in my hand. "It's his change," I said. "But I guess there's no point giving it back to him now."

 **EIGHTEEN**

O kay," Ray said. "Let's go over it one more time."

We were in the bookstore, and it wasn't quite three o'clock yet, for all that it felt like three in the morning. I'd had a rough night with not much sleep in it, and an easy day until the shooting started, and since then I'd been behind my counter with Ray in front of it. He kept asking questions, and I'd have answered more of them if I knew more of the answers.

"So this guy comes in," he said now, "an' you never saw him before in your life."

"Never."

"Big fat guy, all dressed up in a suit an' tie, an' you never set eyes on him before."

"That's what I just told you."

"He never wandered in here before, lookin' to pick up somethin' for a friend in the hospital?"

"If he had," I said, "I'd have remembered him. But it's hard to remember something that never happened."

"Oh, I dunno," he said. "Some people do it all

the time. It's called tellin' lies, Bernie, an' over the years I've known you to be a master of it."

"I'm not lying now," I said. "He came in and played with my cat and told me I had something for him."

"An' you gave him a book."

"Right."

"You never saw him before, an' yet you knew just what book to give him."

"Oh, God. How many times do I have to tell you the same damned thing?"

"Till I understand it, Bernie. So tell me again."

"I had a phone call."

"From the fat guy."

"No, not from the fat guy. From some customer, I think, who asked if I had a copy of a particular book."

"By this Conrad guy. What was his last name?"

"Conrad. His first name's Joseph. He was Polish, and spent a good many years at sea, and ultimately he taught himself English and became a great novelist."

"That's a Polish name, Conrad?"

"He changed it."

"Can't blame him," he said. "Probably full of **Z**s and **Y**s, and you'd have to be Polish yourself to pronounce it, an' even then you might have your hands full. So you said you had this book, an' you put it aside for the guy."

"Right."

"An' when this other guy came in, the fat guy,

you gave it to him instead of keepin' it for the guy who called you."

"I assumed the caller had sent the fat man."

"You ask him what book he was lookin' for?"

"I said the title and he couldn't have been happier. I handed him the book and he held it like the Holy Grail. He asked how much and I told him the price and he couldn't wait to put the money in my hand."

"And then he left."

"First he said goodbye to the cat," I said, "and **then** he left."

"An' got his ass shot off. Why'd you run out after him?"

"He walked off without his change."

"An' you were gonna give it back? You, Bernie?"

"In here," I said, "I'm as honest as the day is long. Even today, which is shaping up to be the longest day of the year."

"How much was the book?"

"Thirteen dollars."

"An' how much did he give you?"

"Fifteen," I said. Honesty, in or out of the bookstore, has its limits. "He gave me a five and a ten and didn't wait for me to give him his change."

"So that's two bucks we're talkin' about, Bernie? You mean to tell me you ran out into the street after him to return two measly dollars?"

"When Abraham Lincoln was a boy," I said, "he had a job clerking in a shop. One day he shortchanged a customer—"

"Abe did? An' here I always thought he was supposed to be honest."

"It was accidental, and the man walked off before Lincoln realized his mistake. So that night he walked all the way to the man's house, in the pitch dark and through deep snow, to return the man's change. And do you know how much it was?"

"Two dollars?"

"A penny," I said.

"A penny? Did it at least have his pitcher on it?"

I gave him a look. "One cent," I said, "but Lincoln knew it wasn't right to keep it, and so he gave it back."

He frowned in thought, or the Kirschmann equivalent thereof. "You know," he said, "I heard that story in school when I was a kid. You figure it's true, Bernie?"

"I think it contains a great spiritual truth."

"What's that mean?"

"In a word," I said, "it means no. I don't believe it."

"I didn't believe it back then," Ray said, "an' I still don't. I think it's like George Washington, coppin' the neighbor's cherry. Makes a nice story but it never happened. Gettin' back to the book, Bernie. It's just another old book off the shelves, right?"

"Right."

"Not rare or valuable or anythin'."

"Not remotely."

"Or why would you be lettin' it go for thirteen

bucks? An' I think you said you owned it a long time."

"Years."

"So it ain't really what the fat guy was lookin' for."

"Good thinking, Ray."

"Now let me ask you somethin'," he said, "which you can answer without incriminatin' yourself. Is there anythin' that I don't know about, and don't need to know about, that you been up to lately? Somethin' that might lead to someone thinkin' you had somethin' they wanted back?"

I didn't have to think long and hard. The only two things I'd been involved in were my adventure Wednesday night, when I'd prowled my way into Barbara Creeley's apartment, and the Mapes burglary, which hadn't happened yet. There was no way either could have led the fat man to my store.

"Not a thing," I said.

"Then it's the Rogovin murders," he said. "They got in an' they killed the people an' they popped the safe, but there musta been somethin' they wanted an' didn't get. Somethin' that coulda been a book."

"A McGuffin."

"What the hell's that?"

"Never mind," I said. "I'd say you're right, they were looking for something at least vaguely booklike."

"Gotta be."

"But not **The Secret Agent,** by Joseph Conrad. That'd be too much of a coincidence."

"What it'd have to be," he said thoughtfully, "is somethin' that they don't know exactly what it is, or else when you handed him that particular book he'da handed it right back to you."

"Or thrown it at me."

"Or at the cat. Though you'd think he'd have smelled a rat when all you wanted for it was thirteen bucks."

Quite so, which explained why he'd assumed I meant thirteen hundred. And even that was evidently a low price for the McGuffin, which explained the enigmatic smile, and the way he hadn't wanted me to see how much money he'd brought along to the bargaining table. God only knows what I could have asked for.

"Maybe he thought I just wanted to get rid of it, and the thirteen dollars was just to save face."

"You couldn't save much face for thirteen bucks. Not much more'n a couple of whiskers. There's got to be two sets of players, Bernie. The ones who hit the Rogovins and the others. My guess is Fat Boy was one of the others, and the ones who hit the Rogovins are the ones who hit him, too."

And who kicked my door in, I thought, since their MO was the same as in the Rogovin home invasion, down to the duct tape on the doorman. But I hadn't mentioned my own break-in to Ray, probably because I'd promised Edgar to keep the

INS away from him. I could mention it now, but then I'd have to explain why I'd held off mentioning it for so long, and it was easier just to avoid the subject altogether.

"Two sets of bad guys," he said, "an' one of them's killed four times already. An' where's Mrs. Rhodenbarr's son Bernie? Right smack dab in the middle."

"Well, I shouldn't be," I said. "I'm only there because you picked me up. They found out I'd been arrested, and they didn't spot it for the police incompetence it was."

"Easy there, Bernie."

"They actually thought you jokers knew what you were doing," I said. "You know what I ought to do? I ought to demand around-the-clock police protection."

"You want it? Easiest thing in the world, Bernie. Come on over to the precinct an' I'll toss you in a cell."

"Very funny."

"Seriously, do you want me to get a plainclothes guy to follow you around? I'd have to clear it with the captain, but it could be done."

That would be peachy, I thought. The guy could tag along when we went up to Riverdale to knock off the Mapes house. He could watch the car, make sure no one ticketed it for parking in a No Burglars zone.

"Thanks," I said, "but I think I'll pass."

•   •   •

I actually did some business while Ray was there. Customers drifted in and out of the store, doing more browsing than buying, but occasionally one brought a book to the counter and I interrupted Ray and rang the sale. Now and then someone asked about the shooting outside, and I agreed it was a terrible thing and let it go at that.

When Ray finally left (though not without promising to return) I had an actual breathing spell and went back to John Sandford. The book was getting exciting, although the main plotline struck me as a little more far-fetched than others in the series. As usual, the point of view shifted back and forth, from Lucas Davenport, Sandford's macho hero cop, to the villain, who was in this case a disillusioned ex-vegetarian Congregationalist minister making his brutal way around Minnesota, slaughtering prominent vegans and organic farmers, butchering them, and eating their livers. Pretty wild, but somehow he made you believe it, and I was starting to get caught up in it when, dammit, somebody else came in the door and headed straight for the counter.

He was a tall man with a neatly trimmed beard, thin as a pipe cleaner, and wearing a three-piece brown tweed suit. His name was Colby Riddle and he was a professor at the New School. I forget what field he was in, but I'm pretty sure it ends in **-ology**.

"Well," he said, "and how are you today?"

And, of course, it was the voice I'd heard on the phone that morning, heard and recognized but failed to place. "Oh, hell," I said. "You've come for the book."

"Is this a bad time, Bernie?"

"No, not at all," I said. "Or at least no more so than any other time. Colby, somebody else walked off with your book."

"Oh," he said.

"I'm really sorry."

"I thought you were going to put it aside for me."

"I did."

"Oh."

"And then someone came in and I handed it to him."

He tried to make sense out of this, and I wished him the best of luck. "You thought he was me," he said at length.

"I thought you sent him. He said he understood I had something for him, and—"

"And you thought I'd sent him, so you handed him **The Secret Agent.** Why didn't he hand it right back?"

"I don't know."

"Because I have to say that it strains the bonds of permissible coincidence that he happened to be looking for the very book I'd asked about."

"He wasn't. I don't believe he knew what he was looking for."

"But you gave him my book and he was satisfied."

"Apparently so."

"He paid for it?"

"Sales tax and all."

"How nice for the governor. Do you suppose he'll bring it back?"

"I'm afraid not."

"Really? When he realizes it's not what he wanted—"

"He's not going to realize it."

"Why, is he brain-dead?"

I decided he was going to hear about it on **Live at Five,** or read about it in the morning paper, so why not tell him now? "Among other things," I said. "He walked out of here, book in hand, and a car pulled up and somebody rolled down the window and blew him away."

"Good grief. You're serious, aren't you? It's not just a ruse to get around the fact that someone else paid more money for the book than the price you quoted to me."

"I wouldn't sell it out from under you," I said. "And yes, I'm serious. You can check out the hole in Cooperstone's window. The bullet that made it missed the guy, but most of the other rounds didn't."

"How shocking," he said, "and how dramatic. More exciting than anything old Joe Conrad ever wrote, I'll have to say that for it. Bernie, I'm sure it's in dreadful taste to bring it up, but when they shot him and he crumpled to the pavement—I assume he crumpled, didn't he?"

"More or less."

"Well, he would have dropped the book, wouldn't he? I don't suppose you managed to retrieve it."

"No."

"But do you think you might?"

"No."

"Oh. Evidence? The police have it?"

"The killers have it."

"The killers?"

"Scooped it up and drove off with it. Broke a few traffic laws while they were at it, but I don't suppose they were much concerned about that."

"They killed the man," he said thoughtfully, "and took my book. Well, not **my** book. I hadn't paid for it, so title hadn't transferred. It was still your book."

"If you say so, Colby."

"Well, let me see," he said, heading for the stacks. "I've got to find something to read this weekend, haven't I?"

I joined him in Fiction. I pointed out what other books of Conrad's I had, but he wasn't interested in them. The appealing thing about **The Secret Agent,** he said, was that it was set on dry land. Conrad's sea stories were just too nautical for his taste.

"Here's Graham Greene," I told him. "I've got a larger than usual stock of Greene, and I think a couple of these are firsts."

"Oh, God," he said. "Not Graham Greene."

"Don't care for him?"

"The salient fact about Graham Greene," he said, "is that his characters get less joy from adultery than the rest of us do embracing our wives. No, I'll pass on Graham Greene."

He settled for one of Evelyn Waugh's Guy Crouchback stories, I forget which one. He'd read it, but didn't own it, and enough time had passed so that he could happily read it again. The prospect pleased him so much that he decided it was time to go on a Waugh jag, and accordingly he picked out three more books and wrote out a check for the lot. "But I do still want **The Secret Agent**," he said from the doorway. "If someone happens to bring in a copy—"

"It's yours," I assured him. "And nobody'll get it away from me, either."

 NINETEEN

I was getting ready to close when Ray Kirschmann turned up like the bad penny he is. "Perfect," I told him. "Just the man I was hoping to see."

"Yeah?"

"Absolutely," I said. "You're just in time to help me with my bargain table."

"I'd be glad to, Bernie."

"Good. You take that end—"

"Except I ain't supposed to lift nothin'. Doctor's orders, on account of my back."

"If our roles were reversed," I said, "and I tried an excuse like that on you, you'd want to know the name of the doctor. Never mind, I don't want to hear it. You can just stand there and watch me work."

"Fair enough," he said, and did just that. The least he could do was hold the door for me, and he did, being a great believer in doing the least. Inside, he leaned his bulk against my counter while I did what I do to settle Raffles in for the night.

"Soon as you're ready," he said, "we can go over

to that gin mill where you an' Shorty go every night.
I was gonna head there myself an' surprise you."

"I wish you had."

"Yeah? Why's that? You like surprises?"

"I like them when they happen to other people,
and you're the one who would have been surprised,
Ray, when we didn't show up."

"You don't like that place no more?"

"Carolyn's got a previous engagement," I told
him, "and I don't feel like drinking alone."

"So you'll drink with me, Bernie. Lock up an'
let's go."

I shook my head. "Not tonight, Ray."

"Not tonight? Ain't it Friday?"

"Yes," I said, "and thank God and all that, but I
don't feel like a drink tonight."

"Cup of coffee, then. Over on University, there's
this place opened up that's supposed to be good."

"It's not bad. A little expensive, though."

"No problem," he said. "You're buyin'."

I was buying a grande latte for each of us, it
turned out. I'm sure they'd have been cheaper with
English names. I brought them to the table he'd
picked out over at the side, and told him Colby
Riddle had come looking for his copy of the Conrad
novel.

"So it's as I figured," I said. "A legitimate customer ordered the book, and I assumed the fat man
was there to pick it up, and he assumed it was what
he was looking for, because he didn't know exactly

what he was looking for. All he knew was that I had it."

"But you say you don't."

"If I did," I said, "you'd be the first to know. People are getting killed over it, whatever it is, so why would I want to hang on to it? I'd turn it over to the proper authorities."

"That'd be a first. This customer of yours got a name?"

"He'd almost have to, Ray. These days it's almost as hard to go through life without a name as it is without a Social Security number."

"You wanna tell me his name, Bernie?"

"Can't."

"Can't? What do you mean, you can't?"

"My lips are sealed," I said. "Don't you read the papers? There was a case in Denver where the cops tried to make a bookstore owner divulge what books one of her clients had bought. He was a dope dealer, and they wanted to prove he'd bought a copy of **How to Make Crystal Meth in Your Very Own Kitchen.**"

"Who'd publish somethin' like that?"

"That may not be the exact title. The point is, Joyce Meskis took a stand, and it must have cost her a fortune in legal fees, but she won. And if she could put her life on the line for the principle of the Freedom to Read, I don't see how I can do less."

"What a load of crap," he said. "What's this Polack Conrad have to do with cooking crank at home? You're blowin' smoke, Bernie, but it don't matter. You don't want to tell me the name, that's fine. I'll tell you a name instead. How's that?"

"You've lost me, Ray."

"Arnold Lyle."

"Arnold Lyle."

"Ring a bell?" I shook my head. "How about Shirley Schnittke?"

"Arnold Lyle and Shirley Schnittke. Schnittke?"

"I think I'm pronouncin' it right."

I suppose it was possible, although when he tried for Mondrian it always came out Moon Drain. "Arnold Lyle and Shirley Schnittke. I can see the two names carved into the trunk of a tree, with a heart around it pierced by an arrow. Who are they, anyway?"

"Remember Rogovin's first name?"

"Give me a moment, it's on the tip of my tongue."

"Spit it out, why don't you?"

"Lyle," I said. "Arnold and Shirley are the Rogovins?"

"They were," he said. "Now they're toast. Fingerprints came back, and that's who they turned out to be, with records almost as long as yours. They both came over from Russia a few years back and went straight to Brighton Beach. There's a lot of hardworkin', law-abidin' Russians in Brighton Beach, but he wasn't one of 'em an' neither was she."

"He came over from Russia with a name like Arnold Lyle."

"Naw, he changed it when he got here. Changed it legally, which musta made it the last legal thing he ever did. Far as anybody knows, Schnittke's the name she was born with."

"Some people are just lucky that way," I said.

"They took that apartment less'n a month ago. Sublet it, signed a one-year lease, an' paid cash. Don't ask me where they came up with the name Rogovin."

"Maybe they were thinking of Saul Rogovin."

"Who the hell's that?"

"He pitched for the Buffalo Bisons fifty years ago," I said. "Or maybe Syrell Rogovin Leahy. She's a writer, and I've actually got a book of hers in the store."

"That's nice, Bern. Let's stick with their real names, Lyle and Schnittke. Names don't mean nothin' to you, huh?"

"Not a thing."

"They musta already owned the safe. The rest of the furniture came with the place, but we got in touch with the owner, an' she don't know nothin' about a safe. An' we contacted the companies in town that sell safes, an' nobody sold 'em one."

"That's interesting," I said, although I'm not sure it was. "Why are you telling me all this, Ray?"

"That's a question I oughta be askin' myself, Bernie."

"And?"

"First off," he said, "I'm pretty sure you didn't have nothin' to do with this."

"So am I, and it seems to me I told you that early on."

"Yeah, but when I start automatically takin' your word for anythin', it's time for them to ship me to the funny farm. This time, though, it looks like you're tellin' the truth. An' I figure it's an opportunity for the both of us."

"An opportunity?"

He nodded gravely. "Over the years," he said, "you an' I done pretty good together, Bern."

"On balance," I said, "I'd have to agree with you."

"There's somethin' here that a lot of people want. Whatever it is, they want it bad enough to kill for it."

"And that looks like an opportunity to you? To me it looks like an opportunity to leave the country."

"If I was to break this case," he said, "it'd be a real good collar. Now that we know who the Rogovins are, an' what with all that shootin' in the street, it ain't my case anymore. Major Cases took it over. But that don't mean I can't put in a little work on it, an' if I was to crack it open, well, it'd look pretty good for me."

"I'm sure it would. Where do I come into it, Ray?"

"Not every case gets solved," he said. "Good police work only goes so far."

"A lot of the time," I said, "it goes too far."

"You'd think so, wouldn't you? Thing is, you got Lyle and Schnittke in the middle of this, you're talkin' some kind of organized crime. A lot of the time you can't close those cases, even though you got a pretty good idea who did it. But whether we close it or not, there could be a nice payoff in it, Bernie."

"If we were to find what everybody's looking for."

"Bingo," he said.

"You still don't know what it is, do you?"

"No. How about you?"

"Not a clue."

"Well," he said, "one of us might learn something. What do you say we pool our information? You find out somethin', you let me know. An' the vice is versa, as far as that goes."

"And if there's a payoff?"

"Fifty-fifty," he said. "Except the credit, which I'll take, because it wouldn't do you much good. Unless we could get the mayor to give you a citation, Citizen of the Week or somethin', but I'd have to say it's a long shot, what with your record an' all. But a straight fifty-fifty split on the cash."

"That's fine," I said. "I'll go along with your tailor on that one."

"My tailor? What are you talkin' about? I don't have a tailor."

"Really? I figured Omar the Tent Maker got all your business."

"Is that a crack? An' who the hell is he, anyway?"

"It's sort of a crack," I said, "but nothing too serious. And he's toast now, like Arnold and Shirley, but back when he was still fresh pita bread he was a Persian poet named Omar Khayyám, and he said a lot of good things. 'Take the cash and let the credit go' was one of them."

"The cash an' the credit, huh?" He considered the matter. "Well, he's no tailor of mine," he said. "I want 'em both."

There's a store on 23rd Street off Fifth Avenue that sells prepaid cell phones. There are, I'm fairly sure, similar establishments all over town, but you generally only notice that sort of place when you're in the market, and even then your eyes can skip right over them. I'm sure I'd have found one on 14th Street, just a few blocks from where Ray left me to sip the dregs of my four-dollar latte, but it seemed simpler to go to the place I knew about, and I did.

I gave the clerk some money and he gave me a phone that would stop working after I'd spent a certain number of minutes talking on it. I forget how many minutes I had coming, because I knew I wasn't going to use more than the merest fraction of them. There was only one number I was planning to call, and I didn't expect to call it more than once or twice, maybe three times at the outside.

I left the store with my new cell phone in my breast pocket, and I just started walking, and after

I'd gone a couple of blocks I realized where I was headed. I looked at my watch, and I had plenty of time, and this seemed like a reasonable way to kill it. I let my feet keep on walking in the direction they seemed to have chosen for themselves, and before very long I was standing diagonally across the street from a white brick building at the corner of Third Avenue and 34th Street. I'd walked past that building Wednesday night, I'd walked all over the damn neighborhood, but I hadn't had any reason to notice it.

I looked it over, and all it looked like was a white brick apartment building of the sort that went up all over the city around forty years ago. Ugly no-frills architecture, cheap construction, ceilings as low as the building code permitted, and walls you could detect a fart through, even if you were deaf. They don't build 'em like that anymore, and it's a damn good thing.

I considered going over and having a word with the doorman, who was on the sidewalk smoking a cigarette. But what could I ask him, and what would he be likely to tell me? Nothing, I was sure, that Ray didn't already know.

Not that I expected anything to come of the partnership he'd proposed. Still, somebody had killed the Rogovins (whom I was going to have to learn to think of as Lyle and Schnittke). And the same people—the perps, if you will—had traumatized Edgar the Doorman, sacked my apartment, stolen my emergency fund, and shot holes in a good customer of mine. (I'd never seen the fat man before, but anybody who's in my store for less than five minutes and manages to spend $1300 is a hell of a good customer. Besides, Raffles thought he was a prince.)

If I could help Ray nail the bastards, or if we could take some money away from them, or both—well, that was fine with me.

I walked around some more, wondering just how many security cameras were recording my movements. All of these infringements on our privacy are making it particularly difficult on people who are doing something they shouldn't be doing, so I suppose it's not surprising the crime rate is dropping. Pretty soon every criminal in a position to make a choice will choose to go straight, or at least to go into the world of big business, where criminal conduct rarely leads to anything so extreme as a jail sentence, and where security cameras aren't a factor.

This is the sort of musing best done in a place where alcoholic beverages are sold, and before I knew it I was in just such a place myself, an upscale saloon called Parsifal's on Lexington a few doors south of 37th Street. It was that transitional hour when the less hardy members of the local workforce were ready to head home, while the crowd of drinkers who lived in the neighborhood had not yet arrived in full force. Thus there were seats at the bar, and I took one and ordered a Perrier. The bartender, a tall blonde with cheekbones you could cut yourself on, brought Pellegrino, squeezed a wedge of lime in it, collected a couple of bucks for it, and left me to drink myself into a stupor.

It would have been in a place just like this, I thought, that Barbara Anne Creeley would have met the deep-voiced chap who'd slipped her her first Rohypnol and then a token of his esteem, or lack thereof. I wondered if he might be fishing the same waters again, and I looked around, wondering what I thought I was looking for. Since I hadn't seen him and had nothing to go by but his voice, I couldn't very well expect to recognize him.

But I could recognize Barbara Creeley, and did, standing at the bar with one foot on the rail, not five stools away from mine.

Except it wasn't her, as a second glance quickly established. This woman was a little older and a little heavier than the woman into whose apartment I'd recently broken, and her face was harder and her hair shorter. The more I looked, the less resemblance I could see.

I scanned the rest of the room, but largely as a matter of form. I knew she wasn't there, and I was right. But I also felt absolutely certain that this was a regular stop of hers. It might not be where she met the Rohypnol guy—**the roofer** is how I found myself thinking of him—but I thought it very likely was. If I hung around long enough, and poured down enough of the Italian fizzy water, one or both of them was almost certain to turn up.

Why, I wondered, would I want to run into either of them?

But I didn't have to know the answer to that one, did I? I had things to do, and it was time to go do them. I drank down most of my Pellegrino, scooped up most of my change, and went home.

 **TWENTY**

By 8:45 I was sitting behind the wheel of a bronze-colored Mercury Sable sedan. It was parked with its front bumper about eight feet from the only curbside fire hydrant on Arbor Court. That's closer than the law allows, but that was the least of my worries, because the car was stolen.

I somehow doubt that too many traffic cops and meter maids work Arbor Court—how many of them even know where it is?—but if one turned up I was ready, parked so that I could see anyone, on wheels or on foot, who happened to turn into the little street. I didn't have the key in the ignition, because I hadn't had a key in the first place, but it wouldn't take me more than a second or two to start the car up, and I'd do that the minute a cop came into view.

For ten minutes no one turned up, cop or civilian, and when someone finally did I started up the Sable and honked the horn, because it was Carolyn. She looked around, saw nothing familiar, and kept walking. I honked again and she spun around, frowning, and I lowered the window and said her name.

"Oh," she said. "Neat car, Bern. Where'd you get it?"

"Seventy-fourth Street. I borrowed it."

"Oh yeah? Who from?"

"Beats me."

"That means you stole it."

"Only technically," I said. "I intend to give it back."

"That's what embezzlers always say, Bern. They were planning to give the money back. Somehow they never get around to it."

"Well, I fully intend to give this one back," I said. "Cars are a pain in the neck in the city. Where would I park it? It costs a fortune to garage them, and if you park them on the street—"

"People 'borrow' them," she said, "and take them to chop shops."

"You know," I said, "you're sounding less and less like a henchperson, and more and more like Ray Kirschmann."

"That may be the nastiest thing you ever said to me," she said, "but I think maybe you're right. I'm sorry, Bern. I got a little confused. I wasn't sure you were coming."

"I said I was."

"I know, but what with everything that happened today I thought you might change your mind. That fat guy getting shot right in front of you."

"Riverdale's miles away."

"I know, but—"

"And I need the money."

I also needed the psychological lift of winning one for a change. I'd started off hiding under the bed, and things had gone downhill from there. Since then I'd been hassled by the cops, burgled by brutes, and given a supporting role in a drive-by homicide. It was time for me to make something happen instead of waiting to see what happened next. Maybe I couldn't bomb Iraq, but I could damn well burgle Mapes, and I wouldn't even have to wait to find out what the premier of France thought of it.

"Wait here," Carolyn said. "I'll just be a minute. Don't you dare go without me."

I got on the West Side Drive. The Sable rode well and handled nicely, and the traffic was almost light enough for Cruise Control, but not quite. I caught a light at 57th Street and glanced over at Carolyn. "I gather she didn't stand you up," I said.

"Not at all, Bern. What I did do is sit up."

"Sit up?"

"And take notice. I got there first, but only by a minute or two. I walked right into the lobby of the Algonquin, just like Dorothy Parker and Robert Benchley before me."

"And Alexander Woollcott, and George S. Kaufman . . ."

"And all those guys, right. So I took a table in the lobby, and this waiter straight out of a London men's club came over and asked me what I wanted to drink, and I didn't know."

"That's a first."

"Well, there's a bar off the lobby, where you'd go for a drink, and there's the lobby, where people meet for tea. Now most of the people having tea were actually having it in martini glasses. Tea's more or less an expression there. But what if she really intended to have tea, and there I am, looking like a drunk?"

"Didn't your Date-a-Dyke ad say you love scotch?"

"I know, but I wasn't sure I should love it on the first date. You know what they say, Bern. You never get a second chance to make a good first impression."

"Is that what they say?"

"I think so. While I was weighing the pros and consequences, this woman walked in the door and made a beeline for my table. She didn't even take a minute to scan the room. She zoomed right in on me and came over."

"She was just passing by, and thought you'd be the perfect person for a serious talk about Amway products."

"It was GurlyGurl, Bern."

"And did she live up to her screen name?"

"She's pretty great looking. Taller than I am, but

who do you know that isn't? Dark hair, real nice figure, peaches and cream complexion, big gray
eyes—"

"Gray?"

"She said they used to be blue, but the color
faded out of them. Have you ever heard of that
happening?"

"With hair."

"I guess it can happen with eyes, too, and Miss
Clairol's no help if it does. She'd just come from
work, and she said she hoped I hadn't been waiting
long, and I said I just got there myself, I hadn't even
ordered yet, and she said . . ."

Di dah di dah di dah. She fed me the conversation word for word, and a court reporter couldn't
have done a better job of it. I stopped listening,
because I was caught up in the physical description.

Hair, figure, complexion, eyes—granted, it could
fit any number of women, but I'd had the feeling for
a while now that there was a great big coincidence
hovering just out of sight, waiting patiently for the
chance to coincide.

I tuned in again, and she was telling how they'd
ordered drinks after all. "She asked what I wanted,
and I said I'd probably have a cup of tea, and she
said she thought I liked scotch, and I said I did, but
tea's nice sometimes, and she said she's a big tea
drinker herself, but after the week she'd just had
scotch would sure hit the spot, and I said in that case
I didn't figure one drink would hurt me. Because I

know you don't drink before a job, Bern, and I shouldn't either, but it would be different if I was going into the house. I'm not, am I?"

"No, I'm on my own for that part."

"That's what I thought, so I figured one drink would be fine."

"So you had a drink."

"Well, two."

"I thought you just said—"

"Bern, who has one drink? It's like one pant or one scissor. They come in pairs. Nobody has just one drink."

"Somebody must," I said, "or where would the expression come from? 'I think I'll have a drink.' **A** drink. Not two drinks, not six drinks, not ten drinks. 'I think I'll have a drink.' People say it all the time."

"Uh-huh, and then they say 'I think I'll have another.' **A drink** is just the stepping-off point. Anyway, we had two each, and I ate a whole dish of mixed nuts to soak up the alcohol, and I'm fine."

"You seem okay."

"That's because I am okay. And I'm not driving, so I don't have to worry about a Breathalyzer test, and I'm not going into the house, so what's the problem?"

"I don't think there is any. I gather the two of you hit it off."

"I like her, Bern. And I think she likes me."

"You made a good impression."

"And a good thing, because that's something you only get one crack at."

"Where does she live?"

"Manhattan. Hey, I knew that going in. I didn't want to meet her and be crazy about her and then discover she's GU."

"Geographically undesirable. It's a curse, all right. I met a girl once and we hit it off, and she wouldn't tell me where she lived. She'd always meet me places, or come over to my place."

"Brooklyn?"

"Way the hell out in Queens," I said. "You had to take the subway for days, and then you took a bus, and then you walked ten blocks. That was the end of that."

"But if she was willing to come into the city all the time—"

"When they're that GU," I said, "you wind up under all this pressure to live together, because otherwise one person's spending half their life in transit. I figured it would save a whole lot of aggravation to break up."

"Wow."

"Besides," I said, "she had this whiny voice, and I thought I could get used to it, and then one day I realized I didn't want to get used to it. In fact what I didn't want was to hear it long enough to get used to it." I took the cell phone from my pocket, put through a call to the number I'd programmed in earlier. "So that was that," I said, while the phone rang in the house on Devonshire Close. It rang four times before a machine picked up, and I listened to what I supposed was the recorded voice of Crandall Rountree Mapes, inviting me to leave a message. I hung up in mid-invitation.

"Well, GG's not GU," Carolyn said.

"GG?"

"As in GurlyGurl. In fact she's pretty desirable all across the board."

"No whiny voice, huh?"

"A nice voice. Kind of throaty."

"She could live in Manhattan and still be a long ways away. Washington Heights, say."

"Washington Heights isn't that far. I had a girl-friend in Washington Heights."

"That's what I was referring to."

"Well, it was a disaster, but you couldn't blame it on the neighborhood. It was just a disaster. Anyway, she lives closer than that, because she walks to work, and it only takes her fifteen minutes."

"Where does she work?"

"Forty-fifth and Madison. That's why she picked the Algonquin. Why?"

"I just wondered. So if she lives fifteen minutes from there, she could live in the East Sixties."

"I suppose."

"Or the West Fifties."

"So?"

"Or the East Thirties."

"What are you getting at, Bern?"

"I just want to make sure," I said.

"You want to make sure of what?"

"That she's not who I'm afraid she is."

"Huh?"

"Because it would be a coincidence," I said, "but coincidences happen all the time, and I've had the feeling one's on its way right about now. And if it turns out that she's who I think she is—"

"Who do you think she is?"

"This would be a lot easier," I said, "if the two of you had told each other your names, but as it stands—"

"We did."

"You did?"

"Of course we did, Bern. You only keep it anonymous until you actually meet. We told each other our names right away. Before the old guy brought the drinks, even."

"What did you say your name was?"

"I said it was Carolyn, Bern. Carolyn Kaiser. Not very imaginative, I know, but I just went and pulled a name out of the air, and—"

"What did she say?"

"She said, 'Hi, Carolyn.' Taking me at my word, not suspecting for a moment that I'd lie about a thing like that, and—"

"What did she say her name was?"

"Lacey Kavinoky," she said, "which rhymes with okie-dokey."

"You're sure?"

"That it rhymes? Positive, Bern. No question in my mind."

"I mean—"

"I know what you mean. Am I sure it's her name? I'm sure it's what she said. Was I supposed to ask to see her driver's license? Are you gonna tell me who you were afraid she was?"

"Barbara Creeley."

"Barbara Creeley. The one who got—"

"Burgled and date-raped. Yeah, you don't have to tell me. I know it's ridiculous."

"I think it would have to make a lot more sense," she said, "in order to be no worse than ridiculous. There are eight million people in New York, Bern. What are the odds?"

"Eight million in the five boroughs," I said. "Only two million in Manhattan, if that many."

"One in two million?"

"Half of the two million are male," I said. "Of the one million left, by the time you cross out the ones who are under twenty and over fifty, and the married ones, and—"

"I see where you're going with this," she said, "and you're still nuts."

"You're right."

"Anyway, forget it. Lacey's not Barbara."

"I know."

"It would not only be a coincidence, it'd be a dumb one."

"I know."

"I sound like I'm pissed off, don't I? I'm not. I'm just sort of incredulous, that's all."

"Whatever you say."

"Her name's Lacey Kavinoky," she said, "and she's cute and bright and genuinely nice. And she's gay, Bern, and she knows it. She's not one of those oh-I-always-thought-it-might-be-interesting-to-try-being-with-a-woman women. She's not one of those variety's-the-spice-of-life women, either. She's like me, she's got nothing against men, and high on the list of things she doesn't hold against them is her beautiful body. You remember that song?"

"I remember."

" 'If I said you had a beautiful body, would you hold it against me?' Well, if you told her, Bern, she wouldn't."

"Great."

"But she might hold it against me. We'll see. But there's one thing I can tell you for sure, and that's that she's not Barbara Creeley. She's Lacey, Lacey Kavinoky, and if anybody date-rapes her it's gonna be me."

● TWENTY-ONE

We stayed with the West Side Drive while it became the Henry Hudson Parkway, and we kept going north and crossed the Harlem River into the Bronx. I took the 232nd Street exit and wound up on Palisade Avenue. The long narrow green strip of Riverdale Park was on our left, with the Metro North tracks between the park and the Hudson River.

I'd studied the route on the map, but there were enough one-way streets to get me disoriented, and it took a little while to find Devonshire Close. While I drove around looking for it, I told her about my mission Wednesday night, scouting the terrain and probing the Mapes defenses. The doors were out, I said, because the alarm system was one I couldn't sabotage from outside, and all the windows were wired into it, and the coal chute, my old ace in the hole, had been trumped by bricks and cement.

"I give up," she said. "How are you gonna get in?"

I told her I'd show her when we got there, and shortly thereafter we did just that. Before I made the turn into Devonshire Close I got out my cell phone and tried the number again, and got the machine again. This time I waited for the beep and said, "Dr. Mapes? Are you there? Please pick up if you are. It's pretty important."

No one did, and I broke the connection. "In case he was screening his calls," I said.

"That's great," she said, "but now your voice is on his answering machine. How smart is that?"

"If it's still on there when I leave," I said, "then it could be a problem."

"You're going to erase it. That's fine if it's digital, but the old machines that use tape don't really erase anything. When you tell them to, you just program them to record over the old message when somebody leaves a new one. So what if it's a tape machine?"

"I'll steal the tape," I said.

I drove into Devonshire Close and spotted Mapes's house right away. While I couldn't have sworn to it, it looked to have the same lights on as it had two nights ago. There was a parking spot open in front of the house, and another across the street, but I did what I'd already decided to do and made the turn into Mapes's driveway. I drove all the way to the back and parked in front of the garage, leaving the motor running.

Carolyn was saying something, but I ignored her and got out of the car. The garage door was down, and didn't budge when I tried to lift it. There was a little door on the side of the garage. It hadn't been locked Wednesday night and it wasn't locked now, though the kind of lock it was likely to have wouldn't have delayed me long. Unlocked, it delayed me not at all, and I went inside and found first a light switch and then the button to raise the garage door. I killed the light once the door was up, got back in the car, drove into the garage, pulled up alongside (and felt insignificant next to) the Lexus SUV, and cut the engine.

I started to get out of the car. Carolyn hadn't moved. She said, "Bern, are you sure about this? We're in the belly of the beast."

"Not the belly. The house, where I'm going, that's the belly."

"So what's this? The jaw, and we're wedged here like a wad of tobacco, with nothing to look forward to but a lot of chewing and spitting. We're parked in the garage of the house you're gonna break into. What if somebody comes?"

"Nobody's going to come."

"What if somebody passes by and sees the car in here, and knows it's not their car?"

"Nobody can see anything once the garage door's closed."

"You're gonna close the garage door? Then if anything does happen, we're trapped."

"No," I said. "We're not trapped. The car is."

"But that's where you're leaving me, the last I heard."

"You wouldn't have to stay in the car. You could stand over by the side of the garage, where you could keep an eye on things. The only thing you have to be concerned about is if someone pulls into the driveway."

"And then what do I do? Start up the engine and let the carbon monoxide solve all my problems?"

"Then you hit the horn," I said. "Three blasts, loud and long."

"That's the signal, huh?"

"That's the signal. You sound the alarm and then you bail out."

"How?"

"Through the backyard. There's a Cyclone fence about five feet high. You can climb a fence, can't you?"

"Probably, if there's an irate homeowner coming after me. Then what? I just run away?"

"Discretion," I said, "is the better part of burglary. Run until you hit the sidewalk on the next street over, then just walk until you get somewhere."

"Where? I don't know my way around here."

"Just sort of drift until you get to Broadway, and then catch the subway. Nobody's going to be chasing you. And this is all academic, anyway, because they're not coming home until we're long gone."

"Whatever you say, Bern. Only I wish I felt as certain as you sound. Now how are you gonna get in? You were about to tell me."

"I'll show you," I said. She got out of the car and I led her out of the garage, pressing the button to lower the garage door on our way out. We started down the driveway, and when we'd covered almost half the length of the house, I stopped and pointed.

"There!" I said.

"There? That's the side door, Bern, and you just said it was hooked into the alarm system."

"To the right of the door."

"To the right of the door? There's nothing to the right of the door."

"Immediately to the right of it," I said, "at eye level. What do you see?"

"Damned if I know. A white wooden rectangle. If it was closer to the ground I'd say it was a pet door, but the only pet who could jump through it at that height would be a kangaroo, and it's too small for kangaroos. What the hell is it, anyway?"

"A milk chute," I said.

"A milk chute? I still don't know what that is."

"It's a sort of a pass-through," I said. "It's about the thickness of the wall it's in, with a door on either side. The milkman opens the outer door and puts the milk in, and the householder opens the inner door and takes it out."

"People still get milk deliveries?"

"Not that I know of," I said, "but they did when these houses were built, and a milk chute was pretty much standard equipment. I suppose the houses that got aluminum siding jobs had their milk chutes covered up, but you're not going to see much aluminum siding in Riverdale, and certainly not on a stone house. Even if you remodel, the way they did when they closed off the chute to the coal cellar, you wouldn't bother to get rid of the milk chute. It's not hurting anything, and what else are you going to do with the space, and how could you fill it without making a mess of the exterior wall? Didn't you have a milk chute when you were a kid?"

"In a twelfth-floor apartment on Eastern Parkway? The milkman would have had to be a human fly."

"Well, I grew up in a house," I said, "and we had a milk chute, and one day I came home from school and my mother wasn't home and the house was locked. And I got in through the milk chute."

"How old were you, Bern?"

"I don't know. Eleven? Twelve?"

"You were smaller then."

"So?"

"So you've grown, and the milk chute hasn't. Look at you. You'll never fit through that thing."

"Sure I will," I said. "I've grown some since I was twelve, but that wasn't the last time I wiggled in through the milk chute. I was still getting in that way when I was seventeen, and I had my full size by then. And even when I was twelve people never believed I could do it, because it looks as though you won't fit, and then you do."

"What's on the other side of the milk chute?"

"I'll be able to tell you later. But what's usually there is a closet."

"Suppose it's locked?" I gave her a look. "Sorry,

Bern, I forgot who I was talking to. If it's locked you'll unlock it. Suppose, well, suppose you can't get through the thing after all?"

"Then I'll come back out," I said, "and think of something else, and if there's nothing else to think of then we'll go back home and call it a night."

If you can get your head through an opening, the rest of the body can follow.

That's a basic guideline, and it's obviously not universally applicable. If you weigh four hundred pounds, your head is going to slip through apertures that will balk at accepting your hips. (I considered the fat man who'd overpaid so generously for **The Secret Agent**. A camel would fit more easily through the eye of a needle, I thought, than would he through a milk chute.)

It's a good general principle, however, and newborns prove it every day. Raffles seems to know it instinctively; if his whiskers clear an opening he'll follow them through, and if they don't he'll step back and think of another way to go, or decide he didn't really want to go there anyway.

The Mapes milk chute was large enough to accommodate my head, whiskers and all. I put on my gloves and got down to business.

The milk chute had a little catch that you turn prior to pulling the door open. It's not a lock, just a device to keep the thing from swinging open in the wind. The catch didn't want to turn, though, and then the door didn't want to open. Time and paint had made them both stuck in their ways, but a little pressure (and the tip of a knife blade) led them to change their attitude.

The chute's inner door had a catch as well, but it was on the side away from me, to be opened by the person retrieving the milk. I had my tools in hand, and a thin four-inch strip of flexible steel slipped the catch as if it had been designed for that specific purpose. The inner door opened, but when I pushed it I felt resistance before it had swung inward more than a few inches. It was a yielding, spongy sort of resistance; I could force the door farther open, but when I let go it would spring back.

I used my little flashlight, and saw right away what the problem was. The milk chute opened into a closet, as I'd expected, and the resistance was being supplied by an overcoat.

I reached a hand in, shifted things around, and created enough of a space for the door to swing all the way open. I returned my tools and penlight to my pocket, kept the sheer Pliofilm gloves on, and then proceeded to poke my head into the opening and follow it with as much as possible of the rest of me. I drew my shoulders in, making myself as narrow and eel-like as possible, said a quick and urgent prayer to St. Dismas, and commenced wriggling and squirming for all I was worth.

And I have to say it brought it all back. Not just that first magical moment of youth, when I'd thrilled at having discovered a way to get into a house I'd been locked out of. There was nothing illicit or dangerous about that first time, I'd been locked out by sheer accident and had every right and reason to be inside, but the thrill had been there from the beginning, and everything that came after grew out of that initial venture.

In no time at all I was playing with locks and teaching myself how to open them, sending away to the correspondence schools that advertised in **Popular Science** and enrolling in their locksmithing courses, pressing my mom's house key in a bar of soap and filing a duplicate to match the impression.

And if I hadn't been locked out that fateful afternoon, would I have escaped a life of crime? Somehow I doubt it. There are, as far as I know, no felons swiping peaches from the family tree. Both the Grimeses and the Rhodenbarrs boast generations of law-abiding folk, content to play by the rules and trade an honest day's work for an honest day's pay. I, on the other hand, am a born thief, the sort of reprehensible character of whom it is said that he'd rather steal a dollar than earn five. (That's not literally true, I'm nowhere near that bad, but I'd certainly rather steal five dollars than earn one.) And I do possess an innate knack for getting into places designed to keep me out. I studied locks, I practiced opening them, but the lessons came easy to me. It is, I blush to admit, a gift.

I don't often think back to those early days, but then I don't often crawl through milk chutes. So I let all of this go through my mind, and it was a mind that might have been better occupied with the task of getting through the milk chute as quickly as possible. Because, as you can readily appreciate, one is at one's most vulnerable during the transitional interval when one is neither inside nor outside of the house. If someone were to come along while my head was in the coat closet and my legs suspended above the driveway, I'd be hard put to explain what I was doing there and unable to run off and do it somewhere else.

But I couldn't hurry through, because I'd somehow reached a point, half in and half out, where I'd achieved an undesirable state of equilibrium, an unwelcome stasis. Wriggling and squirming weren't getting me anywhere, and I couldn't grab onto something and pull myself through because, damn it to hell, I'd put my arms at my sides in order to fit my shoulders through, and now my arms were pinned there by the sides of the milk chute.

All I had to do, I told myself, was the right sort of wriggling. If I set about squirming in an ergonomically sound manner, so as to build up a little momentum, why in no time at all . . .

Hell.

It wasn't working.

For God's sake, was this how it was going to end? Half in and half out of somebody else's house, unable to move in either direction, with nothing to do until Mapes and his wife came home and called the cops? If this had happened when I first tried this stunt, back in my pre-salad days, my whole career in burglary might have ended before it had begun. If it hadn't happened then, why did it have to happen now?

I might have had further thoughts on the matter, might even have enjoyed the irony of it all, but right about then a pair of hands came along and grabbed me by the ankles.

TWENTY-TWO

I hadn't heard a car, hadn't heard so much as a foot-fall. My head was in the closet, literally if not figuratively, with coats and other outerwear all around it, so that would tend to muffle the sound. And it's not as though I was listening hard all the while. I was too busy with my wriggling and squirming, not to mention my remembrance of milk chutes past, to have been keeping an ear open. Had Carolyn honked the horn? Three times, I'd told her, loud and long. But would I have heard it if she had? The car was in a closed garage, and I was in a coat closet. Maybe she'd honked and I hadn't noticed.

The hands on my ankles might as well have been bands of steel. My heart sank, my mind froze, and all I could do was hope Carolyn got out in time, and that she'd think to call Wally Hemphill for me.

Hours passed, or maybe they were only seconds. And a voice said, "It's me, Bern."

And that's all she said. There were any number of other things she could have said, and I'd have had to listen to them, but she didn't, and that is just one

more reason why Carolyn and I will be friends forever. She didn't say another word, but what she did
do was tighten her grip on my ankles and give a little push, and that was all it took. I landed facedown
in a dark closet, and I couldn't have been happier
about it.

Forty minutes later I unlocked the side door, the
one adjacent to the milk chute, and let myself out of
the house. I'd found the control panel for the alarm
system in the entry hall next to the front door—
that's where they usually put it, so the homeowner
can punch in his code when he walks in the door. I'd
studied the Kilgore system, and knew it had zones;
you could set it to bypass certain zones, so that you
could open a second-floor window for ventilation
without setting off a ton of bells and whistles. I
worked out what zone the side door was in,
bypassed it, and let myself out of the house.

Like most homemakers, Mrs. Mapes kept extra
grocery bags in a kitchen cupboard. I'd helped
myself to four, because what I was taking was heavy
enough to warrant double-bagging. I tucked each of
two shopping bags into each of two others, filled
them up with what I'd found in the safe in the master bedroom, added one other item I could hardly
leave behind, and carried everything out of the
house and up the length of the driveway to the
garage, where Carolyn let out a breath she must

have been holding for the greater portion of the time I'd been inside.

"I was beginning to worry," she said. "You were in there for almost an hour."

"It was forty minutes," I said.

"That's almost an hour. Here, let me get the door for you. You want me to push the button for the garage door?"

"After I get these in the car." There was a release button for the trunk lid, especially convenient if you don't have a key. I pressed it, put the bags in the trunk, and got behind the wheel. Carolyn pressed the button, and by the time the garage door was up she was in her seat next to me. I started the car and backed all the way out of the garage, leaving the motor running while I pressed the button a final time to lower the garage door. I was still wearing my gloves, and I used my gloved hands to wipe off surfaces she might have touched.

She noticed this, and told me she was pretty sure she hadn't touched anything. "Well, just in case," I said, and went back to the side door, using my picks to relock it. Carolyn had closed the milk chute door earlier, after I'd cleared it, and I opened it long enough to wipe it free of prints, then closed it and fastened the latch to leave it as I'd found it. I'd already refastened the catch on the inner door.

I got in the car again, backed the rest of the way out of the driveway. There was no traffic on Devonshire Close, which was good and bad—there were fewer passers-by to notice us, but we were correspondingly more noticeable to anybody who did. Soon, though, we were on another street— Ploughman's Bush, it must have been—and before long we were on Broadway, heading south toward Manhattan.

We could have gone home the same way we'd come—the Henry Hudson, the West Side Drive— but something kept me on Broadway, moving at a sedate pace, stopping for red lights, resuming our journey when they turned green. It's a venerable old road, Broadway, running from the foot of Manhattan clear up to Albany. I'd read an article written by a fellow who walked the length of it— not from Albany, but from the Westchester County line. He'd told about what he'd seen, and the history of it all, and I gather you could see quite a bit on a walk like that. You can probably see a fair amount driving, as far as that goes, but I wasn't paying attention.

"Bern?"

"What?"

"Is something wrong?"

"No. Why?"

"You're not talking."

"Oh," I said. "You're right, I guess I'm not."

"So I thought maybe something was wrong."

"No," I said. "Everything's fine."

"Oh."

"There was a whole lot of money," I said. "I guess he got paid in cash fairly often, and the trouble with cash is you have to launder it. Either that or declare it, and then you have to pay taxes on it, and then what's the point? But until you figure out how to launder it, without paying as much in laundry bills as you'd have had to pay in taxes, well, you can just stow it somewhere."

"And that's what he did?"

"He stowed it in his safe, and that's the wrong word for it, because it wasn't. I thought I might have to pull it out and take it home where I could work on it in private, and that would have been fine, but once I took the seascape down from the wall and went to work on it, it was about as hard to open as the milk chute."

"And you didn't have to crawl through it, either."

"Aside from the cash," I said, "he had the usual things you keep in a safe. Stock certificates, the deed to the house, a couple of insurance policies, other important papers. And some of her jewelry. She had a little rosewood chest on top of her dresser, and it was full of jewelry, but she kept some of her better pieces in the safe."

"I'll bet they're not there anymore."

"You'd lose. I left the papers, and I left all the jewelry."

"That's not like you, Bern."

"All things considered," I said, "I'd just as soon the police never hear about what we just did. Not that they're likely to figure out who did it, let alone prove it, but they can't begin to investigate it if they don't even know it happened. If I took the jewelry,

Mapes would have a reason to report it. It's probably insured, and they can't make a claim unless they file a report. But if all I take is cash, and it's cash he never declared, what sense does it make for him to bring the police into it? He's not insured for the loss, he can't logically expect them to recover any of it, and all of a sudden he's got people from the IRS wondering where the cash came from."

"So you think he'll just bite the bullet and keep smiling?"

"He'll probably piss and moan," I said, "but he'll do it in private. He probably thought of the cash as easy come, and now he can think of it as easy go."

"That's great," she said.

"Yeah."

"It really is. The shitheel's out a bundle, and he can't do a thing about it. How much is it going to come to, do you have any idea?"

I shook my head. It was a mix of bills, I told her, from hundreds all the way down to singles, some in rubber-banded stacks, some crammed into envelopes, some loose. I figured it was more than a hundred thousand and less than a million, but I was just guessing.

"Enough so that you can give Marty his finder's fee and still have a lot for yourself."

"Don't forget your cut," I said.

"It shouldn't be much. All I did was keep you company."

"All you did," I said, "was save my life. If it

wasn't for you I'd still be half in and half out of the closet."

"I had a girlfriend like that once, Bern. It's no fun. Okay, I was helpful, but I didn't take any risks."

"If you'd been caught, what would you tell them? That you were only keeping me company?"

"No, but—"

"Marty gets fifteen percent off the top. You get a third of what's left after his fifteen percent comes off."

She was silent while she did the math. "I don't have pencil and paper," she said, "so maybe I got this wrong, but the way I figure it I'm getting something like thirty thousand dollars."

"It'll probably come to more than that."

"Gosh. You know how many dogs I have to wash to make that kind of money?"

"Quite a few."

"You said it. Bern? What'll I do with all that cash?"

"Whatever you want. It's your money."

"I mean do I have to, you know, launder it?"

I shook my head. "It's not that much. I know, it's a fortune, but you're not looking to buy stocks with it. You just want to be able to live a little better, without worrying whether you can afford an extra blue blazer, or tickets for **The Producers**. So you'll stick it in a safe-deposit box and draw out what you need when you need it. Believe me, if you're anything like me, it'll be gone before you know it."

"That's a comfort."

We stayed on Broadway all the way to my neighborhood, where we picked up Columbus Avenue and cruised past Lincoln Center. The plaza was crowded with people on their way out, and for a moment I thought **Don Giovanni** was over, but it was too early for that. There was a concert in Avery Fisher Hall tonight, too, and it had just let out, and if I'd stolen a cab instead of the Sable I could have had my pick of fares. I passed them all by and headed for the Village.

"Bern? If I'm in for a minimum of thirty thousand, you're going to get upwards of sixty. Right?"

"Right. I figured two-to-one was fair, but if you think—"

"No no no," she said. "It's more than fair. But that's not where I was going. The thing is, if you're getting all that money, and you don't have to deal with a fence, you don't have to worry about the cops—"

"So?"

"So how come you're not happy?"

"I'm happy."

"Yeah? You don't seem happy to me. You seem . . ."

"What?"

"Preoccupied, Bern."

"Preoccupied," I said. "Well, I guess maybe I am."

"Do you want to talk about it?"

"Eventually," I said. "But here's what I'm going to do right now. First I'll drop you and the money at your place. I've been getting too many visitors lately and I don't want to have piles of cash around the apartment, not until the traffic thins out and I have a new cupboard built to hide stuff in. I'll drop everything, and then I'll take the car back, and do something about the phone. And then I'll come down to Arbor Court again. And there'll be coffee made, and maybe something from the deli, and I'll sit down with a cup of coffee and put my feet up. And then we can talk about what's preoccupying me."

⊙ TWENTY-THREE

When I got back to Arbor Court, there was a whole buffet arranged on the plywood slab that topped the tub. Beef with orange flavor from Hunan Pan, pumpkin kibbee from the little Syrian joint, cold cuts from the Korean deli. "It occurred to me that neither of us had dinner tonight," Carolyn said, "and that I was hungry enough to gnaw wood, and you probably were, too. But I didn't know what you wanted, so I just walked along Hudson Street and bought some of everything."

We filled plates and emptied them, while her two cats, Archie and Ubi, gazed at us as plaintively as the kids in those Foster Parents Plan ads. It didn't work. Archie's a Burmese and Ubi's a Russian Blue, and neither one looks as though he's missed a meal since his first victory over a ball of yarn.

We had, however, and ate as if determined to make up for it. There was food left when we'd finished—she'd bought a ton, as one does when one shops while hungry—and some of the leftovers went in the fridge, and the rest went to the cats.

"Look at those drama queens," she said. "Now that the food's in their bowls, they stroll over to it as if it's the last thing on their minds. 'Oh, what have we here? Food, is it? Well, I'm not terribly hungry, but I'll just force myself so her feelings aren't hurt.'"

"That's what I did," I said. "I forced myself. Now I think I'll force myself to have a cup of coffee."

"Well, I made some, because you said to. But won't it keep you awake?"

"I hope so," I said.

"Miles to go before you sleep?"

"Miles and miles. I don't suppose you had time to count the money, did you?"

"Count it? I didn't even want to look at it. I left the two bags in the closet, right where you put them, and before I went shopping I stuck a chair in front of the closet door. Like that would make a difference."

"It would have been a bad time for a burglary. Some junkie kicks the door in, hoping to grab a portable radio he can sell on the street for ten bucks, and hello, what have we got here?"

"That's what was going through my mind."

"Well, the chair would have stopped him," I said. "You were clever to think of it."

I got the bags from the closet and drank two cups of strong coffee while we counted. The dope traffickers don't bother counting, they just dump the cash on a scale and weigh it, knowing that you get so many bills to a pound. That works when they're all the same denomination—for those guys, it's hundreds—but the Mapes haul ran the gamut from singles all the way up, and the only scale in the place was the one in the bathroom, and neither of us knew how many bills made a pound, anyway. So we sorted them by denomination and counted. It took a long time, but counting money is not an unpleasant task, not if you get to keep what you count.

We'd each pick up a stack and count it, then write the total on a sheet of paper, then reach for another stack. When all the stacks were counted I added up the numbers on the sheet of paper and wrote the total at the bottom. I showed it to Carolyn and her eyes got very big.

"Two hundred thirty-seven thousand," she said. "Even?"

"I rounded it off."

"That's almost a quarter of a million."

"Pretty near."

"My God, it's a fortune."

"Keep it in proportion. It's the price of a large studio apartment in a good building."

"That's one way of looking at it," she allowed. "But since I'm not shopping for a place to live, there's another way I like better. It's enough to pay the rent on this place for a thousand months. How many years is that?"

"More than eighty. Of course even with rent

control, you'd have some increases over the years. Figure sixty-five years."

"That's plenty, Bern. Sixty-five years from now I'll probably want to move over to the Village Nursing Home, anyway. I just hope they'll let me bring the cats. Anyway, not all of this is mine. How much have I got coming, can you figure it out for me?"

I could, with pencil and paper, subtracting Marty's share and dividing the remainder by three. Her end, I was able to tell her, came to $67,150.

"I'm rich, Bern."

"Well, you're richer than you were a few hours ago."

"I'm richer than I ever was. Bern, I'm scared to have the money in the house."

"It should be safe here. Your locks are good ones. You're on the ground floor, but you've got bars on your window. Most important, no one's got any reason to think you've got anything worth taking."

"Thanks a lot."

"You know what I meant. There's a lot of money here, but you and I are the only ones who know about it, and I don't plan to tell anyone."

"Neither do I. And I know it's safer than your place. But the closet, Bern? Isn't that the first place they'd look?"

She had a point. I asked her if she needed a bath. "Not desperately," she said. "Or do I?" She raised an arm, sniffed herself. "Nothing that would make a billy goat leave the room," she said. "I'll have a bath before I go to bed. Why?"

"Have it now."

"Huh? Oh, I get it."

"I'll turn the other way," I said, "and bury my nose in a book. I wish I had the one I was reading. The new John Sandford."

"I bought it, Bern. I read it, I finished it a week ago. I was gonna ask if you wanted to borrow it."

"I would have, if I'd known. A copy came into the store, and I started it the other day. The one where the guy's killing vegetarians."

"That's the one. I wanted to kill one myself once. I had this sweet young thing over for dinner, and I splurged and bought a gorgeous beef Wellington at Ottomanelli's, and I bring it to the table just in time for her to tell me she doesn't eat red meat. 'Take it home with you,' I wanted to tell her, 'and leave it out on the counter for a week, and it won't be red anymore. It'll be nice and green and you can pretend it's a vegetable.' Did you find it yet? I think it's on the top shelf."

"I've got it."

"I loved it. I think the best scene's where he gets the diet doctor, the one who has all his patients eating nothing but bean sprouts and celery."

I told her I hadn't gotten that far yet, and she said she'd stop before she spoiled it for me. I got caught up in the book and read until she told me I could turn around now, that she was all bathed and dressed.

"And I took a towel," she said, "and dried the tub. How's the book? Enjoying it?"

"Yeah, it's terrific."

"I think it may be his best. I even like the title. **Lettuce Prey**. The tub's all ready, Bern."

I put the two bags of money in the tub, put the cover on, then took it off again. "It's a shame your cats know how to use the toilet," I mused.

"It is? I always thought it was a blessing. Oh! If we covered up the money with Kitty Litter, anybody who looked would just figure it was one big catbox."

"That's what I was thinking."

"They'd also figure my cats were cleaner than their owner, because what would I use for bathing? But the hell with the good opinion of burglars. Present company excepted, of course." She winked. "The deli's still open. You think one bag's enough? Or should we get two?"

Two bags did the job. Anybody who took the lid off the bathtub—and why anybody would do that was beyond me—would put it back on in a hurry. We could have upped the verisimilitude quotient by encouraging the cats to use the thing, but Carolyn drew the line at that. It had taken her long enough to teach them to use the toilet, and if they switched to the tub she'd have to put them to sleep and start over with two new kittens.

"I think we're set," she said. "Oh, I forgot to ask.

His answering machine, that you left a message on. Did you get the tape?"

"It was digital, so all I had to do was erase it. And I got rid of the cell phone. Nowadays it's the easiest thing in the world for them to find out the source of an incoming call. Even if you don't have Caller ID, or if it just registers as **Unknown Caller,** the cops can pull the LUDS and know exactly who called and when."

"I know, they do it on **Law & Order** all the time."

"But with a prepaid cell phone," I said, "all they can find out is where the phone was sold, but not who bought it. So I dumped the phone, and that's the end of that."

"You just threw it away?"

"I could have, but it seemed wasteful. All of those prepaid minutes. I left it on the subway on my way down here. Somebody'll find it and call his mother in Santo Domingo for free."

"That was thoughtful, Bern."

"I was almost thoughtful enough to top up the gas tank on the Mercury," I said, "but not quite. I managed to find a parking place just a few doors down from where it was when I borrowed it. And I put back the ignition cylinder that I'd pulled. The owner won't know the difference."

"Except that it's not where he clearly remembers parking it. So he'll just think it's early Alzheimer's. Bern, what happened?"

"Huh?"

"You were preoccupied," she said, "and now you're not. What happened?"

"I'm still preoccupied," I said. "I just put it on the shelf."

"You did?"

"Literally," I said, and went to the closet. I'd taken something besides the money from the Mapes house, had tucked it into one of the bags before I left the house, and had removed it from the bag when I put it and its fellow in the closet. I'd put it on a high shelf, out of harm's and Carolyn's way, and now I took it down and handed it to her.

"It's a book," she announced. "Hardbound, no dust jacket." She squinted at the spine. "**The Secret Agent,** by Joseph Conrad. Isn't that the title of the book you sold to the fat man?"

"For thirteen hundred dollars."

"And you found a replacement copy in Mapes's library? That's handy, Bern. Now you can make that customer happy. What was his name again?"

"Colby Riddle."

"Right, and how'd I forget it? Ought to be an easy name to remember. Well, you said you had a feeling there was a coincidence waiting to show up, and I'd say this qualifies, wouldn't you? Or did he have such a huge library the book just about had to be there?"

"He had a very small library."

"Yeah? Then it was a real coincidence."

"More than you know," I said.

"Bern, you're kidding."

"Look on the flyleaf. It's priced at twelve dollars, and you can probably recognize the numerals as mine. And it wasn't in the bookcase, either. It was downstairs, on the desk in his den."

"It's the same book."

"Right."

"Not just the same title, but the same book."

"Right."

"Bern, that's more than a coincidence. That's . . . Bern, how the hell did it get there?"

"I don't know," I said, "but you wanted to know why I was preoccupied. That's why."

# TWENTY-FOUR

The fat man took the book."

"Right."

"But he didn't have it long. Whoever shot him took it and drove off with it."

"Right."

"The fat man thought it was something else, and so did whoever killed him and took it away from him."

"Right."

"And then it wound up in Mapes's den. Was it Mapes in the car? Did Mapes kill him?"

"He's a shitheel," I said, "but Marty never called him a thug. The man's a plastic surgeon. He uses a scalpel, not an AK-47."

"Is that what the fat man was shot with?"

"It was some kind of automatic weapon. You hold the trigger and the bullets keep coming out. All I know about guns is that I like to stay away from them."

"Me too. Either Mapes was in the car, or the guy in the car took the book to Mapes."

"That sounds logical."

"But the book's connected to the Rogovins, except that's not their real name. I forget their real names."

"Lyle and Schnittke."

"What have they got to do with Mapes?"

"I don't know."

"Well, I don't know anything. Who were the people in the car? I mean, were they the same ones who killed the Rogovins? Lyle and Schnittke, I mean. Are they the ones who killed Lyle and Schnittke?"

"That's what I thought. Now I'm not so sure. My apartment was tossed by the people who killed Lyle and . . . you know what? I'm going to call them the Lyles. I don't know if they were married or living together or just good friends, but I'm sick of saying Schnittke."

"It doesn't roll trippingly off the tongue, does it?"

"No, it doesn't. Anyway, the same people did those two things, because they gave both doormen the same treatment."

"Sort of a signature. They're the ones we've been calling the perps."

"Right, the perps. I don't know who's who, Carolyn. It's all too deep for me. All I know is the book was in Mapes's den, and it shouldn't have been there."

"And you took it."

"I know, and don't ask me why. It may not have been the brightest thing I ever did. I broke into his house and emptied his safe, and I was nice and anonymous about it, and then I took the book, and that narrows the suspect list from all burglars to a burglar with a particular interest in a particular book by Joseph Conrad. I might as well have taken along an etching tool and signed the safe."

"Bern, he just lost a quarter of a million dollars."

"Not quite."

"Close enough. He just lost the price of a studio apartment—"

"Well, a pretty nice studio apartment, in a good neighborhood."

"—and you think he's even going to notice the book is missing, or give a rat's ass about it if he does? Besides, the book's not the McGuffin. It's a fake McGuffin, and people only want it until they find out it's not what they want."

"Isn't that true of everything?"

"Bern—"

I got to my feet, holding my hands palm-outward to ward off more questions. "It's too deep for me," I said. "All of it."

"Where are you going, Bern?"

"A bar."

"You're gonna get drunk? You can stay right here, Bern. I've got plenty of booze in the house."

"But no softballs."

"Huh?" She waved the thought away, like a pesky fly. "You just drank a quart of coffee, and now you're going out drinking? You'll get falling-down drunk, and you'll lie there with the shakes from the coffee. I don't think it's a great idea, Bern."

"I'm not going to get drunk," I told her. "I'm barely going to drink. I'm going to a bar in Murray Hill. I want to see just how far coincidence goes these days."

I took a cab to Parsifal's. That's the only sensible way to get there from the West Village, especially at that hour, and when I thought about the money in Carolyn's bathtub, I figured I could afford it.

It was late, but when I'd been there earlier, guzzling Pellegrino, it had felt like the kind of joint that keeps selling booze as long as the law allows. The law in New York lets you keep going until four every night but Saturday, when the bars have to close an hour early, at three in the morning. (When you're dealing with drinking laws in New York, counterintuitive is definitely the way to go.)

The crowd at Parsifal's was a little lighter than it had been earlier, but these people made up for it in volume, as their alcohol intake raised their personal decibel levels. Collectively, they added up to something well below your average wide-open motorcycle engine, but a long ways up from the well-bred purr of a Rolls-Royce. I could still hear myself think, though why I would want to was another question.

The same blonde bartender was on duty, and I don't know how she remembered me, but she proved she did by asking me if I wanted a Pellegrino. I shook my head and said I'd have scotch.

"Good for you," she said. "Any particular brand? The bar pour is Teacher's."

"You don't have Glen Drumnadrochit, do you?"

She wrinkled her nose and said she'd never even heard of it, and I wasn't hugely surprised. I'd only come across it once, at an eccentric bed-and-breakfast in the Berkshires,* and when I came home I had three bottles of it in my suitcase. I made them last as long as I could, but they were gone now, and I wondered if I'd ever taste anything that good again.

The thought alone spoiled me for Teacher's, and I asked for a single malt, and they had a decent selection of them. I settled on Laphroaig, perhaps out of pride in my ability to pronounce it, and ordered a double. It's got a distinctive taste, one that you have to acquire. I'd acquired it some years ago, but it had gone the way of the Drumnadrochit, so I took a sip and set about acquiring it all over again. Slow sipping, that's the way to do it. You take little sparrow-sized sips, and you keep telling yourself you like the taste, and by the time you get to the bottom of the glass, it's true.

I took a first sip, and thought **Yes, that's Laphroaig, all right. I'd forgotten what it tastes like, but that's it, and I'd know it anywhere.** Later

*The Burglar in the Library

I took a second sip, and was able to decide how I felt about the taste. I decided that I didn't like it. Somewhere around the fifth sip, it had achieved the virtue of familiarity. I was accustomed to it, and the question of whether I actually liked it no longer seemed pertinent. It was like, say, a cousin. **The man's your cousin, for God's sake! What do you mean, you don't like him? You don't have to like or dislike him. He's your cousin!**

I was almost ready for a sixth sip of Cousin Laphroaig when a woman marched up to the bar and settled herself on a seat two stools from mine. It was getting on for two in the morning, but she looked as though she'd just come from the office. She was wearing a pants suit of charcoal gray flannel, and her dark hair was done up in a knot on the top of her head, and you already know who she was, but it took me a minute, because the last time I saw her—the only time I saw her—she had her hair down and her clothes off and her mouth open.

The big blonde knew her, and knew her drink. "Hi," she said. "G and T?"

"Heavy on the G," the brunette said. "Just a splash of T."

"You got it. Little late for you, isn't it?"

I was watching out of the corner of my eye, so I didn't actually see the brunette roll hers, but I think she probably did. "I didn't think I was going to get here at all," she said, "and I was starting to wonder if you did takeout."

"I don't think the State Liquor Authority would go for that."

"I wonder if the time is right for a test case?" By now the gin and tonic was mixed and on the bar before her, and she took it up and put away more in one swallow than I'd managed in my five delicate sips. "Ahhhh," she said, with real appreciation. "I needed that. Sigrid, back in the days before you decided on a career behind the stick—"

"Hold it right there, huh? Being a bartender's not a career, and I didn't decide on it."

"You didn't?"

"Of course not. Nobody does, not in New York. You decide on a career in the arts, and you wait tables to make ends meet, and it begins to dawn on you that bartenders make more money and don't have to work as hard, plus they never get yelled at for dropping a whole tray of pasta dishes on a table full of people from Ridgeway, New Jersey—"

"Did that happen to you?"

"No, but it could have. So you go take the course at the American Bartenders School, which isn't exactly rocket science, and you get a job when you graduate, and you mix martinis and screwdrivers, which isn't exactly brain surgery, and you quit when the boss puts his hand up your skirt—"

"Did that happen?"

"No, but it could have. So you get another job, and you finally find a place where they treat you right, and one day you notice you haven't been on an audition or a go-see in months, and for a while you feel guilty about it, and then you feel guilty that you don't, and then that's it, you're a lifer, you'll be mixing Salty Dogs and Harvey Wallbangers until the cows come home. But that doesn't make it a career."

"Wow."

"I'm sorry," Sigrid said. "Way too much information, huh?"

"No, actually it was pretty interesting." She drank some more of her gin and tonic, and I seized the moment to take a sip of my Laphroaig. It was definitely improving.

"I don't know what got me started," Sigrid said. "Except it's been a long night, and it didn't help that there was a guy hitting on me about an hour ago."

"Oh, come on. That must happen to you all the time."

"It does, but most of them take no for an answer, and the rest generally take **fuck you** for an answer. This guy thought he was God's gift, and he couldn't believe I didn't see it. Come to think of it, he's been in here before, and—"

"And what?"

"And nothing." She grinned. "My train of thought just pulled out of the station, and I wasn't on it. You know, you were starting to ask me something, before I went into my rant."

"I was? Oh, right. I just wondered if you ever gave any thought to going into the law, and I guess you already answered that. You set out to be an actress."

"Actress and model, actually."

"Oh? I can't believe you didn't get modeling jobs."

"The camera likes you to be really thin, and so do the misogynists behind the cameras. I got work anyway, but nobody ever wanted to use me more than once. I had a bad attitude."

"Oh."

"I still do, but it's okay for a bartender, especially if you've got the tits to go with it. But no, I never thought about becoming a lawyer. Why?"

"Because tonight I was beginning to wish I hadn't, either. Though this"—she raised her now-empty glass—"is definitely helping."

"Another? You got it. And how about you? You all right with the Laphroaig?"

I said I was fine, and she went off to assemble another gin and tonic.

"What did she just call your drink?"

"Laphroaig," I said.

"That's what it sounded like. Is it some kind of cordial?"

"It's scotch. It's a single malt from the Isle of Islay."

"Is that near the Firth of Forth?"

"It would have to be, don't you think?"

"I guess. Is it good?"

"It's getting there. I figure another three sips and it'll be excellent."

She nodded judiciously. "It's an acquired taste, and you haven't quite acquired it yet."

"No."

"But you're getting there."

"It improves with each sip."

"Thus the small sips," she said. "If you were doing shots, you'd be blotto before you got anywhere close to liking it."

"That's exactly right. What was so horrible about your evening?"

"Just that I never thought I was going to get out of the damn office. I'm a lawyer. You probably figured that out."

"I took two and two," I said, "and I put 'em together."

"I'm with this firm about ten blocks from here. Very convenient, walk to work, and most of the time the work's fine, but every now and then you get one of those deals that has to close, if it goes past deadline everything's screwed up and you have to start over, and sometimes it's even worse than that, so we had one that had to close by midnight, and of course everything went wrong."

"Of course."

She reached and picked up the gin and tonic that had magically appeared in front of her. Sigrid, having noticed that the two of us had struck up a conversation, had set it down and moved off without a word. I don't know if they teach that in American Bartenders School, but they should.

"It was a transaction involving a hotel in

Shreveport, Louisiana, and it could have been worse. We could have had to go to Shreveport for the closing. But since the buyer and seller both live within a few blocks of each other on the Upper East Side, we decided, hey, whatthehell, we'll do it right here."

"And whom were you representing? The buyer or the seller?"

"The lender. Like, who cares who gets the better of the deal, because our client's just holding paper. Anyway, wheels are coming off left and right, and it has to close but it looks like it won't, and on top of everything the paralegal I'm working with is a moron, because the one I like, the one who always gets everything right, has to leave the goddam office at six oh fucking clock to go on a date." She held her glass aloft. "Pardon my Latvian, but I get carried away just thinking about it."

"Latvian?"

"I got in the habit of not saying French. You know, like Freedom Fries?"

"Oh, right."

"Which is getting old now, but I like the way it sounds. 'Pardon my Latvian.' You take really small sips, don't you? How was it that time?"

"Almost delicious. I'd offer you a taste, but you'd hate it."

"Never mind then." She looked at me, her brown eyes intent. "I'm Barbara," she announced.

"Bernie."

She thought about it. "Barbara Creeley."

"Bernie Rhodenbarr."

"I don't know that name."

"You're not alone. Millions of people don't. Why, in China alone—"

"And you don't look familiar, either. I could swear I've never laid eyes on you before."

"You and all those folks in Shanghai."

"Unless I saw you in my peripheral vision or something. Do you come here often?"

"No. What's your sign?"

"Yeah, I can't believe I asked a question like that. 'Do you come here often?' And anyway that's not how it feels."

"How what feels?"

"The feeling," she said. "I have this feeling that I really know you on some almost mystic level. More than that, I have the feeling that you really know me." She frowned. "This is ridiculous. I didn't think I was feeling the drinks, but evidently I am. I'm babbling away like an idiot."

"More like a brook."

"What a sweet thing to say! Bernie?"

"Bernie."

"If you drink up I'll buy you another La-whatchamacallit."

"Laphroaig," I said. "But one's plenty. Why don't I buy you another of those instead?"

"Thanks, but no. I'm not really much of a drinker, although you wouldn't know it by the way I made the first one disappear."

"You needed it."

"I guess. I'm in here more nights than I'm not, but it's rare for me to have more than two drinks. Although the other night . . ."

"What?"

"Well, it was weird. I had my usual two drinks, nothing fancy, plain old gin and tonic, and I think I must have had a blackout."

"Oh?"

"I can't even remember leaving the bar. I woke up with the worst hangover I ever had in my life. I mean, I don't have hangovers. I don't have blackouts, either. I think the only time I had one before was in my freshman year in college, when we played this version of Truth or Dare where you kept having to take a drink. God only knows what I drank that time, but it was a whole lot more than I had the other night."

"Ah, youth."

"I was young, all right. And I didn't have a hangover, I woke up feeling fine, but I didn't remember the last hour or so of the evening. But everybody told me I was perfectly fine, I didn't do anything weird or outrageous."

"No harm done, then."

"But the night before last," she said, and frowned. "You weren't here that night, were you? Wednesday, it would have been."

"The only other time I've been here," I said, "was earlier this evening. I stopped in after work and had one drink."

"Laphroaig?"

"Pellegrino water. You can't really develop a taste for it, but you don't need one."

"You just drink it. And you liked it here and came back."

"Uh-huh."

"After work, you said. What kind of work?"

"I have a bookstore."

"Really? Are you Mr. Barnes or Mr. Noble?"

"Well, nobody ever called me Mr. Noble. Actually I'd have to say I'm more like Mr. Strand. It's a secondhand bookstore. But a whole lot smaller than the Strand."

"It sounds like fun. Half the lawyers I know would love to quit and open a used bookstore. The other half can't read. Where is it? Right here in the neighborhood?"

"Eleventh Street between Broadway and University."

"And you dropped in here after work?"

She was wasted on real estate deals, I decided. She should have been taking depositions and cross-examining witnesses. I'd been in the neighborhood delivering a book to a good customer, I told her, and Parsifal's had caught my eye.

"And you popped in for a Pellegrino."

"For a Perrier, actually, but Pellegrino's what they had."

"And you're adaptable." She put her hand on mine. It was just conversational, but I've noticed something. When a woman starts touching you, it is a Good Sign.

"This is really strange," she said. "See, I didn't go home alone Wednesday night."

"You're just saying that to shock me."

"Silly," she said, and touched my hand again. "There's no reason for you to be shocked, but I am, a little. Not at the idea of going home with somebody. I mean, if two grownups get a sort of mutual urge, what's wrong with that?"

"Nothing that I can think of."

"But I don't **remember** it, Bernie! I don't know who the guy was or what happened, and **that** shocks me. In fact it scares me a little. Who the hell did I bring home? It could have been Mr. Goodbar." She'd been looking down, and now she raised her eyes to mine. "It wasn't you, was it?"

"I wish."

"That's the second really sweet thing you've said in, what, ten minutes? Bernie, I know it wasn't you, there's no way it could have been you, you've never even been here before. But why do I have the feeling we've been—"

"Lovers?"

"Well, intimate, emotionally if not physically. I had that feeling the minute I walked in here."

"Past lives," I said. "Karmic ties."

"You think?"

"What else could explain it?"

"Do you feel the same way, Bernie?"

Somehow I'd taken her hand, and I liked the way it felt in mine. There was something going on, and it had been so long that I didn't recognize it at first.

"This apartment you took someone home to," I said. "Is it nearby?"

"Right around the corner."

"I wonder," I said, "if I'll have the feeling I've been there before."

"Do you think it's possible, Bernie?"

"I think we should find out."

"I think you're right," she said. "I think we owe it to ourselves."

⦿ TWENTY-FIVE

If it's all the same to you, or even if it's not, I'll omit details for the next half-hour or so. Suffice it to say that there are certain things which, unlike a taste for Laphroaig, don't wear off and needn't be reacquired. Things which, once learned, are never forgotten. Like falling off a bicycle, or drowning.

"One thing's certain," she said. "It wasn't you."

"What wasn't me?"

"Wednesday night. I mean, I knew it wasn't, but now I really know."

"How's that?"

"If it had been you," she said, "I'd have remembered."

"If it had been me," I said, "I wouldn't have waited until tonight to refresh your memory."

"It was the damnedest thing, Bernie. I woke up with a splitting headache, and of course I'd forgotten to set the alarm, so I had to rush to get to the office. I swallowed some aspirin and took a quick shower and was out the door without my usual cup of coffee. I hopped in a cab, hit the Starbucks across the street from my office, and was at my desk at nine o'clock."

"I'm impressed."

"And I sat there wondering what had happened. I knew I'd been talking with somebody at the bar, but I couldn't picture him or remember anything about him. And the next thing I remembered was waking up with a headache."

"So maybe you didn't bring him home after all."

She shook her head. "I thought of that myself, but when I got home last night I could tell that someone had been here the night before. Whoever he was, he'd evidently made himself at home. It's sort of creepy. I mean, he'd been in my things, and he'd moved stuff around."

"Creepy's the word for it."

"My jewelry was arranged differently from the way I'd left it. But he must have just poked around, because he didn't take anything. But you know what he did take?"

"What?"

"Well, you're going to think I'm crazy, but he took my electric shaver."

"I don't think you're crazy. I think he's crazy. Why would he—"

"I know, it's strange, isn't it? But I looked everywhere and I can't find it, and it's always in the same spot, on the shelf in the bathroom. A little Lady Remington, shaped to fit a dainty feminine hand. I mean, what kind of man would want something like that?"

I took her dainty feminine hand in mine. "Not the kind who'd want to come home with you in the first place."

"Exactly. The only thing I could think of is he took it home for his girlfriend."

"Talk about creepy."

"Well, if he wanted a souvenir, wouldn't he take something more intimate, like panties or a bra?"

"That's a point."

"He went through my purse, but he didn't take any money. I actually had more money than I thought I did. So he wasn't your basic crook. Have you ever been robbed?"

A couple of times, but rather than recount either of them I made one up. "A few years ago," I said. "A burglar came in off the fire escape. He dragged my TV over to the window, but I guess he decided it was too heavy to carry and left it there. He took a combination radio and CD player that I'd just bought, along with the CD that was in it at the time, and which I had a hard time replacing." It's funny how a lie can build up a momentum all its own. I reined it in, and, if you'll allow a change of metaphors, turned the wheel hard right. "He got a few dollars, too, whatever I had around the house. But the thing that bothered me, because there was no way I could replace it, is he took my high school ring."

"That's really funny."

"It is? It didn't seem funny at the time."

"No, funny peculiar, not funny ha-ha. Because I can't find **my** class ring."

"You're kidding. You don't think it was the same guy, do you?"

We both laughed, and she said she wasn't sure he'd taken it, that it might have disappeared a while ago. "Because he left a really good pair of earrings, and a watch, and a bracelet I never wear, but it's gold, and there are all these gold coins on it. I mean, anyone who looked at it would know it was worth some money. And class rings, well, the gold is no better than ten karat, and the stone is glass."

"Sounds like the one I lost. If it brought ten bucks in a hock shop, the pawnbroker was generous. What color was it? Maybe he liked the way it went with your pink electric shaver." I rolled onto my side, put a hand on her. "Barbara, those GTs have worn off by now, right? I mean, you'll remember this in the morning?"

"How could I forget?"

"I was just thinking that maybe we should make sure."

"Oh," she said, and reached for me. "Oh, my. What a lovely idea."

Afterward I got into my clothes while she lay in bed with her eyes closed. She'd taken her hair down when we'd walked in the door, just before she turned to come into my arms, and it was spread out on the pillow now the way it had been when I got my first look at her. She'd been naked then, too, but this time I didn't feel the need to cover her with the sheet. Somehow it no longer felt invasive to enjoy the view.

I was heading for the door when she said, "Bernie? How'd you know it was pink?"

I didn't know what she was talking about. The only pink thing I could think of at the moment . . . well, never mind.

"My shaver," she said. "The one he took. How'd you know it was pink?"

Oh, hell. "You said it was pink," I said.

"I did?"

"You must have."

"But I always thought of it as fuchsia. That's what the manufacturer called it, so if I described it that's what I would have said."

"Maybe you did, and I just registered it as pink."

"Yeah, but I don't think I did."

"Oh," I said. "Are you sure you didn't black it out? No, really, I may have just assumed it was pink. I don't think I've ever seen a woman's razor that wasn't. Do they even come in other colors?"

"Sure."

"Oh. I thought they were all pink. Why? What difference does it make?"

"No difference," she said, sleepily. "I just wondered, that's all."

TWENTY-SIX

The trouble with Thank God It's Friday, I've occasionally thought, is that it's all too often followed by Oh Rats It's The Weekend. Free time is only a godsend when you've got something interesting to do with it. If you've got nothing to do, decent weather lets you do it outdoors, and if you've got time on your hands at the beach or in the park, you may not even notice how bored you are. But when all it does is rain there's no escaping it.

It started raining an hour or two before dawn Saturday, just about the time I was getting out of a cab on West End Avenue. Edgar was manning the door, and he greeted me with a warm smile and an umbrella, though without a mustache. He told me I hadn't had any visitors, and I was glad to hear it.

I went to bed, and when I got up it was still raining, and the apologetic young woman on the local news channel said it was likely to keep on doing just that until Monday morning at the earliest. The sports guy said something about dampened enthusiasms, and the anchorman groaned, and I turned off the set.

I went out for breakfast, although what they were serving by then was lunch. Whatever they wanted to call it, I ate an omelet and drank some coffee and read the **Times**. The news was boring or horrible or both, and the movie listings held nothing that I felt like seeing.

When I got home the phone was ringing. It was Carolyn, reporting that no one had broken in to raid the bathtub while she slept. "But don't think I didn't check," she said, "and I didn't just lift the lid. I stuck my arm down into the Kitty Litter and made sure there were bags under there."

"I'm surprised you didn't haul them out and count the money."

"I might have, if I'd thought of it. Listen, when can we get rid of it?"

"Get rid of it?"

"You know what I mean. Oh, before I forget—I don't know if you're planning to open up the bookstore today, but I fed your cat, so don't let him con you into opening a second can for him."

"That cinches it," I said. "Nobody's going to brave a downpour to buy a secondhand book. I'm not going to bother opening up. How about you? You doing any business?"

"I'm not even trying. I decided to give myself a mental health day. And no, I didn't make a special trip just to feed Raffles. I had some appointments booked, and I needed to call them and cancel. They were relieved, because who wants to take out a dog on a day like this?"

"The Mets are rained out at Shea," I said, "and I couldn't find a movie I want to see."

"There's always the John Sandford. Oh, you left it down here. And you've got another copy at the store, don't you? But you're not going there. Well, as of last night you're in the chips, Bern. Do you feel rich enough to buy another copy?"

"Rich enough, but not crazy enough. I don't want three copies. I've only got two eyes."

"And one pair of lips to move. You should have taken my copy along with you last night. In fact I thought you did, but it's right here where you left it."

"I didn't want to carry it around."

"What, carry? Didn't you just get in a cab?"

"Right."

She thought about it. "But you didn't go straight home."

"Right again."

"Oh, that's right—you said you were going to a bar. You also said you weren't going to get drunk."

"And I didn't. And I know you're going to find this contrary to nature, but all I had was one drink."

"So you got home at a reasonable hour."

"No," I said, "because I didn't go straight home from the bar."

"Oh, God. Don't tell me you went on the prowl

again, not after the haul we made last night. You'd have to be out of your mind."

"I went on the prowl," I said, "but not to burgle."

"What else would you . . . oh, I get it. Well?"

"Well what?"

"Well, did you get lucky?"

"A gentleman never tells," I said. "Yes, I got lucky."

"Anybody I know?"

"Almost."

"Almost? What the hell does that mean?"

"Well, she works at a law firm at 45th and Madison," I said, "but not as a paralegal. She's a full-fledged lawyer, insofar as lawyers get fledged, and she's in the same firm with GurlyGurl."

"That's impossible."

"Why? Because there are eight million people in New York?"

"It's just a pretty big coincidence, that's all. I have a Date-a-Dyke date with one woman, and the same night you get to go home with somebody from the same law firm."

"I gather it's a good-sized firm. Even so, it's a pretty big coincidence. But I know a bigger one."

"What's that?"

"She took me home to her apartment," I said, "but what she didn't know was that I'd been there before."

"You'd been to her apartment but she didn't know it. Oh, for God's sake. Don't tell me."

"Okay."

"Are you kidding? **Tell me!**"

I told her in person, but before I made the trip downtown I called 1-800-FLOWERS, then hung up while they were telling me my call might be monitored. She lived in a brownstone, with no doorman and a grouch for a downstairs neighbor, so I didn't want to send flowers unless I knew she'd be home to receive them.

So I called her and caught her on her way out the door. She had a wedding to go to out on the island and she was running late. "But I thought it might be you," she said, "so I picked up the phone."

I told her I just wanted to say what a good time I'd had, and she said the same, and I suggested dinner the following evening. She said she'd be staying over that night, and there was a brunch on Sunday she was supposed to go to, and it was hard to say how late it would run, or whether she'd get a ride back or have to take the train. We left it that she'd call when she got in, or knew when she was going to get in, and if it wasn't too late and I hadn't made other plans, we'd get together.

So I didn't have to call 1-800-FLOWERS after all. No point—they'd only waste their fragrance on the desert air.

The way it was raining I'd have been happy to take a cab to Carolyn's, but enough other New Yorkers felt the same way to drop the number of empty cabs below the Mendoza line. I couldn't find one, and I didn't waste too much time trying. I had my umbrella, and it kept me dry all the way to the subway.

"It's a pretty big coincidence that they both work at the same place," Carolyn said, "but it's not a coincidence you went home with her. Because you were looking for her, weren't you?"

"Well, kind of. Parsifal's struck me as the kind of place she'd be likely to go, but I figured I was about as likely to run into him as her."

"Him? Oh, the date-rapist. How would you know it if you did?"

"By his voice, if I heard him talk. I have a feeling he was in there earlier, and that I didn't miss him by much."

"What makes you say that?"

"Just a hunch. Anyway, it's not important. Boy, do I hate rainy weekends."

"You and everybody else, Bern."

"Especially this one. But I'd hate this weekend even if the sun were out. Everything's just stuck."

"Stuck?"

"The money's stuck in the bathtub. We can't rent a safe-deposit box and put it in the bank because the banks are all closed until Monday. And everything else is stuck, too. Barbara's stuck out in Long Island at a wedding, and Ray's not working. He sometimes works weekends, but not this one, naturally. I called the precinct, and they said he was off today, and I called his house in Sunnyside and nobody answered."

"What did you want him for?"

"I thought he might know who the fat man was, or what the Lyles had that the perps wanted. He can't know much less than I do, but I know something he doesn't know, and that's that the Conrad book, the false McGuffin, wound up at Mapes's house."

"You can't tell him about Mapes."

"I can't tell him about Mapes the Burglary Victim, but why can't I clue him in about Mapes the McGuffin Recipient? Besides, if I can give him something, maybe I can get something from him."

"What makes you think he knows anything?"

"Even if he doesn't there's something he can find out for me. But not unless I ask him, and I can't do that until I know where he is. I wish I could get in touch with him. Why are you looking at me like that?"

"I just never thought I'd hear you say that, Bern."

"I hate weekends," I said. "You know what we could do? We could go someplace."

"In this weather? Where would we go?"

"How about Paris?"

"For the weekend?"

"Sure. We'll take the Concorde. A suite at the George Cinq, dinner at Maxim's, a cruise on the Seine, a stroll down the Boul' St. Germain, a **café au**

lait avec croissant at Les Deux Magots, then back on the plane and we're home again."

"That would cost a fortune."

"As it happens, we've got a fortune. We could swing it. Say fifteen to twenty thousand apiece for round-trip Concorde tickets, a thousand a night for a decent suite, half that for dinner—I'll tell you, for fifty thousand dollars we could have a memorable weekend."

"Uh, it sounds great, Bern, but—"

"But we can't do it," I said, "because the Concorde isn't flying anymore. And anybody who tries to buy any airplane ticket for cash, let alone thirty or forty thousand dollars' worth of cash, is going to spend hours answering questions in a room full of uniforms. Besides, we'd need to take a cab out to JFK, and how would we get a cab on a day like this?"

"And you've got a date tomorrow night with Barbara Creeley."

"She'll never make it back from the island in time, not in this weather. Man, do I hate weekends."

There was one thing I could do, though not without getting wet again. While Carolyn was getting wet herself, picking up dry cleaning around the corner, I made a small withdrawal from the stash of money in her bathtub. I could have done it while she was there, but I wanted to avoid having to explain why I needed it. And not long after she got back I put the Sandford novel aside yet again and walked up to 14th Street and took one bus east to Third Avenue and another bus uptown. I got off at 34th, walked up and over, and let myself into Barbara's brownstone.

I went upstairs, past the Feldmaus apartment, and remembered to open only the two locks she was in the habit of locking, which saved me a little time. I was in and out in under five minutes, and when I hit the street I couldn't think where to go next. Back to Carolyn's? Down to the store? Uptown to my place?

I went around the corner to Parsifal's, wondering what kind of a crowd they'd get on a rainy Saturday afternoon, and found that they got a sort of rainy-Saturday-afternoon crowd. There's something warm and welcoming about a bar on a day like that, but after you get over being warmly welcomed, you notice that everybody there gives off an air of desperation.

I'm sure I was no exception myself. I took a stool at the bar, where Sigrid's role was now being played by a black woman with short curly hair that either she or God had colored red. She was as tall as Sigrid and had the same cheekbones, along with the same subliminal message: **Sleep with me and you'll die, but it'll be worth it.**

I ordered Laphroaig and took a long time drinking it, meting it out in small sips. I was making progress, or it was; by the fourth sip, it tasted pretty decent.

While I sipped at it, I worked my way around the bar, talking to no one but listening to everybody. I was hoping to hear a particular low-pitched voice, but didn't really expect to. There was no one in the place who looked like my image of the man, and there was no one there who sounded like him, either.

Most of the time I wasn't listening that hard, anyway, because I was busy thinking. You ought to be able to work this out, I told myself. The whole thing was full of coincidences, and when you have that many of them, sooner or later they start fitting together in meaningful ways. That's what I told myself, anyway, but I kept turning the pieces around in my mind, and I couldn't quite make anything out of them. It was like a jigsaw puzzle, I decided, with some pieces missing. If I got hold of the missing pieces I might still be stumped, but at least I'd have a shot at it.

I went to the phone, dropped more coins into it than it used to cost, dialed a string of numbers that I remembered only because I'd dialed them twice already today, and listened to the phone ring in Ray Kirschmann's house. If a phone rings and there's no machine to answer it, does it make a sound? I decided it makes the sound of one hand clapping, which was about as much applause as I was capable of today, anyway. It rang until I was tired of listening to it, and then I hung up and went back to the bar. There'd been a sip or two left in my glass, and there'd been more cash on the bar than I would have left for a tip, but the bartender (whose name I hadn't caught, but I was pretty sure it wasn't Sigrid) had thought I'd left and taken it all away.

I really hate weekends.

TWENTY-SEVEN

The rain stopped sometime after midnight Saturday, too late to do most of the city any good, and started up again before dawn, in plenty of time to ruin Sunday. I went out for breakfast and came home with the paper. I still didn't have either copy of **Lettuce Prey** at hand, but the Sunday **Times** was enough to see anybody through a rainy Sunday, and clear into the middle of the week. Even after I'd tossed all the advertising supplements in the recycling bin, and added those sections like **Jobs** (which I don't want) and **Automobiles** (which I don't need), I still had enough paper left to make a person have second thoughts about freedom of the press.

I settled in with it, pausing now and then to try Ray Kirschmann in Sunnyside. Around eleven his wife answered, just home from church. No, she said, Ray wasn't home. He'd had to work, he hadn't even been able to go to services with her. I gave her my name and number, and she said she'd pass them on to him if he called in, but she sounded as though that wasn't likely to happen.

I tried the precinct and left a message there as well, and went back to the **Real Estate** section, where there was an inspiring story of a couple who'd searched high and low for a place that would accommodate both their hobbies, although they preferred to call them areas of interest. He built elaborate layouts for his model trains, while she collected weathervanes and old farm equipment. For a mere eight million dollars they'd bought an old warehouse in Nolita, which is not, as you might suppose, a Nabokovean tale about a prepubescent girl who won't have anything to do with Humbert Humbert, but a realtors' term for the emerging area north of Little Italy. By acting as their own general contractor and doing most of the work themselves, they'd managed to hold the cost of the gut rehab they'd done to another four million, so—well, you can run the numbers yourself and see what a bargain they'd got, with enough square footage to give him the HO-gauge equivalent of fifty miles of railroad track, while she had plenty of room to show off her treasures, including one of the very first McCormick reapers.

I called Carolyn. "What I want to know," I said, "is where do they find these people?"

"Huh? Where do who find what people?"

"Page four of the **Real Estate** section."

"I'll call you back," she said.

It was close to fifteen minutes before the phone rang, and I picked it up and said, "Well, it took you long enough. After we finish the remodeling, what do you want to do—play with your trains or go cut the wheat in the back forty?"

There was a long, thoughtful pause, and then a voice not at all like Carolyn's said, "It didn't take me long at all, not once I got your message. An' the rest of what you said must be in English, because I recognize all the words, but I don't know what the hell you're talkin' about."

"Oh, Ray. I thought you were Carolyn."

"I'm a foot taller'n she is an' a lot heavier, an' I got a deeper voice. Not to mention the fact that she's a woman, for all the good it does anybody. Most people don't have a whole lotta trouble tellin' the two of us apart. You called me, Bern. You got somethin'?"

"I might," I said.

"It took a while findin' out who he was, Bernie. He had a wallet with enough cash in it to choke a goat, but not a lick of ID anywhere in it, or anywhere else on him."

"No money belt?"

"Not unless he was wearin' it underneath his skin, because the last I seen him he was bareass naked on a metal table with a doctor diggin' bullets out of him. We ran his prints, of course, but he didn't have none."

"The man had no fingerprints?"

"He had 'em on the tips of his fingers, like everybody else except your occasional visitor from outer space. But he didn't have 'em on file, so when we ran 'em we didn't get nowhere."

He bit into a doughnut, chased it with a gulp of coffee. He'd picked me up in a city car, a Chevrolet Monte Carlo that must have been confiscated from somebody buying or selling low-grade cocaine, and now we were in a restaurant near the Manhattan side of the Williamsburg Bridge. Ray was partial to it, for reasons that remain unclear to me. We'd picked up our coffee and doughnuts at the counter and taken them to a table, on which Ray was now putting his cards.

"So we had nothin' to go on," he said, "an' we ID'd him anyway."

"How?"

"Good police work," he said. "How'd he get to your store? Well, you don't see too many fat guys on the bus or the subway, unless that's all they can afford, an' I already told you about his wallet."

"How much was he carrying?"

"I didn't weigh him, but he had to go over three hundred pounds. Oh, money?" He held his thumb and forefinger half an inch apart. "A wad this thick. Eighty-seven hundred bucks, all in hundreds, an' that's not countin' what he had in euros. That's a man who can afford to take a cab, but I knew right off that's not how he got there."

"How'd you know?"

"What's he gonna do, get a cabby to break a hundred? He didn't have any small bills, Bernie. What that tells me is he's got a car. He drove there, an' he's plannin' to drive straight home, wherever home is." He shrugged. "Course, we checked cabbies, too, lookin' for somebody who dropped a fat guy on your block of East 11th somewhere around lunchtime. You go through the motions, but I knew he drove."

"Unless he walked."

"A guy with his build?"

"I don't know, Ray. The man was light on his feet."

"Every fat man's light on his feet, Bernie. They gotta be or they wouldn't have a leg to stand on. Anyway, even if you had a point, it's a mute one. We found the car."

"Oh."

"He left your place walkin' east, an' he was gettin' ready to cross the street when he got blown away instead. So that tells me to look south an' east of your bookstore, an' what did we find on 10th Street between University an' Fifth?"

"A car?"

"A Buick," he said, "pulled up smack dab alongside a fire hydrant."

"It's good you got there before the traffic squad towed him."

"Couldn't happen, Bern. He had DPL plates. Diplomatic immunity might not keep him from gettin' shot full of holes, but it kept his car from gettin' hauled off to the pound. It mighta kept us from searchin' his car, I'm not too clear on the rules, but as fate would have it I had the car open before I even noticed the DPL tags. Careless of me."

"But convenient."

"Photo ID in the glove compartment, a driver's license plus his credentials from the Latvian embassy. Guy's name is Valdi Berzins, an' accordin' to the embassy he had somethin' to do with the Latvian mission to the UN, but nothin' too important. That was all we got from him outside of his address, which was a hotel, the Blantyre on East 51st Street. He had a room there by the month. Not a bad hotel, but not the Carlyle, either. Only thing we found in the room was a scrapbook of newspaper clippings, an' the last I heard they were lookin' for someone to translate 'em."

"Pardon my Latvian," I said. "I assume that's the language they're in?"

"Some's Russian, goin' by the letters. They're in that alphabet they got, that's like Greek but worse."

"Cyrillic."

"No, I'm pretty sure it's Russian. The others are in our alphabet, for all the good it does. An' there's one in English, speculatin' that the Black Scourge of Riga might be hidin' out here in America."

"The Black Scourge of Riga. Did they give his name?"

"Yeah," he said, "an' it's a whole string of vowels an' consonants. He's some kind of war criminal, would be my guess."

"Another doddering old European who might

have been a concentration camp guard. Whatever he did, he probably can't remember doing it." I thought a moment. "How old was Arnold Lyle?"

"I forget. Why?"

"Because he changed his name from something, and it probably had vowels and consonants in it. If the Black Scourge of Riga was a war criminal, he'd have to have been at least twenty-five in 1945, and probably older than that. Otherwise he'd have been the Junior Assistant Black Scourge of Riga. But say he was twenty-five. That would make him what, eighty-four?"

"Forget it. Lyle was fifty tops."

"It was just a thought. There's a connection there, Ray. Not to the clipping about the Black Scourge, but some kind of connection tying Berzins to Lyle."

"They're both Russians."

"Except for Berzins, who's Latvian. But Latvia was part of the Soviet Union back when there was such a thing. Not originally, because it was independent between the two world wars, but then the Russians took it over along with the rest of the Baltics. Ray? How hard would it be to get into the murder apartment? The one at 34th and Third?"

"It's a crime scene, Bernie. It's sealed."

"Oh."

"Why?"

"I'd like to get in there."

"Oh, well, we'll just ask permission from the guys in Major Cases. 'Bernie here's a convicted burglar, plus he's an early suspect in the case, an' he'd like to poke around the crime scene. Any of youse got a problem with that?' "

"I thought we could do it off the books."

"Sneak you in, in other words. Why?"

"Two people died in that apartment," I said, "plus the doorman downstairs. They all got killed because someone went there looking for something."

"Which we don't know what it is."

No, but I was beginning to have an idea. "We know they didn't get it."

"Bernie, I saw the safe. It was cleaner'n a whistle."

"So if the McGuffin was in the safe, the perps got it."

"Who the hell's McGuffin, an' where'd he come from?"

"It's a name," I said, "for the thing everybody wants, because we have to call it something and we don't know what it is. If it was in the safe, they got it. But suppose it wasn't?"

He frowned at me. "Why'd they have a safe an' not put the thing inside? Unless they didn't have it in the first place."

"A possibility," I admitted, "but I think they had it, and I think they were planning to sell it, and they bought the safe so they could keep the money in it when they got paid, because they were expecting a lot of money and they'd be getting it in cash. But suppose they kept the McGuffin somewhere else?"

"Then the perps got it. They tortured Lyle an' Schnittke until they handed it over, an'—"

"Did you find evidence of torture?"

"No, just a couple of bullets in their heads."

"That may have hurt," I said, "but it wouldn't have made them talk."

"Then they talked without bein' tortured, or the perps found the stuff on their own, and you know how I know that? Because if it was there an' they missed it, then **we** would have found it."

"I know they didn't find it, Ray. Otherwise they wouldn't have looked for it in my apartment."

He sighed. "It was us tossed your place, Bernie. We had a court order, it was all opened up above-board."

I told him about the second search, and when he protested that I hadn't reported it, I told him about Edgar the Doorman and the INS.

He looked hurt. "We wouldn't rat a guy out to those assholes," he said. "Half the guys on the force are Irish, an' half of them got a relative with a fishy Green Card or none at all. All the same, I can see why he'd be worried. But I have to say you're right. Same MO with the doorman means the same bunch of mopes, and if they found it they'd quit lookin'. So you know what I think? I think it wasn't there in the first place."

"Because the murder scene was searched by trained police investigators."

"Right."

"What were you looking for, Ray? And where did you look for it?"

"I can answer the second part. We looked high and low, searched the place top to bottom. What were we lookin' for? We'da known if we found it."

"I'm a trained burglar," I said, "and I know more places to hide things than you do, and more places to look for them. And I even have a sort of an idea what I'm looking for."

"An' you want me to sneak you in there. Against all rules, in a case that ain't my case anymore."

"Right."

"Get me two more of those crullers," he said. "With the chocolate on 'em, an' the jimmies." I went and fetched them, and he ate them without a word. Then he drank down the rest of his coffee and got to his feet.

"Well, what the hell," he said.

There were things I wanted to look at before I started hunting the McGuffin. First was the lock on the door to the Lyles' apartment. You can pick a lock without leaving traces, if you're careful not to scratch the face of the cylinder. But the cruder forms of entry all tend to involve gouges of some sort or other, and I couldn't see any, or any scratches, either. It looked to me as though the Lyles had let their killers in.

Ray had badged his way past the doorman, picking up a set of keys in the process, and the two of us had pulled down all the yellow CRIME SCENE tape from the door, and I balled it up and pocketed it for disposal later, far from the scene of the crime. After I'd studied the lock, he opened it with the key, and in we went.

The forensics team had long since come and gone, but it was still hard to resist an impulse to mince around on tiptoe. I did pull on a pair of Pliofilm gloves, which got a raised eyebrow from Ray, but I couldn't see any reason to leave a print behind, and several reasons not to.

"The Lyles let them in," I'd told Ray before we entered, and after a close examination I said as much for the safe. "Either Lyle opened it for them, or he told them the combination and let them do it themselves. But nobody blew it or peeled it, and I don't think there are fifteen people in America who could open it without force and violence."

"Fifteen, huh? You an' fourteen others?"

"It wouldn't be easy. The thing is, if they were good enough to get through this safe, they wouldn't have kicked my door in. I had a good lock on there, but it would have been child's play compared to this baby."

It wasn't locked, so I didn't have to show off. I opened the thing, and it was as empty as he'd said it was.

"If it was like this when Lyle opened it for 'em," he said, "an' if they looked all over an' still didn't find it, why the head shots? I can see doin' one of 'em, to show the other one you're serious, but why cap 'em both?"

"Head shots," I said.

"That can't be news to you, Bernie. I told you, an' even if I didn't you'da got it from TV or the papers. They were both shot in the head, and with the same gun. And no, before you ask, it wasn't the same gun as killed Berzins. That was a Lindbauer TDK on full auto. Lyle and the lady were shot with a .22 caliber pistol."

"Your crew searched the place."

"I told you that."

"But neatly," I said, looking around. "You put things back where you found them."

"It's a crime scene, Bernie. You don't touch it until the forensics guys are done, an' then you do what you have to do an' put everything back where you found it."

"That's what you did at my place," I said. "But it's not what **they** did."

"They made a mess? Yeah, you said they did."

"But they didn't make a mess here. Aside from a pair of dead bodies in the living room, I'd say they left the place pretty much as they found it. Which means they didn't search it, and what does that tell you?"

"That they got the damn thing outta the safe, just like I told you right from the beginning."

"But I already explained why they couldn't have. So that leaves another possibility, and it's the only one I can think of."

"Let's hear it."

"They got something," I said, "and they thought it was the McGuffin, and at that stage they had no reason to leave the Lyles breathing."

"Bang bang."

"And away they went, and it wasn't until hours later that they found out they didn't have what they wanted. Because it's still here."

He took his time thinking it over. "Okay," he said at length. "I can't find the holes in that, so all you gotta do is prove the pudding. If it's here, show it to me."

Twenty minutes later, we stood looking down at four photos which I'd laid out on the dining room table. They were color prints, four inches by five inches, and looked to have been taken by the same camera. All four were framed with Scotch tape that held them to pages recently torn from a book. If you looked closely, you could see another thickness of tape, half as wide, which suggested that they'd been mounted somewhere else, then cut loose and mounted anew. The book from which they'd been most recently removed was **QB VII**, by Leon Uris. I'd read the book years ago and remembered it fondly, and it had bothered me to rip out the pages, especially with the author having died not long ago. But it was a book club edition and its dust jacket was missing, so it could have been worse. I'd put it on the table next to the photos, where it sat looking deceptively intact.

The photographs showed two faces, full-face and

profile. Both faces, stern and expressionless, were those of middle-aged white men, and they filled the photos; if anything of either man existed below the chin, you couldn't have told from these pictures. Madame Defarge might have just plucked them from the basket at the base of the guillotine.

"There," I said, triumphantly. "Head shots."

 **TWENTY-EIGHT**

give up, Bern. Who the hell are these guys?"

"That's what Ray wanted to know," I said. "He also wanted to hang on to the photos, but I pointed out they might be evidence someday, so he couldn't just come up with them. He had to find them somewhere, in the right time and the right place, when finding them was something he was legally authorized to do. This way, I said, he had plausible deniability. I think he liked the sound of it."

"I don't blame him. I like the sound of it myself. You got any idea who these bozos are? Because I wouldn't know where to start guessing. You look at them and at first glance they look like brothers, or maybe cousins, and then you look again and see how different they are. The noses are different, the mouths are completely different, this one's jowly, this one's got a higher forehead, the other's got a scar, they're different around the eyes—you know, when you add it all up, they're barely members of the same species, but there's a similarity about them, and I don't know what it is."

"Same pose, for one thing. Same expression, or lack of expression."

She nodded. "Same overall shape of the head, too."

"Ray said they were brothers, but with different parents."

"Ike and Mike, they look alike. Except they don't. Ike here looks older, doesn't he?"

"Well, he's a blond. They're supposed to have more fun."

"Mike's definitely younger. If he were a woman you'd say his hair was mouse-colored, but you don't hear that with guys. What would you call his hair color, sandy?"

"I guess."

"It's funny," she said. "He's got less hair than Ike, but he looks years younger. I wonder why."

"Maybe he was born ten years later than the blond guy."

"That would explain it, Bern. Or maybe it's clean living. A healthier diet. More vegetables. Plenty of exercise, regular dental checkups. Assuming either one of them even has teeth. They've both got this cold closemouthed stare, and I think that's what makes them look alike, even though they don't. Bern, how'd you know where to look for the photos?"

"I gave Berzins a book," I said, "and he was happy to pay thirteen hundred dollars for it, and I suppose he'd have gone as high as ten thousand, because that's what he'd brought along with him. He didn't care about the title or author, and when I said the title he must have thought I was talking about him, because that's what he was, a secret agent of some sort."

"And then they shot him and took the book from him—"

"And took it to Mapes's house in Riverdale. Or to Mapes, anyway, for him to take home. They didn't say, 'A book? We don't need no stinking books,' and throw it in the garbage. They figured it might be what they were after, so I thought about that, and I decided it might be something you could hide in a book. And then I realized it was probably photos, which you can definitely hide in a book. Then you stick the book in the middle of a bookcase, and nobody thinks to look for it."

"Like the Poe story."

" 'The Purloined Letter.' Yes, the same idea. The apartment was a sublet, remember, and the original tenants had left the books in the bookcase. They were readers, too, so there were plenty of books. Ray said he and his buddies lifted them out a handful at a time and checked to make sure nothing was hidden behind them. That was reasonable if you didn't know what you were looking for, but it was just a waste of effort in this case. Some cop had that copy of **QB VII** in his hand and didn't have a clue what he was holding."

"So you went through them a book at a time."

"It didn't take long. You just open the book and riffle the pages. If there's anything in there, you know right away. The hard part was finding the right book, which happened fairly early on, and then checking all the others to make sure it was the only one like that."

"I don't know if I would have had the patience to do that, Bern."

"I didn't get to think about it, because Ray just kept going, picking up books and riffling them, showing me what painstaking police work looks like. The least I could do was follow his example. And of course there were no more books with photos taped to their pages, but that way we were positive."

"Just four photos," she said. "Two for each subject. I asked before if you had a clue who they were, and I don't remember what you said."

"I didn't say anything."

"Oh."

"Your computer working?"

"Is my computer working? Of course it's working. I was just online, and I checked my buddy list, and guess who else was online? GurlyGurl, so we IM'd back and forth for a while. We've got a date for Tuesday night, unless she has to work late." She grinned. "She was bitching about one of the lawyers who keeps piling work on her, says she's a real ovary-buster. I bet I know who she means."

"Maybe we'd better not go on any double dates just yet."

"My thought exactly. She likes me, Bern. Isn't that neat?"

"Very."

"Why'd you ask about my computer?"

"Because you're better on it than I am," I said, "and I thought maybe you'd like to do a little research."

Ray had brought along a fresh roll of CRIME SCENE tape, and after he'd used it to reseal the apartment he offered to drop me at Carolyn's. He got as far as Sheridan Square and told me I was on my own, claiming that he always got lost in the crooked little streets. He may just have been in a hurry to get home. It was still raining, so I was glad I had my umbrella.

Before I got out of the car I reached in my pocket and remembered what I'd been carrying around ever since I spoke to him hours ago. "You could do me a favor," I said. "Do you think you'd be able to run a print for me?"

He looked at me and made me repeat the question. Then he said, "Could I run a print? Nothin' to it. Could I run a print for you? Now that's somethin' else again. Whose print and where'd it come from?"

"If I knew whose print it was," I said reasonably, "I wouldn't ask you to identify it for me. As for the rest, you don't want to know."

"Meanin' you don't want to tell me. I dunno, Bernie. I'm bendin' a whole lotta rules today."

"Rules were made to be bent."

"Well, you're right about that," he said, and held out his hand, and I filled it, and he looked at what he was holding and then at me. "I dunno, Bern," he said. "This yours? Could be you're as light on your feet as Valdi Berzins."

Now, while Carolyn settled in at her computer, I made a few calls on her phone. I reached Marty Gilmartin at home, asked him a couple of questions to which he gave guarded responses, and made a date for lunch the following day. He asked if The Pretenders was all right, and I said it was always fine with me. I might be pressed for time, I said, in which case we could make it a drink or a cup of coffee instead of a full meal, but it would be good to get together.

I hung up and called Barbara Creeley, and when I'd said hello she said she was hoping I'd call. "I called you about half an hour ago," she said, "but I got your machine."

"I was out," I said. "Still am."

"I'm home."

"I figured that," I said, "right about the time you picked up the phone."

"Oh, right, of course. That was dumb of me, saying I'm home. I mean, you called me, so of course I'm home."

"I wouldn't say it was dumb."

"You wouldn't?"

She sounded shaky. I asked her if she was all right.

"I guess so. Do you still want to have dinner?"

"That's why I was calling. I was hoping you'd be home, and that I could take you out someplace for something nice."

"Okay."

"Okay?"

"Well, sure. I mean, I'm home. And yes, dinner would be nice."

"Great. What time's good?"

"What time? I don't know. You say."

"Uh, seven?" That would give me plenty of time to go home and change. "Is that good?"

"Seven's fine."

"Should we pick a place? It's Sunday, so not everybody's open. Do you have someplace you particularly like? Or do you want to meet at Parsifal's, and we can figure out where to go from there?"

There was a pause, as if two questions at once was too much to deal with. Then she said, "Could you just come over here?"

"If you'd like."

"That would be good, Bernie. You'll come over here at seven?"

"I will."

"You know the address?"

"I do."

"I'll see you at seven, then. Or earlier, if you'd like. Whenever you're ready, just come over. I'll be right here."

She hung up. I sat there holding the phone for a long moment, and then did the same myself.

"I've got to run home," I told Carolyn. "I need a shave and a shower. I've got a date."

"With Barbara? That's great."

"Let's hope so," I said.

TWENTY-NINE

It was a little before seven when I mounted the half flight of steps at the brownstone on East 36th Street. I rang and she buzzed me in, and when I got to her floor she was waiting in the doorway. She wore a dress with a bold geometric print, the kind of thing Mondrian might have done if he hadn't been so firmly committed to the right angle.

I told her I liked her dress. I'd noticed it before, actually, and had admired it then, but it did more for her figure than for a hanger in the closet, which is where I'd seen it. She said she'd taken it to Long Island, to wear at the Sunday brunch, but an informal poll indicated that most of the other women would be wearing jeans or a skirt, so the dress went back in the suitcase. She didn't know where we'd go tonight, but she could put on something else if I thought she was over- or under-dressed.

I was wearing a blazer and gray slacks, and I had a tie in my pocket, so I figured we were all right for just about any setting. I said she looked great, and she did, but there was an uncertain air about her that matched what I'd heard over the phone. She led me into the apartment, and there was a touch of awkwardness, the to-kiss-or-not-to-kiss moment. We'd been to bed two nights ago, but we really didn't know each other, so would it be presumptuous for either of us to expect the other to fall into a clinch? I hesitated, and she hesitated, and I reached for her and she came into my arms and we kissed.

It was a nice embrace, and a lingering one, but when we drew apart she still seemed troubled, and I asked her if everything was all right.

"Yes," she said, and thought about it, and said, "No," and thought about that, and then frowned. "I don't know," she said finally.

"What's the matter?"

"I'm a little scared."

"I can tell. Of what?"

She'd been avoiding my eyes, but now she met them. "Bernie," she said, "have you ever had the feeling that you could be losing your mind?"

"Sometimes I'm not sure I ever had one in the first place," I said. I glanced at her bed, and thought about the time I'd spent not in it but under it. "Sometimes I know I'm doing something that's really nuts, but I can't seem to keep myself from doing it."

"You mean like eating dessert when you'd decided earlier not to have dessert, and you really don't even want it, but there it is and you eat it?"

"Something like that," I said, "but on a grander

scale. Like it's a really rich dessert, and I'm a diabetic, and I eat it anyway."

"You're diabetic?"

"No, that's just an illustration of the relative degree of craziness I'm capable of."

"That's what I thought, but I wanted to make sure. Everybody has that sometimes, don't they? But this is different. I really think I might be losing it. First that blackout when I only had two drinks, which can't be a good sign. And then this. Can I tell you what happened?"

"Sure."

"Sit down. Can I get you anything to drink? There's different kinds of soda, or I could make you a cup of tea. Or coffee, but it'll have to be instant."

"I'm fine."

"I wish I could say the same. Bernie, when I woke up Saturday morning I thought about what we'd talked about, about how I brought someone home the night I had the blackout, and how he'd gone through my things but didn't take anything, except for my Lady Remington. And I thought about my missing class ring, and I went through my jewelry more carefully. All my good stuff was there, but I was definitely missing a pair of earrings, and a couple of silver bangle bracelets."

"More souvenirs."

"And nothing I couldn't live without, but it was still disturbing."

"Of course."

"And then I remembered the money."

"In your wallet? You said it was all still there."

She shook her head. "The other money," she said. "I never keep cash in the house, there's no need, not with an ATM two blocks away. But for a week or so I'd had a lot of cash on hand. Well, not a fortune, but I think you could call it a substantial amount. It was over twelve hundred dollars."

"That's substantial. In cash, anyway."

"That's what I mean. It was enough so that I found a place to hide it. I put it in the icebox, in the freezer compartment. I don't know, maybe that's the first place a burglar would look."

Not the first place, I thought, but right up there.

"Why I had the cash in the first place," she said, "is that Alison Harlowe's wedding was coming up, and she was one of the last of our crowd to get married. And she and Scott were torn between a big wedding and a honeymoon in Europe, they couldn't really afford both without going into debt. So word got around, and we all agreed that the gifts would be cash, but not individual gifts from individual friends, because that would feel like the opening scene in **The Godfather,** with everybody coming around with envelopes.

"So I volunteered to take the collection, and I got in touch with everybody, and people gave what they wanted, and the average gift was a hundred dollars, and by the time everybody was present and accounted for, the honeymoon fund came to almost nine thousand dollars."

"That's impressive."

"Most people gave me checks," she said, "but more people than I would have guessed gave me cash, and the cash amounted to over twelve hundred. I put the checks in the bank, and I don't know why I didn't do the same with the cash, but there's something about cash, do you know what I mean?"

"Definitely."

"It's like having a secret, or a concealed weapon, or something. It fit neatly into this brown envelope, and I tucked it away in the freezer, and I liked having it there."

"It beats Pop Tarts."

"And it's less of a temptation in the middle of the night than a pint of Häagen-Dazs. I suppose I would have put it in the bank eventually, but for the time being I figured it was fine where it was. And I sort of forgot about it. When I first started checking things to see what was missing, when I checked my wallet and counted the cash in it, I didn't even think of the money in the freezer. Maybe that's a sign all by itself that there was something wrong with me."

"Doesn't sound alarming to me. It slipped your mind, that's all."

"Or maybe it was my mind that was doing the slipping. Anyway, yesterday after I checked my jewelry drawer I thought about the wedding. The way we worked it, I was supposed to write one big check to cover everybody's contribution, and I'd done that, and mailed it in plenty of time so that they'd have it in the bank before the wedding and honeymoon. But getting packed for the wedding made me think about the check, and that made me think of the cash, and I got this sinking feeling in my stomach and went to the freezer."

"I guess it wasn't there, or you wouldn't be telling me about it."

"I took everything out of the freezer, including a beef brisket I never get around to cooking, and it's probably like frozen mastodon meat, it's been in there so long. I really searched, because I so much wanted the money to be there. I mean, I was probably ready for a new electric shaver anyway, and when am I ever going to wear a class ring from Bennett High? But twelve hundred dollars is a lot of money."

"Sure it is."

"And I felt really stupid for keeping it there in the first place. I'd put the checks in the bank right away, and it would have been the easiest thing in the world to do the same with the cash. But no, I had to hang on to it. Cold cash, frozen assets—God, I was so damn stupid."

"Cut it out," I said. "You know what you're doing? You're blaming the victim. You didn't do anything wrong. Some unprincipled son of a bitch"—Bernie by name, I thought—"stole something from you, and you think it's your fault. It's not. It's his."

"If the money hadn't been there—"

"But it was, and it had every right to be, and he had no right to take it. If you'd left it in plain sight on the kitchen table you could blame yourself, maybe, but you didn't. You put it in the freezer where he had no business looking, and he poked around and found it and took it. Barbara, it's really not your fault, and it certainly doesn't mean you're losing your grip on reality."

"I know," she said, and swallowed. "There's more."

"Oh?"

"When I got home this afternoon," she said, "I opened the freezer. Don't ask me why."

"Okay."

"No, I know why. I had the harebrained thought that maybe it would be there this time. So I opened the freezer."

"And?"

"And there it was."

Right where I'd left it the previous afternoon, while she was out on Long Island. "You're kidding," I said. "So it had been there all along, huh?"

"Bernie, I swear I took everything out of the freezer. Everything."

"Even the mastodon meat."

"Everything. I stood there looking into this completely empty compartment, and it even crossed my mind that it would be a good time to defrost it, but instead I put everything back. That money wasn't there, Bernie."

"Okay."

"Do you believe me?"

"Sure."

"And it's there now. Do you want to see it?"

"No, why would I want to see it?"

"So you'll know I'm not crazy. Except you'll know the opposite, that I **am** crazy. Here, I want to show you. See? Do you want to count it?"

I put a hand on her arm to steady her. "Put it away," I urged.

"It comes to exactly twelve hundred and forty dollars. Are you sure you don't want to count it?"

"I'm positive."

"It must have been there all along. It couldn't go away and come back. But how could I have missed it?"

There were, I told her, any number of logical explanations. She challenged me to name one.

"The money could have dematerialized," I said. "Then it reappeared."

"Something like that could happen?"

"Who's to say it couldn't? Look at it this way, Barbara. If you hadn't checked yesterday, it could have dematerialized and reappeared without your knowing anything had happened."

"But things don't dematerialize. Nothing ever dematerialized before."

"I had a pint of Häagen-Dazs do just that once. It was gone, and I swear I didn't touch it."

"I'm serious."

"Well, don't be," I said. "I'll tell you what most likely happened. You were preoccupied and panicky when you looked for the money yesterday. It was there, and you took it out of the freezer along with the rest of the food, and it just didn't register that that's what it was. And when you put everything back, it was still just another Stouffer's TV dinner for all the notice you gave it. It was right in front of your eyes, but you didn't see it, and that happens all the time."

"And it's not a sign of Alzheimer's? Or a brain tumor?"

"Afraid not."

"I know you're right," she said. "That must be what happened. Although I sort of like your first theory, about dematerialization and all. Poof! It's gone. Poof! Poof! It's back."

"Ricky Jay does stuff like that all the time. It's just magic."

"Well, that explains it. You know what? I feel better now. Where should we eat?"

We ate at a French place, where she put away a big dish of cassoulet while I had the steak frites. We each had a dry Rob Roy first—I ordered one, and she thought it sounded like a good idea. We decided our dishes called for a robust red, and agreed on a Nuits St.-Georges that turned out to be a splendid choice. It may not have been the meal I'd envisioned in the imaginary weekend in Paris I'd suggested to Carolyn, but there was nothing wrong with it.

I grabbed the check, but she insisted we split it, and sounded as though she really meant it. She got out a credit card. I had plenty of cash, so I let her charge the whole thing and gave her my half in green.

She brandished the bills before putting them away. "I'm a little nervous," she said. "Are you sure they're not going to dematerialize on me?"

"Always a risk."

Back on 36th Street, she led the way up the two flights of stairs and had a little trouble getting the key into the uppermost lock. **Let me,** I might have said, and taken the keys from her, and unlocked the locks for her. But of course I didn't do that, and the key slipped in and the lock turned.

And she had no trouble at all getting the second key into the bottom lock. It went right in as if drawn by a magnet, or an irresistible impulse. But then it wouldn't turn.

"Damn," she said, and forced it, and of course it snapped in the lock.

"Oh, hell," she said. "Look what I did? Shit piss fuck. Pardon my Latvian, but what a stupid thing to do." She looked at the lock, looked at what was left of the key. "I don't believe this. We'll have to call a fucking locksmith. God fucking dammit."

A curious calm settled over me, though I'll be damned if I know why. I took hold of her shoulders, said "Easy, easy" with the certitude of a horse whisperer, and moved her gently to one side. I drew my tools from my pocket, selected a small pair of needlenose pliers of the finest German steel, and extracted the broken-off bit of key from where it was lodged. I presented it for inspection like a dentist with a drawn molar, dropped it into my outside breast pocket, and bent to the all too familiar task of opening her lock.

It didn't take long. When the door was open I straightened up and motioned her inside, but she stayed where she was, wide-eyed and open-mouthed. "Come inside and sit down," I said. "There's something I have to tell you."

 **THIRTY**

A burglar," she said. "I never met a burglar before. But how can I say for certain? I wouldn't have known you were one if you hadn't told me."

"You must have had your suspicions when I opened your lock."

"I don't know what I thought. That this wasn't happening, that I really had lost my mind and I'd never be able to find it. Or that maybe you were just this incredible storybook hero, a man for all seasons able to cope with anything."

"What kind of hero hides under the bed?"

"A smart one. Is there really room under there? I've heard of women who always check the bed to see if there's a man under it. I thought it was a joke, but now just watch, I'll be doing it myself. What's the name of the drug he gave me?"

"Rohypnol. Roofies for short."

"The date-rape drug. What a bastard he must be. Pardon my Latvian, but what a motherfucking cocksucking shiteating cuntrag asswipe." She took a breath. "Whew! I got carried away there. Pardon my Latvian, or did I say that already?"

"You can say it all you want."

"I brought one stranger home with me, and there was another one already here. Suppose I'd come home alone. What would you have done?"

"Pretty much the same thing, when I missed my chance to get out the window. Incidentally, you're taking a big chance keeping it nailed shut like that. Suppose there's a fire?"

"There are two windows side by side."

"Right, and they're nailed shut."

"I bet I can tell you which one you tried."

"Only one's nailed shut? I'll be a ringtailed son of a bitch."

"It's a good thing you picked the one on the right, or you'd have gone out the window with all my good jewelry. How come you put it back, anyway?"

"Because I felt sorry for you. Because by the time he left and I got out from under the bed I felt as though I knew you, and I don't take things from people I know."

"You kept the money."

"Well, I didn't know you that well. And it was only money, it wasn't something personal like jewelry."

"My dad gave me the charm bracelet. He was a coin collector, and he'd add a coin for birthdays and other occasions, or just because he'd picked up something at a show. I never wear it because it looks dorky, but I'd hate to part with it. I probably ought to keep it in a safe-deposit box. It must be worth a few dollars."

"The diamond earrings, too."

"I know. They were my grandmother's, and I'd hate to lose them. But I wear them sometimes, and that would mean having to go to the bank first."

I told her about hidey-holes, and that I'd make one for her.

"My hero," she said. And her eyes got this look in them, and it seemed like a good time to kiss her. And, well, one thing led to another.

"That's how you knew it was pink," she said.

In light of the particular activity that immediately preceded this remark, it took me a second to realize she was talking about her Lady Remington.

"You took it," she said, "so of course you knew what color it was. Why do you suppose he smashed it? He likes his women hairy?"

"Quite the contrary. He threatened to shave you."

"To **shave** me? Where would he—oh."

"Right."

"In that case I'm glad he broke the shaver. I've already replaced it, and God knows how long the other would have taken. I guess he broke the thing because he's all those things I already called him, but why did you take it?"

"To keep you from wondering why it was broken."

"So I wouldn't know just how bad a night it had been. That's the same reason you straightened up. And you put the jewelry back because you're a sweet man. You may be a criminal, but you're too much of a softie to be a hardened criminal."

"Sometimes I tell myself I'm not really a criminal, I'm just a man who performs criminal acts."

"Oh, I like that."

"And then I tell myself that's a load of crap."

"I like that, too. You put the jewelry back because you felt like you knew me, but you kept the money because it was only money, and then you put it back. Because we'd slept together?"

"I suppose so. And you hadn't noticed it was gone, and this way it would be back before you missed it."

"Except it wasn't, but how could you know I would look between the time we talked on the phone and the time you got here to replace it?"

"I should have expected it."

"Why, Bernie?"

"Because it's a coincidence, and I've had a run of them lately. If I'd known you'd missed the money, I don't know how I would have handled it. I'd have found some way to give it back to you, but not in a way that would leave you doubting your sanity."

"You were Gaslighting me, and you didn't know it. I like the explanations you came up with, incidentally."

"They were the best I could do on the spur of the moment."

"Dematerialization's cute, but the other was actually plausible enough to make me feel better. The idea that I could have taken the money out and put it back without it registering. I suppose that would be a form of hysterical blindness, wouldn't it? But I didn't really get hysterical until I came home and the money was there again, so would it still be hysterical blindness?"

"Maybe it's more along the lines of an emotionally detached retina."

"That sounds right. Wow, you've had a busy few days, haven't you? Wednesday night you broke into my apartment, except that's the wrong word for it, because you didn't actually break anything. The only thing that got broken was the Lady Remington, and you're not the one who broke it. Whatever we call it, you were here Wednesday night. Then Friday you picked me up at Parsifal's, or I picked you up—"

"We picked each other up."

"—and we came back here. Then Saturday you came back to return the money, and—I just thought of something, Bernie. He took the money from my wallet, didn't he?"

"Yeah, but fortunately he left the credit cards."

"That's not the point. He took the money, and I didn't think it was more than eighty dollars or so, but there was more than that in there the next day. You replaced it, didn't you?"

"Well, yes. Out of the twelve-sixty from the fridge."

"And then you replaced the twelve-sixty. You lost money on the deal."

"I'm a pretty good burglar," I said, "but not a great businessman."

She had a curious expression on her face. I'd seen something similar on Mindy's face, of **Mork & Mindy,** when she would look at Robin Williams. **You're from outer space,** she seemed to be saying, **but you're kinda cute.**

She drew a breath and said, "And now it's Sunday, and you've entered my apartment twice tonight. The first time I let you in, and the second time you let me in. And in the meantime you've been running a bookstore? Where do you find the time?"

"Barbara," I said, "you don't know the half of it."

I guess I felt like talking, because I went pretty much nonstop for the next half hour or so. By the time I was finished, she knew it all.

THIRTY-ONE

Monday morning Carolyn and I counted money. We went straight to her bank, where she sat down with an officer and did what you have to do to rent a safe-deposit box. They only had the smallest size available, but that was all she needed to hold the $65,000 in large bills she'd brought along. That wasn't the full amount of her share, she had another two grand and change, but the rest was in small bills and she'd keep it around the house and spend it.

She left to open her salon, while I caught a cab uptown. The subway would have been faster, but not with what I was carrying. The Number One train stops at Broadway and 79th, and for years now I've had a safe-deposit box at a Citibank branch on that very corner. I could have been there in ten minutes on the train, but I'd worked too hard stealing the money I was carrying to risk letting some common thief take it away from me. While the cab ride took longer, I got out of the cab only ten dollars poorer than I got into it, and that was fine with me.

I went into the bank, sat at the appropriate desk,

and signed **William Johnson** on the signature card. That was the name I'd taken the box under, purposely picking something eminently forgettable, although I didn't have to worry about forgetting it myself. Bill Johnson was my scoutmaster when I was in Troop Seven, and I always liked the man. I was as surprised as anyone when those stories got around.

The bank officer had never seen me before, but she compared my signature to the others on the card, and led me into the vault and used my key and hers to get my box out. It was a large one, at least ten times the size of Carolyn's, but it was easy for Ms. Chang to carry because it was empty. I never keep anything in it for any length of time, because it's only safe from other thieves, not from the cops or the IRS, who can get a court order to open it with no trouble at all. The only reason they've never opened my box is that they don't know about it, but sooner or later they'll find out, and I want it to be empty when that happens. So I only use it as a temporary cache, where I can stow something while I figure out a better place for it. If I'd had my hidey-hole it would have gone there, but for now it could sit in the vault.

Ms. Chang led me to the little room where I locked myself in and transferred an even $125,000 to it from the Ultrasuede attaché case I was carrying. My full share had come to just under $135,000, but I'd already spent some of that, and the rest of it was in Carolyn's tub, hiding out under the Kitty Litter.

That left Marty's share, which was still in the attaché case when I left the bank. It came to just over $35,000, enough to justify another cab down to the bookstore. I opened up, but didn't bother with the bargain table, as it was getting on for eleven by then and I'd only be dragging it inside in another hour. Carolyn had already fed Raffles, though that didn't stop him from rubbing against my ankles, trying to hustle me out of an extra can of Nine Lives. It works more often than not, but this time I didn't fall for it.

I opened the attaché case and got out the material Carolyn had downloaded from a few different Internet sites and printed out for me. I'd scanned it earlier, but I gave the several sheets of paper a closer reading this time around, while the world of readers and book collectors failed to beat a path to my door. I was going through the material a second time when the bell above the door announced a customer.

"Welcome," I said, without looking up. "Have a look around, and let me know if there's anything I can help you with."

"Not much chance of that, Bernie. Far as I can see, there's nothin' here but books. Whatcha lookin' at?"

"Nothing interesting, Ray. Just printed matter, like a book but without the binding." I folded what I was reading and moved it out of harm's way. He tried to get a look at it without being too obvious about it, failing in both respects, but did notice my attaché case on the floor behind the counter.

"Nice briefcase," he said. "I think I seen it before."

"Well, it's possible. I've had it for years."

"Got any bunnies in there, Bernie?"

"Bunnies? In an attaché case?"

"Like I said, I seen it before, an' more'n once you've been known to yank a rabbit out of it. If you're gonna do it again, I want to be around when it happens."

"It seems unlikely," I said, "but if any rabbits are yanked, you'll have a front row seat."

"Back row's better, Bernie. So's I can block the doors." He leaned in, dropped his voice. There were no customers in the store, but maybe he didn't want Raffles listening in. "I ran the prints on that shaver. You can have it back, but I'd get a new one if I was you. The case is cracked an' it don't work."

"I know. Did you get an ID on the prints? That was fast."

"Computers," he said. "They speed up everything, even the response time from Washington. Course it's even faster when you don't have to go to Washington, which is the case if the prints match up with somebody local that we already got a sheet on."

"I thought they might."

"There were some partials, probably a woman's from the size of 'em. They didn't ring a bell, an' I didn't send 'em to DC on account of I figured the others were what you were interested in. They were the ones on top, an' they were nice an' clear, an' they damn well did ring a bell. The name William Johnson mean anythin' to you?"

"Not a thing."

"Yeah, right. You better not play poker, Bernie. The other players'll know what you got before you do. Well, this Johnson's the last person to handle the damn thing. Is that what you figured?"

I should have expected something like this, given the run of coincidence I'd had all along. And it was a common name, which was why I'd picked it for my safe-deposit box. Even so, I hadn't expected it to come up less than an hour after my first visit to the box in ages.

"It couldn't be the same William Johnson," I said. "The reason I reacted—"

"I'll say you reacted. You looked like you swallowed a bad clam."

"That was my scoutmaster's name when I was in the Boy Scouts, Ray. William Johnson. I was just thinking of him not an hour ago."

"Yeah?"

"And he got in trouble, so he could have had a sheet. But it wasn't in New York, so I don't think it could be the same man. How old is the one who left his prints on the shaver?"

"Thirty-four."

"Different person. The man I knew, well, he'd have to be in his sixties by now. This one has a record? I can't say I'm surprised."

"What do you know about him, Bernie?"

"Until a minute ago," I said, "I didn't even know his name."

He looked at me for a moment, then shrugged. "Okay," he said. "I ain't sayin' I believe you, but you found that book about the quarterback, so maybe you know what you're doin'. This Johnson's been arrested half a dozen times, charged with assault an' menacin' an' a few counts of disorderly conduct. What he is, he's a pain in the ass."

"Has he done time?"

"You only do time if you're convicted. He never even went to trial. His uncle's Michael Quattrone, an' I think you probably heard of him."

"Investments," I said.

"That's what he calls it. He's been associated with some boiler-room operations over the years, where they got a bunch of guys workin' the phones, lettin' you in on the ground floor for some stock they're pushin'. Soon as you bite it goes straight to the basement. Guy's mobbed up, an' we think he's runnin' a laundry for his friends."

"Laundering money, you mean."

"You want to get your shirts washed, take 'em to the Chinaman down the street. You want to make some drug money look like you came by it honest, maybe Quattrone can help you out. No indication this Johnson's a part of it, beyond takin' a desk an' phone in the boiler room now an' then. He's Quattrone's sister's kid, an' that means anytime we pick him up he gets a lawyer who's real good at makin' charges go away. Mostly he picks up jobs when he needs 'em, workin' for a truckin' company, or as a bouncer at a nightclub."

"A mover and shaker," I said. "You happen to know where he lives?"

"Last address we got's in the West Fifties. You want it?"

When Ray had left, after reminding me that he wanted to be there at rabbit-pulling time, I hauled out the phone book and had a look. There was no shortage of Johnsons, and a fair number of them were Johnson William or Johnson W, but none showed the West 53rd Street address Ray had supplied. I wasn't hugely surprised. Johnson's last address was almost three years ago, and somehow I didn't see him as the type to stay in one place long enough to put down roots.

I picked up the John Sandford novel, found my place, and stepped right back into the more logical world of Lucas Davenport. But I had to leave after a couple of pages, because it was time for my lunch with Marty.

THIRTY-TWO

The Pretenders have a rule against conducting business on club premises. Obviously they don't monitor conversations at the bar or around the billiard table to make sure no one's talking about auditions or offering a look at a script. What they want to avoid is the appearance that business is being done, and toward that end they make you check your briefcase at the door. Accordingly, I'd left the attaché case at the shop, having transferred Marty's share to a pair of plain white envelopes. I handed them to him once we were settled in with our drinks.

"These are yours," I said, and he lifted the flap on one just enough to see that it was full of currency. His eyes widened the slightest bit, and he put the envelopes in his pockets and patted them through the fabric of his suit jacket.

"Now there's a surprise," he said. "I hadn't even known you'd, uh, taken up the good fight."

"Friday night."

"Extraordinary. And I gather you were success-

ful. Highly successful, judging from the girth of
those envelopes."

"They could be all singles," I said, "but they're
not. Yes, I'd call it a great success." I told him how
much he'd find in the envelopes, and that it repre-
sented fifteen percent of the total sum.

"How marvelous," he said. "All of it a total loss
for the shitheel, that's the best part of it."

"For me," I admitted, "the best part is the
money."

"You had every right to keep all of it, Bernie. I'm
quite certain I offered to waive my own interest."

"You did, but why should you? It wouldn't have
happened without you."

"I'm glad you feel that way." He patted an envelope. "It's not as though I'll have trouble finding a
use for it."

We worked on our drinks—a martini for him,
white wine for me—and chose our lunch selections,
which Marty wrote down on a check for the waiter.
I'm not sure why they do it that way, the waiters can
hear as well as anybody else, and could presumably
either remember the orders or write them down
themselves. I think they like to have things they do
differently just so the members will be in no danger
of forgetting that they're in a private club, not just
another restaurant.

After the waiter had left, slip of paper in hand, I
asked Marty if he'd had any further contact with
Marisol.

"No," he said, "nor do I expect to. That's a

closed chapter, Bernie. She chose another man, and it's a choice she was entirely free to make. I emerged from the experience with a strong desire to punish him, which I have to say we've done, but no desire to chastise her, or to get her back. As I said, a closed chapter."

"I'm glad to hear that," I said, "but I wonder if we could peek at a page or two."

"What do you mean?"

"I have a question or two about Marisol. Her mother's from Puerto Rico?"

"Well, of Puerto Rican descent. I believe she was born in Brooklyn."

"And the father's from northern Europe."

"One of the Baltic republics. Quite a mixture, wouldn't you say? Fire and ice."

"You don't remember which Baltic republic, do you?"

"There are three, aren't there? Two of them start with **L**, and it's one of those, which is just as well as I can't recall the name of the third. Eritrea? No, that can't be right."

"Estonia."

"Estonia, of course. Where's Eritrea? No, don't tell me, because wherever it is, her father's not from it, or Estonia either. Does that help?"

"It could. Did you ever tell me her last name? Because I can't seem to recall it."

"I probably didn't, and you'll understand why. It's Maris."

"Maris? What's the matter with Maris? I mean,

Roger did all right with it." I thought for a moment. "Oh."

"Oh indeed. Marisol Maris. I thought she might change it, but she wouldn't hear of it. She thought it would look distinctive on a marquee or in a list of credits without striking one as absurd. And I suppose she's right. Now that her name's no longer going to be coupled with mine, I can view it more objectively."

I could see his point. There was something almost irresistibly awful about the conjunction of Marisol Maris and Martin Gilmartin.

"She wanted to honor both parts of her heritage, the Puerto Rican and the Lithuanian. Or is it Latvian?"

"It would almost have to be."

"It would?" He frowned, then shrugged it off. "She told me she was lucky, that her mother had wanted to name her Imaculata Concepción, but her father drew the line at that. Good for him, I'd say."

"And how old is she, Marty?"

"Unsuitably young," he said, and smiled. I asked him what that came to in human years, and he said she was somewhere in her mid-twenties. I did the math and put her date of birth somewhere in the late Seventies, which ruled out a conclusion I'd been about to jump to. Unless—

How, I asked, had her parents met? In this country? Or, uh, somewhere else?

"In Brooklyn," he said, too polite to ask why the hell I wanted to know. "He came over in the late

Sixties or early Seventies. He was in Toronto for a chess tournament and defected, and then managed to immigrate to the States. He was living in Bay Ridge, and she was in Sunset Park, just a few blocks away, and they met and fell in love." He cocked his head and looked at me. "If you want to know more," he said, "you'd have to ask her. I assume she's kept the apartment, although it'll be up to the shitheel to send in the check each month. Would you like me to give you the address?"

That was the second conversation in a row to end the same way, with someone offering to furnish an address. One more and I'd be willing to add it to the list of coincidences, but for now it didn't seem all that remarkable. But I did take down Marisol Maris's address, and her phone number, too.

I went straight back to the store, and the most interesting thing that happened all afternoon took place between the covers of **Lettuce Prey**. I marked my place and closed the book with fifty pages to go, stopping only because I was late for my standing rendezvous at the Bum Rap. When I got there Carolyn was already at our regular table. She wasn't alone, but looked as though she wanted to be.

I said, "Hi, Carolyn. Hi Ray," and took a seat with her on my left and him on my right, perfectly placed to be the umpire if they decided to have a tennis match.

"It's good you're here," Ray said. "Short Stuff

an' I was just beginnin' to get on each other's nerves."

"It must be the weather," I said. "The barometric pressure or something. You normally get along so well."

"The more small talk you make," she said, "the longer he's gonna stick around."

"I'm about to tear myself away," he said. "Bernie, you remember those newspaper clippin's in the fat guy's wallet? Well, they translated the Russian ones, an' they were all about the Black Scourge of Ringo."

"Riga."

"Whatever. They got somebody workin' on the others, workin' on findin' someone who can translate 'em, but I'd give you odds they're the same."

"No bet."

"Just as well, 'cause I'd be takin' your money. See, they're in our alphabet, an' none of the words look like what you or I'd call a word, but there was one that I recognized from the translations, on account of it's a name."

"Kukarov."

"Now how in hell did you know that?" He held up a hand to forestall an explanation. "Never mind, Bernie. You got somethin' goin', and that's all I gotta know. Any minute now those rabbits are gonna be flyin'."

When he cleared the door Carolyn said, "Of course he walked off without paying for his beer.

You know something? I'd have bought him a whole case to get rid of him."

"Oh, Ray's all right."

"No," she said, "he's not. Where did the flying rabbits come from, anyway?"

"He wants me to pull one out of my attaché case."

"You've got a rabbit in your attaché case?"

"Or out of my hat, and I don't have a hat, either. He wants me to get everybody in a room and unmask a killer, and I don't see how I can."

"Because you don't know what happened."

"Oh, I've got a pretty good idea what happened," I said, "and how it happened, and who made it happen. But this isn't the usual kind of case, where there are all of these suspects and one of them did it."

"There aren't really any suspects, Bern."

"I know. Usually all sorts of people walk into the bookstore, and one of them turns out to be the killer. This time the only person who walked in was Valdi Berzins, the fat man from the Latvian embassy, and he can't be a suspect because he got killed right away."

"So what are you gonna do?"

"I shouldn't have to do anything," I said. "I already made a big score, and got away clean. I even got a girlfriend out of the deal. It's not a great way to meet girls, I wouldn't recommend it to anyone, but in this case it worked out fine. I actually told her

the truth about myself, which is something I generally tend to avoid, but I had no choice, and so far
she seems to be able to handle it. So I could stop
now and let the police work it out or not work it
out, and everything would be fine."

"But you won't, will you?"

"I might."

"Yeah, right," she said. "Fat chance, Bern."

I called Barbara, and when the machine picked up I
rang off and tried her at the office. It looked like a
late night, she said, and I said that was probably just
as well, as I had some things I ought to take care of.
She was a sworn officer of the court, she reminded
me, so if the things I had to do weren't legal, she'd
prefer not to have foreknowledge of them. I told
her not to worry her pretty little head, and she gave
me a suggestion which, on the face of it, struck me
as physically impossible. "Pardon my Latvian," she
added, and we agreed we'd talk tomorrow.

I took a bus to 34th Street, had a slice of pizza
and a Coke, and transferred to a crosstown bus to
Lexington. I walked into and out of half a dozen
saloons, including Parsifal's, but didn't spend more
than a couple of minutes in any of them. I did make
a few phone calls, including one to Crandall Mapes
in Riverdale. A man answered, and I said, "I'm not
sure I have the right number. I'm trying to reach
Clifford Mapes, the composer."

"I never heard of him," he said. "I didn't even

know there **was** a composer named Mapes. What sort of music does he compose?"

"Oh, no music," I said. "He composes limericks. He's brilliant at it."

"Good for him," he said, and rang off, and I wasted a good twenty minutes fiddling around with the rhymed saga of a poor fellow named Mapes, who got into some terrible scrapes. Either that or he had a few narrow escapes, as you prefer. The last line might have involved women with curious shapes, or pissing all over the drapes, but the couplet in the middle was hopeless and I finally ordered myself to drop it. It's yours, if you want to mess with it. Feel free.

The other calls were to the number Marty had given me, and I got to hear the recorded voice of Marisol Maris, inviting me to leave a message. She had a nice voice, and if there was any trace of San Juan or Riga in it, I couldn't hear it. She sounded like any sweet young thing from Oakmont, PA.

I didn't leave a message, not even a fake one to see if she was screening her calls. She was an actress, she wouldn't screen her calls, she'd grab the phone the minute it rang, as sure as hope springs eternal. If the machine was picking up, that meant she was out—and not with Mapes, who was home in his big old house on Devonshire Close, trying not to think of a limerick with his name in it.

I walked uptown and west, passing through Times Square, and stopping whenever I found a working pay phone to try her number again. I had my finger poised to break the connection the instant I knew it was the machine answering. If you're quick about it, you get your coins back. I got it right all but one time, which struck me as pretty good, since you only get your coins back somewhere around sixty percent of the time from a New York pay phone even if there's no answer at all.

I got so good at it that, when I called from a phone mounted on the exterior wall of a bodega at Ninth Avenue and 46th Street, I rang off and scooped up my quarters only to realize belatedly that it wasn't a machine that had just answered. It was the same voice as the one on the machine, but it was live and in person, and I'd hung up on it all the same.

I tried the number again—I was in no danger of forgetting it—and this time her "Hello?" had an edge to it. "Sorry," I said. "That was me a moment ago, and I'm afraid we got disconnected."

"I wondered what happened."

"It's good you're home," I said. "Stay right where you are. I'll be there in a few minutes."

I got over there in a hurry. The building was your basic Hell's Kitchen tenement, with four apartments to a floor, and the bell for 3-C was marked MARIS. I rang, and her voice over the intercom was inaudible over all the static. "It's me," I said, accurately if not helpfully, and she found that sufficiently reassuring to buzz me in.

I took the stairs two at a time, and the door marked 3-C opened just as I was reaching to knock on it. The young woman who opened it was tall and slender, with the sort of awkward grace that gets called coltish. She had Baltic blue eyes and honey blonde hair and high cheekbones and rich tawny brown skin and a generous, full-lipped mouth that made you grateful the Supreme Court knocked out all those dumb laws against the very thing that mouth put you in mind of.

She looked frightened, but not necessarily of me. "Who are you?" she demanded. "Why are you here? What do you want?"

"My name is Bernie Rhodenbarr," I said. "And I want to talk to you about Valentine Kukarov."

She took a step backward, put her hand to her remarkable mouth, and burst into tears.

THIRTY-THREE

It was after ten when I left Marisol's apartment. I walked back to Ninth Avenue and hailed a cab, something I seemed to have been doing a lot that day. Sometimes I'll go weeks without taking a taxi, and all of a sudden I was flagging them left and right.

This one let me off in front of Parsifal's, where an owlish young fellow looked as though he couldn't believe his luck, either at having a cab drop right into his lap that way or at the young woman who was draped on his arm and ready to share it with him. I wished them well and went on inside.

Sigrid's shift hadn't started yet when I'd come in earlier, but she was behind the bar now, serving drinks to the Thank God Monday's Over crowd. I eyeballed the room, then went and found a spot at the bar. She came over and said, "It's either Laphroaig or Pellegrino. What kind of a mood are we in tonight?"

I felt more like a glass of brandy—it had been a long day—but it would have been gauche to suggest it. I went with the Laphroaig, and when she brought it I crooked a forefinger and motioned her in close. "Late Friday night," I said, "I was talking with a woman named Barbara. Dark hair, had it up in a bun—"

"I remember."

"You were starting to tell us about a guy who came on strong earlier in the evening," I said, "and then you did a quick one-eighty and changed the subject."

"Oh?"

"It was pretty smooth," I said. "She didn't notice it, but I did, and that might be because I was looking for it. My guess is you were behind the stick two nights earlier, and he was the same guy she went home with that night, and as soon as you made the connection you dropped the subject."

"That's your guess, is it?"

"It's an educated guess."

"Well, you seem like an educated guy. Maybe you're even smart enough to tell me why you and I are having this conversation."

"I'm hoping you'll help me find him."

"Why would I want to do that?"

"I know his name," I said. "Mine is Bernie Rhodenbarr, and that's all you'd have to know in order to track me down. But his is William Johnson, and he's not the only one in Manhattan."

"You know more about him than I do," she said. "I didn't even know his name until just now. And you still haven't said why I should help you find him."

"He took Barbara home and fed her a couple of Roofies, and when she passed out he raped her."

"Christ in the foothills."

"Then he helped himself to a few souvenirs and went home."

"What a son of a bitch," she said. "I wondered what his game was. I knew there was something creepy about him, but that goes beyond creepy."

"I don't think it's the first time he's used that kind of pharmaceutical assistance," I said, "and I don't think it'll be the last. I'd like to do something about it."

"Jesus, I'll say. Something that involves surgery, I would hope. Hang on a second."

She went down the bar to attend to someone who'd run dry, and I worked on my Laphroaig. "I don't know how you can drink that," she said on her return. "It tastes like medicine to me."

"Strong medicine," I agreed.

"The thing about alcohol," she said, "is it doesn't wear out its welcome. You work in a pizza place, within a couple of months you lose your taste for pizza. You tend bar, you drink as much as ever."

"Have something."

"Not till my shift ends, but thanks. You said you wanted me to help you find God's gift to women. I'm game, but I can't think how. You're not a cop, are you?"

"No."

"I didn't think so. You could be a private eye. I've known six of them, and I swear the only thing they've got in common is the state gave all six of them a license."

"That lets me out," I told her. "They'd never give me one."

"Bad moral fiber?"

"Worse than that. A felony conviction."

"No kidding. It wasn't rape, was it, or something nasty like that? Then I won't ask what for. I still don't know how I can help."

"You could describe the guy. I don't have a clue what he looks like."

"Barbara won't tell you?"

"Barbara doesn't remember a thing."

"Then how in hell do you know his name? And how do I know it's the same guy as the one who hit on me?"

"You saw the two of them leave the bar together, remember?"

"Oh, right. But maybe she ditched him and went somewhere else and picked up some other boy wonder, and he was the one who fed her the Roofies. I just wish you could mention one thing about him so I was sure we were talking about the same person."

"He has a very deep voice."

"Yeah, that's him, the son of a bitch. Now how on earth do you happen to know that?"

"That's confidential."

"Confidential, huh? Hang on." She went away and came back just as I was having another sip of my medicine. "I could describe him," she said. "He's about six-three, very big in the chest and shoulders, with the kind of muscular development you get in the gym, and probably not without anabolic steroids. Biceps like Popeye when he's full of spinach."

"Tall and muscular," I said.

"Dark complexion, as if he goes straight from the gym to the tanning salon. Black hair, and he parts it on the side and slicks it down with mousse or goo or something, so it wouldn't move in a hurricane. Has a big jaw, not enough to remind you of Jay Leno, but it's out there. Eyes are set deep, with a little bit of a slant to them."

"That's a pretty good description."

"You think? It seems to me it would fit a lot of people. You couldn't pick him out of a lineup, could you? Oh, I know!"

She turned around and came back with an order pad and a pencil, tore a sheet from the pad and turned it over on top of the bar. "I took a course," she said. "Drawing on the right side of the brain. The trick is getting into a right-brain mode. Do you mind?" She picked up my glass of Laphroaig and downed it in a single swallow. "Yuck, I don't know how you can stand that stuff. Just give it a minute. Okay, I think I'm shifting into a right-brain frame of mind."

She began sketching, and I watched, fascinated, as Barbara's date-rape date took shape upon the slip of paper. "He's a good-looking guy," I noted. "You wouldn't think he'd have trouble getting girls on his own."

"I suppose so. Not my type, though." She turned the pencil around, erased an area around the mouth, then tried it again. "I like older men."

"He's thirty-four."

"Well, he was born about thirty years too late. 'If you're not gray, please go away.' That's my motto."

"Really."

"Older men know how to treat a woman," she said. "On the one hand they pamper you, and at the same time they see right through your bull-shit. They may think it's charming, but they know it's crap. The worst thing about this job is the crowd's too young. I never meet anybody I'm inter-ested in."

"The only older guys I know," I said, "are either married or gay."

"You can keep the gay ones, but married's fine. I'm a lot happier with a man who's got a wife to go home to." She frowned at the drawing, turned it to face me. "It's getting close," she said, "but it's not quite right, and—well, fuck me with a stick." She picked up her drawing, crumpled it in her fist, and flipped it over her shoulder onto the back bar, where it nestled between bottles of Jim Beam and Maker's Mark.

"Hey," I said. "Even if it's not Van Gogh, I could use it."

"You don't need it. Don't turn around, not just yet. You'll never believe who just walked in the door."

•   •   •

Of course I believed it. I should have expected it. With the long arm of coincidence rolling the dice, how could William Johnson fail to make an appearance just as Sigrid was putting the finishing touches on his portrait?

And, granted a look at the original, I have to say she'd turned out an excellent likeness. Up close and in living color, there was a quality of spoiled self-indulgence she hadn't quite captured, a look around the mouth reminiscent of some of the Roman emperors. And not Marcus Aurelius, either. More like Nero, say, or Caligula.

He was wearing a muscle tee, sleeveless to display his delts and triceps and skintight to showcase his pecs, along with tight black jeans to show off his glutes. He had a deep tan already, and it wasn't even summer yet. He surveyed the room purposefully, then headed for the back, where two women were seated together at the bar.

"Here we go," Sigrid said. "He's found his quarry."

"That's if he can split them up."

"If he drugs them," she said, "he may not have to. He can take them both home."

"They've got short hair," I pointed out.

"So? Oh, they might be gay? I don't think so, but once he slips them the Roofies, does it really matter?"

"Good point. What do we do?"

"I don't know. Don't you have a plan?"

"I was going to follow him home," I said, "and find out where he lives. But that won't work if he goes home with them instead."

"And it won't be the evening they're hoping for, either. C'mon."

"C'mon? C'mon and do what?"

"Improvise," she said. "Go help him hit on them while I take care of everybody's drinks."

She was, as I already knew, an actress and a model. She'd also demonstrated an enviable facility for drawing faces. I was willing to believe she had multiple talents, some of the more interesting of which I'd never learn about because I was too young for her. One of them, it turned out, was close-up magic. I don't know how she did it, but after two rounds of drinks Audrey and Claire and I were clearheaded enough to drive an obstacle course, while William Johnson was a coma looking for a place to lie down.

The two women, who'd thought Johnson and I were at least promising, found his sudden lapse into word-slurring eye-rolling idiocy more than a little disconcerting. Sigrid acted as though he pulled this all the time.

"Oh, not again," she said, in a voice that carried throughout the room. "He's a nice enough guy, but that's the last time he's getting a drink in here. Bernie, grab him, will you? Before he slides off the stool and lands on his empty head."

She came around from behind the bar, deputized one of her regulars to cover for her, and the two of us each got an arm under one of his and walked him out the door. He was a big guy, but she was a big girl, and must have had muscles even if they didn't show the way his did. Between the two of us, we had surprisingly little trouble walking him down the block and around the corner. There was a narrow alley on 37th Street, running between a pair of apartment buildings; I'd spotted it while on the prowl, and that's where we took him now.

Some of the city's native fauna scuttled out from among the garbage cans when we maneuvered him to the rear of the alley. We got maybe three-fourths of the way there, turned him around, and gave him a light shove, and he landed on his rear end and clunked his head on the brick wall. He wound up sprawled there, his oversized jaw slack, with drool leaking out of the side of his mouth.

"Jesus, what a charmer," she said.

I bent over him, came up with his wallet. Without thinking I scooped out the bills, gave half to her, and stuck the rest in my pocket. "He got drunk," I explained, "and passed out in an alley, and some lowlife rolled him." She looked at the money for a moment, then put it away, while I went through his wallet looking for a current address. His driver's license had him living on 40th just off Lexington, and he'd renewed it less than a year ago, so it was probably current. I was going to write it down, but it was easier to take the license along with me, and while I was at it I took his credit cards.

That brought a raised eyebrow from Sigrid. "I'm not going to use them," I said, "but he won't know that, will he? He'll have to go through the hassle of calling the card companies."

"Good," she said. "Look at him, the misogynistic son of a bitch. I could kick him in the balls and he wouldn't even feel it. Or would he?" She decided to find out, and the result of the experiment was inconclusive. He groaned, but didn't really stir.

"He'll feel it when he wakes up," I said.

"God, I hope so. Look at him, will you? He makes an almost perfect picture. It's just a shame he didn't puke on himself." She thought a moment, said, "Well, I can fix that," and stuck a finger down her throat, anointing him generously with the missing element.

"Adolescent bulimia," she explained. "I outgrew it years ago, but you never forget how. Like falling off a bicycle."

"Or drowning."

"Exactly. I'd better get back to Parsifal's before Barry gives away the store." She pinched my cheek. "You're cute. It's a shame you're not twenty years older."

"I'm aging as fast as I can."

"You haven't got an uncle with a roving eye, have

you? Oh, I know what I wanted to ask you. That noise when we first walked into the alley, sort of something scuttling away? Was that rats?"

"I'm afraid so."

"Good," she said. "Let's hope they're hungry."

THIRTY-FOUR

The lock on William Johnson's front door was nothing special, but for some reason it gave me a hard time. Working away at it, I wondered why I hadn't had the sense to fish his keys out of his pocket while I was rolling him. It certainly would have made things easier.

Once I was inside, my first thought was that I was too late, that someone somehow had beaten me to it. The apartment, a large L-shaped studio, looked as though it had been lately tossed by a team who'd taken the verb literally, picking up everything mobile and flinging it somewhere. It would have been just one more coincidence to add to the string, and it took a few minutes to realize that I was Johnson's first and only illicit visitor. The place was a mess because that's the way he kept it. Maybe, I thought, he hadn't meant any harm when he dumped Barbara's jewelry drawer on the floor. Maybe he wasn't vandalizing the place after all. Maybe he was helping her redecorate.

The state of the place made my task harder than

it might have been. It's not easy to look for something when you have to include the floor among the places to be searched. Nor, oddly, is it as easy to leave things as you found them, because how can you tell when they're back where they belong?

I did the best I could, and didn't linger. According to Sigrid, he'd wound up with a double dose of Rohypnol, with the capsules intended for both Claire and Audrey somehow winding up in his glass. It had certainly been enough to knock him cold, but who knew how long he'd stay that way? I wanted to be gone before he came back.

On my way out, I took time to pick his lock again, leaving that too as I'd found it. It was quicker the second time, but would have been quicker still with his key. Then again, I consoled myself, if I'd taken his keys he'd have missed them, and might have suspected that whoever had taken them would head straight for his apartment.

I walked for a block or two, buoyant with the heady sensation I get from illegal entry. It was cool enough so that I stuck my hands in my pockets for warmth, and realized I still had his credit cards. I was going to throw them away, but I decided that would be wasteful. Just because I wasn't inclined to run around charging DVD players and iBooks to Wee Willie Johnson, why should I deprive some other citizen of the pleasure?

I left the cards here and there, out in plain sight, where whoever came along could pick one up and do as he pleased with it. A person with a conscience as overdeveloped as Johnson's upper body could seek out the card's owner and return it. One who was merely honest could simply leave it where it lay. And a truly enterprising individual, a passerby with energy and the will to better himself, would max out that card as quickly as possible.

When the cab stopped for me, I would have loved to go straight home and call it a night. Instead I gave the driver an address on Park Avenue that turned out to be between 62nd and 63rd.

The building I wanted was a fully serviced luxury apartment house, with a concierge on the front desk and an attendant in the elevator. The only way to get into a building like that is through subterfuge; ideally, you find a bona fide tenant to invite you in, and make a little detour on your way out. That's hard to arrange on the spot in the middle of the night, and I hadn't had time to set anything up. I was, God help me, on the prowl again, and I didn't see any way to avoid it if I was going to make this work.

Fortunately, I didn't have to get past the desk, or take the elevator anywhere. On either side of the building's entrance was a staircase descending a flight to a suite of basement offices, all of them occupied by members of the medical profession. The one I wanted was on the left, and if I got down the stairs I'd be all right. No one at street level could see me while I worked on the lock, and I couldn't believe there would be a burglar alarm on the door.

What there was, and I could even see the goddam thing, was a security camera. I didn't care what wound up on the tape, because no one would look at it unless a crime was committed. I planned on committing one—I'd do so the minute I opened the door, and might even fit the definition of criminal trespass when I went down the stairs for no legitimate reason. But if all went well no one would know I'd been there, so why review the night's tapes?

The danger lay in being caught in the act, which could happen if the concierge was looking at the closed-circuit TV monitor on his desk while I was passing in front of the camera. They don't sit there and stare at it by the hour, they'd go nuts if they did, but all it takes is a glance at just the wrong time, and they pick up the phone and call 911, and another hapless burglar gets free room and board as a guest of the governor.

I found a pay phone, made a phone call, and came back to where I could watch the building. When the guy brought the pizza, I made my move, and I was down those stairs in a hurry. The lock was a cinch, and it took me hardly any time to find everything I was looking for. I took a sheet of paper from a desk drawer and wrote down what I needed to know, and I folded it up and put it in my pocket, and that was all I took. Unless they counted the letterhead, no one could possibly know they'd had a visitor.

So I was out of there in a hurry. I was tempted to

leave the door unlocked, but I'd done everything else right, and I didn't want to stop now. I picked it shut and walked quickly up the stairs and away from there. This was the dangerous part, because from where I stood there was no way I could see if the concierge was busy, but when I was clear of the place and took a look back, it was clear I'd had nothing to worry about. The pizza guy was still there, talking away on his cell phone, while the concierge stood there with his hands on his hips, and it looked as though it might take them a while to sort it all out.

I caught a cab and went home.

I would have loved to stay there. My humble abode had never felt so welcoming, nor had my bed ever looked so inviting. I decided to stretch out for just a minute, and I told myself not to be an idiot. I put some coffee on and took a quick wake-up shower while it brewed, then threw a couple of ice cubes in it so I wouldn't have to wait for it to cool.

Was there no way I could avoid another trip to Riverdale?

None I could think of. I spent a few minutes preparing the parcel I would take with me, then bit the bullet and got to it. I walked around until I found the Mercury Sable, opened its door, diddled its ignition, and drove it the nine or ten miles to Riverdale, found Devonshire Close without getting lost, and parked the car not in Mapes's driveway—

the unfamiliar noise of a car in their own driveway might wake Mapes or his wife—but two blocks away. I walked the two blocks, well aware of the impossibility of appearing innocent walking residential streets at that hour. I went up the driveway to the side door, and looked longingly at it. I'd set the alarm to bypass that door, and unless someone had noticed, it was still like that. But I couldn't find out without opening the door, and if they'd changed the setting—well, that was a sentence I didn't want to finish.

That left the milk chute. Let's just say I didn't get stuck this time. Not on the way in, and not on the way out, either.

I drove home, parked the car right where I'd found it—who'd grab a parking space away from me at that hour? I got myself home, exchanged a friendly word with Edgar, and went straight to bed.

THIRTY-FIVE

Bern, I hate to say it, but you don't look so hot."

"That's good."

"It is?"

"I don't feel so hot, either, and I'd just as soon be consistent. I ran myself ragged until daybreak, and I was tired enough to sleep until nightfall, but I made myself set the alarm and forced myself to get out of bed when it rang. Don't ask me how."

"I won't," she said. We were at the Poodle Factory. I'd opened up at eleven, having stopped on my way down to pick up a new prepaid cell phone on 23rd Street. I made a few calls with it, then picked up lunch at Two Guys from Kandahar, and brought Carolyn up to date while we ate.

She said she couldn't believe I'd gotten so much done in one night, and when I thought about it, neither could I. "I kept wanting to call it quits," I said. "When the poor bastard showed up from Twenty-four/Seven Pizza, I wanted to walk in there, pay him for it, take it home, eat it, and go to bed."

"Instead you broke into Mapes's office. Swipe any drugs while you were there?"

"I told you, I didn't take anything."

"You went through all that just to look at his appointment book."

"I had to, in order to schedule things. I couldn't set up a big showdown at a time when he was going to be busy giving some kid from Larchmont a new nose in time for her Sweet Sixteen party. I needed to know his schedule before I did anything else."

"And you called him this morning? How did you know what to say?"

"I didn't. I played it by ear. 'Mapes? I think you know who this is.' And evidently he thought so, too, because we went on from there."

"Was that the voice you used, Bern? Were you trying to sound like anybody in particular?"

I thought about it. "Maybe Broderick Crawford," I said. "Playing a heavy, not being one of the good guys in **Highway Patrol**. Basically I was trying to sound menacing."

"Well, you picked a good voice for it. Did you use it for the other calls?"

"No, because I wasn't sure menacing was the way to go. With some of them I wanted to sound ingratiating, and with others I just wanted to sound like a reasonable man with a reasonable proposition. It was strange, because I was calling people I didn't know."

"Telemarketers do that all the time, Bern."

" 'Hello, Mr. Quattrone. How are you today?' "

"I know, I can't figure out why they do that. The

only person who ever starts a conversation by asking me how I am is some dimwit on Montserrat trying to sell me a time share in Omaha."

"Are you sure it's not the other way around? The thing is, they want you to think they're having a conversation with you, but most of them have never had one, so they're at a loss. I was at a loss of my own, because I was cold-calling people without knowing whether they were interested in what I had to sell. If not, I just wanted to move on to somebody else. The hard part was deciding whether they were expressing genuine bafflement or just playing dumb. Anyway, I told them the time and the place, and we'll see who shows up."

"How many people are coming?"

I hauled out my list. "The names with a check mark are ones I called this morning. I'll ask Ray to round up the ones with a star."

"Hey, I'm on the list. You want me there?"

"Of course."

"How come I don't get a check mark or a star?"

"Because I didn't call you this morning," I said patiently, "and I didn't think it would be necessary to have Ray bring you. I figured I'd just tell you about it, and you'd come."

"No problem," she said, scanning the list. " 'Barbara Creeley.' I guess you'll tell her, right? She's a lawyer, she's got meetings and closings all the time. Will she be able to come?"

"I hope so. It's not a dealbreaker if she can't, but I'd like to have her there."

" 'GurlyGurl.' You put **Lacey** on the list? And how come you wrote down her screen name?"

"Because I didn't get much sleep last night and I'm a little rocky this morning and I couldn't think of her damn name."

"Don't bite my head off, Bern."

"I'm sorry. I thought you might like having her there, and it might be interesting for her. She's not tied into any of it, but there's a coincidental connection in that she works with Barbara. I figured it would be up to you to invite her, and it's your call to make. Personally, I'd just as soon have a lot of people in the room."

"Should I bring my cats? Just a little joke, Bern."

"Ha-ha."

"Man, you're nicer company when you've had a full night's sleep, aren't you? This is a long list, isn't it? Let's see who else is on it."

"This here is some list," Ray Kirschmann said. "How you gonna fit 'em all in this guy's house?"

Just bring them in through the milk chute, I thought. "It's a big house," I said. "Anyway, they're probably not all going to come. Some of the people I invited sounded as though they didn't know what I was talking about, and they'll probably find something else to do tomorrow afternoon."

"Weather report says there's a fifty percent chance of rain tomorrow," he said, "which is a lot like sayin' they don't know what the hell it's gonna do. Rain or shine, that's a lot of people to send clear up to the Bronx. I never heard of the street. 'Devonshire Close.' Close to what, Bernie?"

"Close to Ploughman's Bush," I said, "if that helps. They call it a close because it's closed at one end."

"You mean like a dead-end street? Why not come out and say so?"

"I suppose they could have," I said, "but I guess the developers felt it would be harder to sell houses on Devonshire Dead End."

"Either way, it's a Roach Motel for cars. They get in but they can't get out. I don't know if that's good or bad."

"I don't either, Ray. I'm starting to have third thoughts about the whole business."

"You mean second thoughts, don't you?"

"I already had those. I've taken it to the next level. The whole thing could fizzle."

"You mean you might not come up with a rabbit?"

"I'm not even sure I've got a hat."

He looked troubled, perhaps imagining how he'd come out of it if my magic act fell flat. Then he brightened. "Aw, you'll pull it off, Bernie. You always do. An' if you don't, well, hell, there's names on this list we could just arrest on general principles."

I made some more phone calls during the rest of Tuesday afternoon, and even went out to issue a couple of invitations in person. I met Carolyn at the Bum Rap, talked some more about the following day's agenda, and went straight home. I was in bed by 7:45, and asleep by 7:46. I slept the clock around, waking up a few minutes after eight.

I showered and shaved. I broke some eggs in a bowl, swirled them with a whisk, tossed in some shredded cheese and a pinch of celery salt, added a soupçon of curry powder, and made better scrambled eggs than I could have gotten around the corner. I made coffee, too, and there was nothing wrong with that, either.

Washing up, I caught myself whistling, and was amused to realize the melody was that of "Put on a Happy Face." I checked the mirror, and damned if I hadn't followed the song's advice. If my face looked any happier I could get a job as a village idiot.

I felt, I realized, uncommonly good—rested, of course, but also energized and optimistic. I was in high gear, and I felt as though nothing could stop me.

Of course I hadn't left the house yet.

# THIRTY-SIX

There was a bell, of course, but I used the lion's head door knocker and gave it a couple of good thumps. I heard footsteps, and then the door opened, and the man who'd opened it must have whistled a different tune at the breakfast table, because the face he was wearing didn't look much like a smile button. I could only hope he didn't have a gun in his pocket, because he didn't appear at all glad to see me.

"Mr. Rothenberg," he said.

Well, a lot of people get it wrong. Aside from relatives, I've never come across another Rhodenbarr. I suspect the name was the gift of an overworked immigration officer at Ellis Island, but what it may have been before then is anybody's guess. People who hear it are apt to turn it into something else, while people who encounter it in print tend to mispronounce it. I don't know why, it's simple enough, ROAD-in-bar, but for some folks it turns into a tongue-twister.

"It's Rhodenbarr," I said. "And you're Dr. Mapes."

He was, but my saying so didn't make him visibly happier. Aside from the downcast expression, I'd have to say he looked pretty good. I knew he was around Marty's age, but his face was younger than his years, with no pouches under the eyes, no loose skin hanging like crepe on his neck, and a minimum of the little lines that life etches into people's faces.

His hair was dark, too, and he had a full head of it. Younger than his years, I thought, but they showed in the stoop of his shoulders and the liver spots on the backs of his hands. He might have sipped from the fountain of youth, and even splashed some of its waters on his face, but he hadn't gone for full-body immersion.

He led me inside to the living room, where his wife was waiting. She'd set out a plate of sandwiches with their crusts cut off, along with a thermos of coffee and a pair of bone china cups and saucers. She invited me to make myself at home, and said she'd just leave us men alone, as she had to be off right away if she was going to be on time for her afternoon bridge game.

I decided that Mrs. Mapes, like her husband, looked young for her age, and then I wondered how I could know that, since I had no way of knowing how old she was. Then I worked it out that her face, firm and unlined, looked younger than the rest of her. She had a dumpy figure and an old lady's walk, but if you just looked at her face . . .

And then, of course, the penny dropped. The man was a plastic surgeon, for God's sake. You'd expect him to give his wife the most youthful face his craft could furnish. And, while he would hardly operate on himself, surely he'd avail himself of the services of a skilled colleague. It wouldn't inspire confidence in a prospective patient to confront a plastic surgeon with his face sagging halfway to his waist, with a wart here and a wart there and deep wrinkles all around. It would be as disconcerting as a visit to a snaggle-toothed dentist. But the occasional nip and tuck, along with periodic injections of Botox, could make the years go away. Mapes's own face was his own best advertisement.

And as for the hair, dark and abundant . . . well, damned if the old goat wasn't wearing a rug. It was a very good one, but once I looked for it I could spot it for what it was, and right away I felt a lot more in control of the situation. Nothing gives you the upper hand like knowing the other guy is wearing somebody else's hair.

We stood around until Mrs. Mapes had backed out of the driveway and driven off. Then he pointed to the spread on the coffee table. "My wife insisted on this," he said. "She believes in applying a veneer of sociability to an essentially commercial transaction, and in this instance a distasteful one at that. But help yourself to sandwiches and coffee, if you like."

"That's awfully gracious of you," I said, "but I've got a better idea. Why don't you clear all that out of here. There isn't nearly enough to go around, and I'd hate for any of the others to feel left out."

"Others?"

"I guess I forgot to tell you," I said. "Company's coming. Let's see, we've got the sofa and the love seat and those chairs. We're going to need more chairs. Why don't you give me a hand, and for starters we'll bring in the six ladderbacks from the dining room."

"What are you talking about? I don't want any other people coming here."

"You didn't even want me," I said, "but that's the way it goes. They're on their way, and I couldn't stop them now even if I wanted to. Come on, Doc. Don't just stand there looking young. Grab a chair."

I'd come up on the subway arriving right on schedule at one o'clock. It took a while to fill the living room with chairs, and we'd barely finished before the early birds began to show up for their worms. They kept coming, by ones or twos or threes, and I took over the duties of our reluctant host, meeting them at the door and ushering them to their seats. Most of them just went where I pointed them and waited in patient silence, but now and then somebody wanted to know just what the hell was going on. I told them more would be revealed.

Barbara Creeley was there, and so was Lacey Kavinoky, and neither knew what to make of the other's presence. GurlyGurl turned out to be every bit as attractive as Carolyn had said, and closer to Laura Ashley than L. L. Bean. She sat next to Carolyn on the love seat, but had drawn a few inches away from her when Barbara arrived.

Ray showed up with a trio in tow, including William Johnson (the date-rape artist, not the safe-deposit boxholder) and a pair of police officers, out of uniform but unmistakable all the same. One was a woman, and you could still tell she was a cop. I don't know what it is that gives them away. Maybe it's the way they stare at people without the least embarrassment.

The pair split up, each electing to remain standing, one alongside the front door, the other in the archway separating the living and dining rooms, and stared hard at the rest of us. Meanwhile Ray took an armchair and put his feet on the matching ottoman, pointing Johnson to the straight-backed wooden chair on his left. Johnson looked all right—he'd had thirty-six hours to shake off the effects of the Rohypnol—but he walked carefully, rather like a man who'd been kicked in the groin.

Next through the door was Marisol Maris, living up to her name, with her sea-washed blue eyes and her sun-warmed brown skin. Wally Hemphill had brought her, on my instructions. There were a few people who might need a lawyer by the time the day was over, but she was the only one who deserved a good one, and he might as well be with her from the jump.

They chose the couch, with Wally on one end

and Marisol in the middle, and the seat beside her was claimed in a heartbeat by the next person who entered. He was a wispy young man with a wispy blond beard, and you probably would have guessed he was a painter even if he hadn't used his blue jeans as a drop cloth. He was Marisol's first cousin, from the old neighborhood in Brooklyn, and you'll know which side of the family he was on when I tell you his name, Karlis Shenk.

So far everybody had rung the bell, but the next person used the knocker. I got the door, and in came three men in suits. The first and third were young and muscular, and if they didn't spend as much time in the gym as William Johnson, they still looked capable of holding their own in a shoving match. Their suits were bargain specials from Men's Wearhouse, while the man in the middle's had been made to measure. He was well-groomed and clean-shaven, and he looked like a successful businessman, and I suppose that's what he was. He was also Johnson's uncle, and his name was Michael Quattrone. He looked around, and the seat he picked was one that gave him a good view of the room while presenting his back to the room's sole unbroken wall. His two companions stayed on their feet, and posted themselves alongside the two standing cops.

They were followed moments later by two more men in suits, but the new arrivals looked like neither businessmen nor muscle. They had to be government employees, and they were, as I learned when one of them showed me his federal ID. He withdrew it before I could catch his name, and I never did learn it, so I can't give it to you. His partner didn't show me any ID, or much respect, either, and they both found seats and sat on them like wannabe models in posture class.

Next came a tall, wraithlike man with a precise black goatee and close-cropped black hair topped with a beret, also black, which he took off upon entering the house. His slacks and turtleneck were black, as were the carpet slippers on his feet. He might have been a monk of some particularly ascetic order, or perhaps a Greenwich Village bohemian left over from the 1950s, but then he wouldn't have been accompanied by a pair of hoodlums. His name was Georgi Blinsky, and mothers in Brighton Beach invoked it to scare their children.

Blinsky looked around the room, but the only person he seemed to notice was Michael Quattrone, whom he acknowledged with a curt nod. Quattrone nodded back at him, and Blinsky found a chair and sat in it, while his two thugs posted themselves at the room's two entrances, where they glared at Quattrone's thugs and ignored the cops.

Next came Colby Riddle, who'd just wanted something to read. He used the lion's head knocker, but very tentatively, and was equally tentative when it came to mounting the threshold and coming into the house. "I'm still not sure why I'm here," he said. "But here I am."

I picked out a chair for him, not wanting to confound him with choices, and got back to the door in time to open it for Sigrid Hesselblad, who was wearing a Brooks Brothers shirt with the sleeves rolled up and a pair of jeans out at the knees and no makeup and no lipstick, and who looked drop-dead gorgeous.

Next up was a Mr. Grisek, a short and pudgy fellow dressed like a pre-Glasnost delegate to an Eastern Bloc conference on tractor maintenance. He was in fact a Latvian diplomat, and he had a one-person entourage, and that one person deserted him at the door, returning to sit behind the wheel of the limo parked across the street. Grisek didn't seem to know anybody in the room, nor did they know him; he took a seat and waited for something to happen.

He got there at 2:05, and I decided I'd wait five more minutes and then get the show on the road. I don't know if you've been counting, but I think that came to twenty-two, including me but not including the guy in the limo. I may be forgetting someone. It was a big room, but we were doing a pretty good job of filling it.

Ray was giving me a look, and people were squirming in their chairs, and it was time to get going or serve them drinks, or else I was liable to find myself facing a mutiny. I moved into position and cleared my throat, and right on cue the doorbell rang. It was Marty Gilmartin, looking splendid in a powder-blue cashmere jacket over pale gray flannel slacks. His shirt was open at the neck, and he was wearing an ascot, and was the rare sort of man who could do so without looking like a dork.

"I'm sorry I'm late," he murmured. "I had a cabdriver from hell, and he must have been trying to find his way home." I told him he was just in time, and he found himself a seat. He must have noticed Marisol Maris, and he'd have had to have spotted Crandall Rountree Mapes, aka The Shitheel, but he gave no sign of it.

My throat was already clear, but I cleared it again and got everybody's attention. There was any number of ways I could have started things off, but there's a lot to be said for tradition, and sticking with the tried and true.

"Good afternoon," I said. "I suppose you're wondering why I summoned you all here . . ."

THIRTY-SEVEN

Once upon a time," I said, "there were three independent republics on the southern shore of the Baltic Sea. Lithuania was on the west, Estonia was on the east, and the one in the middle was Latvia. They came into independent existence at the end of the First World War, and disappeared again at the onset of the Second. When Germany invaded Poland in 1939, the Soviet Union grabbed up the Baltics. Then, when Hitler went to war with Russia two years later, the Wehrmacht marched through the Baltics on their way to Stalingrad."

The Latvians in my audience seemed to be paying the most attention to this little history lesson, and they were the ones who already knew it.

"When the Nazis retreated," I went on, "the Red Army marched in again, and the Soviets established each former republic as a member state of the USSR. But the hunger for independence never died in those countries, as evidenced by the rapidity with which they broke free when the Soviet Union began to fall apart under Gorbachev.

"Almost half a century before that, when the war ended, partisan bands hid out in the forests of Latvia and launched periodic assaults upon the Soviet occupying forces. For over twenty years these Latvian wasps went on stinging the Russian bear. They couldn't turn the tide, they were just a handful of poorly armed idealists, but they knew all they had to do was survive. As long as they were out there in the woods, the spark of Latvian independence could never be entirely extinguished."

I looked around. Marisol had tears in the corners of her blue eyes, and her cousin Karlis looked as though he might burst into applause. Mr. Grisek, the Latvian attaché in the bad suit, was paying close attention, but didn't seem as emotional about it.

But the rest of my audience was growing restive, with here and there an eye glazing over. I tried to hurry it along.

"Of course the Russians did what they could to squelch the unrest and wipe out the partisan bands. They didn't give it top priority. If it was enough for the partisans to keep the cauldron simmering, so it was enough for the Soviets to keep a lid on it. Different men had that assignment over the years, all of their efforts falling somewhere between failure and success. Then, sometime in the early Seventies, they gave the job to a man named Valentine Kukarov.

"Kukarov was a Russian, born in Tashkent around the time the Russian winter was stopping the Nazi advance in its tracks. He was around thirty when they sent him to Riga, and he'd already achieved a high rank in the KGB. He went after the Latvian partisans the way William Gorgas went after yellow fever mosquitoes in Panama. Anyone suspected of anti-Soviet activity was executed as an enemy of the state. Anyone who might have knowledge of such activity was interrogated, and the question-and-answer sessions often ended in death. He wasn't there long before Latvians started calling him the Black Scourge of Riga, and the name stayed with him when his superiors shifted him to another assignment. He got a promotion, because he'd done what nobody else could do. He didn't stifle the desire for independence, nobody could have done that, but he left the citizenry in no position to do anything about it. Hundreds of partisans had been killed, hundreds more were shipped to the Gulag, and thousands of ordinary Latvian citizens were relocated to remote regions of the USSR, their places in Latvia taken by Russians more likely to be loyal subjects of the men in power.

"Somewhere along the way, Kukarov stopped being all that loyal himself. On an overseas assignment, he got turned by an American agent who got him to double. He went on for a few years playing both ends against the middle, until it was clear that his KGB bosses were catching on to him, whereupon he told his CIA control he wanted to defect.

"They told him lots of luck, but you're on your own. It was one thing to co-opt the Black Scourge of Riga and make clandestine use of him, but it was quite another to welcome him into the land of the free and help him cram for his naturalization test."

"Well, that's the fucking government for you," said Michael Quattrone.

A few heads turned at that, but when he didn't say anything further they turned back to me.

"In 1987," I said, "Kukarov came over on his own. He must have had his pick of fake passports, and an entry visa for the US wouldn't have been hard for him to arrange. He'd already shaved his heavy black beard, and as soon as he got here he bought himself a blond wig, plucked his bushy black eyebrows, and dyed them to match the wig. He wasn't worried that the KGB would stay up nights trying to find him. The only thing he had to worry about was the Latvian-American community, and he wasn't greatly worried, because he'd been careful all his life about not having his picture taken. He was fairly sure nobody had a decent photo of him. They might have a description, but it no longer fit him, so what good would it do them?

"Then Latvia became independent. And, even worse from Kukarov's point of view, the Soviet Union collapsed and access to secret KGB files was suddenly a lot easier to come by. And the KGB had several nice clear photographs of him. Of course he was a little older now, and he kept the eyebrows plucked and dyed, and shaved twice a day, and never went anywhere without the blond wig.

"Add in the fact that more Latvians were finding their way into the country, either as immigrants or as embassy staff. It had been twenty years since the heyday of the Black Scourge of Riga, but that didn't mean anybody was ready to forgive and forget. If someone who knew him when were to take a hard look at him and got to imagining him with dark hair and bushy eyebrows, well, that wouldn't be so great. Where could he go, Australia? There were plenty of Latvians in Australia. And he was past fifty, and too old to start over somewhere new.

"He came up with a way out. Plastic surgery. And which eminent plastic surgeon do you think he picked?"

Mapes knew this was coming, he must have seen it coming a mile off, but he still winced a little. I was more interested in watching some other faces, only a few of which turned to look at the good doctor.

"The physician he chose," I went on, "was a board-certified plastic surgeon with an excellent professional reputation. He did the usual run of nose jobs and facelifts and liposuction and tummy tucks, putting caviar on the table by making the well-to-do a little easier to look at. He also did a good deal of reconstructive surgery on burn victims and accident survivors and children born with facial birth defects. A lot of his work with kids was what lawyers would call **pro bono**. I don't know if doctors would call it that or something else, but whatever you call it he didn't get paid for it."

I glanced over at Marty, who appeared surprised. Nobody, I'd have to tell him, can be a shitheel a hundred percent of the time. It's too exhausting.

"Somewhere along the way," I said, "this doctor became first acquainted and then involved with what we might call the criminal element. Maybe he found criminals fascinating. Many of us do. Or maybe he just saw a way to turn an extra dollar, a dollar to be paid in cash, and one he could thus forget to report when he filed his tax return."

The two government men tried to keep straight faces, but they weren't very good at it. I had their attention now, and it showed.

"He did some favors. Took out bullets and cleaned the wounds without making a report, the way the law says you have to. Maybe he wrote out a few death certificates, putting down cardiac arrest as the cause of death. Well, it always is. If somebody cuts your throat or puts a bullet in the back of your head, you die when your heart stops beating. So he wasn't exactly lying . . .

"Still, he was heroically overqualified for that sort of work, and it was only a question of time before someone made better use of his abilities. He became the man to see if you wanted to change your face to one the law wouldn't recognize. The people who needed his services would pay big money, and they'd pay it in cash, and wouldn't try to deduct it from their own taxes, either. And there was no hospital cutting into the pie, because he had to do the work in the privacy of his own office. That was generally safe enough with facial surgery, and if anything went wrong, well, he could just fill out the death certificate appropriately. But why should anything go wrong? Nothing ever did, and it wasn't long before he'd paid off the mortgage on the big house in Riverdale and had a nice cash cushion in the bargain."

That got some heads to turn. Whoever hadn't already figured it out now knew that their host for the afternoon was the very doctor I was talking about.

So why not call him by name?

"One day," I said, "Dr. Crandall R. Mapes had a visitor, referred by one of his associates in the world of organized crime. The man wore a blond wig and explained the steps he'd already taken to alter his appearance. But he still had the same face underneath it all, and he wanted a new one.

"Dr. Mapes agreed to take him as a patient, and the two settled on a price. Mapes took pictures, as he always did for every client, a group of shots showing the subject's face from various angles. He studied the photographs at length, devised a plan, and, on the appointed day, performed the first of a series of surgeries upon the face of Valentine Kukarov."

"You're slandering me in my own home," Mapes said, "in front of a roomful of witnesses."

"They say it ain't bragging if it's true," I told him, "and the same thing holds for slander."

"You can't prove any of this." He got to his feet. "Allegations, nothing but allegations. I'm damned if I'm going to listen to allegations." I don't know if he was going for the front door or the dining room, but his body language was saying **See ya later, Allegator.**

He didn't get very far. Before he could take the first step, the two feds rose to their feet, while the two trios of cops and goons at the room's two exits all but linked arms to block his flight. That gave him pause, and then Michael Quattrone said, "Sit down, Mapes," and he sat.

"The operations," I said, "were a success. Dr. Mapes gave Kukarov a new nose and refigured his jawline. He shaved his cheekbones to make him look less Slavic, and took ten to fifteen years off his appearance by lifting what had begun to droop, tightening the loose skin on the neck, and doing a little work around and under the eyes. He got rid of a scar at the side of Kukarov's mouth. Nobody knew about it back in Latvia, he'd grown the beard to hide it, but it was a distinguishing mark in the American version of Kukarov, and Mapes got rid of it for him. He pitched the blond hairpiece, reworked the hairline with a combination of surgery and electrolysis, improved the eyebrows permanently with some more electrolysis, and taught his patient to dye his hair and eyebrows a light brown that was becoming enough while less attention-getting than what he'd had. Besides"—I glanced pointedly at Mapes, who glowered back from beneath his rug—"sooner or later someone recognizes even the best wig for what it is, and starts wondering what you'd look like without it."

"So he fixed him up good," Ray said. "Then what?"

"Then he took some more photographs," I said, "and collected the balance of his fee, and sent the Black Scourge of Riga on his way."

"Excuse me," said Grisek, the man from the Latvian embassy. "Kukarov allowed him to retain these photographs?"

"Certainly not. He'd always been cautious to the point of paranoia on the subject of photos, and now that he had a new face he certainly didn't want pictures of it floating around."

"Ah."

"Mapes insisted on taking the photos," I said, "because he needed them for reference while the work was in progress. The surgeries took months, and he took more shots along the way to chart his progress. And he snapped a last batch upon completion as well, so that he and his patient could view them side by side, Before and After, and see just how substantive a change Mapes had worked in Kukarov's appearance."

"That's standard," Mapes said. "Everyone in the field does it."

"That's what you told Kukarov. And he let you do it because you assured him that, when your work was over, all copies of the photos would be destroyed."

"The man insisted."

"As other men had insisted before him. And you agreed, as you had agreed before. But you didn't keep your word, did you? You held on to four photos, mug shots, really. Before and after, full-face and profile. Just as you kept of all your patients, legitimate and criminal."

He winced a little at the last word, then rallied to tell me what a valuable, even essential, reference library the photos constituted.

"Pardon my Latvian," I said, "but that's a load of crap. You kept the pictures to feed your ego. You knew you shouldn't have the pictures, so you didn't keep them with the rest. Instead you Scotch-taped them to the pages of a book and stuck it on the shelf in your office. Maybe you got a kick out of it, having it right out in plain sight, where anybody could pick it up and page through it. But of course nobody did. **Principles of Organic Chemistry, Volume Two.** Sounds like a real page-turner, doesn't it?"

"They were readily available for reference," he said, "yet secreted so that no one would find them. You said it yourself, Rothenberg." I didn't correct him. The man was hopeless. "Even if you were searching the place, you'd never pick up that book. And no one would stumble on it by accident."

"Suppose they'd read Volume One, and didn't want to miss the sequel? Never mind. Let's say the photos were safe there. But you didn't just drool over them in private. Every once in a while you couldn't resist pulling the book down and showing off. Every now and then you just had to impress some sweet young thing by showing her the dangerous men whose faces you'd rearranged."

"They didn't know the men, they weren't going to tell anybody, it was perfectly safe . . ."

His voice trailed off. Everyone was staring at him now, except for Marty, who was gazing thoughtfully at Marisol, and Marisol, who was examining her feet.

"If it was so damn safe," I said, "how come we're all here? How come four people are dead?" I sighed. "It might have been safe. Unethical, dishonest, illegal, but safe. Except you forgot one thing. You forgot the long arm of coincidence."

THIRTY-EIGHT

I liked the phrase enough to say it again. "The long arm of coincidence. The law has a proverbially lengthy arm, but so does coincidence. I checked my **Bartlett's** this morning, and a fellow named Haddon Chambers coined the phrase back in 1888, in his play **Captain Swift**. He was born in 1860 and died in 1921, and except for his one immortal line, that's as much as I know about Haddon Chambers. Of course you could go and Google him, and you'll probably get his blood type and his mother's maiden name, along with Whittaker Chambers and Haddon's Notch, New Hampshire.

"The long arm of coincidence. There's a hand at the end of that arm, and it's left its fingerprints all over this business. Starting with the time a couple of weeks ago when Mapes took Volume Two down from the shelf to show off to his latest girlfriend."

"That's terrible," Lacey Kavinoky said. "On top of everything else, the man cheats on his wife." She colored, embarrassed by her outburst. "I'm sorry, I didn't mean to pipe up like that."

"How could you help it? It's shocking, and we're all shocked. Still, there's a fair amount of it going around. What's coincidental is that the woman in question was the daughter of a Latvian immigrant."

"And he showed her Cuckoo's pitcher anyway?" Ray said. "Not too bright, is he, Bernie?"

"Not the sharpest scalpel in the autoclave," I allowed, "but all he knew about Kukarov was that he was Russian. The man wouldn't have mentioned the Riga connection, let alone that he was the Black Scourge thereof. 'Now this man,' Mapes told her, 'came here from Russia to make a new life for himself, and thanks to me he doesn't have to look over his shoulder for KGB operatives.' The pictures didn't mean a thing to her, Before or After. But she knew the name. There aren't too many Latvians—or half-Latvians, for that matter—who wouldn't recognize the name of Valentine Kukarov."

Grisek said something in an undertone, but even in an overtone I wouldn't have understood it, because he was speaking in his native tongue. I found out later that it was something along the lines of **May the fires of Hell consume him, starting at the toes and taking eternity to reach his cursed head.** I'd have pardoned his Latvian, but nobody asked me to.

"Marisol was the girl's name. That doesn't sound Latvian, but don't worry about it. She'd heard her father talk about Kukarov, and would have gone to him for advice, but he was back home in Oakmont, Pennsylvania. But she had an aunt and uncle in Bay

Ridge, and they agreed that she had to get hold of those photographs.

"But how? She'd been to her lover's office once, at his invitation. There was no reason for him to invite her again, and no plausible way she could invite herself. The way things stood, if the book disappeared he'd never suspect her; he'd put it back himself before ushering her out of the office. But if she were to pay him another visit, and **then** the book went missing . . .

"Her cousin Karlis came up with the answer. An artist with a loft in Williamsburg, he made an appointment with Dr. Mapes. He showed up twenty minutes early, looking perfectly respectable in his weddings-and-funerals suit, and when the receptionist was out of the room he pulled down **Principles of Organic Chemistry** and popped it in his tote bag. He could have torn out the four pages with Kukarov's photos on them, but maybe that would have taken too much time."

"I never saw the man," Karlis said. "Or the photos. So how would I know which ones to take?"

"But when you showed the book to your cousin, she could point out the photographs Mapes had identified as Kukarov's." He nodded. "Once she did, why not tear out those pages and return the book?"

"What, go to his office again? The one time I saw him I had to make up a reason. I couldn't think of anything. He asked me what I wanted. 'Look at me,' I said. 'What do you think?' Well, he tells me, my nose is crooked, and my ears stick out a little, but these are all things he can fix. Up until then I thought I looked fine. Now every time I pass a mirror I turn my head the other way. I should go back there? Hey, Doc. You know what? Screw you!"

"Your ears do stick out," Mapes said, "and your nose **is** crooked, and I never asked you to come to my office in the first place."

"The book," I said. "**Principles of Organic Chemistry.** After Marisol identified Kukarov, you took it home and gave it to your father."

"So?"

"And he showed it to a man who was living under the name Rogovin, but who'd been calling himself Arnold Lyle. I don't know what his name was originally, or what scam Lyle and his wife or girlfriend were working at the time."

"Hard to say," Ray put in. "He was a guy who took what came along. When opportunity came knockin', he opened the door, even if it was somebody else's apartment."

"The Lyles had sublet a place in Murray Hill," I said, "and whatever they had going on, they were glad to make room for Kukarov. Lyle was a Latvian, after all, and he'd gladly do his part to give the Black Scourge of Riga what he deserved. But Lyle didn't see why they couldn't turn a profit on the deal. Not from their fellow countrymen, but from some parties who might be interested in some of the other fellows who'd posed for Mapes's candid camera.

"So he got the word out, letting a few interested

parties know what he had to sell. I believe you were one of those parties, Mr. Blinsky."

I looked at him, and he looked back at me, and I could feel myself shrinking under his gaze. If you wrote a play called **The Black Scourge of Riga,** he's the guy you'd cast in the title role. His clothes were all black, and so was his hair and beard, and his whole affect was decidedly scourge-like. I was going to tell him he hadn't answered my question, but then I realized that I hadn't asked one, and I decided to move on.

"Marisol had done her part," I said, "but now she was beginning to have second thoughts. She'd grown up hearing about Kukarov's evil deeds, but the closest she'd ever been to Latvia was a weekend in East Hampton, and he'd done the bulk of his scourging before she was born. And what had she done? She'd betrayed a trust, for one thing, and she might have imperiled Mapes's other clandestine clients, men who may have run afoul of the law but who had done nothing to her, or to her fellow Latvians.

"So she did what a lot of people do when they're feeling disturbed. She went out and had a couple of drinks."

Wally Hemphill went into a quick huddle with his client. "She's over twenty-one," he told the room. "If she wants to have a drink it's her business."

"I never said it wasn't."

"Well," he said, "I object to this whole line of

questioning, and I'm advising my client not to answer any more questions."

"I haven't asked any."

"If you do, I reserve the right to object."

I closed my eyes for a moment, but what good did it do? When I opened them, everybody was still there. This next part was tricky, and I hoped he'd shut up so I could get it right.

"She lives in Hell's Kitchen, but she didn't want to go where she might run into someone she knew. So she went east and south a short distance, to a place someone had recommended. A nice place, some of you may know it. She went in and had a drink, and then a man came and bought her another drink, and the next thing she knew she was in bed in her own apartment with a man on top of her, and—"

"Objection!"

I glared at him, and he shrugged apologetically. "You know," I said, "you're not in court, but if you were I'd hold you in contempt."

"I'm sorry, Bernie."

"Just keep a lid on it," I said. "She came out of a blackout, and she tried to make the guy stop, but she couldn't, and then she went back into a blackout, and when she came to hours later he was gone, and so was a piece of jewelry Doc Mapes had given her."

"The necklace," Mapes said, and colored deeply when eyes turned toward him. I don't think he meant to say anything.

"The necklace," Marisol confirmed. "The beautiful ruby necklace you gave me, that I loved so much. I woke up and it was gone."

"And what did you remember?"

"At first," she said, "I hardly remembered anything. I remembered him buying me a drink, and I remembered waking up and . . . and trying to fight him off, to make him stop what he was doing. It was horrible."

"And did your memory come back?"

I saw Wally lean forward, and I was afraid he was going to cite me for leading the witness. But he got himself in check.

"Parts of it," she said. "I was so upset about the book of photographs, and I remember that I talked to him about it. I don't know exactly what I said, but I told him things I should have kept to myself." She frowned. "I don't understand it. I didn't have that much to drink. I never get like that, not on two drinks."

"You were drugged," I said.

"I thought maybe that's what happened."

"The man who drugged you," I said, "and went home with you, and raped you, and stole your necklace. Do you know who he is?"

"I don't know his name. I never saw him before that night, and I never saw him since." She paused, and her timing was right on the money. "Until today, in this room."

"Could you point him out?"

She got shakily to her feet, hesitated, touched her

forefinger to her lower lip, trembled, and then thrust her hand dramatically in the direction of William Johnson. "Him," she said. "He did it."

You'd think the dumb son of a bitch would have seen it coming. After all, it was his MO, and I wouldn't have been surprised if he'd tried to patent it. But he was at a distinct disadvantage, in that he knew for a fact he'd never seen the girl before. With her Northern hair and eyes and her complexion out of the warm South, she wasn't someone he could have seen and forgotten, and he'd certainly remember her if he'd taken her home. He might not know where she was going with all of this, but there was no way she could be coming in his direction.

And here she was, sticking her little finger straight at him.

"No way, man. No fuckin' way. I never saw this chick before in my life."

"Really," I said. "The bar's called Parsifal's. Do you know it?"

"I was there maybe once or twice."

"Ever take a woman home?"

"Maybe. But not this broad. I told you, I never saw her."

"Ever put something in a drink to improve your chances?"

"Hey, c'mon," he said, and flexed some muscles. "You think I need any help?"

"Then you're saying you didn't slip Rohypnol to Marisol Maris?"

"Is that the chick's name? No, I never slipped her nothing. Not what you just said, and not what **she** says I slipped her."

"In fact you never saw her before."

"Never." He changed expressions, trying for sincere. "What happened to her's horrible, but I had nothin' to do with it. You got the wrong guy."

There was a silence, and Sigrid waited a beat before picking up her cue. "Oh, William," she said, exasperated. "You're so full of shit it's coming out your pores."

He stared.

"I've seen you operate," she said. "You're quite the stud, showing off your muscles and chatting up the ladies. You buy them one drink and the next thing I know they're out the door with you. I figured you had a hell of a line, or maybe you were oozing some kind of sex appeal that I couldn't see. I noticed that some of them looked a little woozy on the way out, but I just assumed lust was interfering with their motor skills. It never occurred to me that you were feeding them Roofies."

"This is crazy," he said.

"I'll say it is." To me she said, "He hit on me a few nights ago. I brushed him off, or it would have been my turn to wake up sleeping in the wet spot with my Diamonique earrings nowhere to be found. You came in the night before last, William.

Remember? You tried to pick up two girls at once, and I think maybe they switched drinks on you, because you got a fit of the blind staggers and barely made it out the door."

You could see him processing the information. So that's what happened—the bitches had switched drinks with him, and next thing he knew he was coming to in an alley, covered with his own vomit, with his cash and cards gone and an aching groin that only bothered him on days ending in a **Y**.

And there were people in the room he might have seen before. The brunette, for instance, dressed for success, her hair up. He'd pulled her out of some-place, and it could have been Parsifal's. And even I looked vaguely familiar, like maybe we hung out in some of the same bars. But this chick going on about her necklace and the pictures her cousin stole, he knew damn well he never saw her before in his life.

But I was just guessing. I couldn't really read his mind. For all I knew, he was thinking about super-setting bent-over rows with reverse-grip chins, and what that might do for his lats.

"You went home with her necklace," I said, "not to mention the warm glow that comes from an evening spent doing the Lord's work. And when you woke up you thought about the story she'd told, about a book full of photos of men who'd bought new faces in an effort to keep the past from catching up with them. You figured that kind of information ought to be worth something to the right people, and so you picked up the phone and called your Uncle Mike."

His jaw dropped, but I didn't care if it hit the floor and went through to the basement. I was through with him for now, and turned to Michael Quattrone, who'd been following the proceedings with interest. "Your nephew called you," I said, "and you saw an opportunity. You put the word out, and somebody picked up something about two people named Rogovin in an apartment at Third Avenue and 34th Street."

I'm not sure what my next sentence would have been, but Quattrone stopped me there by raising one well-manicured hand six inches into the air. "You put on a very good show," he said judiciously. "It's instructive and entertaining at the same time."

"Thank you."

"But you've got one thing wrong. My nephew never mentioned anything about Mapes and his photographs."

"You're saying you were unaware of them?"

"I was aware of them," he said. "There's no end of things of which the observant man becomes aware. But I never heard a word on the subject from my nephew." He looked over at Johnson, with something a few degrees cooler than avuncular affection. "My nephew. The son of my younger sister and the man she picked out all by herself and married."

"He didn't call you?"

"I guess he didn't need anything," Quattrone said. "He only calls when he needs something. Money, a lawyer. Something along those lines."

"Uncle Mike—"

"Shut up, Billy." To me he said, "You may have heard of a man named John Mullane."

"The name's familiar."

"He's also known as Whitey Mullane. You watch **America's Most Wanted**?"

Religiously, hoping I won't see myself on it. "Jersey City," I said. "Or was it Newark? He ran rackets there for years, and at the same time he was working with the FBI. And now he's running away from a murder indictment—"

"Four counts, plus other charges."

"—and they update his profile every few months, and John Walsh says how we need to catch this coward, and they never do."

"And they won't," Quattrone said, "as long as they go on looking for the face he doesn't have anymore, thanks to our friend here." A nod to Mapes. "The man's an idiot, but he does good work. Whitey Mullane was like a father to me, I've known him since I was an altar boy, and I have to tell you, if I hadn't seen the Before picture I wouldn't have known the After picture was him."

"You saw the pictures."

"You know," he said, "I don't recall saying that. As I remember, I spoke a sentence with an 'if' in it."

"So you did. Well, last Wednesday some men paid a call on the Rogovins, or the Lyles, or whatever we want to call them. They overpowered the doorman, left him immobile in the parcel room, and went upstairs, where the Lyles opened the door for them. Then the Lyles opened the safe for them, probably at gunpoint. I don't know why the Lyles got themselves a heavy-duty Mosler safe. They didn't need all that just to provide a short-term home for an outdated college textbook. My guess is it was in conjunction with another enterprise of theirs, and they're dead, so it hardly matters.

"Because the visitors got the book, and in return for their cooperation the Lyles got two bullets in the back of the head. Meanwhile the doorman, wrapped up in duct tape, suffocated. Three people were dead, and the book was gone.

"And wouldn't you know it, even while they were going about their business, the long arm of coincidence was reaching to take me by the collar. It turned itself into the long arm of the law, which I'd call a familiar quotation, even though Bartlett doesn't seem to think so. Here's the coincidence. On the night in question, I was taking the air in the same neighborhood where the Lyles lived and died. Half a dozen different security cameras recorded my passing. It doesn't matter why I was there, I had a perfect right to be there, but coincidentally enough I was once convicted of burglary, and my presence on the scene was enough to induce that gentleman there"— I nodded toward Ray, and they looked at him—"to place me under arrest. And that gentleman there"— I nodded at Wally— "secured my speedy release.

But by then the word was out, and people had reason to think I might be involved."

I looked at Michael Quattrone. "If I were to ask you a hypothetical question, do you think it might be possible for you to answer it?"

He smiled without moving his lips. "It might," he said.

"If someone you knew pulled the home invasion on 34th Street," I said, "and if the Lyles let them in and opened the safe for them, why did they have to shoot them?"

"That's easy," he said. "They didn't."

● THIRTY-NINE

Of course we're speaking hypothetically," Michael Quattrone said. His eyes swept the room, pausing on their way to make brief but significant eye contact with Ray Kirschmann and Wally Hemphill. "And, as we've been reminded, this is not a courtroom. No one's taking down what's being said, and I would hope no one's wearing a wire, but even if there's a record kept, we're speaking hypothetically."

"Of course."

"In that case," he said, "let's suppose a certain person was to learn that an old friend of his had photos of his new face floating around, up for sale to the highest bidder. And suppose he found out where the photos were, and when the bidder was going to show up to finalize the transaction. And suppose he sent some friends of his to show up before the bidder, and shortstop the whole operation."

"Taking the photos by force," I said, "before the other party could arrive to pay for them."

"Something like that," he agreed. "Now, if anything like that happened, I imagine this certain person's friends would have immobilized the doorman, so as to come and go unannounced. And I imagine the people in the apartment—you've been calling them the Lyles—"

"Or the Rogovins. As you prefer."

"Let's call them the Rogovins, then. It's such a stereotype otherwise, isn't it? Criminals with foreign-sounding names that end in a vowel. Like Lyle." Once again he managed to smile without moving his lips. "Let's say Mr. Rogovin heard a knock on the door and opened it, thinking he was about to get rich. A couple of guys came in, and as soon as they opened their mouths he knew they weren't the men he was expecting. But what could he do about it? He opened the safe for them, and they took the book and the money."

"Wait a minute," Ray said. "What money?"

He chose his words carefully. "I would have to assume there would have been money," he said. "Why lock a chemistry textbook in a safe? But if you already had a sum of money in there, you might as well put the book in with it."

"How much money?"

"I can only estimate. Perhaps as much as twenty-one thousand dollars. Or as little as nineteen thousand."

"In round numbers," I said, "twenty thousand."

"In round numbers. Perhaps the high bidder paid some earnest money in advance, to bind the transaction. Perhaps the money was the proceeds of some other enterprise. I'm sure the men who took it thought of it as a welcome if unexpected bonus."

"My original question—"

"Was why did they kill the Rogovins. My answer was that they didn't. They left them trussed with tape, which held them while they had a quick look around the apartment to see if it held anything else worth taking. It would also keep the Rogovins incapacitated while they quit the building and left the area. After that, what threat did the two of them represent? They could hardly file a police report. In any case, they didn't know the identities of the men who robbed them. Killing them would just generate heat, and to no purpose."

"And the doorman? He suffocated before the cops found him."

"That was unfortunate," Quattrone said. "It was an accident, and it should never have happened." His eyes flicked ever so briefly toward the doorway, where one of his goons was looking at the floor with the fascination of someone who had never seen carpet before. "I wouldn't be surprised," he said, "if the person responsible didn't very much regret what happened."

"Someone shot those two people," I said. "They were all taped up, and they'd been shot in the head. If it wasn't your hypothetical men—"

"It wasn't."

"—then who was it?"

"Bern?" I turned at Carolyn's voice. "The high bidder," she said. "He was on his way over, right?"

"Of course," I said. "There was a second party of visitors to the apartment on East 34th Street. The doorman was still **hors de combat,** so all they had to do was walk in and go upstairs. They'd have found the door unlocked and the safe wide open and the occupants all taped up. Maybe they took the tape off one of their mouths long enough to get some questions answered. They wouldn't have liked the answers, wouldn't have been happy to go away without the book of photos, and without a chance of recovering the twenty grand they'd paid in front. Whether that was half in advance or payment in full, it was a big chunk of dough, and there was no way to get it back."

I could feel eyes staring at me, and they were Georgi Blinsky's. "You were the high bidder," I told him. "You showed up to keep the appointment. When the Lyles couldn't supply either the photographs or the money, you executed them and left."

"You can prove nothing," he said. "You have no evidence and no witnesses. When all of this was taking place, I was with large party at Georgian nightclub on Oriental Boulevard. Many people will swear to this."

"I'm sure they will. Why kill them?"

He looked at me, as if he found the question disappointing. Then he said, "No book, no money. So? No witnesses, either. But I was with friends, in nightclub. I can prove this, and you can prove nothing."

• • •

"The next thing that happened," I said, "is that my apartment was broken into. It had already been searched by the police, but the men who broke in probably didn't know that. My doorman was trussed up and locked in the parcel room, the same as the Lyles' doorman, so it seems safe to assume the same people were responsible."

"I can see where you'd assume that," Michael Quattrone said.

"They tore the place apart. What do you suppose they were looking for?"

"The missing photos," he said without hesitation. "Whoever sent them must have heard about these photos of a missing Russian, and none of the pictures in that chemistry textbook looked like they could have been that man. And there were pages missing from the book, as if somebody had torn them out. Four pages, which would work out to one set of four photos."

"And you had a use for them?"

"A lot of people wanted them. It's human to want what everybody wants. Besides, who's to say what else a person might find in a burglar's apartment? It seemed worth a visit."

And while they were there, I said with my eyes, **your ham-handed thugs broke open my secret cupboard and took my money.**

When you find money, his eyes answered back,

you take it, and if I were you I'd be glad they left you the passports.

Funny how much information can be exchanged without a word being spoken . . .

"I'm having trouble following this," Lacey Kavinoky said. "I mean, maybe I'm not supposed to follow it. I'm not sure what I'm doing here in the first place. But I thought the photographs were in the book. But I gather some pages were torn out. Those were the photos of this Russian? The Black Scourge of Riga?"

"That's right."

"Who tore them out? And why?"

"The Lyles," I said. "They were Latvian patriots, after all. They might try to get some money for Kukarov's photos, but they'd make sure they went to a good home—somebody who'd track the man down and bring him to justice."

A nod from Grisek confirmed my supposition.

"So they removed those four pages," I said, "and cut the photos free from the backing, and taped them to the pages of another book."

"The one about the quarterback," Ray Kirschmann said.

"You know," I said, "you used that phrase once before, Ray, and I didn't know what the hell you were talking about, so I let it pass. But now I get it, and **QB VII** isn't about a quarterback."

"It ain't?"

"It's a novel by Leon Uris, based on what he

went through when some Nazi sued him for libel. The title is the name of the British courtroom where the trial took place."

"Well, how's anybody supposed to know that, Bernie? An' who gives a rat's ass, anyway? What I want to know is why didn't the poor saps turn the book over to this Blintz guy so's to keep from gettin' shot? It was still there in the bookcase, right where anybody could find it."

"Not just anybody," I said. "It took a skilled professional, gifted with imagination and resourcefulness. You're being too modest, Ray. When you told me how you went through every book in the bookcase until you found one with torn pages bearing telltale tape residue, it was clear what had happened. Somebody had found those photographs and spirited them away."

This was all news to Ray, and I could see him working hard to adjust to new realities. Well, who told him to mention **QB VII**?

"It wouldn't have saved them," I said, moving along smoothly, "and they must have known that. And who's to say they had a chance to raise the subject even if they wanted to?"

"So this guy took the book," Lacey said, pointing at Quattrone, "and that guy murdered the man and woman," she went on, nodding at Blinsky, "and the photos were still in the apartment. Right?"

"Hypothetically," said Michael Quattrone.

"Hypothetically," I agreed.

"Whatever," she said. "But if somebody found them, and tore them out of the book, they aren't there anymore. Right?"

"Right."

"Okay," she said, and flashed a smile at Carolyn. "I like to understand stuff. That's all."

I like to understand stuff, too, especially if I'm called upon to explain it. But sometimes you can start with the explanation and wait for the understanding to come along in its wake. That had worked once already—until Quattrone spoke, it hadn't occurred to me that the Lyles could have had a second set of visitors after the first set made off with the book.

So I pressed on.

"Wednesday the Lyles were robbed and murdered," I said, "and Thursday I got arrested and burglarized, and Friday morning coincidence once again hove into view. I got a phone call from a customer of mine, and perhaps he can tell us what he asked me for."

"I guess it's my turn," Colby Riddle said. "I certainly thought my request was innocent enough. I'd called your bookstore, Bernie, and I asked if you had a particular book."

"Not **Principles of Organic Chemistry,** I don't suppose."

"I'm afraid not. Nor **QB VII,** by the much

lamented Mr. Uris. I asked for a book by Joseph Conrad."

"I don't suppose you remember the title?"

"**The Secret Agent.** You determined that you did, and said you'd set it aside for me. I said I'd come by and pick it up when I had the chance, and I suppose we exchanged further pleasantries, though perhaps we didn't, as that's as much as I can recall."

"That may have been all there was," I said, "because I didn't know who you were."

"Why didn't you ask my name?"

"Because your voice was familiar, Colby, and you sounded as though you assumed I'd know who you were, and I didn't want to appear boorish. I'd hardly had any sleep the night before, so I wasn't at my best. I was sure I'd know you when you showed up."

"And so you did, Bernie. But you didn't have the book anymore."

"Because I'd given it to a man named Valdi Berzins," I said. "Mr. Grisek, I believe you may have known him."

The Latvian nodded, looking unhappy. "A good man," he said. "A fine man. A patriotist."

"It was he to whom the Lyles had promised the Kukarov photos, wasn't it?"

"He did not tell me the detailings," Grisek said. His English was unaccented, but also unorthodox. "And always he looked on the side where the sun was. 'The photos have been thieved,' he told me, 'so I will make my deal with the thief. And perhaps he is less of a thief than the man he took them from.' You know this book, **The Power to Think Positive?**"

"That's **The Power of Positive Thinking**," I said, "by Norman Vincent Peale. A great bestseller in its day. I've got two or three copies in the store, and I suppose I ought to put them on the bargain table, but I somehow feel I owe it to the author to think that someone'll come along and pay full price for it."

"Valdi Berzins was positively thinking, Mr. Rhodenbarr. He went to your bookstore with money to pay for the book. And instead he was killed."

I said I saw it happen, and one of the women said it must have been awful for me, and I said it was worse for Berzins. "He came into the shop and said I must have something for him. And I didn't know what he was talking about, and then I remembered Colby Riddle's phone call, although I still didn't know who'd been on the other end of the phone. I knew it wasn't Berzins, the voice was wrong, but he seemed so confident I would know what he wanted, and that was all I could think of. I said the book's title, and that seemed to make him happy, and he sure didn't argue about the price. He paid me a hundred times what I asked him for, evidently assuming that I was leaving off the word **hundred** to save time. I realized this just in time to run outside after him and watch him get killed. If there hadn't been a parked car in the way, I might have been killed along with him."

"Who killed him?" Grisek demanded. "Who killed my friend Berzins?"

"That's a good question. Here's another. Why did he assume I'd know what book he wanted? And, when I mentioned the book by name, why did it make him happy?"

"You said **The Secret Agent,**" Carolyn said, "and that was him. He thought you were recognizing him for what he was."

"That's what I thought at first, but it doesn't add up. It still doesn't explain why he thought I'd have a book for him, or why he was happy with the one I handed him. He didn't flip through it looking for pictures. He just paid for it and left. Colby, what made you ask for that particular book?"

"I'd been looking for a copy. It's a book, and you're a bookseller, and so—"

"You don't much care for Conrad."

"I don't like his sea stories. I'm told **The Secret Agent** is the sort of book the man might have written if he'd never gone to sea. I thought it worth a try."

"And worth a phone call."

"Why not?"

"But I think you already got a phone call," I said. "From a plastic surgeon."

"Bernie," he said, "you can't be serious. I may look like a candidate for plastic surgery, but I'm afraid I lack the requisite vanity. Am I to assume the plastic surgeon in question is our host, Dr. Mapes? Why would you think I even know the man? How would we have met?"

"At school," I said, "or on a bus, or in an Internet chat room, with both of you pretending to be lesbians. But if I had to guess, I'd say your dermatologist referred you. Maybe you had a suspicious mole on your face, in a spot that was sufficiently visible to warrant a plastic surgeon's doing the work."

"How could you possibly know something like that?"

"Just a wild guess. What I can't figure out is how you knew Valdi Berzins."

"I didn't."

"You must have. The two of you probably had a friend in common, some professor teaching a course called **Latvian as a Second Language**. One way or another, you knew both of them. And you called Mapes, or Mapes called you, and he let you know about these photos, and that he had a few hundred thousand dollars in a wall safe in his bedroom, and—"

"Hold it right there," said one of the government men. They were both on their feet. One of them was holding a gun, while the other brandished a piece of paper. "I was wondering when you'd get around to the reason we're here. A couple of hundred thousand dollars in undeclared cash, that sounds about right." He whirled on Mapes. "Crandall Rountree Mapes? I'm from Internal Revenue, and I have here a court order authorizing my partner and I—"

My partner and me, I thought, you federal dimwit.

"—to search said Devonshire Close premises. Sir, I'd like you to escort us upstairs and open the safe for us."

Mapes had weathered everything up to this point. Now it was as if the hand of fate had come at him with a scalpel and savaged all the fine work some colleague had done for him. He aged ten years just like that, and his color faded even as the perspiration poured out of him.

He was sputtering, something about an attorney, and the IRS man told him he could get one later, but in the meantime they were damn well going to have a look at that safe. Wally Hemphill scanned the piece of paper and told Mapes yes, they had the authority, and there was nothing he could do but keep his mouth shut.

"The rest of you wait down here," the other IRS agent said.

And off they went.

 **FORTY**

They weren't gone long, and when they came back, well, as Carolyn has been known to say, the worm was on the other foot. The IRS robots looked thoroughly disgruntled, so much so that it was hard to believe they had ever been gruntled to begin with, while Mapes had somehow reclaimed the face someone had constructed for him.

"Well, I told you," he said. "And now you can tell the rest of these ladies and gentlemen. Was there any money in that safe?"

They glared at him.

"I'll take that as a no," he said. "Insurance policies, stock certificates. A few pieces of jewelry, none of them terribly costly, and all of them purchased for my wife with after-tax dollars. That's what you found, and what I'd said you would find. But you found not a drop of this mysterious cash."

"Don't think you're getting off that easy," one of them said. "You can expect to be audited for the rest of your life."

Mapes drew himself up to his full height and

glared down at them. "That's enough," he said. "You've exercised your warrant and exhausted my patience. I want you to leave."

And I guess they didn't care about the missing photos, or who killed Valdi Berzins, or any of the rest of it. If the cash was gone, so were they, and that was the last we saw of them.

By walking upstairs and coming down five minutes later and a quarter of a million dollars poorer, Mapes had suddenly blossomed as a folk hero, a little man who had taken a stand against the machine. Michael Quattrone was telling him that the Feds pulled shit like that all the time, and that he could recommend a lawyer who would run rings around them. Wally Hemphill told him there was a limit to how much they could harass a person, and they might have crossed it; he told Mapes he should talk to Quattrone's lawyer.

I wasn't much surprised that the safe in the bedroom was empty—after all, as you'll recall, I was the one who had emptied it. But what relieved me enormously was the extent to which Mapes was relieved. He was so happy to be off the federal hook that he hadn't yet had a chance to wonder where his money had gone. That meant this was the first time he'd opened the safe since my visit, and that meant the rest of the plan had a chance of working.

First, though, he tried to throw us out. "I want to thank you all," he said, "for your support just now. But I don't need to keep you any longer. I think you should go."

"Oh, I dunno about that," Ray said. "Seems like we're just gettin' warmed up."

"I'll admit I'm growing interested myself," Michael Quattrone said. "I think our friend here should continue."

I was glad to hear I was his friend, and by implication everybody else's. I'd taken a seat, but I got up now and faced them. "Getting back to you," I said to Colby Riddle, who looked as though he'd hoped I would have forgotten him in all the excitement. "Mapes called you. He mentioned money, whether there's any in the safe right now or not. And he mentioned me, because he'd read the same newspaper stories as everybody else. You were a scholar, a book person. I owned a bookstore not far from where you taught -ology, and—"

"Ology?"

"Well, whatever. It ends in -ology, doesn't it?"

"It's comparative linguistics."

"I stand corrected," I said, "though that's even better, come to think of it. You'd have friends in all languages, including Latvian. Mapes thought you might know me, and he was right, but you also knew some Latvians, and you knew Valdi Berzins was after the Kukarov photos.

"Mapes wanted them back. He had a pretty good idea what kind of treatment he could expect from the Black Scourge of Riga if they got into the wrong hands. He called you, hoping you could do something. You knew there was an opportunity here, you could smell it, but what action could you take?

"First, you called me. There was a chance you could keep out of sight altogether, so you didn't bother to identify yourself. You asked for a particular book, one by an author in whom you have no interest—"

"I don't care for the sea stories, I told you."

"You don't care for Conrad, period. You once quoted a line from **Heart of Darkness**—'The horror! The horror!' According to you, the horror was the way the man wrote."

"Did I say that? I can't say I recall it."

"Well, I can. You asked if I had **The Secret Agent** only because you knew the answer would be yes. It was right in the middle of the section you always go to, and it's been there for years. If by some chance I'd sold it since your last visit, you'd just ask for something else. But I hadn't, and you didn't, and I set the book aside for you.

"Then you got in touch with Berzins. I had the photos, they were in a book called **The Secret Agent,** and all he had to do was pick them up and pay for them. You figured I'd hand him the book, and he'd look through it and throw a fit, and I'd ask him what the hell he expected for twelve lousy dollars, and he'd walk out knowing he'd had a shot at the photos, but now they were gone.

"But Valdi Berzins was a positive thinker, and Norman Vincent Peale would have been proud of him. It didn't even occur to him that he wasn't getting the photos when he bought the book. He knew others were after them, knew they might show up at my store at any moment, so he was quick to pay for his purchase and get out. When he asked the price I said 'Thirteen' and left out the word **dollars,** and he thought I left out **hundred** as well. Of course I might have meant thirteen thousand, but that was more than he had, so he thought positively and counted out thirteen hundred-dollar bills and took a hike."

"And they killed him," Grisek said mournfully. "They killed this good man."

" 'They,' " Sigrid said. "Does this 'they' have a name?"

"Not one that I can supply. At least two people were in a car that pulled up at the curb halfway down the block from my store. When Valdi Berzins walked out the door, the car shot forward. Berzins was gunned down, and either the gunman or another passenger snatched up the book he was carrying, still in the brown paper bag I'd put it in."

"That's how it musta happened," Ray said. "But you ain't tellin' us nothin' new, Bernie. Who was in the car an' what happened to the book?"

"I can answer the second part, and maybe the rest will become clear. What happened to the book? Well, one way or another, it wound up here."

Mapes shook his head. "Ridiculous."

"Oh? I wish I'd been with you when you opened the safe for the IRS boys. But no, I don't think that's where you'd keep it. It's a book, so you'd hide it with your other books. Have you got a den, Doc?"

He didn't answer right away. Then he asked me to tell him the book's title again, and I did, and he said he had a copy of **The Secret Agent,** that he'd owned it for years. He'd read it in college and still had it.

"I'll be doggoned," I said. "Another coincidence."

"And that's all it is, damn you. Maybe Riddle asked for that book because he knew I had a copy. There must be hundreds of copies of the book in New York."

"Enough so that I've never been able to sell mine," I said, "until someone came along and gave me thirteen hundred dollars for it. How much did you pay for your copy?"

"I've no idea. A couple of dollars."

"I think it was a little more than that. I think you paid a pile for it, but then you weren't buying the book. You were buying the photos."

I'd just given him an out, and he grabbed it. "I can prove you're wrong," he said, and hurried through the dining room to the den, and came back triumphantly, book in hand. "Here," he said. "Here's the damned book. And if you can find any photos in it—"

He riffled the pages and stopped in abject horror.

Gently I took the book from his hand and flipped it open to show a mug shot of a blond man in profile, with a scar alongside his mouth. It was fastened to the page with Scotch tape, as were three more photos which I found and displayed.

"No," he cried. "No, that's impossible." He grabbed for the book, but I snatched it out of his reach. He stepped back, plunged a hand into his pocket, and the book wasn't the only thing he'd had in the den, because when his hand came out there was a gun in it. It wasn't a very big gun, but they're all huge when they're pointed at you.

This one wasn't pointed at me for long. "You **bastard**," he cried, and he could have meant me, God knows, but as he spoke the words he whirled toward Colby Riddle and fired the gun. "Son of a fucking **bitch**," he yelled, and pumped two bullets into Georgi Blinsky, and looked around for someone else to shoot.

The cops and goons all had their guns drawn, but we were all in a circle, and no one wanted to risk a shot because a miss could kill the wrong person. "You started this," he screamed, "you brainless spic whore!" and took careful aim at Marisol Maris.

Whereupon Wally Hemphill, marathoner turned martial artist, leapt from the sofa, whirled like a dervish, and delivered a spinning back kick that knocked the gun from his hand, following it with a move I couldn't follow that sent Mapes reeling across the room, right into the arms of a cop and two thugs. The thugs slapped him silly, the cop cuffed him, and Ray Kirschmann read him his rights. I hadn't paid attention to Miranda for a while, and noted that Mapes had a nice long list of rights. Somehow, though, I didn't think they were going to do him a whole lot of good.

FORTY-ONE

Thanks, Maxine. You're a lifesaver, and don't ask me what flavor, it'll give me ideas. Bern, pick up your glass. Here's to crime."

"And punishment," I said, and we touched glasses and drank.

"Punishment," she said. "Well, sure, why not? For them that have it coming, that is."

We were in the Bum Rap, you will not be surprised to learn, on a Thursday evening just a week and a day after I'd gathered much of New York's population into the living room of the house on Devonshire Close. It was not the first time Carolyn and I had sat down together since what a less original narrator might characterize as **that fateful day,** since we'd kept our standing lunch date more often than not. It wasn't even the first time we'd met for our after-work drinks date at the Bum Rap. But there'd been time constraints, or people around, on other evenings, and lunch wasn't right for the conversation we had to have. It was somehow necessary that there be glasses in our hands, and scotch in those glasses.

And this seemed like the time and place. Neither of us had anything to do for the next hour or so, nor was anyone likely to pull up a chair and horn in. And we had scotch at hand, and if it somehow disappeared, the faithful Maxine would see that it was replenished.

"Bern," Carolyn said, "there are a couple of things I'm not sure I understand."

"I'm not surprised. There are things I don't understand myself."

"A lot of things came out in Mapes's living room, and I was following along okay, but it was confusing. And then the way it ended, with the shooting and all, it seemed like some ends were left dangling."

"Like participles," I agreed. "No question about it."

"And then there were the things that came out that weren't true."

"Lies, we call them."

"Well, I wasn't going to say that. It seemed a little harsh."

"But accurate," I said. "There were basically three kinds of information dispensed that afternoon. Some of it was true, and some of it was guesswork, and some was utter fiction."

"That's what I thought, Bern. But now that it's over, I'd love to know the pure and simple truth."

"According to Oscar Wilde," I said, "the truth is

rarely pure and never simple. Some of it we'll never know, because the only people who could tell us are dead. But I can certainly tell you what I know. Where do you want me to start?"

"With William Johnson," she said. "Billy the Nephew. Talk about your impossible coincidences. He didn't date-rape Marisol, did he?"

"No, of course not. He never saw her before in his life."

"But she said he did."

"Does that mean it must be true?"

"She was very convincing, Bern. I was watching her, and she had tears in the corners of her eyes."

"Everybody was watching her," I said. "The girl has presence. Carolyn, she's an actress. She was acting."

"Well, she fooled me. I knew what she was saying couldn't possibly be true, and I believed it anyway. You must have told her what to say."

"When I saw her," I said, "she fell apart. Because of what she'd done, violating her lover's confidence, four people were dead, including Valdi Berzins, a genuine Latvian patriot."

"And a positive thinker."

"That too. She felt guilty, and when I suggested she might be able to do something to make it right, she was eager to help—especially when I told her what kind of a fellow Johnson was and what he'd pulled on Barbara Creeley. We worked out a story, and she gave me the ruby necklace Mapes had given her."

"And you planted it in Johnson's apartment."

"When I let myself in, after I'd left him in the alley swathed in Sigrid's puke."

"I can't believe she did that."

"She's a resourceful woman," I said, "with a tendency to get straight to the heart of the matter."

"She backed up Marisol's date-rape story, too. And she was pretty convincing in her own right, Bern."

"She's an actress herself, even if she doesn't go on auditions anymore. I didn't coach her, just let her know what to expect, and she did a great improv. But then she'd improvised beautifully getting Johnson out of Parsifal's and into the alley, so I could get his address."

"Because you had to get into his place."

I nodded. "I had two things to do there. First, I had to plant Marisol's necklace where he wouldn't come across it himself in the next day or two, without concealing it so well that the cops couldn't find it when the time came."

"And it came soon enough. Ray was reading him his rights before the bodies were cold."

"I'm not sure of that. Before Colby Riddle's body was cold, maybe, but I have a feeling Georgi Blinsky's body was somewhere around room temperature long before Mapes started tossing lead around the room. That Russian was the coldest man I ever saw."

"He looked good in black, though. What else did you do in Johnson's apartment?"

"I found Barbara's class ring from Bennett High."

"And gave it to her?"

"Just the other night. I have to say she was impressed."

"I bet she was. Maxine?" She pointed at our glasses, and got a nod of assent from Maxine. "Reinforcements are coming, Bern. I've got some more questions."

"Shoot."

"Colby Riddle. When did you start to think he had something to do with it?"

"Well, I always wondered," I said. "He never called me about a book before. It's rare that I get a phone call from someone who's just looking for a reading copy, and **The Secret Agent**'s in print in trade paperback, so anybody hunting for it could just drop into the nearest general bookstore, or get online and pick it up from Amazon. But Colby was always an odd bird to begin with, and we were up to our eyeballs in coincidences anyway, so I didn't dwell on it. I didn't really tie him in until I let myself into Mapes's office."

"You went there to check out his appointment book, and pick a time that would work for the showdown."

"And while I was there, I had a look at his files. I was looking for Kukarov, not really expecting to find anything, not under that name. And I didn't, of course. But then I looked up a few other people, and the only one I found was Colby. And he'd been there for just the reason I'd said. He had a growth removed from his cheek two years earlier."

"That could have been a coincidence too, couldn't it?"

"I suppose so, but I figured he was tied in."

"Yeah, I guess not even coincidence has arms that long. Hey, thanks, Max. Bern, we're not gonna die of thirst after all."

I took a sip of my drink just to make sure.

"Bern? Summarize what happened, will you? Not with William Johnson, I get all that. But the rest of it, with the photographs and the people getting killed and all."

I thought about it. "Well," I said, "there are a couple of versions. There's what I laid out, which is how the cops have the case written up. And there's what Ray knows is really true. And then there's what's even truer, that Ray doesn't know about. And then of course there are the things I did to make it happen."

"Uh-huh."

"So which would you like to hear?"

She grinned. "All of 'em, Bern."

"The Lyles got the photographs pretty much the way it came out in Mapes's living room. Marisol told her cousin Karlis, and he made a fake appointment with Mapes and swiped the book when no one was looking. He got it to his father, who in turn got it to Arnold Lyle."

"Okay."

"Lyle talked to more people than he should have,

and made arrangements to sell the book to Georgi Blinsky."

"**Principles of Organic Chemistry,** you mean. That book."

"Right, Volume Two. The book Mapes taped the photos in. First, though, Lyle removed the Kukarov photos from the book, but he liked Mapes's system, so he taped them into another book, one belonging to the owner of the apartment he'd sublet, and stuck it back in the bookcase."

"And that was **QB VII**."

"Uh-huh. Now the way I told the story, Ray found the book in a careful search of the apartment after the murder, but the photos were already missing."

"Ray couldn't find a black cat on a white sofa, Bern."

"This is the official story, remember? Ray found the book, but the photos were gone."

"Who took them?"

"Good question. First, though, the home invasion and the murder. Michael Quattrone's men were responsible for the home invasion part, as he more or less admitted, albeit hypothetically. The cops can't make a case against him and won't try, but they know his guys did it. And the doorman's death was accidental. It was homicide, that's what you call it when someone's killed in the commission of a felony, but nobody meant for it to happen."

"That must make the doorman feel a lot better."

"Quattrone wound up with **Principles of**

Organic Chemistry, which by now contained Mapes's mug shots of everybody but Kukarov. His main goal was to destroy the ones of Whitey Mullane, his friend and mentor, and my guess is he'll trash the others as well, if he hasn't already. They'd be worth something to a blackmailer, but that's not his line of work, and anyway he doesn't know who the people are."

"And after his men left?"

"Blinsky and his crew got there, too late to pick up the book, or to recover the twenty grand they'd already paid the Lyles. So they shot them, which I suspect they were planning to do all along, book or no book. I don't think Georgi Blinsky was a very nice man."

"Then I won't feel too bad that he got killed. What about the photos of Kukarov?"

"What about them?"

"Well, I know what happened to them. They were in the Leon Uris book waiting for you to find them. I know that because you told me, and Ray knows it because he was there. But what do the cops think happened to them?"

"They think they disappeared."

"Just like that? Poof?"

"No one's too clear on the details. Maybe when they took the tape off his mouth Lyle told Blinsky where the photos were."

"And Blinsky took them. And put the book back where he found it?"

"Does that seem unlikely? How about this—

Lyle taped the Kukarov photos in **QB VII**, then thought better of it and cut them out again. He put them somewhere else, and gave them to Blinsky, hoping it would lead the man in black to spare his life. ”

"That's a little better, but—"

"Carolyn, it didn't happen, so what difference does it make **how** it didn't happen? Somebody got the photos, and whoever it was he doesn't have them now, so what do the cops care?"

"I just wondered, that's all. But I see what you mean. ”

"Now what comes next? Colby Riddle, I guess, and Valdi Berzins. Well, you know how the story goes there. Mapes called Colby, who agreed to help out, probably for a substantial consideration. ”

"Money, in other words. ”

"What could be more considerate? Colby got me to set a book aside for him, then told Berzins to go in and ask for it. Meanwhile, a car full of Russians was waiting for Berzins to come out of my store. ”

"How'd they know to wait for him there?"

"They knew about me from the newspaper article," I said, "or they knew about Berzins and tailed him to the bookstore. He was waiting around on the sidewalk while I had lunch at your place, so that would have given them time to get into position. Both explanations play out about the same, so you can take your pick. ”

"Okay. ”

"Then Berzins came in, picked up the book,

overpaid or underpaid for it, as you prefer, and went out to meet his death."

"In a hail of flying bullets," she said. "A Russian shot him, right?"

"Right."

"And then jumped out and picked up the book."

"Right."

"So how did it get in Mapes's den?"

"Well, that's hard to say for sure," I said, "because all the people involved are dead."

"Not Mapes."

"He's refusing to answer questions. And nobody much cares, because he killed two men in front of a roomful of witnesses, including three cops and two members of the New York bar."

"And a paralegal," she said, "and someone who works behind a New York bar, and a lot of others besides. But they must have some explanation."

"The Russians," I said. "I'll tell you, they make even better villains now than they did during the Cold War. They shot Berzins, and they wound up with the book, and they already had the photos. They taped the photos into **The Secret Agent,** and sold the package to Mapes."

"If they already had the photos, why shoot Berzins?"

"That's a good question. Hmmm. Okay, try this: Colby and Mapes didn't know the Russians already had the photos, so Blinsky killed Berzins and grabbed the book so he'd have a plausible explanation for how the photos came into his possession."

"I'm not sure that makes perfect sense, Bern. Thank God it doesn't have to. But getting back to Mapes. Why would he come back with the book? He'd have to know the photos were in it, and he looked completely surprised when they showed."

"That would have been a problem," I acknowledged. "He could have been planning to remove the photos, and somehow forgot that he hadn't gotten around to it yet. Or he could have been brazening it out. Remember, the photos were taped securely to the pages. You could give them a fast riffle without revealing anything. He gambled that you could, anyway. And on the off chance that it didn't work, well, he brought his gun along for backup."

"Or Colby could have put the photos in the book without telling him, Bern."

I nodded. "Much better. Colby thought he was doing Mapes a favor, and Mapes saw it as betrayal, and that's why the first person he shot was Colby. That's good, Carolyn. If they ever ask me, I'll trot that one out for them. But I don't think they will."

"So that's the story," she said. "The Russians sold the book back to Mapes. For the money in the wall safe, I suppose. And then he lost it and shot everybody, because he saw the walls closing in on him."

"And he'd have shot Marisol, too," I said, "if Wally hadn't blown out a knee and switched to martial arts. Marathon training just doesn't do much for you in close-quarters combat."

"Wally was terrific, Bern." She picked up her

glass, drank deep. "And so was everything you just told me. Now tell me what really happened."

"Well," I said, "to begin with, I had the photos."

"Right."

"Of course I didn't get them until after Berzins was killed. That was on Friday, and Ray let me into the taped-up crime scene on Sunday afternoon."

"I'd forgotten that part."

"Colby never knew Berzins. I was just blowing smoke when I said he did. He knew Mapes, and after Mapes called him, asking what he knew about a bookseller named Rhodenbarr, Colby wanted to make sure the store was open. So he called, and when I picked up the phone he had the answer to his question. Then, to give himself an excuse to stop by later on, he asked for a book he already knew I had."

"Because he'd seen it in the section he always browsed. But if Colby didn't know Berzins, how did Berzins know to ask for the book?"

"He didn't."

"He didn't what? Didn't know or didn't ask?"

"Both. He knew I had something to do with the burglary—even though I didn't—and he combined positive thinking with diplomatic caution. He left his ID and his regular wallet in his parked car and came to me with nothing but ten thousand dollars and a bellyful of self-confidence. 'I believe you have something for me'—that's what he said. If I told him I didn't know what he was talking about, he'd have gone into more detail. But he didn't have to, because I was obliging enough to turn around and hand him a book."

"And he assumed the photos were in it."

"Wouldn't you?"

"I might have looked to make sure, Bern."

"Even if a fast response would let you get something for thirteen hundred bucks that you'd been prepared to pay ten thousand for?"

"That's a point."

"Then he got gunned down, and somebody picked up the book."

"And there weren't any photos in it."

"Of course not. They saw him come out of my store, and they had to assume he had the photos, because what else would he have gone there for? So they shot him and took what he was carrying, and it was nothing but a Joseph Conrad novel, and not even a first edition."

"So the Russians had the book."

"Maybe."

"Maybe? What do you mean, maybe?"

"I think there was probably a Russian behind the wheel," I said, "and another one firing the gun. But I think there was a third person in the car, and I think that person was Colby Riddle."

"In the murder car."

"That would be my guess. He looked at the book and knew right away what had happened. He took it home with him, or back to his office, and he paged through it and made absolutely sure there were no pictures in it. And then he took it to his friend Mapes's office and let Mapes look, and commiserated with Mapes about the problems they were having. 'Here,' he told Mapes. 'You might as well hang onto this goddamn thing. Call it a souvenir.' "

"And Mapes took it home?"

"And left it on the desk in his den, where I found it that very same night after I cleaned out his safe."

"And you brought it home."

"Which seemed like a mistake at the time," I said, "but I couldn't get over the surprise of finding it there. The last I'd seen of it, someone was snatching it out of a fat man's dead hands for reasons I couldn't begin to fathom. And here it was, on Mapes's desk."

"Wow. And he never knew it was gone?"

"How would he know? It was just an old book, with nothing valuable about it. He could have thrown it out in the first place. He kept it, but that didn't mean he was going to sit down and read it. He tossed it on his desk, and wouldn't have noticed it was gone unless he went looking for it."

"But he could have noticed, Bern."

"I know," I said, "and that worried me, but only a little. Because the last thing I did Monday night—although it was well into Tuesday morning by then—was drive out to Riverdale and let myself into his house for a second time."

"Through the milk chute."

"Don't remind me. It went smoother this time.

Maybe I lost a pound or two, or maybe I improved with practice. I took the book along, and I'd already fixed it up, taping the photos in place. I could have just dropped it on his desk, I suppose, but I didn't want him paging idly through it, so I found a place on his shelf. The spine's dark, you don't notice it right away, but it would show up in a search. If he'd already missed it, well, that might have been tricky, but I knew I was in the clear when he came downstairs after showing his empty safe to the IRS boys. His reaction made it very clear he hadn't had a clue the money was missing. That meant he hadn't missed the book, because if he'd been aware that something had disappeared, the first thing he'd have done was check the safe to see if anything else was gone."

She took it all in, and asked a few more questions, and I did the best I could to answer them. Then she pointed out that Ray knew I'd had the photos. So how did he think they'd found their way into the book, and the book onto Mapes's shelf?

"Ray's a practical man," I said. "He's not as stupid as you think he is."

"He couldn't be, Bern, or he'd die because he forgot to breathe."

"He only thinks about things if he has to," I said. "He knows I had the photos, and if he thought about it he'd wonder how they got where they did, and how I knew they were there, and, well, any number of things. But what he wanted me to do was pull a rabbit out of a hat, and I did, and he wasn't about to ask who the rabbit's father was, or how much I paid for the hat. Instead he concentrated on the fact that he'd brought in a fellow the press is calling the Date-Rape Bandit of Murray Hill, at the same time that he was solving a crime Major Cases had yanked out from under him."

"So he came out of it okay."

"Smelling like a rose."

"I could say something," she said, "but it would reveal me as a mean-spirited human being, so I'll keep it to myself. And you know what? I'm glad Ray came out of it okay. I mean, you and I did all right, didn't we?"

"My Get Out of Dodge fund is replenished. And I've got money in the bank, and I just yesterday got a line on a carpenter who'll build me a hidey-hole every bit as good as the one Quattrone's clowns wrecked."

"And you've got a girlfriend."

"Oddly enough, I do. And I don't have to worry what she'll think when she finds out I'm a burglar, because she already knows."

"And it doesn't bother her?"

"Sooner or later it will, and sooner or later the relationship'll fall apart. But for the time being she's okay with it."

"I'm happy for you, Bern. She's really nice."

"So's Lacey."

"Yeah," she said, beaming. "We both did fine.

I've got a safe-deposit box stuffed with money, plus I've got a really neat girlfriend who thinks I'm pretty neat myself."

"I gather LBD's not a problem at this stage."

She blushed, something she doesn't do often. LBD stands for Lesbian Bed Death, a name coined to describe the curiously sexless state of so many long-term lesbian relationships. It seems to me heterosexual couples have the same problem, but we don't have a cute term for it. We just call it marriage.

"I thought Marty and Marisol might get back together again," she said, changing the subject deftly. "But I guess that's a thing of the past, huh?"

"They were both ready to move on. And they didn't have trouble finding somewhere to move. Marisol's seeing a lot of Wally these days."

"I guess it's hard for a woman to resist someone who just saved her life."

"And hard for a guy to resist someone whose life he just saved, especially if she looks like Marisol. It's got him over his hopeless crush on that Chinese waitress, so now he's not spending all his time at that dopey teahouse."

"That's good."

"And he's keeping up his martial-arts training, which is also good. On the downside, he's studying Latvian."

"Why? Marisol speaks perfect English."

"I know that," I said, "and so does Wally. That's just the way he is. Pardon my Latvian, but the other day he wished me **Dauds laimis jaungada.** That means Happy New Year."

"Really? When do Latvians celebrate New Year?"

"January first, remarkably enough, so he was eight months early."

"Or four months late."

"Look, he's happy. Meanwhile, Marty and Sigrid couldn't be happier. He's the married older man she always wanted, and she's the hot gorgeous blonde everybody always wanted."

"Including me, Bern, but I've got my hands full just now. Is that why you invited them to Riverdale? Because you figured they'd be right for each other?"

"Well, I had to have Sigrid there to back up Marisol's date-rape story. And I thought Marty deserved a chance to see the shitheel get what was coming to him. But yeah, I sort of had it in mind that the two of them might hit it off."

"What a storybook ending," she said, and sighed. Then she straightened up and leaned forward. "Bern, the photos. What happened to the photos?"

"You saw them. In the copy of **The Secret Agent.**"

"Right. What happened to them after Mapes and Johnson went off to Central Booking?"

"Oh," I said. "Well, I sort of took them."

"Sort of? What do you mean, **sort of?**"

"When no one was looking," I said, "I picked it up. Otherwise it might have spent the next fifty years in an NYPD evidence locker."

"And you wanted it for a souvenir?"

I shook my head. "I already gave it away."

"You gave it away. Wait a minute, let me guess. You gave it to the little man from the Latvian embassy."

"Mr. Grisek."

"So they'll hunt down the Black Scourge of Riga after all."

"They'll try. He seems to have pretty good survival instincts, but they're highly motivated. So we'll see."

"Wow," she said, and leaned back in her chair and stretched like a cat. "Gee, look at the time. I guess we don't need another round of drinks, do we? We had two already."

"Three."

"Really? Was it three?"

"I'm afraid so."

"It's funny how you can lose count. Three. You know what that means?"

"No, but I'll bet you're about to tell me."

"It means we had two drinks," she said, "and then had a third."

"So?"

"Two drinks, and then one drink."

"So?"

"So that one drink seems incomplete, doesn't it? Because you know my theory about how there's no such thing as one drink." She waved a hand, crooked a finger. "Maxine!"